IN THE ARMS OF A HIGHLANDER

Brodie moved toward her, and the heat of his hazel gaze burned her up from the inside out.

Softly, he slid his fingers down her cheek before brushing his thumb along her lips. Her eyes locked on his, and he felt her shiver and her body stiffen, but she did not pull away.

Before her nerves took over, Brodie claimed her mouth once again with his own, deliberately using his own desire to ignite Shinae's. With a gentleness he had not known he was capable of, he continued kissing her until Shinae relaxed into him, her mouth softening . . .

Books by Michele Sinclair

THE HIGHLANDER'S BRIDE

TO WED A HIGHLANDER

DESIRING THE HIGHLANDER

THE CHRISTMAS KNIGHT

TEMPTING THE HIGHLANDER

A WOMAN MADE FOR PLEASURE

SEDUCING THE HIGHLANDER

A WOMAN MADE FOR SIN

NEVER KISS A HIGHLANDER

THE MOST ELIGIBLE
HIGHLANDER IN SCOTLAND

HOW TO MARRY A HIGHLANDER

IN THE ARMS OF A HIGHLANDER

HIGHLAND HUNGER
(with Hannah Howell and Jackie Ivie)

Published by Kensington Publishing Corp.

In the ARMS of A HIGHLANDER

MICHELE SINCLAIR

**ZEBRA BOOKS
KENSINGTON PUBLISHING CORP.**
www.kensingtonbooks.com

I dedicate this book to women everywhere.
If you are fighting cancer, continue to fight as hard
and as long as you can.
Your life is precious to those who love you.
If you are a survivor of cancer,
do what you can to help others still in the fight, and
most importantly—continue to survive.
If you just know someone who is fighting cancer,
check on them often (text, call, email, or visit).
Continually let them know
that they have made an impact in this world
because in the dark days,
we forget. Your outreach encourages us
considerably by showing we are not alone,
and we have not been forgotten.
Cancer and the methods
to fight it decapacitates the mind and the body,
which isolates us more than we ever say aloud.
To Carrie and Emma, a special thanks
for helping me to unravel some of the more gnarly
twists and turns this story took.
And last, this is for you, E and H.
Remember how much I love you—forever and always.

PROLOGUE

Shinae felt no resistance as her dirk easily sliced through the English soldier's neck. He slumped lifeless to the floor just as she heard a scuffle several feet behind her. Quickly twisting around, she regripped the small knives in both of her hands in preparation for the next attacker. He was much larger than his comrades, with dark hatred in his eyes.

He returned her level stare and flexed his muscles in an effort to remind her that his size gave him a significant advantage over her lithe frame. He took a step forward and then another. Shinae remained motionless until he lunged for her and then easily spun out of his path. Encountering only air when he forcefully came forward, the English soldier stumbled, and Shinae wasted no time severing his spinal cord at the back of his neck, once again proving that bigger did not mean faster.

Ignoring the thump as the limp form joined the three soldiers she had already dispatched, Shinae's vivid green eyes quickly glanced around the abbey's large dining hall. Her fellow nuns had taken the opportunity to escape when she had confronted the attackers. For a brief second, Shinae wondered what her fainthearted abbess would think if she had stayed and witnessed her deadly abilities. Would it matter to her that Shinae had saved the lives of her fellow nuns by giving them time to flee?

Shinae did hope they had made it to safety even though she doubted a single one would have actually mourned her death. None of them were friends—with her or one another. The abbey's austere environment did not lend to such niceties as smiles, words of comfort, or general cordiality.

A loud clink of a sword against the stone floor echoed behind her. On instinct, she ducked as she turned, narrowly avoiding a sword meant for her neck. At first the invading English soldiers had laughed at her, standing by herself holding only a dirk and a *sgian dubh*. In her hands, the long Scottish dagger was especially deadly when coupled with its shorter version.

The English had foolishly attacked one at a time, but seeing how quickly she had dispatched the first one, the next two approached together and more cautiously. To their surprise, it gave them no advantage. Hesitation was a deadly mistake in a knife fight, as they soon discovered.

As she stood back up from her ducked position, Shinae slashed her advancing attacker with what she hoped was a painful blow across his side. Seeing the relatively small amount of blood on him, she knew instantly it had been too shallow to be a crippling strike.

His dark gaze darted toward the door behind her and

back again. Seeing Shinae still standing and his fellow soldiers dead at her feet, the fear in his small eyes belied the smirk on his face. It was clear to her the coward had hoped that one of his comrades would have succeeded in killing her and was waiting for additional men to burst into the dining hall.

"Unlike them," he said, signaling with his beady eyes the men she had dispatched, "I'm not a mere foot soldier, but a trained English knight. Let me pass and I'll order my men to let you live."

Shinae just watched him, strangely calm.

His voice was deep and authoritative, but she could tell he was lying. Perhaps he was an esquire in hopes of someday becoming a knight, but he wore a gambeson and no armor, not even a basinet to protect his head.

The man tightened his grasp on his sword's handle and swung again. This time Shinae was ready for him and drove her dirk into his armpit and upward of his fighting arm, while at the same time she sliced his abdomen with the *sgian dubh* in her left hand. Neither were death blows, but the one across his gut would most likely turn deadly if not treated quickly.

The soldier took a step back and glared at her as he fought to keep his sword from falling. Shinae debated whether she should leave him to die a long death or let her dirk fly right into his chest, ending his misery and any chance to be a threat again.

Seeing she was going to attack, he suddenly hunched over, pressed his free hand against his stomach wound, and took an unsteady step backward. "You do not want to kill me. I'm important," he huffed in pain. "I know things your king would be interested in. Help me and I will tell you what I know. Don't and . . . and you will wish you had."

Shinae eyed him and knew, unlikely as it was, he was telling the truth. Like her father, she had an instinct about people that had, over time, proven nearly infallible. She thought of it as her inner angel, giving voice to God's guidance. It was not by a look or information gleaned from brief contact that she could discern someone's motivations; it was something she just knew. Unfortunately, the knowledge could not be summoned on command. Yet, when her inner voice gave direction definitively one way or the other, it was never wrong. And today it was telling her that this man was not lying. The soldier may not be an English commander, as he claimed, but he had information as if he were one.

The malevolent look in his dark eyes and the tight grip he had on his hilt also made it clear he intended to see her dead.

Shinae waved her hand over the bodies around her. "What use do I have to save someone who attacks godly women who pray to the Lord?"

His eyes narrowed as he glanced down at the death she had caused. His gaze slowly traveled up her bloodied, white-robed form. "You're no nun," he scoffed.

Somewhere underneath the four lives she had already ended were her wimple and veil. She did not care much for their loss. Both garments had been poorly made. All the nuns had to make their own habits, which consisted of tunic, cincture, wimple, and veil. Hers were passable, but Shinae was not nearly as skilled with a needle as she was with a dagger. Still, even bloody, it was obvious she was wearing the white habit of the order.

"But I am," Shinae responded as a slow smile curved her soft mouth. "I just wasn't always one."

"And you won't be one for much longer," he snarled. "There's no escape and my men are coming." Using all his fury, he blocked the pain and regripped his sword, hinting that he was about to attack.

Unconsciously, Shinae spun her small dirk in her palm. Unlike her younger sister, Mhàiri, she had always enjoyed the touch of a blade in her hand. It did not make her feel powerful, but rather gave her a sense of peace. For the past few years, holding a knife was the one thing that made her feel like she still had some control over her life—that the Church had not totally erased who she was.

Until now, she had never wielded a blade in self-defense. Then again, she had never needed to either.

For all the defense training her father had made her and her sister do in her youth, Shinae never really thought she would use it. Her father was a very successful traveling merchant and had made sure both his daughters could protect themselves if ever necessary. After the death of her mother, he had left Shinae to live with his sister in a small community nestled in the Highlands. Shinae had been on the verge of womanhood and he had thought it best. Four years later, her younger sister joined her at the priory.

Her aunt had been part of a group of God-fearing men and women who did not believe in making monastic vows, but in serving the Lord by helping those in need in the community. Shinae committed herself to the life and continued to stay with them after her aunt passed away in her sleep. Her sister continued to stay as well but had been far too spirited and willful to join the priory as a member. She contributed, but had been far more interested in drawing, reading books, and learning than spending her days caring for others.

All was well until five years ago. The priory had been one of the few left in Scotland, and after it caught on fire and burned to the ground, there had been nowhere for them to go.

Despite the dire circumstances, Mhàiri had refused to leave her things. Shinae had resolved to stay with Mhàiri until an older priest, who had vowed that a powerful Highland clan—the McTiernays—would keep her safe and her books secure until their father came and got her. Meanwhile, the Catholic Church had also come to the priory's aid and promised they would allow Shinae to continue helping others if she took her vows and moved to an abbey in Scotland's Lowlands. It had been an empty promise. The times Shinae had been able to leave Dryburgh Abbey had been rare and brief. She had wanted to serve God by helping people, not live in servitude and austerity.

A year later, Shinae had learned through eavesdropping on the elders in the dining hall that rather than reuniting with their father, her sister had met a McTiernay Highlander who supposedly appreciated Mhàiri's talents, as well as her quick, often sharp wit. Shinae would have liked to have met Conan McTiernay, for rumors and gossip did not present the best impressions of him when it came to women. Shinae could not imagine Mhàiri giving up her precious freedom for such a Highlander, not after so vociferously refusing every man who had asked for her hand in marriage—many of whom had been quite handsome and wealthy. But her father had assured Shinae a couple of years later, during his one sanctioned visit, that Mhàiri's marriage was a good one. Her sister and Conan McTiernay worked as equals and their passion for each other reminded him of what he and her mother had shared. Shinae was happy for Mhàiri but shuddered at the idea of marriage, much preferring giving and supporting others. Helping others gave her peace and contentment like nothing else.

Passion was not something Shinae had ever experienced, but it was not due to a lack of opportunity. While she was with the Culdees, her lithe figure, silky skin, long dark hair, and uncommonly light green eyes, had consistently attracted men to ask for her hand in marriage. They had always made it clear how much they appreciated her striking features, but none had endeavored to see past her physical appearance. Many had mistakenly thought to persuade her to accept their proposals by acting on their passion, but they promptly learned Shinae was not someone who could be manhandled. Not surprisingly, their interest faded almost immediately.

Supporting village clansmen and women had been different. They had appreciated her assistance, and Shinae had enjoyed getting to know those in the community. Helping others had been why she had joined the Culdees and, eventually, the Catholic Church. She knew most women wanted marriage and a family, but Shinae far preferred being a spinster than receiving the unwanted ardor of man. It was helping do God's work that made her happy.

Or it had.

Now, being eight and twenty years old, Shinae frequently questioned her decision to join the Church. Outwardly, she looked and acted the perfect nun, for doing so made life easier. But internally, her thoughts had never been in line with the St. Augustinian order.

After leaving the priory, she had been sent to Dryburgh Abbey. As part of the Premonstratensian order, the cloister followed the Rule of St. Augustine, where the nuns wore white, not black, and adhered to statutes that made their life one of great austerity. Shinae had agreed to take the vows because the order highly believed in pastoral ministry with a duty to preach and support those outside the monastery walls.

While not an enclosed religious order, Shinae oftentimes thought it might as well be for the few times she was permitted to help those nearby. She had not been allowed to attend Mhàiri's wedding, her father had been allowed to visit only once, and she had not ever been granted leave to see her sister.

The English soldier snarled, snapping Shinae's attention back to the man still white-knuckling the handle of his sword. He had a renewed focus and was swaying back and forth from newfound manic energy. His injuries should slow him down, but in his state they would only slightly. Shinae knew her limits. She had expert skills when it came to knives, but the length of his sword gave the man a much farther reach. She would need to kill him before he attacked, requiring a very precise throw at a wavering target.

It had been a while since she had thrown a dirk. Shinae had kept both of hers sharp, mostly out of habit and always in secret, when alone in her room at the abbey. Whenever possible, she also practiced the movements she had honed and perfected in her youth. But throwing? It had been nearly five years since she had had the opportunity.

"A nun who kills," the man snarled. "What would your abbess say if she knew she had been harboring a murderer?"

Shinae shrugged, feeling no guilt for those around her who lay dead, and wondered what would bother the abbess more—her killing them or her lack of remorse. Though deaths caused by self-defense were not unlawful or immoral, Shinae suspected the Church would require a lot of penance and her being constantly on her knees in prayer for at least a month.

"Are you not curious what I might know?" He paused, waiting to see if she answered. Shinae showed no interest. "Are you not interested in saving your precious Scotland?"

Shinae continued to remain as she was. He was taunting her to ask questions in return and give his fellow men time to save him, but she doubted they would. The smell of smoke was starting to seep into the dining room, indicating the building had been lit on fire.

In retaliation for the king of Scotland's recent raids, the king of England, Edward II, had ordered his army north, but the Scottish army had stopped their advance in Edinburgh. Forced to withdraw, the English soldiers were burning abbeys as they retreated back south. Despite the English raiding and burning Melrose Abbey and its nearby village less than a week before, Abbot Hugh of Dryburgh had believed the army would continue its journey south, not go west. He had been wrong, and Dryburgh Abbey would soon be nothing but ashes.

Shinae heard a loud thump against the doors. The English soldier also heard it and a slow smile curved his pinched lips. "You are about to die," he said, and then a low chuckle escaped him as the door to the abbey's large dining hall swung open.

Shinae reacted on instinct and threw her *sgian dubh* as hard as she could into the snickering soldier's thigh, causing him to fall. Immediately afterward she spun around and, seeing the silver glint of a large broadsword, she threw her dirk. Over the soldier's shrieks of agony, she heard her blade's thud as it hit the doorframe, narrowly missing its mark.

Cyric Schellden quickly took in the scene before him. He had been too late to help those in Dryburgh Abbey from the English, arriving just as several panicked nuns had emerged from the main building, screaming that one of them was still in the dining hall surrounded by English soldiers. When he opened the hall's doors, he expected to find death—not a dirk-throwing, bloodied nun surrounded by dead bodies. He could only conceive of one logical explanation.

"I thought I knew all of King Robert's spies, but I had no idea he stashed one here disguised as a nun," Cyric stated nonchalantly as he pulled her knife free from the doorframe. Grinning openly at her, he stepped into the room and let the heavy door close behind him. She had the greenest eyes he had ever seen.

"Who are you?"

Her question was direct and simple, and Cyric could answer it one of many different ways, for he was many people. He was a husband, a father to the sweetest two-year-old daughter, and one of King Robert's royal attachés. But right now, he was a man on a mission to warn a friend, an ally, and one of Scotland's most powerful Highland chiefs that his family was in great danger.

The royal court had successfully kept secret that the English had infiltrated many of the major clans. In the last year, the sudden collapse and death of lairds or their kin who helped fight to win Scotland's freedom had died mysterious or untimely deaths and the royal court was on edge. When, by whom, and how—poison, disappearance, a suspicious fall—no one could predict the next target, but Cyric was going to ensure Conor McTiernay—a friend and clan ally—was warned.

"Just a soldier hoping to warn the southern abbeys that the English were coming."

Shinae looked at the tall man skeptically. He had black hair, etched facial features, and golden-brown eyes. He was also wearing a plaid she recognized as belonging to one of the more powerful Highland clans. The quality of his leather belt, sporran, and léine all indicated that he was not just a soldier as he alluded. Such finery was worn by nobles and royalty, not army footmen.

"And just why would a royal diplomat be sent for

such a task?" Shinae asked, probing to see if her hunch as to his identity was correct.

Cyric kept his expression the same, ignoring her question. "I was told to come to the dining hall and assist you, but I see our king has chosen his spies well."

Just as he spoke his last few words, an English soldier slipped into the room. He lifted his sword to attack and Shinae opened her mouth to warn the mysterious Scot, but before she could utter a sound, the large, dark-haired man deftly whipped his sword around and removed the English soldier's head.

Shinae blinked as something whizzed by her head, and less than a second later, the clank of a falling sword followed by a new, very loud screech echoed in the dining hall. The English soldier she had injured had pulled her knife free from his leg and had been preparing to throw it. Now, he was hunched on the floor with her dirk protruding from his hand.

The Scot walked over to the wounded man, whose shrieks became louder, changing to pleas for his life. "Help me. I know things. Things your king will want to hear about why so many—" and began to scream when the Scot grabbed Shinae's dirk and removed it before tossing it to her. Next, with the hilt of his sword, he hit the Englishman in the head causing him to go uncon-scious, ending his cries for mercy.

Cyric did not have to look up to know that the nun was watching him. "Is he the reason you are here?" she asked, pointing at the now-quiet, limp figure on the floor.

Cyric glanced down. "Nay," he replied with a shake of his head, "but he might prove to be useful."

The woman's thin dark brow crinkled in confusion. "Just why is he so important?"

"He probably isn't," Cyric lied, and his posture grew serious.

The smell of smoke was getting stronger and the nun pointed to the door. "We should leave."

Cyric knew she was right, but he was not inclined to leave just yet. Beyond the woman's ability to cause carnage, there was something about this nun—as if he recognized her, though he would swear they had never met. "Do you have a name?"

They stared at each other for nearly a minute before Shinae decided there was no harm in sharing her name. "I have one," she responded with a shrug. "Shinae Mayboill."

As soon as he heard the name, Cyric closed his eyes and rubbed them. He was correct that they had never met. But he did know her, or least of her. Shinae's unusual features—dark hair and piercing green eyes— were eerily similar to that of Conan McTiernay's wife. Shinae Mayboill was Mhàiri's older sister, which meant she was definitely not a spy.

"Then you really are a nun," Cyric said with a frown in obvious disappointment. It would have been handy to have a deadly female spy.

"Was," Shinae replied as she wiped her knife on one of the few non-bloody spots of her tunic.

"Why the white garb if you left the Church?" he asked incredulously. It was unheard of.

She nodded her head once. "As of tonight. The sisters

will head to another abbey, I suspect, but I will go to Melrose and help those who are injured before heading south, to my sister's family."

"Your abbess might disagree."

She unconsciously twirled her knife and said, "I doubt it."

Cyric stared at her for several seconds, hiding his mixed emotions as an idea formed. Such a revelation changed everything. He needed to get back to Stirling Castle as quickly as possible to convince the king to support his burgeoning idea. Shinae Mayboill may have been a nun, but she was going to be King Robert's newest spy.

She just did not know it yet.

CHAPTER ONE

Shinae tried to ignore the continual complaints of the woman trudging beside her as the bitter night breeze continued to chill their bones. Isilmë had valid reasons to be grumpy, but after days of hearing about them, Shinae just wanted her uninvited companion to be quiet, for she was miserable as well. Despite it being summer, the day felt more like late fall. The intermittent rain and constant cool wind had started in before dawn, and the dank and unusually cold air had not improved with the sun's rising.

Most days, the foul weather would not be a problem. She would seek or build a shelter near one of the rivers, snare a rabbit, light a fire, eat, and stay warm until the rain stopped. For most of their journey, they had followed the Lieder River and then the Blackadder, which kept them near such resources. Unfortunately, after turning south yesterday, they came to the southern edges of the Lammermuir Hills, which had little to offer but grass and lots of rocks.

"Ow! Slow down!" Isilmë wailed. Shinae did not stop or look back. An old woman with a bad hip could have traveled farther than they had in the last week.

The trip from Melrose to Lochlen Castle should have taken approximately three days on foot, but with their slow pace, it was taking much longer. And on days like today, it was hard not to think they should have been warm, dry, and full from dining on delicious foods but they were close now, so close that Shinae did not want to stop; walking was the only thing keeping them from being even colder.

Shinae expected to catch a glimpse of the lit sconces of Lochlen Castle with each peak they passed and forced herself to keep moving one foot in front of the other despite being wet and nearly frozen. This meant Isilmë had to follow or be alone. So, she also kept walking . . . and complaining.

Shinae had not wanted a traveling companion and had hoped the abbess would force Isilmë to remain with her and the other sisters when they all left the morning after the fire. Maybe Dryburgh Abbey would be habitable again someday, but it would not be anytime soon, so everyone had headed south to join the sisters at Jedburgh Abbey. Then, on the brink of their departure, the shortest of the nuns had shocked everyone when she declared that she too was renouncing her vows and joining Shinae. Suddenly, she too had a great desire to help the injured villagers at Melrose. Unfortunately, the frazzled abbess had no desire to even try to make Isilmë stay with the other sisters. It was almost as if the harsh woman was glad both of them would no longer be in her care.

To Shinae's surprise, and despite her and Isilmë being her opposites in almost every way, they slowly developed a unique bond that was oddly comforting. At least it had been. Now, they were both too cold and wet to be civil, and where Shinae had kept her suffering mostly to herself, Isilmë voiced every cross thought in her head.

With each step, Shinae silently wished she had already arrived at Lochlen. When they first started to make their way to where the castle was located, she had held no animosity that the journey was taking longer than anticipated. She—a simple, half-Scot, half-Gypsy ex-nun—had been given a mission. One she did not want but could not refuse. Her sister's husband, and therefore her sister, were in grave danger, and Shinae was tasked to tell absolutely no one but them about the strange message Cyric wanted her to relay.

Lochlen Castle was the home of Colin McTiernay, the Lowland chieftain of a powerful clan into which her sister had married. Cyric, who was some close family friend, had estimated it would be a slow but easy two-to three-day journey to the east by foot.

The very first morning she should have realized that the journey would be neither short nor easy.

Within an hour of their journey, the sky had become overcast and the air had become cooler. Neither she nor Isilmë was physically prepared to walk long distances day after day, and the dank air made it even more difficult. However, by midday they had made it to Leader Water and turned north leaving the River Tweed behind.

That was when it started to rain. It was a light rain, but it was enough to make them put on their cloaks to stay dry.

Shinae and Isilmë had gone through the rubble at Dryburgh when all had left and found multiple odds and ends, including a lump of soap, a brush, candles, a few bags, blankets, and two cloaks that had belonged to taller-than-average monks. Shinae did not mind the hem dragging behind her, but Isilmë had wisely trimmed hers and did not have to deal with having to constantly pull the hem free when it got snagged on some root or stick. But Shinae had melted the beeswax from the few candles that had survived the fire and rubbed them on the hood and shoulders of her cloak. When she had offered to do the same for Isilmë, she refused, saying that it made the material stiff and uncomfortable. Seeing the beads of water run off Shinae's cloak as hers grew damp had made Isilmë, understandably but annoyingly, snappish.

They had started walking even closer to the Leader Water's winding shore so the overhanging branches could protect them from getting too wet. It was not the ideal way to travel, but nonetheless, they had been making progress until Isilmë caught her foot on some fallen branches and twisted her ankle. Not badly, but enough that continued use would have made the injury much worse, possibly halting their journey for a week, if not longer.

They had decided to just stop and make camp where they were. It had easy access to the river, and all the foliage kept them fairly hidden. Always traveling from one village to another as a child, Shinae had spent the first dozen years of her life building shelters, starting fires, trapping rabbits, and sleeping out in the open. So when they had stopped, she had not hesitated and started to erect a small shelter to protect them from rain. By the time she had caught a rabbit, the rain had stopped, and with a little patience she finally got a fire going. They stayed there two days . . . two very sunny, warm days when all Isilmë's chatter would have been easier to endure if they had been walking. The morning of the third day, Isilmë agreed she was healed enough to continue if they went slowly.

The sky had been a beautiful shade of blue with just a few clouds. Periodically, they had halted briefly for Isilmë to rest her ankle, and by midafternoon she had needed to stop. Each night, Shinae had been able to quickly capture and skin a good-sized rabbit that would feed them that night and the next day. Once she got a fire going, Isilmë would find a small but sturdy branch to cook the meat, and at night they would sleep beneath the stars. With no shelter to be built, Shinae opted to bathe in the river. Upon seeing her clean, Isilmë decided she wanted one too. They both wished that they had remained dirty.

When she borrowed Shinae's soap, Isilmë had taken it and their entire bag along with her. It would not have been a problem if she had just left their things on the shore, not on a rock close to where she was bathing. By the time she realized all their possessions had been taken by a strong current in the river, it was too late. They both had only the clothes they were wearing and Shinae's *sgian dubh* strapped to her waist inside her tunic and the dirk strapped to her thigh.

The fifth day they reached Blackadder Water and Shinae knew they were close. If they increased their pace, they would be at Lochlen Castle before sundown, which was good because the vegetation and their easy food sources were gone. The landscape had changed to large, treeless hills, making one feel like they were traveling in circles. Small game was still around, but there were only prickly bushes here and there, which provided no shelter from the wind and burned fast. Keeping warm throughout the night meant one of them had to wake every few hours to feed the fire.

Today should have been the last day of their journey, with them having arrived at Lochlen Castle hours ago. But early that morning the skies had opened up and a heavy rain had come down for over an hour before lessening into a soft drizzle. Hard rain, then drizzle occurred all day until the late afternoon, when another downpour came, this time with a cold wind.

Without the sun, she and Isilmë could not get dry, and being hungry only added to their discomfort. Animals had gone into hiding and dry firewood was impossible to find. Even if they had found some food, they would not have been able keep the fire going to cook anything. They were freezing, starving, and exhausted.

Isilmë started to fret once again. "I'm cold and any minute it is going to pour down on us again," she huffed. "And I know you believe it is all my fault."

"I do not," Shinae muttered. It was inarguable that they would have arrived at Lochlen Castle and been safe from the miserable weather if Isilmë had not gotten hurt. But it was also true that such an accident could have happened to anyone, including her.

"If we do not get there soon, you will have led us to our deaths," Isilmë grumbled in an accusatory tone.

Shinae took a deep breath and remained silent. Isilmë's bitter complaints were no longer irritating but infuriating, and her last comment was not entirely inaccurate. The sun had dropped below the horizon and the temperature was dropping with each minute. Already wet and cold, if she and Isilmë stopped moving and fell asleep in this wind, it really was plausible they would not live to see the morning. Reaching Lochlen Castle was imperative. Not just for their survival, but her sister's.

"Just think, you could have joined the nuns and be well fed and warm at Jedburgh Abbey."

Isilmë's grimace turned even more sour. "Another abbey is the *only* place worse than where I am right now." The vehemence in her friend's voice was unmistakable. Shinae was not going to pry. Like her, Isilmë's reasons for leaving the order were her own.

Except being close in age, they had little in common with each other. Shinae had a happy childhood and traveled a great deal in her youth as her father was a traveling merchant. Isilmë had a very different upbringing, growing up at the abbey, and knew no other life. Consequently, at seven and twenty years old, she had few skills and lacked the knowledge it took to lure unmarried men who were seeking a wife to her side.

The one talent Isilmë did possess was her exceptional skills with a needle and thread. Her clothes were always perfect. Shinae thought it pointless to put such tedious effort into making a habit. No matter how well crafted, the garment would still feel restricting, the headdress more than a little uncomfortable. And that was why the moment she had decided to leave the Church, Shinae had not returned to wearing her wimple, veil, and scapular.

Isilmë, on the other hand, had continued to dress exactly like she had while living at the abbey. With only her face visible, one could just see Isilmë's round, freckled cheekbones and pink lips that were meant for smiling and laughter, not the somber life of a nun. It was not until she had hurt her ankle that she finally gave up the headdress, revealing she was a hidden beauty.

Isilmë only saw herself as short, curvy, and freckled, and the color of her hazel eyes was common among Scots. Her one vanity was her auburn hair—thick, vibrant, and just a tad wild. Like Shinae, Isilmë must have refused to cut her hair very short like most nuns did. Shinae had been scorned by the abbess for being rebellious, and while amicable in most things, cutting her hair was never going to be one of them.

The largest difference between them was their manner of speaking. Shinae preferred to have a calm voice and spoke directly and concisely when needed, keeping most of her thoughts or opinions to herself. Isilmë could not be more different. Never at a loss for words, she was gregarious to the point that it rankled many people's nerves. As a captive audience for the past several days, Shinae could do nothing but listen. But she also understood what compelled her friend's constant babble. Growing up in the Church, Isilmë had been verbally stifled her entire life, which had only intensified her need to vocalize every thought, emotion, and opinion to anyone within hearing distance.

After five days of travel, it was hard to say if Shinae wanted warmth or silence more. Neither was possible until they reached Lochlen.

* * *

Brodie pushed his blue-and-white kilt back down in frustration. The wind wanted to undress him and, aside from the chill in the air, he was not the type to wander around in only a léine. He turned north, glad to be heading away from the castle lights and into the darkness. He had endured hours before he had been able to escape Lochlen Castle's walls and its inhabitants' overwhelming cheerfulness. The rain from earlier had stopped, but it was threatening to return as clouds started to block the night sky. Periodically, the moonlight peeked through, enabling him to see into the distance, but one had to know the area well when outside the village at night to keep from getting lost.

"Where are you going?" The jaunty question erupted beside him.

Brodie's gold-brown eyes gave his friend a hard stare, making it clear he wished to be alone. "I left without telling anyone for a reason."

Dunlop chuckled. "Aye, it was so clear that I thought you were practically begging me to follow."

"I wish to be alone." Brodie's low voice rumbled with displeasure.

"Probably, and who could blame you? That Callum boasts enough confidence and good looks to fill two great halls, let alone one." He paused, then added, "The *pol thoin's* is also too observant."

It was partially true. Callum's abundant self-assurance in any setting was often irritating, but tonight he had unwittingly brought up some sensitive topics. It rankled that the esteemed Schellden commander could see the truth of situations he knew little about.

After an eight-year hiatus from being a commander for Colin McTiernay, Brodie had abruptly returned to Lochlen Castle. That was three months ago. All knew this. What they did not know was that he had returned to the McTiernays after being dismissed as Laird Donovan's presumptive heir. This was known only to very few—none of whom would have shared that information with anyone. Yet Callum had correctly guessed at the truth and boldly asked him why the laird had made such an unexpected decision. Brodie had silently risen, left the gaiety of the great hall, and left.

Truth was, he did not know why Mahon had told him to leave.

Dunlop gave his friend a light punch on the arm. "You should be finding a willing woman to lose yourself in. Nothing like being in the soft arms of a curvy female to make you forget your troubles."

Brodie said nothing. He had not been with a woman since his return and Dunlop no doubt correctly suspected that he had not lain with one for far too long before that.

The years had not changed his friend much. Dunlop still had his easygoing demeanor, which hid the true force of his nature. His dark hazel eyes saw far more than people realized until his sarcasm gave him away. It always held more truth than was comfortable and tended to put people on edge. Just like it did now.

"I don't need a woman. I need to think and be alone."

"So you say," Dunlop replied with a shrug.

If anyone did understand him, however, it was Dunlop. Eight years ago, they had been close friends, until an unusual opportunity had separated them. Three months ago, unexpected events had thrown them back together. Despite the near decade of separation, Dunlop acted and probably believed that their friendship had changed very little. And, in a way, he was right.

When he had left, Colin McTiernay was the new laird of the Dunstan clan. Colin had taken over as a McTiernay chieftain of his wife's clan upon her father's death. At that time, Brodie had been a member of Colin's elite guard. Now, eight years later, Dunlop was still a commander but with more seniority, significantly more responsibility, and the confidence to match such a position. Brodie, however—who was three years older than his friend—was now nothing more than a displaced soldier with little possibility of becoming an elite guard again. He was not even sure he wanted his old position. At one and forty, he helped where he could and supported the McTiernay commanders where needed, glad to help the clan and its army as needed.

"Come, let's return."

"You should have worn a hat," Brodie chided.

Dunlop issued him a scowl. Nearly bald since his early twenties, Dunlop had compensated for his thinning hair by growing a thick, brown, slightly gray beard. The little hair that he did have grew only on the sides of his head, which Dunlop routinely shaved. And yet, while baldness was not attractive on some men, Dunlop thought it improved his appearance to women. His smooth head and bushy beard had always made him look older than his age of which he took advantage. Brodie suspected that even now only a few knew exactly how old he was.

Brodie, on the other hand, kept his face shaven and possessed thick, shoulder-length, dark blond hair that had been a much lighter color when he had served Colin McTiernay. Under Donovan, it had darkened, and to hide the few grays, he usually tied it back at his nape.

Another significant difference was their height. Dunlop was almost three inches taller, but Brodie had always outsized his friend in girth, and despite the years and age, he was still considered one of the strongest among Lowlanders. Only a few could best him in strength, and not reliably. He would have been considered quite the catch upon his return to the clan, but his once-attractive face had disappeared. Now people only saw dark emotions in his expression. Time and experience had left no trace of his previous jovial personality.

For the next hour, Dunlop and Brodie walked in silence. A sudden gust of wind caused Brodie to look up. Clouds were getting thicker and he could feel the moisture in the air rising. It would soon be raining again, and this time it would be heavy, concealing most, if not all, of the moonlight.

"Leave now and you might make it back before the storm hits," Brodie suggested. "Frank's cottage is near, and he told me earlier that he'll be staying with his eldest daughter throughout the festivities if I need to be alone."

Several of the farmers who lived a ways from the castle were staying with friends or family who lived in the village next to Lochlen, so they could enjoy the rare nighttime celebrations. It was not often that multiple feasts were held this time of year. Lammas Day, a holiday celebrated in August, was a single festival to mark the annual wheat harvest. This August, however, was unusual. Colin McTiernay had invited all his brothers to gather together to enjoy the holiday at Lochlen Castle.

Fierce winter snowstorms the past few years had made it impossible to travel long distances even in the Lowlands from November to April, and if the winter trend continued, it would be the same this year. As a result, none of the McTiernays had been all together since the last McTiernay marriage five years before. So instead of gathering for Christmas at McTiernay Castle, Colin had sent word to his brothers suggesting they bring everyone together in August to help celebrate Lammas at Lochlen. With the mild weather, all could make the journey—even the youngest—and celebrate the first wheat harvest festival of the year together.

Brodie thought it a fine idea until he remembered Colin had six brothers, five of whom had children. For the last couple of weeks, the McTiernays had kept coming and coming—all very boisterous and annoyingly merry. By the noise, one would assume every family had arrived simultaneously when Conor, the clan chief, his wife, and four children came through the gate. The noise had been loud and boisterous. But for a week, more McTiernays came, each with noisy children—most of them small with piercing shrieks of laughter or distress. Only Conan and his wife, Mhàiri, had yet to arrive, and no one knew just when they would get there.

After the families' immediate euphoria upon arrival, Brodie had hoped that the noise would calm, but if anything, it had continued to rise. Colin and his wife, Makenna, had five children, and his siblings brought eleven more. To find any peace and quiet, one was forced to leave the castle.

After a few minutes of walking in silence, it was clear that Dunlop was not returning back to Lochlen. "Know that if there is only one bed, you're sleeping on the floor."

Dunlop once again shrugged his large shoulders. They had both slept outside many times over the years so sleeping on the floor was not a concern. "As long as there is a fire and shelter from the rain," he said in hopes that his friend would finally break down and talk.

It was not that Brodie was unwilling to discuss Laird Mahon Donovan and what had happened, he just did not know what to say that Dunlop did not already know. He just had never dreamed he would be back on McTiernay land.

Brodie stopped walking and squeezed his eyes shut. He had been a fool to think a non-Donovan would be named Mahon's heir. Brodie may have lived among them for years, but he was a Dunstan by birth and a McTiernay at heart.

Colin McTiernay—born and raised a Highlander— had married Makenna Dunstan and, upon her father's death, took over leading the clan. Within a couple of years, he'd won the hearts of most clansmen and women, and the clan was now referred to as the Dunstan-McTiernays, a clan under the powerful Highland McTiernays.

The takeover had been far from trouble-free, but eventually it had been done, and with Mahon's support. Brodie had just assumed it would be the same for him when the laird finally announced Brodie as his heir.

But he had not, and the only man Brodie could think of who might be named Mahon's heir was Taveon. Just shy of six feet, his girth was muscular. His long, black hair and brown, almond-shaped eyes made him nauseatingly attractive to women.

He was not only a true Donovan, Taveon was an excellent swordsman, and the men liked him. It was why Brodie had made him a commander. Taveon was also considerably overconfident and needed to mature at least several more years and fight in a few battles with true enemies, before he would truly be a good leader. All this Brodie had thought was obvious to Mahon. But when Mahon suggested Brodie return to Colin McTiernay, Taveon's usually congenial expression turned smug at the idea of being named as the Donovan heir. It had felt like betrayal then and still did now. Pride compelled Brodie to say nothing and simply leave the clan. Arguing would have been pointless. Thankfully, Colin had welcomed him back, allowing his commanders to decide on Brodie's role and responsibilities.

Thunder cracked and lightning lit up the sky. Brodie shifted his thoughts to start searching for Frank's cottage, or at least signs of where it should be. It was close, but he could not yet see it with clouds blackening the surroundings. Dunlop glanced around as well. Pointing southwest, he said, "It's over the next hill."

Brodie grunted and followed in silence. Despite his years away, he knew the land and felt comfortable walking among the hills even in the near darkness, but Dunlop had lived in this part of the Lammermuir Hills since birth. He knew every rock, bush, and cottage. He could practically be blind and still find his way around.

Brodie began heading in the direction Dunlop had indicated as lightning lit up the clouds, revealing a huddled silhouette to his right. He stopped and stared into the darkness to see if he had been mistaken. Another flash. He had not. It was a drenched figure barely shuffling along in the same direction he and Dunlop had been going. He could not imagine who would be venturing out in this dangerous weather, when even animals knew to find shelter.

The crumpled figure suddenly collapsed.

Brodie ran forward, with Dunlop on his heels.

CHAPTER TWO

Brodie reached the huddled figure and could just barely make out that she was a woman, drenched and shivering. Muddy footprints showed that if she had managed to keep walking in the direction she was headed, she would have passed Lochlen Castle without even knowing it.

He picked her up, surprised to find her lighter than he thought she would be in her sopping garment. Lightning between the clouds followed by earsplitting thunder started to come more often in the sky, and any moment now another torrent of rain would be released.

Brodie turned about to head to the cabin when Dunlop pointed to the woman's filthy white tunic and said in an incredulous voice, "She's a nun."

Another crack of thunder filled the air and the wind picked up. Brodie nodded. "We need to get her to Frank's cottage."

He started to move, and the woman suddenly opened her eyes. Her teeth were chattering so much, she could hardly speak, and yet she began to squirm, somehow finding the energy to resist being held.

Giving up, she murmured, "Isilmë."

Her voice was so quiet, he could barely tell if she had even said anything. Her body shuddered violently, and Brodie began to walk more briskly, feeling an urgency grow inside him. She needed to get warm and dry before she caught ill.

Brodie felt a cold finger curl around the edge of his léine. She gave it a tug and then tugged again. When he slowed and gave her attention, she whispered hoarsely, "Find Isilmë."

Again, lightning struck between the clouds, lighting up the night sky, and in that brief second, he saw her index finger pointing in the direction from which she had come and the greenest eyes he had ever seen.

Brodie paused as he grasped what she meant. "Is someone traveling with you?" He stared at her, waiting for an answer, wondering if she was conscious.

Brodie looked curiously at Dunlop, who shrugged. "I have not heard of any nuns in this area." Brodie agreed. He did not know of a family with a daughter who had taken any vows, but that did not mean there wasn't one.

Then she barely opened her eyes once more and gave a small nod. Brodie felt Dunlop's large hand squeeze his shoulder to get his attention.

"Someone needs to find her friend. I was going to go back for help, but that'll take too long." Dunlop's voice had been solemn, depicting the seriousness of the situation. They both knew if her friend was similarly drenched, death would most likely take her before the sun rose.

"You go. I'll get this one to the cottage," Brodie replied, holding the now-limp, unconscious form.

Dunlop held out his hand as he felt the first few drops of cool water splash on his palm. It was summer, but this storm's wind could still chill a person to death if they were not protected or moving. "Frank's home is on the other side of the hill. Get her there. I'll either join you with the other one or find shelter. What's coming is going to be a deluge no one should be out in."

Brodie heard the rapid plopping sound of Dunlop's retreating footsteps and then turned to make his way to Frank's cottage. His friend knew the area thoroughly, and even in the dark, Dunlop could search far more quickly than he could. Brodie hoped he found the second nun alive.

The thought sent a bolt of urgency through Brodie as he pulled the nun tighter to him. "You're safe now," he whispered as his own steps, once aimless and unhurried, now had purpose and speed.

He could not remember the last time he felt truly needed, and every instinct drove him to protect the woman in his arms. It had been pure luck he had seen her. If he had not, it would have been days before someone found her body, puzzled as to who she was and why she had been out in the storm. Questions he too wanted the answers to, but first he needed to get her safe and warm.

Slowly, consciousness came back to Shinae, but she kept her eyes closed and her body still. A fire was crackling, and she was lying on a lumpy but surprisingly comfortable mattress stuffed with wool. Someone must have found her and Isilmë and brought them to safety.

Shinae reached instinctively for her *sgian dubh* and upon feeling only skin, her eyes popped open. She had not a stitch on her. Isilmë should be going off in a torrent about her unclothed state, but there was only the sound of the fire.

Glancing around, it was clear Isilmë was not there, and that she was in someone's home, not in one of Lochlen's bedchambers. Someone had found her, brought her to their cottage, and undressed her. And the sound of someone throwing a log into the fire meant they were still there, not out searching for her companion.

Shinae tightened her fists on the edges of the blanket covering her and pulled it tightly around her as she sat up. She turned her head toward the hearth and saw a large man staring into the flames. He was wrapped in a dark, blue-and-green plaid tied around his middle. Their clothes were all around him. A blue and white kilt, a man's shirt, her filthy tunic—all draped on whatever he could find and placed near the fire so they could dry in the heat.

The muscles along his broad shoulders and well-developed arms rippled as he grabbed a poker to stoke the fire. There was something spellbinding about the way he moved. Muscles rippling, powerful, sensuous. All in all, he made an impressive figure. Power and strength radiated from him in waves.

She couldn't keep her eyes from following his every movement and wished she had been awake when he rescued her. Only someone with his strength could have carried her drenched form in the storm to safety. It was almost laughable to think of the monks at Dryburgh carrying her in a storm. Instead, they would have dragged her until giving up. Not a one would care more about her than themselves. They had proven that by their flight during the fire.

He shifted again and returned the poker to its resting place, and then clasped the wooden mantel as he continued staring into the flames heating the room.

Shinae closed her eyes, sucked in a quivering breath, and tried to slow her rapid heartbeat. Just looking at him was actually affecting her. No man had ever done that . . . but then again, they had always been clothed. If her rescuer had been dressed, she doubted she would be reacting this way and almost demanded that he put on his clothes, regardless of their sopping state. But reason took hold. What was the man supposed to have done? Leave her in soaked clothing to die of sickness, undoing his efforts to save her? Not to mention that he had already seen her bare and was clearly not interested.

Shinae coughed and in a raspy voice asked, "Isilmë?"

Brodie heard her question and was flummoxed for a second. He had heard her movements and been preparing for the shrilling he was sure was to come once she realized her naked state. She had been shaking violently when he carried her into the cabin, leaving him no choice but to undress her. Aye, she might be a nun, but it had still needed to be done. He had been telling himself that once she calmed, he would explain that he had disrobed her in the dark and barely saw or touched her form.

"Isilmë," she croaked again, breaking Brodie's line of thought.

Brodie cleared his throat. "My friend went to get her and find them shelter," he said with the certainty he felt.

The woman said not a word, but he could hear her teeth start to chatter. He grabbed his tartan, draped over the chair closest to him, laid it on the floor in front of the fire, and then pointed at the now-empty chair. "Come sit by the fire if you're still cold," he said with his back still toward her.

Shinae did as he suggested, glad he was not looking at her. "Th-thank you and y-your friend," she managed to get out. "We w-would have died."

Brodie instinctively turned to ask just what she was doing out in such weather but stopped when he saw her huddled in the chair, with the dark blue-and-green plaid from the bed wrapped around her.

He swallowed. He deliberately had not tried to ascertain what the woman he had carried out of the storm looked like. He had known enough. She was a nun, and beyond being a female in need of rescuing, she was of no interest to him. In the darkness of the cabin, he had stripped her bare, removed her knives, and put her on the bed, tucking a soft blanket around her. Then he had made a fire, put her clothes out to dry, undressed his own self, laying out his léine and tartan before wrapping a thin McTiernay plaid he had found around his waist. Afterward he had gazed into the fire to warm himself and indulged in some fleeting thoughts about the wayward nun . . . where she had come from and how she had gotten lost in the hills. Beyond that he had not really thought about her at all or even glanced her way.

His mind had quickly drifted back to the reason he

had ventured away from the castle: *What was he going to do?* Because he could not continue as he was—a man without purpose.

Upon seeing her huddled in the chair, however, his thoughts suddenly shifted, and he felt his body come alive after many months of being disinterested in the opposite sex. She was a nun, and he had been expecting her to look like one. But the bedraggled woman looking at him was nothing like the spinster he had envisioned while undressing her.

He had not encountered many nuns in his life, but he had seen a few. Most were wrinkled and wore haggard expressions. This woman, however, not only looked nothing like a nun, she did not behave like one either, carrying weapons that could easily injure her. She may be covered by the blanket from the bed, but underneath it, she was completely bare, as his lower body was now painfully reminding him.

Brodie quickly searched for something to say and saw some bread he had brought with him in his sporran. "Er, um, are you hungry?" he asked much too quickly. "It's a little dry from the fire's heat, but otherwise fresh."

Shinae let go a small chuckle, relieved to see he was also a little shaken at their situation. It did not matter why he was nervous, only that he was, and she could feel her body relax. She curled her feet underneath her and nodded her head. "I couldn't hunt in the rain, and finding sweet cicely and chanterelles has been a luxury the last day. Dried bread will be a delight," she answered with a large smile as she took the bread from his extended hand. It was awkward, but somehow she managed to keep the blanket closed and around her shoulders as she took her first bite. It was delicious. She had only some foraged fruit, herbs, and mushrooms for the last couple of days, and the bread was enough to make her softly moan with pleasure.

Brodie swallowed and took a step back, but his dark hazel eyes were locked on her curled figure. *Nuns looked like that under all that stuff they wear?* Each time she took a bite she had to move her hand, and the blanket opened slightly, giving him a glimpse of her body. Even in her disheveled state, her beauty was unmistakable. She was no longer in her early youth, which made her only more enticing, but neither was she beyond child-bearing years. Her facial bones were delicately carved, her genial mouth, and lashes that swept down across her cheekbones partially hid green, crystalline eyes unlike any he had ever seen.

Shinae popped the last bite of bread in her mouth, moaned once more, mumbling about how she now needed a drink, and then looked at him expectantly.

"Can I have something to drink?" she asked again, suddenly feeling very vulnerable.

The man looked around and with a sigh of frustration upon seeing there was no ale, poured her some water from a bucket into a mug. As she drank its entire contents, she decided she did not care if her shift was still damp. She needed to put it on. Many nuns did not wear them, but she preferred the feel of cambric, not wool, against her skin.

Brodie knew he was staring and that had made her uncomfortable enough to stand up and take her shift from one of the mantel's nails. He watched her feel it, and while he could still see some damp parts, she had obviously deemed it dry enough when she twirled her index finger, indicating for him to turn around.

Needing similar armor, he lifted his léine from a similar nail, turned around, and slipped on the garment, letting the McTiernay blanket fall to the floor. The shirt was long enough to cover him, but it was also thin enough to reveal his aroused self. Seeing a second chair at the small table across the room, he went and grabbed it and put it in the only spot he could—next to hers. By the time he was done, she was sitting back in her chair with the blanket once again around her shoulders, not quite as tightly as it had been.

Brodie wanted to stretch out his legs but could not risk it without exposing how hard he was. It had been too long since he had been with a woman, and she was too pretty. It was going to be difficult to keep himself under control. With her so close, his mind could focus on nothing else. Her long black hair tumbled over her shoulders, as if she had just stepped out of a bath. With her dark coloring and bright green eyes, she was the most unusual-looking Scot he had ever seen.

"I would have thought after taking my clothes off you would no longer have a need to stare at me."

"And were you not staring at me as well?" He glanced over at the bed, indicating that he had been aware she had spent some time looking him over after she awoke.

She almost replied, *what did you expect?* He may not be a young man, but he was a very good-looking one who was still in his prime. Being half dressed, she could not help herself. *Just as he could not help himself,* her inner angel added.

With his elbows on his knees, he turned his head and looked straight at her. She held his look and refused to give in to the need to fidget like a little girl underneath her father's stern stare.

"What causes a nun to be out hunting for her fare alone, in the dark, in a storm? Were you trying to drown yourself?" A loud snap of thunder clapped right above them, followed by the sound of heavy rain, as if to prove his point.

"Ah, but I am not a nun," Shinae corrected him in Gaelic. "Or should I say I am *no longer* a nun," she paused, and with a bit of mockery, added "nor was I alone." A month ago, she had set herself free of her self-donned shroud of meekness and for the last few weeks had felt, acted, and spoken as she used to when she had lived in the Highlands.

"When I found you, *lass*, you were alone," he replied in the Highland tongue, which many Lowlanders did not know. Most Lowlanders only conversed in Scots, especially those who lived this close to Scotland's border with England.

His reminder worried Shinae once again. "Are you sure Isilmë is safe?"

"Dunlop found her and took her to safety," he said with such confidence Shinae could not help but believe him. "He would not stop until he did."

It had been many years since Shinae had been a naïve girl and thought all in the world were kind. But at fourteen, she discovered that not all strangers were well meaning. Thankfully, she had been able to defend herself, but she was glad to have been sent to her aunt at the priory. Since then she had not been alone with a man, and she knew she should be frightened now. But her rescuer's voice . . . it was the same one she remembered when she thought she was going to die.

You're safe now, it had whispered.

The sound was low and full of command, but at the same time soothing. It was full of strength and control—something she suspected this man conveyed even when he said nothing. Her gut told her she was safe then and still safe now.

She nodded her head to let him know she believed him. "My name is Shinae."

Brodie fought back a grin. "Mine's Camdyn, but people here call me Brodie."

Her brow furrowed. "As in Clan Brodie near Auldearn?" she asked with unexpected excitement.

"Aye." His surprise was evident.

"I once knew a young woman from that clan. She would talk of swimming in the River Nairn, which she informed me was how she could tolerate the freezing brooks and rivers of the Torridon mountains."

Brodie started coughing. Supposedly of Celtic ancestry, with Pictish royal ancestors, the Brodie clan was one of the first to settle northern Scotland. The people were incredibly fierce, but small in number. Unless from the area, Highlanders were unaware of the clan. In the Lowlands *no one* had heard of them.

"My mother's father was brother to Laird Brodie and my father was a Dunstan elite soldier. They met at Urquhart Castle when King Robert—who wasn't the king then—held a great meeting of many lairds. Not sure the outcome of the meeting, but they fell in love, married, and moved to the Lowlands, where the Dunstans lived."

"So that is why you are called Brodie?"

He bobbed his head and flashed her a smile. "My mother has called me that since I was a bairn. It stuck, and it reminds me of where I came."

"Are your parents still alive? Do you see them often?"

Brodie glanced at Shinae, and she looked so earnest in her need to hear more that he could not stop himself from obliging.

"We were happy living in the Lowlands under Alexander's lairdship until my father fell fighting for independence in the Battle of Dunbar. I was a young boy on the verge of turning into a man, and my mother was afraid that I might just disappear to join the next fight and get myself killed. She was probably right." He sighed, remembering her frantically packing to leave.

"As soon as she convinced Laird Dunstan to order a couple of soldiers to travel with us for protection, she left for her northern home. I was a year past ten at the time. But in the Highlands, under Brodie tutelage, I learned to expertly wield a sword plus a half dozen other weapons. When I reached twenty, I came back to Lochlen Castle, the home of my father and my birthplace, and joined Laird Dunstan's army."

Shinae imagined him as a young man, skinnier and yet bulging with muscles like he did now. She suspected he had been stronger and faster than most of the Dunstan soldiers. Highlanders were huge and deadly, and Brodie's abilities to use multiple weapons most likely made him one to watch. "Highland trained, you must have risen through Dunstan ranks quickly."

"I did," he replied with a wide, boyish grin. "A few years later, by the time Colin McTiernay arrived, I was part of the elite guard and Dunlop had just been named one of the training commanders." Brodie plucked the blue and white kilt that was hanging on a nail and placed it on his lap before stretching out his legs in front of him. Seeing all was adequately hidden, he leaned back and interlocked his hands behind his head. "We were constantly fighting off English invasions and barely escaping death."

"We?" Shinae prodded.

"Dunlop and me. We could anticipate each other's moves. Those were good days. I miss them," he ended with a sigh.

Shinae wanted to know why he spoke like they were no longer so close, but her inner angel said to wait a while.

"So, do you consider yourself a Highland or Lowland soldier?"

Brodie opened his mouth to say it was his turn to prod into her life when he paused and thought about the answer to a question no one had ever asked before. He shrugged with his chin and replied, "Both. I think of myself as a Lowlander because I am the son of a Lowlander. However, I fight like a Highlander, can speak Gaelic, and feel more at ease around them. Fortunately, the McTiernay-Dunstan army is a combination of both."

He saw her puzzled look and sat up. "That, however, is a story for another time."

Her brow remained furrowed, and he found himself wanting to reach over and rub it away. Brodie could not believe he had been rattling on for so long. He had never been one to talk much and here he was, with a woman he did not know a thing about other than that she was once a nun, who had lived in the Highlands . . . and carried weapons. He suddenly felt very vulnerable. He had just volunteered information about his life few knew to this haphazard-looking female with incredible eyes. If he was not careful, he would not have a secret left.

"So why did I find a dagger hidden in your tunic and another strapped to your leg?"

Shinae's eyes grew large at the amusement she heard, as if she wore them simply to make her feel powerful and not for literal use. "I told you that I hunted for our food. I-I may not be strong enough to wield big swords, but I-I can get rabbit and quail when they are around," she asserted.

Shinae had stumbled over her words, and any hope of that being enough of an answer vanished when she saw that he wore a huge, mischievous grin as he shook his head.

"You don't believe me?"

Women carrying weapons was not that unusual to him. He knew a few who did, many of whom she would meet the next day at Lochlen Castle. The idea was not implausible; it was how she responded that was so comical. Her chin was stuck in the air, her eyes were narrowed, and her back had gone completely straight. He expected that if he questioned her abilities any more she would challenge him. His smile became even larger at the idea and, unable to keep his mirth to himself, he erupted into full-body laughter. Unable to help herself, Shinae joined him. It had been so long since she last laughed out loud. It felt good, and the wall she had instinctively built around herself lost another stone.

"I blathered on and on about myself. It's your turn."

"Aye, but your life is interesting. Mine is not." He crossed his arms and looked at her. Shinae rolled her eyes and then pointed her finger at him. "When you start to yawn, I'll refuse to continue."

She shifted in her chair to a more comfortable position and began as he had, with her parents. "My father is a traveling merchant and met my mother on his travels. He is a brilliant man, and she liked to say that he entranced her with his stories. Anyway, they fell in love, married, and, being a gypsy, she was comfortable traveling all the time. It seemed like a perfect fit, and she went with him, for she was just as full of wanderlust as he was. Inevitably they had me, and four years later, my sister."

"Where were you living then?"

"Nowhere in particular. Father was always moving, and my mother loved the life. We grew up learning how to build shelters, cook outside, and packing up to do it all again the next day."

Shinae could tell that Brodie was both shocked and not in the least bit bored. Encouraged by his interest, she continued. "But as we grew, my mother became concerned about her daughters being able to protect themselves. As a gypsy, her caravan had often been ambushed. She had learned to wield a weapon as a young woman and was determined my sister and I learned as well. Her mother had taught her to use a dagger and she taught us. Like myself, my sister Mhàiri became an expert in their use, but she never enjoyed the feel of a blade, as I do."

Her frame immediately stiffened as she realized what she had just admitted. Brodie sat still as he waited for her to continue, wondering if she really was any good.

"That's it. That is why you found daggers strapped on me," she declared, throwing her hands in the air.

Silence filled the room. Her voice was pleasant and sweet; he bet many a person fell into the trap that she was helpless and needed saving. He was just glad that the one time she actually did, it was he who found her.

The fire crackled. "That explains your distant past, but not how you became a nun and then not," he prompted.

It was too quiet again, and Shinae knew that it would remain that way until she told this portion of her life's story. It was not a secret, she had just never shared it with anyone. Until now, no one had been interested. With a deep breath, she began. "When I was ten and four, my mother caught an illness and passed away. Soon afterward, a man took an interest in me. I did not think much about it at the time. He was easy to dispatch, but soon afterward my father sent me away to his sister. I knew he loved me but I admit at the time I did not understand why I could no longer live with him, though my sister could. Four years later, Mhàiri arrived at the priory— she had just turned four and ten. I suddenly understood. She looked like a blossoming young woman but not at all ready to wed and become a wife and mother."

Brodie let out a snort, as if he were disgusted with the idea of taking someone so young to bed. "Did you like living with your aunt?"

Shinae looked at him, and the heavy look in her eyes

vanished as she thought about the priory and her beloved aunt. "I did. She was part of a Culdee community, who lived separately from the Catholic Church," she said pointedly. "My home was a priory located somewhere in the middle of the Torridon mountains. As I grew older, I came to appreciate their focus on helping others and aiding the community as needed. There, they could devote themselves to God without having to take vows. Though my sister contributed, she was too much like my parents, with the constant desire to travel. So, when my aunt passed away, I agreed to join Mhàiri. She could explore the Highlands, I would help start other Culdee communities before they all disappeared.

"But before we could leave, the priory caught fire, which left us needing to find another place to live. Mhàiri was befriended by a clan, but before she could be reunited with my father, she married a McTiernay Highlander who I hope appreciates her talents, and her often-sharp wit."

Brodie wanted to bang his head against the mantel for being so obtuse. Shinae was the older sister of Conan McTiernay's wife. It had been approximately five years since he had seen Mhàiri periodically during the weeks before their wedding ceremony, but she was not someone easily forgotten. Dark-framed eyes, small-boned, tiny waist with a full figure—he had thought Conan a lucky man. But Shinae . . . she had all the same features yet somehow they were much more appealing.

Once again, his body was revealing the direction of his thoughts. "You don't sound very sure that he does," Brodie stated as he pulled in his legs and sat upright in his chair.

"I had heard a few rumors that did not lead me to believe he would make a good husband. But then, neither can I imagine Mhàiri giving up her precious freedom to just anyone after absolutely refusing to even speak to a man who wasn't part of the priory." She turned her head to look Brodie directly in the eye and added, "Many of whom were not only nice but quite handsome and wealthy."

A frisson of jealousy suddenly went through him. The emotion was unexpected. She was speaking of her sister, but it was visions of Shinae being swarmed by men asking for her hand flashing through Brodie's mind.

"My father assured me—the one time we were allowed to meet—" she scoffed, "that it was a good match."

"And you decided to join the Catholic Church."

Shinae took a deep breath and exhaled slowly. "They told me that not only would I have shelter and food and the ability to worship God, but have opportunities to support nearby villagers in times of need."

Brodie almost choked when he thought of the Church helping others. Maybe a clan's priest was generous with the time, but abbeys were full of those who preferred isolation, if not demanded it.

"Let me just say that it was not the life I was promised," she whispered.

With the Culdees, Shinae thought she had found the passion married men and women felt for one another in her love and passion for the Lord. Giving and supporting others gave her peace and contentment like nothing else. Like Mhàiri, men had always made it clear that they appreciated her looks, but never saw past her physical appearance. Even those she had tried to get to know had not been able to rein in their sex drive. But with those she helped, it was different. It was why she joined the Culdees and eventually the Catholic Church. Serving others was a different kind of passion, and it had made her happy. Now, at eight and twenty years old, Shinae planned to find her sister, share Cyric's secret, and then leave to join their father once he was located.

Realizing that Brodie was waiting for her to finish, Shinae cleared her throat and started to speak again. "So, when the English lit Dryburgh Abbey on fire, I decided it was my chance to leave the Church and make the journey to Lochlen to visit my sister." She stopped there and prayed he would not ask about how she knew Mhàiri and Conan McTiernay were to make an appearance sometime this month.

Brodie did indeed want to know how Shinae knew her sister was going to be visiting Lochlen this month. Maybe if he had not witnessed her fight to keep from yawning, he might have pushed her to reveal more. But seeing Shinae's eyes close and her head fall to the side, his need to see to her well-being, however, won the fight.

He took one last, long look at her face, committing it to memory in case he woke finding tonight all a dream. Then he slipped a hand underneath her and carried her once more to the bed, tucking her blanket around her before forcing himself to stand by the hearth and stare into the flames, contemplating his future.

A future he was certain had just changed.

Shinae watched in horror as her knife sliced through the English soldier. Blood splattered everywhere—her face, her tunic, and her hands were covered in the man's blood. The soldier, now on the ground, started to speak, taunting her that soon her sister would be the one lying dead, and it would be all Shinae's fault. Shinae could feel herself screaming at him, but he only smiled, as if he knew she would not succeed. But she had to and vowed she would.

Brodie shook Shinae more firmly, finally getting her to blink, her brows pinched in confusion. Her fearful eyes were wild and filled with liquid as tears began to fall. Without thought, he slid in behind her, turned her so that he could see her face, and held her tight, whispering over and over again that she was safe.

Shinae clung to his léine and his words, but they did not make her forget what she had dreamed. "I need to find Mhàiri," she mumbled.

"Shh. It's still dark outside, but when the sun rises, we will go to Lochlen and wait for Conan and your sister."

"You know who I am?" she asked in a panic.

"Aye, you have the same features."

"You know my sister?"

"Somewhat. I met her when she wed Conan. Since then they have been traveling. But they promised they would come and should be arriving at Lochlen any day now."

"She is not there yet?"

"Not yet," he replied and felt her entire form go limp in relief. Her need to get to Lochlen and see Mhàiri had an urgency that was not about her missing her sibling, but of something else. Something that made her uncomfortable.

"Go back to sleep. I will stay and keep you safe."

Shinae shook her head. "I cannot. I keep seeing—" She stopped when she realized she was about to reveal something that Brodie would pursue until he knew the whole thing. But she had promised Cyric to keep the king's warning a secret until she met with Conan and her sister.

"Seeing what?" he asked softly.

"The abbey burning," she lied, and somehow knew Brodie was aware that she was not telling the truth. Thankfully, he did not push her to say more. In her vulnerable state, she probably would have divulged why she was really there. If she was wise, she would dress and not say another word to the man. Instead, she snuggled closer to him.

When he did not pull away, a peace filled her that she could not explain. Her reaction to him was even a larger mystery. She liked men, but she had never been physically attracted to one. She certainly had never opened up to one. And yet within hours of meeting Brodie, she had revealed more of herself to him than anyone outside her family . . . and it had felt good when she had.

Until a few hours ago, she had found talking to men rather boring, shallow, and repetitive. But not Brodie. She did not know why, but she wanted to listen to him talk again, get her mind off the visions of her nightmare still repeating in her mind.

Brodie pulled back a few inches and was about to stand, for he knew he was in dangerous territory, about to do something he would regret. But Shinae refused to let him go, and without warning, she pulled him back and pressed her lips against his.

Unable to push her away, he caught Shinae's face between his hands and kissed her slowly, taking his time, letting her feel the endless need inside him. His body grew tight; his control was on a knife's edge and yet he did not want to stop and continued to brush his mouth lightly across hers. Never did he think that a simple kiss would leave him wanting. Aye, it had been months since he had been with someone, but that had been to release a physical need. This was different, which did not make sense. He knew Shinae only a handful of hours and yet his physical desire for her was enormous. When she kissed him, there had been no thought, no caution, only realization that she wanted the same as he—to know what it would be like.

He nipped playfully at her lower lip, and when her mouth remained closed, he could tell she was an innocent. Her body, however, was reacting on natural instinct. Her arms stole softly around his neck, and a moan of despair escaped her throat. The soft, primal sound almost ended any control he had. Forcing himself to slow, he released her lips, kissed her brow, and then went to sit back down by the fire.

When at last his lips released hers, Shinae's chest heaved with the effort it took to breathe. That was not the peck of comfort she had expected. She had been kissed before, but none had caused her body to tremble and ache with the need to take it further. Until just now, her complete lack of response to a man's kiss was one of the reasons she really thought her life was with God, supporting the Church.

"I'm sorry," she said in a soft, self-loathing tone.

Brodie was not sure what Shinae was sorry about, for he certainly wasn't that she had kissed him. He had been dying to do so ever since he had gotten lost in her green eyes.

"I honestly don't know why I did that," she continued.

"It wasn't all you," Brodie growled, disturbed that she might be regretting the embrace. Then he remembered that it was not so long ago she had been a nun. From her closed-mouth response and the desire she had conveyed, he somehow assumed she had never been kissed before . . . then again, it would also make sense if she had. She had initiated the embrace and her moans indicated that she was willing to deepen the kiss and take it further if he had not pulled away.

"Aye," Shinae agreed, "but it was I who started something you would not have."

Brodie was not too sure about that, but he did not want to scare her by telling her he had been on the edge of wanting her. He had not hesitated even a second when she reached out for him.

He stood up, went to the hearth, and began to rub the back of his neck.

Shinae began to fidget in the silence. "Say something."

He blinked and turned around. "Like what?"

"A-anything. Tell me . . . about the family my sister married into."

Brodie was glad she offered a topic that was not about himself or her, and quickly started to comply with her request. "You lived in the Highlands, you had to have heard of them." As he uttered the last word, he wanted to kick himself. He wanted to prolong the discussion of this subject, not end it.

"Very little other than that they are a large clan." She yawned.

He smiled and continued, thankful that he had a topic he could ramble on about without any sexual inferences. "Aye, the McTiernay clan is indeed very large and very powerful, and with close allegiances to several other large, powerful clans. The chief of the McTiernay clan is Conor, and it was his wife, Laurel, who invited your sister to live with them until she and one of his brothers fell in love." He shook his head as he remembered the event.

"You were there? At the wedding? Tell me everything you can remember."

"Hmmm, it was probably one of the most significant events that has occurred in the Highlands for I don't know—decades. Aye, there have been fierce battles with many impactful deaths. I'm sure there have been many important weddings and bairns born, but *Conan pledging himself to one woman*? This was something practically all of Scotland had to see. Laurel had put a pause to the ceremony until all arrived, which took a few weeks. We men got together to pass the time, and I recall winning a few rounds of the caber toss. . . ."

He stopped when he saw that she was waving her hand for him to stop. "Not that. What was Mhàiri wearing? How did she do her hair? What did she say?"

Brodie's brow furrowed. He had no idea how to answer such a request. First, he honestly could not remember that day at all, he had drunk so much ale later that night in celebration. When they had met a week prior, he could recall her being very pretty with unusual eyes, her arguing with Conan quite loudly one time about the long wait, but not much beyond that. Second, she was marrying a McTiernay, which meant she was *not* someone you ogled.

"For details, you'll have to ask the McTiernay wives."

Shinae looked frustrated. "At least tell me about the ceremony."

Brodie wanted to make her happy, so he tried his best to remember. "As I was saying, it is highly unlikely Scotland will ever see such an event again. I can't recall the number of people who came to see the most ill-mannered, arrogant, condescending Highlander get married." Brodie looked at Shinae, pointed his finger at her, and said, "Actually, it was not Conan they came to see but your sister. They wanted to meet the woman who not only captured Conan McTiernay's heart, but who truly loved him in return. Something all thought impossible. Including me."

Shinae's eyes popped open wide. "The rumors were true? My sister actually married such a man!" she exclaimed. "I know she can be a bit eccentric—"

"And stubborn, willful, and, well, let me just end by saying that she is perfect for Conan. Makes me think that it's possible God did make a woman for every man." Once again, his thoughts drifted to Shinae, wondering if just possibly she was the woman God made for him.

"Or maybe he made a man for every woman." Shinae's hand flew to her mouth, covering it. All the thoughts she used to keep buried were just popping out. Seeing him chuckle, Shinae rallied, "My father said they were good together, but I don't want to talk anymore about him."

Brodie briefly looked up and said, "Thank you, Lord," before he returned his focus to her.

"Continue telling me about this Conor and his brothers. Are they all as infamous as my sister's husband?"

"Aye. There are seven McTiernays in total and all are well known for one reason or another. Tomorrow, you will meet five of them. The second oldest, Colin, is the laird of Lochlen and is married to Lady Makenna. Both are easy to spot. She has bright red hair and he is the only McTiernay with short brown hair. Something about his youngest son, Alec, always pulling at it. Conor is the clan chief. You'll know him because he is the only one with gray eyes, the other brothers' are a piercing blue."

Shinae chuckled. She could only imagine the mayhem a bunch of children playing made. "How did someone from the Highlands become laird of a Lowland clan?"

"He married Diedre, the eldest daughter of the Dunstan chief and, as her father only had daughters, it was presumed that Colin and she would produce the next heir. Unfortunately, Diedre was never very strong and died a year into the marriage. Colin was then forced to marry Laird Dunstan's youngest daughter to save the clan from being torn apart by others wanting Lochlen. Lady Makenna is very different from her frail sister and I honestly did not think a man who loved Diedre could fall in love with her youngest sister, but I was wrong, for they have a *lot* of loud offspring."

Fascinated, Shinae prompted him to tell about the others.

"Then there is Cole, and for all his professing how

much he hates the English, he went and married an Englishwoman, Lady Ellenor, who is best of friends with Conor's wife, Laurel, and she is *also* English. Craig and Crevan are twins and actually married twin sisters—"

Shinae put her hand up for him to pause. "Do *all* the McTiernays' names begin with a *C*?"

Brodie snorted. "Aye, and Laurel liked it so much, she followed the tradition by naming all four of her children with a B," he answered, rolling his hazel eyes, indicating what he thought about the idea.

"Anyway," he continued, "Cole is the McTiernay chieftain of Torridon, who is from the area where your priory was located. You know about Conan and your sister. Clyde is the youngest McTiernay, and I cannot tell you much about him other than that the last I heard he was fighting the English, Irish, and reivers for years— anywhere he can wield his sword. As far as I know, he has not returned since he left as a young man and no one knows where he currently is."

"I hope they like me," she whispered, failing in her attempt to stifle a yawn. Shinae felt her eyes getting droopy but did not want Brodie to stop talking. His voice had a deep, timbre that soothed her. She lay down and curled into the blanket. "Keep going."

Brodie obliged, seeing that Shinae would soon be asleep. He told her about all the brothers and what he knew of their wives, everything from how they looked to their personalities. Then, he started to describe the other two McTiernay chieftains—Hamish and Dugan— but she was asleep before she even heard their names.

He sat down by the fire and tried to doze off when he heard a noise. He craned his head back and confirmed that Shinae was still asleep; however, her teeth were chattering so loudly, he was amazed that she had not reawakened.

Brodie threw two more logs on the fire and slipped in behind her. Throwing her blanket over them followed by his, he curled his arm gently around her and hoped his body heat would soon warm her up. Shinae unconsciously moved closer to him and snuggled her back against his chest and slowly stopped shaking. Never had anything or anyone felt so good, and while Brodie knew he should go back to his chair, he could not convince himself to leave her side and fell asleep.

Brodie's head was pounding along with the striking sound at the door. He ignored it. The incredible feeling of the woman in his arms was incomparable to anything he had ever felt. Whoever was at the door was ruining the most glorious night of sleep he had ever had.

Refusing to move, he muttered, "Just ignore it," and decided to thrash his friend the next time they sparred. And he meant it. Dunlop might be equally skilled at fighting, and a bit taller, but Brodie was undeniably stronger. And in his current mood, Dunlop would never waken him from a night's sleep again.

Loud pounding again filled the cottage. This time the commotion was enough to awaken Shinae. Now, he was seriously irritated and bellowed, "*Mo chreach,* Dunlop!"

Shinae's compulsion was to snuggle closer and ignore the noise. She could tell Brodie felt the same when his body suddenly stiffened just as another, much higher-pitched voice was heard. It belonged to someone he could not ignore, and neither could she.

"If you do not open this door right now and prove to me that my friend is well and unharmed, you will not only answer to the Lord our God but to me!"

Shinae took in a deep breath and let it out slowly. Brodie had been right. His friend had not only found Isilmë but had been suffering from her constant hounding that he get her proof Shinae was safe. "I mean it!" Isilmë cried out. "If you have touched a single hair on her body—"

"I'm fine!" Shinae shouted.

"Well, at least we know they are in there," Dunlop said in a jovial voice, which only aggravated Isilmë further.

"Not good enough! She's my friend, and if anything happened to her—"

Dunlop snorted. "What? What is a little freckled thing like you going to do about it?" Shinae could hear scuffling, followed by an "Ow! What was that for?"

Isilmë returned his snort, and Shinae could imagine her tapping her foot with her arms crossed. "What kind of soldier are you?" Isilmë sniggered. "Can't even handle a little kick to the shins."

Dunlop's voice suddenly changed to a much darker tone. "I'm a damn good one, and you're lucky Lady McTiernay is not here or—"

"Or what?" Isilmë returned, clearly unafraid of pending threat.

"Or I'll turn you over my knee and swat you with my sword. Nun or not."

"*Trasna ort féin!*"

"Ah, lass, that's no way to talk to your *hero*," he countered with discernable mirth. "It's what you called me over and over again after I saved your life, and you know it. So, no more name calling or I'll take you back where I found you and send one of my men to get you when you have calmed down."

Isilmë scoffed, and Brodie almost shouted out that his friend was not teasing when Isilmë, who was either oblivious or foolish, dared Dunlop to make good on his threat. "Do it, then, because. . ." but before Isilmë finished her warning, Dunlop swooped her up in his arms and placed her on his shoulders, ignoring Isilmë's shouts and efforts to get free.

Brodie was sure Dunlop was going to leave and relaxed at the thought of being alone once again with Shinae. Unfortunately, that flicker of excitement disappeared at the sound of hooves being pulled to a stop and someone dismounting.

"Well, it seems my message made it to the castle," Dunlop quipped loud enough so that he could be overheard.

Knowing what that meant, Brodie sat up and pointed at their clothes. Shinae bobbed her head in silent agreement. They were just about to rise and dress as fast as they could when Dunlop kicked the door open. In walked one of the loveliest women Shinae had ever seen. She was tall and slender, with long, wavy, pale gold hair with strawberry highlights, and her blue-green eyes looked like the color of the North Sea right before a storm.

"I am Lady McTiernay," Laurel announced, taking in the scene.

"You are correct," she directed to Isilmë. "Your friend is indeed in trouble, but nothing a little wedding at sundown cannot solve."

CHAPTER THREE

Brodie sent a silent thought of thanks to the Lord for Lady Laurel's impromptu appearance. She had brought an extra horse along with her entourage and left them behind upon their departure. When she had seen his and Shinae's . . . state, his mind had raced, thinking of ways to explain, to convince her and everyone that the situation was not what it appeared. And then, Lady Laurel had unknowingly come to his rescue and declared he and Shinae were to wed at sundown. Once they both nodded, Laurel had turned and ordered everyone to leave, and that Brodie and Shinae would *soon* follow. The meaning behind the emphasis on the word "soon" was not missed by the couple.

Glad Shinae was riding in front so she could not see his face, Brodie could not stop smiling. He had no place he needed to be, and he was enjoying the feel of her, Brodie let the horse amble along as he tried to figure out what to say. He knew he should tell her that no matter what Laurel said, Shinae was under no obligation to marry him. Their position may have looked compromising, but nothing had really happened between them. And yet he could not make himself say the words for fear she might choose freedom rather than marriage.

Shinae swallowed, glad she was riding in front so she could not see his face. Most likely it was worrisome, as was hers.

What happened to the easy banter they had shared last night? But deep down, Shinae knew. She had agreed to Lady Laurel's declaration way too fast, practically leaping on the idea, which probably obligated Brodie into agreeing as well. Her mind encouraged her to say something, for the silence was oppressive; however, her faithful inner voice that guided her was saying that marriage to the man sitting behind her would be a dream come true—a dream she never knew she had. She should be feeling ashamed, nervous, and yet she felt none of those things. Last thing she wanted was to have him tell her that he had changed his mind.

In the distance, smoke could be seen from village cottages that surrounded a much larger castle than Shinae expected. "Is that it?"

"Aye, that's Lochlen," Brodie answered and with a heavy sigh, added, "with all of Colin's brothers, their wives, and children. I warn you, for the next few weeks, the inner ward will be in a state of constant chaos. But I vow that when the laird's siblings leave, it will only be the frivolity of his children to be endured."

Shinae could tell Brodie was genuinely unexcited to return, and why should he be? She, on the other hand, was eager to get to Lochlen Castle and all the mayhem Brodie dreaded. After being in an abbey for five years, Shinae was looking forward to some noise and merriment. "How many children are there?"

"Too many," Brodie grumbled and instantly regretted it. All the cheerfulness and constant buzz of familial activity might not bother him as much with Shinae at his side. "Over a dozen adults and at least that in bairns."

Shinae sat in stunned silence. That was a lot of people, and she wondered if there was enough room for her and Isilmë, or if they would have to pray for a generous clansman. But on the heels of that thought came another—she would not be sleeping with Isilmë; she would be sleeping with someone else—her husband. Until last night, she had not slept with anyone since her youth, and it was her sister, usually under their father's wagon. Now, her place would be where Brodie slept. "Where does everyone slumber for the night?"

Brodie gave her a slight squeeze and as if he could read her thoughts, whispered in her ear, "Don't worry, Lochlen has enough room for everyone. Most McTiernay clansmen and women sleep in their homes outside the curtain walls, but wherever we go, it will be together, and I will keep you safe."

Brodie smiled as Shinae sat straight when Lochlen Castle came into view. The massive gatehouse towers awed most the first time they approached the stone fortress. Shinae kept looking back, her mouth slightly open, but it was her emerald eyes as they approached the outer gates that showed her awe the most. "It's enormous," she whispered as they went through the outer gate.

Brodie brought the horse to a halt, dismounted, and helped Shinae slide down before handing the reins to a stable boy. Then, hand in hand, they walked from the middle ward through another set of massive gatehouse towers to the inner ward. Shinae slowly turned around, taking it all in.

Brodie started telling her about what she was seeing. "After the Viking raids, Malcolm III was one of Scotland's first rulers to defy the Norman kings of England, who were reluctant to accept Scottish independence. Malcolm's leadership inspired the construction of many keeps, including Lochlen, named after the small lake located southwest of the castle's town wall. It was continually fortified for over two hundred years to what it is today."

The well-fortified castle was nestled just on the southern edge of the Lammermuir Hills. An odd-shaped outer wall fit the rolling contours of the land and housed the many cottages for castle staff, soldiers, and those who did not need large sections for land, as farmers required. Six massive towers formed the castle's trapezoidal-shaped inner ring. Four drum towers secured each corner and two substantial gatehouse towers allowed entry to the inner ward.

"As you can see, Lochlen was built in phases over several generations."

"It is so much larger than I imagined." Most castles she had seen in her youth, while traveling with her father, were large, single-tower keeps. This was far different. She pointed to the dark tower that stood out from the rest.

"At least one of them had a sense of humor," Shinae said, pointing to the black structure. "That has to be the only one of its kind, in Scotland at least."

"Aye, when *Tòrr-dubh* was built—"

Of course, that would be its name, Black Tower. Shinae almost chuckled out loud, but she was able to swallow her mirth after years of compressing such an emotion. Unfortunately, she did not fool Brodie.

"I thought the name somewhat . . . predictable as well." He looked down to find her smiling at him. Even with her dirty garment and hair that was wild from not being brushed, she was the most beautiful woman in the world.

"I mean, they could have called it the 'formidable tower.'"

"That is much better. The children call it the scary tower so it fits."

"Oh no. It is not scary, but an elegant structure that indicates impregnability."

Brodie could not help himself and burst into laughter. "Laird Ranald Dunstan would be proud to hear you say that. For when he had it built, he thought the dark stone would make the tower indestructible. Rumor is that it took nearly three years to mine and haul enough stone from the mountains of Skye only to discover that the dark stone was not just hard but near impossible to cut and shape. Pride made him finish the tower's exterior out of the wicked rock, but the rest of the castle was built from local limestone."

Lady Makenna's great-grandfather decided Lochlen's inner ward was not large enough to handle the clan's growing needs and had ordered a second curtain wall to be built. Through the crenels, she could see the shadows of other soldiers still at their posts. The number of men on duty may be slightly lower than normal, but every tower and section of the inner and outer curtain walls was manned.

Since Forfar Tower's erection, the laird's sons and daughters had resided in its walls. Its counterpart, Canmore, housed the laird's solar and his connecting day room as well as the lady of the castle's bedchambers and meeting room. Standing on either end of the fortified gatehouse, the towers secured the interior castle ward.

"Will we be staying there?"

Brodie froze for several seconds. *Will* we *be staying there?* she had asked. He had thought about their wedding night quite a bit on their quiet ride back, but he had not once considered just where they were to sleep. The gatehouse towers typically provided the sleeping accommodations for most of the soldiers when they were assigned to guard Lochlen. The other towers were for visitors and people of importance. The bottom gatehouse floors were for storage, guards, a weapons stash, and machinery to operate the portcullis.

Brodie had been sleeping in the gatehouse, where soldiers were at least six to a chamber. He was not sure how Lady Makenna was going to arrange things, but one thing was for certain: He needed another place to rest his head that was not just private but much larger than a makeshift bed.

He paused for a moment, then said honestly, "I doubt it." He needed to change the topic and suddenly he thought it might be a good idea to stop ignoring Callum, who had been waving at him to come to the great hall since their arrival.

Callum Schellden was large and muscular, and had too much reddish-brown hair for a man. His singular turquoise eyes drew the eye of every woman around him, married or not. In other circumstances, he might have liked the good-looking Highlander. As a commander and a soldier, Callum was very capable, but the thought of him flirting with Shinae was more than bothersome— more like self-inflicted torment.

Shinae must have noticed where he was looking. "Who is that man?" she asked with more interest than Brodie liked. *He* had been the one who had saved Shinae, and until she was in all ways his, that seducer of pretty women was not getting anywhere near his soon-to-be wife.

"Just one of the men who has come with the McTiernays to make merry," he replied, wearing a dark scowl. Callum's main job was to ensure the safe travel of the McTiernay twin brothers, Craig and Crevan, and their families. At Lochlen, he periodically helped with security, but the majority of the time he wandered about the clan to make eligible women jolly and a nuisance of himself.

Shinae heard Brodie's gruff reply and felt his hand possessively on her back, pushing her in another direction, wondering if her inner angel was right. Could he be slightly jealous of the tall man?

Brodie's goal was to change her line of sight and

block Callum's. Suddenly, he broke out into a large grin. This was his lucky day. He was not going to have to search for Lady Makenna; she was standing in the inner ward with the other four McTiernay wives and her friend, Isilmë. He escorted Shinae to them and all the chatter stopped. Their attention was solely focused on the great hall.

He turned and saw Callum still waving at him, but more vigorously. Why did the man look like a fool when he could just run over and tell him what was so urgent? He was about to return his attention to Shinae when Colin and Conor stepped out of the hall and signaled for him to come. When a chief and chieftain gestured for one to come, it meant you stopped what you were doing and joined them. It also meant something was wrong. McTiernay commanders and the steward handled most clan problems, and for this to involve him—an ex-commander—meant the situation was serious.

Brodie acknowledged their request with a single nod of his head. All three went back into the hall and pulled Shinae away from the women and quickly whispered, "I must go. You know Laurel already, and the others are McTiernay wives as well. They will help you and introduce you to everything."

Brodie briskly walked across the ward. To what, he had no idea. He hated leaving Shinae so abruptly, but he had no choice but to head to the great hall, praying that whatever was happening would not take long. He had plans at sundown.

Shinae watched as her intended walked toward large wooden doors, located across from the main keep. His frame just seconds ago had been relaxed and comforting. Then, without warning, it had gone stiff with considerable tension. Something serious had happened, and she worried whether it was going to interfere with their pending nuptials.

Before she could give in to the urge to run up and get his assurance, thin fingers lightly curled around her arm and gave her a tug toward the chapel. "Come on, Shinae," Isilmë hissed.

Brodie entered the hall and quickly dodged the sharp table's edges until he reached the main one, where the laird, his lady, and their most important guests usually sat when dining. Now, however, it was filled with Colin's commanders, plus his McTiernay brothers. All were standing around a large piece of vellum that depicted a map of the clan's lands, as well as the lands of those meeting its borders. Brodie went to stand with Dunlop, who barely acknowledged his presence.

"Over a half dozen cows were stolen from here." Colin was laird of the Dunstan-McTiernays, and it was his extended family who had come to visit.

All seven of the McTiernay brothers were known for their strategic abilities in battle, but Colin did not want to draw blood to resolve the situation. "We have multiple herds located throughout our lands, so the loss of cattle is not going to leave my clansmen and women to go hungry this winter, but it will impact the size of the herd as all seven are pregnant." Brodie listened stone-faced. Colin's cows mated in June. It would take a few years to recoup the loss. "News that I overlooked such a theft would spread rampant, practically begging for others to try it as well. Before that happens, I want to speak to the one most likely to have taken them."

"Aye," Conor agreed. "If possible, let's avoid carnage and death." As the chief of all the McTiernays, Conor's word had great influence, but it was Colin's stock and it had happened on Colin's land. He was leading the discussion and would be making the final decision.

Colin slid his finger down the map to a spot just beyond the McTiernay borders. "This strip of land belongs to Laird Jamie Denholm. His keep is almost a day's ride east of our order. Here is where we corral the herd that was robbed. Next to this portion of our border on a fairly high hill is where Aaron Denholm and his family live." Brodie stayed silent, but it was a clear line from Aaron's home to the corral. To take seven springing heifers over such difficult land would be daunting, requiring each one to be led individually. The land to the south was covered in jagged rocks, and the only thing that grew there was black bearberries. "I hope I am wrong, for Aaron has a dovecote he uses to communicate with his laird using pigeons."

"Clever," Conor said. He had never used pigeons to send messages, but King Robert sometimes did. When it worked, pigeon post was the world's fastest communication system.

"I agreed to ignore one missing cow a year as long as Aaron sends one of his pigeons with a red ribbon around its leg whenever the reivers decide to travel north," Colin confessed. "Such a warning has not been sent for the last three years. I assume that after always meeting my army at our border, they've moved on to other, more profitable areas."

"But the agreement with Aaron is still in place."

"I believe so, but with seven springing heifers suddenly missing, I need evidence that Aaron, not the reivers, was responsible."

This time Cole spoke up. "A face-to-face meeting needs to be had with this Aaron Denholm, as well as his laird," Colin said.

"You don't think this Denholm is involved," Cole clarified.

"Nay, nor do I believe it was the reivers. They haven't traveled this way in a long while. And when they do, they steal in large numbers to make their effort worthwhile. And yet *seven* heifers? This was not an accident. The thievery was intentional, and I need to find out just who is behind this before it happens again."

All present voiced their agreement, and once again Colin took charge. "Craig, Crevan, see this line? It denotes the only navigable path through these two hills. Don't try to go up them with the horses. It is cluttered with jagged rocks, making travel over them by horse a risk to not just the animal but oneself. I need you two to do some scouting. I doubt you will come across reiver activity, but you might spy something else that could explain the theft." Then Colin turned his attention to Brodie and Dunlop. "Conor and I are going to visit Laird Denholm to see if he's made any new alliances and remind the man just who and how powerful the McTiernays are.

You two are to do the same with Aaron Denholm. You both know the area, so get there as swiftly as you can, confirm all aspects of our agreement are still in place, and then get back here as fast as possible. Makenna really might skin me if you miss your own wedding."

"And I might help her," Brodie jested.

"Are you really going through w-with marrying that w-w-woman?" Crevan asked. "I thought o-o-once you got back, you'd change your mind. I mean, you don't even know the f-female."

"Aye," Craig said, affirming his twin's opinion. "Regardless of what Laurel said, you don't *have* to marry. Nobody believes anything happened between you and the nun."

"Ex-nun," Brodie corrected.

"Whatever," Craig said dismissively. "Think about it. You still don't know anything about her. and no one would think less of you if you were to be delayed getting back."

"I am going through with it and I have thought about it. I will not change my mind, and I actually do know enough about Shinae to marry her," Brodie replied crisply.

Colin did not want to become involved. He had been around Laurel long enough to know not to interfere with one of her matchmaker plans, especially if his wife also supported it.

"Any questions?" he asked, redirecting the conversation back to the situation at hand.

With shakes of their heads, the group broke apart and Brodie immediately headed for the stables.

Dunlop quickened his pace to keep up with his friend. "Don't you want to stop somewhere first?" he asked, hinting that Brodie should first talk to Shinae to let her know that he had to leave for a few hours.

"Nay, I will not spend a second doing anything that might keep me from getting back in time."

Dunlop moved past Brodie and stopped in his path, not allowing him to move forward. "Craig and Crevan were right."

Brodie clenched his jaw in anger. "Move out of my way."

Dunlop's expression changed to one of astonishment. "I cannot believe it. You, Brodie Dunstan, actually *want* to be married! And to a nun!" Brodie sent Dunlop a look that would wither most men, but instead of feeling intimidated, Dunlop burst into laughter as Brodie stepped around him.

Brodie pursed his lips and tried to think of a way to explain to his friend that marriage to Shinae was not being pushed on him; rather, he had leaped on the idea. Aye, she had looked like a mess that morning, after a night of twisting and turning, always seeking assurance that he had not left. Only when he had held her close was she calm. It did not escape him he was only calm when he was holding her. Despite smelling like someone who had spent a few days in the outdoors and rain, he wanted to be with her, not just that night but every night. Even now, the thought of her made his whole body tighten with desire.

Dunlop clapped his back. "Marrying a virgin. Oh, what fun you will have tonight."

"You have no honor," Brodie grumbled and then barked loudly, "Be warned, marrying Shinae Mayboill will make me the envy of you and every single man within a hundred miles."

Dunlop threw him a skeptical look. He had seen the lass that morning, and while there was some resemblance to her sister, the ex-nun had a way to go before making anyone envious. But then, stranger things had happened . . . like the feelings her odd little friend aroused in him whenever she got feisty.

Isilmë did not move as Shinae watched Brodie head to the great hall. She knew Shinae wanted answers, but her own anxiety needed answers as well. Until she learned that her future—including where she was going to sleep that night—was not in peril, her worry was only going to continue to grow. The McTiernays considered Shinae family because she was the sister of Conan McTiernay's wife. She would not be turned away, even if she did not marry the big, bulky commander who had rescued her. Isilmë did not have the same reason to be confident. No one had sprung up out of the earth eager to marry her, and she was not sure she wanted one to.

It had not been until her ride back with Dunlop that Isilmë realized her own future was not at all clear. An unwanted baby, she had been raised to be a nun. She had no family. She had no idea how to act in the real world, or what to wear, or when it was inappropriate to talk, especially with her superiors. Knowing how to pray, sew, and garden was the sum total of her knowledge.

When Dunlop had found her huddled form, Isilmë had not yet succumbed to the idea of death. He had carried her to the closest cottage and woken the family. It was early in the morning, but the couple had welcomed them inside. The farmer's wife had given her an overly large shift and an arisaid to wrap up in, offering their barn to sleep in once they got warm. Isilmë, imagining Shinae dying somewhere in the rain, was grateful for their offer but insisted Dunlop take her to the castle to get her help. Even when he explained her friend was "safe" with Brodie, Isilmë was not comforted—mostly because she herself felt vulnerable, not having her friend there to vouch for her.

Isilmë gave Shinae's arm another jerk, and she finally broke her gaze and looked where they were headed. The lady of the Castle—Makenna or Laurel, for they both acted as if they were in charge—had asked her to watch for Shinae's arrival and bring her to the chapel.

As they followed the five McTiernay women into the chapel, Isilmë tried once again to assess who was in charge. She assumed the beautiful but commanding blonde was in charge as she was the one who had declared that Shinae and Brodie must be married. But it was the fiery redhead with curly hair who was yelling at a loud and overactive group of children across the inner ward.

With a warm smile and soft voice, she said, "Isilmë, I know that we only just met, but I am Lady Makenna, and this is my lively home." Without warning, the redhead came forward and embraced Shinae and then her in a warm, but very brief hug. Her thick, red hair was curly, and her smile and green eyes reflected the earnestness of her welcome. It only lasted a second, though. Her smile remained, but she took several steps back and joined the other women, who also wore similar pleasant expressions but clearly were reluctant to come any nearer.

"Greetings, Lady Makenna. I'm Shinae."

Makenna smiled at her friend. "As you are Mhàiri's sister and therefore family, please just call us by our names. You really do look so much like Mhàiri, but her eyes are darker," she said while shooing the group of children their way.

"I noticed you gazing at the great hall. Don't worry, they won't be long. You will meet all the men later tonight, after your ceremony," someone, who had light, tawny-colored hair and hazel eyes, said. She was looking at Shinae when she spoke, and Isilmë was feeling as she usually did, like a ghost.

"Raelynd, don't scare her or there might not be a ceremony!" hissed another woman of the same coloring. Isilmë assumed they were sisters.

With hands on her hips, Raelynd hissed back, "If telling her that she will meet and be inundated by more people than she has ever known scares her, Meriel, she is not going to survive a week!"

Isilmë stood opening and closing her mouth at the idea, not knowing whether she should speak. She wanted to be around people and have conversations, but the noise of Lochlen Castle's inner ward was not just chaotic but deafening. Very different from the abbey. Though the shouts filling the inner ward were generally happy sounding, the loudest ones were mostly coming from a gaggle of small children who, without doubt, were on their way to join them.

"*That* is what is going to scare her," another woman mumbled. Isilmë agreed, but looking at Shinae, she saw an eagerness to meet them.

When one of the young girls shrieked, a half dozen large dogs tied up outside one of the towers started barking, increasing the noise. As if Lady Makenna was oblivious to what was happening around her, she continued her introductions, which Isilmë knew would only need to be repeated later. "Raelynd and her sister, Meriel, are like all of us—McTiernays by marriage. And—"

"So sorry, Makenna," Laurel interjected, clearly distracted. "Conor is over there hollering at me and getting agitated that I am not coming." She paused at Makenna's look of disbelief. "You'll be fine. Take them to their temporary bedchambers and ensure baths are waiting for them. And Meriel, can you find something for them to wear before—"

The man who had been impatiently waiting for her suddenly roared out Laurel's name again, clearly impatient. "I'm coming!" she bellowed back and started moving to what had to be her husband. Isilmë wondered how such a loud sound could come from such a thin, delicate-looking woman. Laurel had sounded mad, but her storm-blue eyes had been sparkling, so it remained unclear if Lady Laurel really was angered by the rude interruption.

"And the answer to the questions all of you are asking

yourselves is aye, I am sure. Very sure. And after a short argument with my husband about me not being at his beck and call, I shall return."

Isilmë stood silent as Shinae said her goodbyes and wished the woman luck. Isilmë was not sure if she was shocked into silence by the woman's abrupt departure or if she was carrying on a shouting match where all could hear and see. "What do you mean, you're leaving? So help me, Conor . . ."

Waist-length, wavy, pale gold hair with strawberry highlights bounced with every step she made across the courtyard. Tall and slender, Isilmë could not remember ever seeing a woman look so fierce and delicate at the same time. No wonder she had caught the eye of the Highland chief.

"I've known her for years and it still boggles me how Laurel can do that," Makenna said softly.

"Argue while walking?" Raelynd chuckled. "I am an expert. Ask Crevan."

"Aye, you are, but Laurel does it like nobody else."

"I wonder if I look that magnificent when Cole and I get into it." The voice had an English accent and it belonged to another pretty woman. This one had long, chestnut hair and large eyes. With her short, full frame, Isilmë felt like she was back at the abbey, being overlooked, disappearing into the crowd.

"Of course we do," Meriel piped in with a mischievous gleam in her eyes.

Ellenor's face erupted into a large grin. "I think Cole likes to upset me just so we can make up. I'll admit that I don't mind."

Isilmë could not believe what she was hearing. Dunlop had told her all the McTiernays were madly in love with their spouses. But if that was how men and women expressed their feelings, she was not sure Shinae was going to tolerate matrimony for very long. The woman was incredibly good with knives.

Makenna turned back to the group, as if the last several minutes had never occurred and continued where she had left off. "And to my right is Ellenor, Cole's wife."

Isilmë stretched to look behind Shinae's tall frame and watched an overactive group of children slowly making their way over to them. All the women, including Shinae, were acting as if they could not hear them or the couple shouting at each other by the great hall. Older boys were pushing one another as they walked, clearly a contest of who could knock down whom. Older girls were ambling behind them, whispering and giggling, and the younger ones were running around in circles, screaming as they chased the boy who had what looked to be a little girl's ribbon.

The boisterous group of children continued with their own bickering until they came to a stop right in front of them. The youngest girl with red hair said, all chipper, "Hi, Mama. We are here, like you asked."

"Thank you, *an-éadan*," Ellenor said as she gave her "redbird" a hug. Another young girl, who looked about nine years old, pulled back, plugging her nose. "Mama, why did she do that to her hair?" she asked, pointing at Shinae.

Horrified, Shinae elbowed Isilmë. "Why didn't you tell me how awful I look?"

Isilmë answered honestly. "I thought you knew," she hissed back.

Isilmë knew she and Shinae had an outdoorsy odor about them, but Dunlop had not said a word. She had assumed the rain had lessened the effects of days of walking and sleeping outdoors. Based on people's reactions, she had just gotten used to their odor. She suddenly wished she could bathe and wash her clothes in a river.

"These are all of our children," Makenna announced and very quietly started counting. "Where's Aislinn?" she asked. Her red-headed daughter had her father's blue eyes, but had her thick unruly red hair and usually was easy to find.

As soon as Makenna asked where her eldest was, Laurel began looking around for hers. "And *where* is Brenna?" Except for her unusual silver eyes, which she got from her father, Brenna was the spitting image of herself at that age with her long wavy pale gold hair with strawberry highlights. She then looked at her youngest daughter and into her gray eyes. She was an incredibly smart child and when those pools of mercury twinkled, she was scheming. Right now, however, they just stared back at her as she unconsciously fingered her dark brown hair.

"I don't know," Bonny answered. In a few months, Bonny would be two and ten years old, three years younger than her sister, Brenna. "Ellie and I were not invited to go with them."

"Aislinn said there was not enough room for us," Ellie added petulantly. Only one year younger than Bonny, she looked like a smaller version of her mother Ellenor but with the McTiernay brown hair. She was clearly not happy that she had been left behind, and kept angrily swatting at one short piece of hair that kept escaping her braid. Until a few months ago, she had a habit of chewing on her hair, until one day a piece just broke off in her mouth.

"They both most likely snuck off in one of the carts to watch the harvest," Meriel chimed in.

Makenna snorted, uncaringly at how unladylike she sounded, so Meriel tried again. "They *are* at the age when staring at men working outside can be quite appealing to young women."

"Ha!" barked one of the two older boys. The brown-haired, brown-eyed boy bent over laughing and started teasing his tall friend, who was undoubtedly a McTiernay. "Hear that, Braeden? You are the same age as your sister. Is *that* why you were showing off for Fio—"

"I am going to knock your teeth out, Gideon!" Braeden bellowed and started chasing Gideon, who raced to the open gatehouse.

Without warning, the younger four boys in their dwindling group ran after Braeden, not wanting to be left out. A woman with mouse-gray, wiry hair who had been standing across the inner ward talking with another woman suddenly broke into a run after them. She was far sprier than she looked, especially wearing an arisaid.

Makenna, Meriel, and Ellenor started shouting for them to return, indicating that the boys belonged to them. Giving up, Ellenor sighed and said, "I'm so glad they are old enough to play together during this visit. Last time, they were too young."

"The two older boys belong to Lady Laurel," Raelynd said with a heavy sigh, tucking a strand of dark blond hair behind her ear. "Well, the taller one does. She allowed Braeden to invite his best friend—Gideon—thinking the company would help occupy them both and keep him from being a nuisance around the soldiers."

Ellenor bobbed her head in agreement. "It was a great idea that went frustratingly wrong. The two boys cause twice as much trouble, which only encourages the younger boys to misbehave by mimicking them."

"There are so many of them," Isilmë mumbled. Families, children, barking; it was far different from living in the abbey.

Shinae nodded her head. "Don't you just love it?"

No, Isilmë almost said aloud. One or two well-behaved children she would not mind, but beyond that was too many. It was clear from her friend's expression that Shinae disagreed.

"Actually, when you include the little bairns, there are sixteen McTiernay children here altogether," Makenna said. "Next time we get together at Conor and Laurel's, they'll be old enough to join the others. Now *that* will be true chaos. Not only are there the two other chieftains who are not with us, but the children have enjoyed making new friends so much that Laurel plans to invite the McTiernay commanders to come as well. Can you imagine *another* sixteen children around here?" The tone of Makenna's voice conveyed happiness at just the thought.

"Where are the others?" Shinae wondered out loud. Isilmë was shocked. Shinae had lived in the quiet of the abbey for five years and therefore was not accustomed to the noise either. Why she would be interested in more little noisemakers was a mystery.

Makenna retucked the same loose strand of her red hair behind her ear. "The three youngest are with their nannies."

"My twins, Aeryn and Laire, are nearly three, and Makenna's little Alec is almost four," Raelynd explained, but the multitude of names was making Isilmë's head spin. She glanced at Shinae and saw no confusion at all. The woman had to be pretending. No one could remember all the faces and names. Then it hit her that all of them were *married*. She felt like several stones just landed on her shoulders as she realized there were even *more* faces and names to memorize. Not to mention where did everyone sleep?

She must have been mumbling her thoughts aloud, for Makenna giggled and said encouragingly, "Don't worry if you cannot remember anyone's names. You will learn them quickly, I'm sure."

Ellenor started laughing. "The most frustrating of us will be the most memorable, but you will get to know us all much sooner than you think."

"Just be glad you do not have to figure out bedchambers for everyone!" Raelynd teased their hostess, knowing the painful exercise in patience Makenna had had.

Makenna let out a soft groan at the reminder of the argument she and Colin had that morning about their two new arrivals. "If Colin had to make the sleeping arrangements, half of us would have nowhere to lie down. Lochlen is a sizable castle for the Lammermuir Hills. Most local lairds only have tower keeps or donjons due to the rolling hills, whereas Lochlen has four sizable towers. It's not immense like Laurel's home." Then she quickly looked back and verified Laurel and Conor were still out of hearing range.

Isilmë wondered why Makenna even had to look. Their argument was not as booming as it was, but it was loud enough to know that it was still ongoing.

Shinae pointed at the large gatehouse towers, and Makenna shook her head. "Those are occupied by Colin's soldiers, who are ordered to protect Lochlen. You wouldn't want to stay there as it is right now. The smell alone would curdle milk."

"We can barely manage when Laurel's family visits us, as Caireoch Castle has only three towers," Raelynd interjected. "Crevan and our family stay in one, another is used for storage and guests, and our messy relatives inhabit the other," she said, pointing at Meriel, who just shrugged at the comment.

Isilmë got the strange feeling that her and Shinae's arrival was actually the cause of this conversation. "I love my home, and I am not sure I can manage anything as large as McTiernay Castle with its seven towers, but there would be plenty of room here at Lochlen if my husband was not *the most inflexible, immovable, mulish man of all the McTiernays*," Makenna huffed. The other women rolled their eyes, and Isilmë guessed that each thought that their husband was more stubborn.

"We would have plenty of space if Colin would have shooed out the soldiers who sleep in the gatehouse towers, but he gave me his I-will-not-budge, not-even-a-little glare when I asked him to move them elsewhere before everyone came. I needed to set up the chambers, but most of all I needed time to cleanse them of the men's stench. But Colin refused! He yelled that I had four towers in which to figure out the problem *without* affecting *his* men. The children are having to sleep practically on top of one another, but thankfully they seem to enjoy it. I have saved one space for Conan and Mhàiri when they arrive, but now you two are here."

Isilmë inhaled deeply and held her breath in fear that Shinae was about to volunteer them to stay outside. *She* might not have minded, but Isilmë did. Her room at the abbey may have been small and sparse, but it was dry, and she had her own bed! She had experienced sleeping outdoors and wanted no more of it.

"At first, I thought we would have to put you and Brodie on the first floor of the Pinnacle Tower," Makenna continued, talking to Shinae. "It holds much of the castle's food, and after celebrating Lammas Day and the start of the harvest last night, much of it was consumed, so there is room there. But Father Tam came to my rescue . . . well really *your* rescue, Shinae, and offered his chambers at the chapel. After everyone leaves, we will find you and Brodie permanent accommodations. The father meanwhile is going to stay with the tower warden, who could use someone near to help him."

"Don't look alarmed," Raelynd whispered in Isilmë's ear. "He is just getting old."

Isilmë almost corrected her and said she did not fear where Shinae was sleeping but herself. She had forgotten Shinae was to marry that afternoon. Wherever she slept, she would be alone.

A plump woman with graying brown hair walked right up to Makenna and said, "Their baths are near ready, milady, I just need to know where to put them."

"A *bath*?" Isilmë squeaked with glee and grabbed Shinae's arm, giving it a squeeze. They had both been washing themselves in cool river water just as they had at the abbey. And because she lost their one lump of soap, it had not been very effective.

"Ellenor, please take Shinae to the bedchambers on the second floor of the chapel. Meriel, you look close to Shinae in size; see if you can find something in your things for her to wear at her wedding. I'll ask Ceridwin if she would let Isilmë borrow a bliaut. In the meantime, I will take Isilmë to the room I reserved for Conan and Mhàiri." She stopped, and concern filled her eyes. "But when they do arrive, you will have to join the girls. I know it is not ideal, and it won't be long, but . . ."

"I will sleep on the first floor of the Pinnacle Tower," Isilmë said quickly, hoping that idea would still be acceptable despite her being alone. She was just glad Lady Makenna was not sending her out in the village to fend for herself.

Makenna's brows shot up, and Isilmë was afraid she was going to refuse based on her being alone, but instead her face transformed from surprise to delight.

"Our seamstress married this summer and now lives considerably far outside the village. If you don't mind small quarters, you can stay there as long as you like. It has a nice-sized window that allows in a significant amount of light."

Before Makenna could continue praising the features of her tiny room, Isilmë jumped up and down with excitement. "I cannot thank you enough for the offer."

Makenna was surprised by Isilmë's eagerness, yet relieved. "Then despite my husband's frustrating declarations, all is well!"

"What is so important that you need to drag me here?" Laurel shouted as she marched toward the great hall. "I barely was able to meet Mhàiri's sister and her friend before you started wailing like a lunatic. If you need something, go and find Braeden and Gideon or someone else to amuse yourself so I can get ready for the wedding."

"That's going to be very difficult as *I won't be here*."

Laurel stopped and stared Conor directly in the eye for several seconds. "What do you mean, *you won't be here*?" Laurel's voice, which was already loud, started to grow in intensity.

"You think I would go if I did not have a good reason? How long have you known me, woman?"

"I have told you over and over again to *stop calling me 'woman.'* And there is not a reason good enough to abandon your family . . ."

"Brodie is a close family friend, but he is not family."

Laurel smiled at the error, but it held no humor. "Ah, but *Shinae* is. I hope I am there when Conan comes and learns you left just hours before *his wife's sister* says her vows."

"I'm sure he will understand once he learns that none of his brothers were there."

"What?!" Anyone in the vicinity or even close to the inner ward could hear the anger in the single word.

Conor took a deep breath and leaned against the stone wall next to the great hall's doors. Laurel began to pace, and he just watched. After years of marriage, he knew that she was truly mad but would not calm down until she was ready to talk about it. He had one advantage—distraction. He never thought someone else's upcoming nuptials would make him happy, but anything that would shift Laurel's focus from him and to something else was a good thing.

Shinae stepped from the bath and wrapped herself in a linen sheet that had been left folded on top of the bed. Tucking the blanket around her chest so that it would stay, she considered what to do about her eavesdroppers.

She had thought there might be rats living with the priest while she had been in the water, but then she overheard some giggles coming from the room's garderobe. She suspected it was occupied by the older two girls Makenna had inquired about earlier. Shinae was delighted to have a private place to go to the room but was not pleased to have it used to be spied upon. Hoping to teach them a lesson without getting them in trouble with their parents, Shinae slid a chair across the room and positioned it directly in front of the narrow door. She then sat on the chair, making it difficult to open. Hoping that by forcing them to remain cramped in the small, odoriferous room would encourage the girls to do their spying elsewhere, she began to slowly use her fingers to comb out the largest knots in her hair.

After this early morning's events, Shinae doubted she would have much time alone in the future. During her and Isilmë's journey to Lochlen, she had put together a weak plan of how she could identify the would-be assassin. She would chat for a few minutes with the men, starting with those who frequently came in and out of the castle in hopes her inner voice would alert her to potentially corrupt individuals. She planned to think of ideas on how she would go about a task that had been impossible with Isilmë's continual chatter. Her agreement to be married, however, made things even harder. No doubt her time alone would be limited and having two stalkers was not going to help either.

"You can come out," she said, moving the chair back to the small wooden table under the room's one window.

The garderobe door creaked open and two girls on the verge of becoming women stumbled out—one with pale yellow hair and the other red. They took deep breaths of the odorless air and stretched their limbs, each eager to move again.

"How did you know we were in there?" Aislinn asked, shaking her arm to get feeling back in it. Brenna was an expert eavesdropper and they had never been caught before.

"I used to be a nun," Shinae replied. "I talk to God and He talks to me."

Aislinn's bright blue eyes grew wide. Brenna rolled her gray ones and said, "You were squirming and making noise."

Aislinn jutted out her chin. "Well, you said that we would learn something and we *didn't*."

"I didn't know Aunt Makenna would decide to talk outside. I assumed she would do it here, where no one could see or smell her." Realizing the insult she had inadvertently blurted out, Brenna's hands quickly covered her mouth.

"I bet Aunt Laurel knew what we were doing," Aislinn murmured, her arms crossed and her eyes narrowed.

Brenna's brows drew together in a frustrated frown, knowing Aislinn was most likely right. Her parents had never approved of her eavesdropping, but it was a habit she had perfected over the years. Aislinn, however, was unskilled at secretly listening in on conversations.

Thinking they would leave, Shinae started to move to open the heavy door when she heard a splash behind her. Both girls were peering at the bathwater and wrinkled their noses.

"You took a *long* bath."

Aislinn nodded in agreement. "She needed to. We could smell you even in there." She pointed to the garderobe.

"The honesty of youth." Shinae sighed, shaking her head at them. And yet they did have a point. It must have been really dark for Brodie to have agreed to marry her. When she saw herself in the reflective piece of metal hanging next to the door, she had frightened herself. While the bath had helped, until she was able to brush her hair, she would continue shocking people.

"That water is too dirty for anyone else to use. But it smells nice."

"Can you not bathe when you're a nun?" Brenna wondered aloud.

Shinae looked at the bathwater. It was incredibly dirty, more so than she realized. She turned to answer Brenna's question when she saw Aislinn lying on the room's bed, staring at the ceiling. Brenna was still standing, leaning against the mattress. Neither looked inclined to leave. Instead, they both launched into another set of questions.

"Why did you stop being a nun?"

"Did you really walk here all the way from Edinburgh?"

"What did you eat?"

"How long did it take you?"

"Weren't you afraid?"

"Do you really know how to use that?" Brenna asked, pointing at Shinae's *sgian dubh*, peeking out under her habit, piled on the floor. "My mama can throw knives and she is the best at using a bow and arrow, even on a moving horse. Can you do that?"

Aislinn turned around and flopped over on her belly, propping herself up on her elbows. "I didn't think you could quit being a nun. Does that mean you don't love God anymore?"

Shinae blinked at the speed of the questions and realized both girls had finally paused and were waiting for an answer. "Ah, no. I still love the Lord."

Shinae sat down slowly in the chair next to a small

wooden table under the room's one window. They had rattled off their questions so quickly, she was not sure they actually expected her to answer them. Seeing a hairbrush on the table, she said a silent little prayer for the priest to forgive her for using his styling tools and began to brush out her hair. The tangles were worse than she had thought, but slowly, her snarled hair became free.

Both girls just watched her and, after a few minutes, Aislinn pointed at Shinae's habit in a pile on the floor. Aislinn immediately asked, "Did you bring any other clothes?"

Brenna chuckled. "Do nuns even have other clothes?"

"Don't worry about it if you don't. Aunt Meriel has *tons* of gowns and you look about the same size. She won't mind you borrowing some now that you smell better."

"You look like my aunt Mhàiri," Brenna commented.

"She's my aunt, too." Aislinn sounded annoyed, but was quickly distracted by Brenna's next question.

"Why are you really here?"

"My mama said your name is Shinae and you came to see Aunt Mhàiri."

Shinae nodded. "It is and there is a reason I look like Mhàiri . . . I'm her older sister and I came to see her."

"That makes you our aunt!" Aislinn said excitedly.

Brenna crossed her arms. With a disbelieving look, she asked, "Why now? Aunt Mhàiri has come here many times and you never visited then," Brenna pointed out. "Are there other reasons?"

Aislinn gave her cousin a look that said the answer was obvious. "Papa said that Brodie wasn't married because he didn't love anyone." She then linked her fingers together and rested her head on them. "Did you secretly meet when he was working for Laird Donavan? Is that how you know each other? Did you and he fall in love? Is that the reason you are not a nun any longer?"

Brenna uncrossed her arms. "Is that why Brodie is always moping?"

"You are right, Brenna. He was *smiling* when they came into the courtyard. You remember?" She smiled, as if she had discovered a secret. "You finally got away and were able to meet your love."

Brenna tapped her lips with her index finger. "Is Aislinn right? Do you love him?"

"If you get married, does that mean you are staying here, even when everyone leaves?"

The sound of the door opening saved Shinae from having to answer or correct any of their assumptions. She swiveled around to see one of the McTiernay wives carrying several garments.

"*Dia dhuit*, it's just me, Meriel. Sorry for barging in, but my arms are about to drop all of this on the floor." Meriel was using her back to close the door and, once through, aimed for the bed.

Aislinn quickly scooted off and made room for everything her aunt was putting on the bed. Meriel furrowed her brow and put her hands on her hips. "So, this is where you two have been."

"Mm-hmm," Aislinn answered and started looking through the garments. "Ooh, I like this one. You should get married in it," she said, pulling the light blue bliaut against her body.

Brenna shook her head. "Green. She should wear the green one to match her eyes. Oh, look, it comes with shoes!"

Meriel looked at Shinae wrapped in a sheet and ignored the girls. "No one has said this yet, and Laurel would probably box my ears if she knew I was, but you really do not have to do this. Marrying Brodie, I mean. Makenna and Colin know him and say that he is a good man." Meriel shrugged her shoulders. "He may be, but that is not a reason to marry him. It took Craig and me months to realize our feelings for each other, and then only after years of being friends."

"Mama said she and Papa fell in love instantly," Brenna quipped.

Meriel pursed her lips and gave Brenna another fierce scowl. "And that's probably why she suggested this." Turning back to Shinae, Meriel continued. "Where are you two going to live? What if Brodie decides not to stay at Lochlen? Do you really want to marry a soldier who may be hurt or die protecting Lochlen? Do you want to have children? Will this be a handfasting? What about your father? Will he not want to be there to hear you take your vows?" Meriel paused and then sank onto the mattress looking distressed. "I guess what I really mean is . . . should you do this? Do you not want to wait and decide later if marriage is right for you? Brodie broods a lot and you—"

Shinae raised her hand to stop Meriel. She thought the girl's rapid flow of questions could be blamed on their youth, but it was clear loquaciousness ran in the family. That, however, did not render Meriel's questions invalid. In truth, she had not considered many of those questions, and part of her urged her to slow down and do so, but there was one thing she wanted to know first. "Why would Lady Laurel want to box your ears?"

Meriel considered the words she wanted to say and decided there was no way to soften the truth. "Laurel believes you two would not have so quickly agreed if you did not actually *want* to marry. If either of you had hesitated, the other would have pushed back as well. But from what we were told—by Laurel herself—you both truly want to say, 'I do.' Delaying the ceremony would only create doubt and possibly keep you from ever marrying." Meriel bit her bottom lip. "Not all of us are as convinced as Laurel is." Meriel folded her hands on her lap. "But I feel you should not be pressured into such a life-altering decision. So most of us women want to caution you from rushing into taking large steps that will affect your and Brodie's future. You are so beautiful, and you are going to meet a lot of men younger than Brodie who might make you wish you had waited."

Shinae took in a deep breath. Everything Meriel said was understandable and all her questions were reasonable, but her inner voice urged her otherwise. Two days ago, she had never dreamed of ever getting married. Now, she could not imagine avoiding the altar.

Isilmë stood completely still and stared at the wooden door leading to the chapel's bedchambers. Deep down she had been hoping there would be lots of chatter, giving her a reason to leave. Instead, there was only silence on the other side, making her unsure of how to proceed. She and Shinae were slowly becoming friends despite their different personalities. To a degree they trusted each other, but they were not remotely close enough to give each other advice. But Isilmë did not think she could live with herself if she did not at least caution her friend about what was happening.

The man Shinae was going to marry had left that morning with a goodbye and had still not returned, though the ceremony was just over an hour from occurring. Nobody knew where he and most of the McTiernay men had gone, nor when they would return. Shinae had a right to know about his sudden disappearance, but mostly Isilmë hoped that such knowledge might make her friend rethink her decision to marry.

After the second knock, Isilmë heard Shinae shout for her to come in. Isilmë opened the door and her hazel-brown eyes widened in surprise. Shinae had been sleeping in a light shift and was not remotely ready to make promises in front of witnesses.

Shinae lifted her head and then let it fall back down on the pillow. "I'm so glad it is you. You would not believe how many people have stopped by to tell me that I did not have to marry Brodie, as if I did not already know I could refuse."

Isilmë swallowed. That *was* the main reason she was there, and if Shinae knew marriage was not really being forced upon her, why had she agreed to marry a man she barely knew?

Shinae sat up, yawned, and stretched her arms, and

then stared at Isilmë for several seconds. "You look absolutely beautiful. Purple is definitely your color."

Isilmë blinked. For years, those in the abbey whispered about the features they could see—her freckles, her large breasts, her thick red eyebrows, or how short she was. All of it had been in unflattering tones, which had destroyed any thoughts that might be even somewhat attractive. But after one of the maids worked on her brows and showed her how to do her hair using twists, not braids, Isilmë had thought for the first time in her life that she could pass as somewhat pretty.

Makenna had stopped by her room earlier with a complete ensemble belonging to one of her friends, who was supposedly of similar size and height. The deep purple gown was simple, with very few embellishments, and matching slippers. Isilmë got the feeling, looking at it, it was the best dress Makenna's friend owned.

Makenna had explained that she would eventually introduce her to Ceridwin, the wife of one of Colin's commanders, but she was with her two children, both sick from overeating at last night's feast. Meanwhile, until the seamstresses could make her some dresses of her own, Isilmë was welcome to wear Ceridwin's bliaut.

Feeling far more comfortable being alone with Lady Makenna than she had with all the women talking in the hall, Isilmë assured her hostess that she loved to sew and would make her own clothes if there was any material available. Upon hearing Lady Makenna telling her that there were several bolts of cloth that she could choose from, Isilmë had become optimistic for the first time since her and Shinae's arrival. Not only would she be able to create some stunning garments for herself, but she would surprise Makenna's friend Ceridwin with several new bliauts as well. It was the least she could do after Lady Makenna assured her that she was welcome to stay as long as she wanted and to consider Lochlen Castle her home.

"I mean it, Isilmë; you are going to catch many a man's eye tonight," Shinae said and then stretched her arms over head. "Whoever styled your hair knew what they were doing. I wonder if they could do something with mine."

Isilmë doubted that she could interest any man but decided not to argue the point. "I can help, if you would like."

"Could you?" Shinae asked excitedly, moving from the bed to the chair.

"Most of the time I pull the sides back or braid it," Shinae said. Isilmë had guessed as much after spending several weeks working with her in Melrose village, helping those in need after their Abbey was destroyed by the English.

"My hair is so curly, it is hard to work with, but yours is long and soft. Do you want something in particular?"

Shinae shook her head. "Anything you want."

Isilmë started brushing, better understanding why the maid had wanted to style her hair. There was something enjoyable about brushing someone else's hair. At night, when alone in her room at the abbey, she often tried different styles, but her hair being thick and curly, limited what she could do. In her youth, she had pilfered one of the polished plates from the abbey's kitchen to see the results. She knew it had been wrong, but she never once considered returning it.

"Are you nervous?" Isilmë asked.

"Aye," Shinae replied, her fidgeting hands confirming her admission.

When Shinae did not expound further, Isilmë considered letting her know that Brodie, along with several other men, had left. Not wanting to be the one to tell Shinae, she continued twisting her friend's dark hair into a semi-loose, intricate bun. "There."

Shinae rose and went to look at her reflection in the small, highly polished piece of silver hanging on the wall. She had never seen herself with all of her hair pulled back. She thought it would make her feel self-conscious as the wimple had consistently pulled out the hairs framing her face. They were constantly growing back in tight curls until they once again were long and straight. But the soft wisps actually made her look and feel pretty, not odd like had assumed. "You are so talented. If Mhàiri was here, I don't think she would recognize me." She went to the foot of the bed, opened a chest, and pulled out a pale green dress that matched her eyes. "Fortunately, the priest brought his things with him, leaving me a place to store the clothes Meriel gave me." She grabbed a pair of matching shoes and started to dress. "There; how do you think I look? Then again, after smelling and looking so awful this morning, Brodie will probably be relieved" she added, unaware of just how attractive she was.

Isilmë sighed and helped her tie the sides of the bliaut. She knew now why Lady Laurel wanted Shinae to marry so quickly. Every man—single or married—would be unable to take their eyes from her. The castle would be overrun with would-be suitors.

CHAPTER FOUR

"Now, let's begin. We—"

"Thank you, Father Tam, but I need to talk with Brodie before we continue." Shinae could hear the gasps echo in the oratory, as well as the rapid intake of several breaths. The tension she could already feel going through Brodie doubled.

"Do you want to wait?" His voice was pitched low and intense.

Shinae shook her head, uncaring of who heard what she said. With the McTiernay wives nearby, she doubted anything said would remain between them. Colin's family alone was seven with all their children, and Lady Makenna had seemed open to even more. The only thing keeping Shinae from breathing rapidly from nerves was knowing Brodie was *not* one the McTiernay brothers. No wonder he had taken a walk in the rain last night. He had needed to take a breath from the mayhem.

The tightness of Brodie's frame grew noticeable as her face showed the fear of sharing her thoughts, and his eyes grew cold. Oddly, his expression was what calmed her nerves. He was not marrying her because of Lady

Laurel's directive, but for personal reasons, the same as she was.

"Before we make our vows, I need you to know that I am not agreeing to a handfast marriage. I am no longer a nun, but my beliefs have not changed. I will not make vows that will only be held for a year. I do want to marry you, but only if we remain loyal as husband and wife until one of us passes."

Brodie slowly let out the breath he was holding, never having felt so thankful. He never even considered hand-fasting with Shinae. He probably should have after spending only a few hours in her company, but the idea of a marriage no longer filled him with an urge to flee. He did not desire freedom now, nor did he expect to at any time in the future. "I agree, but this marriage will not be in name only, but one where a husband and wife share our thoughts, feelings, and concerns, as well as the same bed."

People gasped and her green eyes widened, followed by a slow smile curving her soft mouth. "I agree."

Her reaction was genuine. Brodie felt the tension in his body change from anxiety to eagerness.

"I have one last question. Please answer truthfully. Do you want children?" She nervously chewed her bottom lip as she looked up at him. "Because I do."

Unable to stop himself, he framed her face in his hands, pulled her close, and fastened his lips tenderly to hers.

When he pulled away, people started to applaud. The sound of Shinae's laughter was soft and melodious, and her eyes lit with mischief. "I think that was a yes."

"Aye, *inam*, it was. I will always be honest with you. Will you be with me?"

Shinae nodded her head, only thinking of him, his kiss, and how her inner angel was saying this was how God intended it to be. All thoughts of why she had come to Lochlen fled her mind.

Brodie turned to Father Tam, who was standing with his mouth open. He was young and inexperienced, but if he was going to be a McTiernay priest, he was going to have to learn to expect the unexpected.

He squeezed Shinae's hand. "Father, we are ready to continue."

"I'll come back after a few minutes and give you some privacy to get ready," Brodie told Shinae, feeling his nerves resurface.

"Thank you," came Shinae's soft response.

Brodie closed the door to their borrowed bedchamber behind him and leaned against the stone wall. Yesterday, he had felt lost and now he was married. The opportunity came and he had leaped in without doing what everyone wanted—to wait. To verify what he already knew. And in a few minutes, he and Shinae would become in all ways husband and wife. And despite all the doubts from others, he still could not believe his good fortune.

When Shinae had walked into the chapel, a strong fission of jealousy had gone through him, knowing that every man there was full of envy. Though she had looked a mess that morning, he could only see her beauty, though it helped having met her sister Mhàiri, who had similar features and was very attractive. But that knowledge had not prepared him for seeing Shinae.

Over the years, when he was Laird Donovan's commander, many men bragged about their women and wives, claiming their beauty incomparable to any other lass. And usually they were indeed very pretty, each possessing a certain allure. Shinae, on the other hand, could not be described with words.

After hearing her agreement to be his wife that morning, his mind had been consumed about her and this moment. He had not thought there would be such celebrating, for he was just a clansman. Then he remembered who his wife was. Having back-to-back nights of revelry was uncommon, but Lady Makenna, with some help from Conor's wife, Laurel, had made it seem effortless. So, Brodie had forced himself to endure the revelry that had so annoyed him the night before.

Tonight, however, the music and the crowds of people dancing did not bother him in the same way. He even suffered the constant flow of men placing long, lingering kisses on Shinae's hand, whispering her good wishes when he knew that was the last thing they were thinking. Not once had he left Shinae's side, in fear that she might be swept away when he returned. Dunlop had finally taken pity on him and announced that the newly married couple needed to spend some time on their own. If Brodie had not been so anxious to leave, he might have struck his friend for his wink to the crowd and playful tone of voice.

Dunlop might have thought it was just months, but in reality, Brodie had not been with a woman in well over a year. It had been convenient that no female had ever truly intrigued him, for he had planned to follow Laird Mahon's lead and never marry. So the level of lust he had upon first seeing Shinae astonished him and still did. Just the memory of her lips was making him aroused yet again. But it was how they were together that captured his heart. He knew then he would do whatever it took to make her part of his life, so when Lady Laurel instructed that they marry, he did not flinch. That afternoon in front of the priest he again realized the gift Lady Laurel had given him by demanding that marriage would occur and that very afternoon. Every single man at Lochlen would have been after Shinae and the possibility he could have lost her to another was terrifying to consider.

He rapped on the bedchamber door once. Unable to wait until Shinae called out that she was ready, he opened the wooden obstacle and closed it after him.

Shinae stood in the middle of the room in front of the hearth. Her hair was down, and her feet were bare, but otherwise she remained clothed.

"Do you need more time?" Brodie choked, thinking he would die if she said she did. Just looking at her in her shift he could barely control himself. He had not even touched her and already his body was raging. Taking deep breaths, he promised himself that he would take it slow and ensure her pleasure first. They were married now and their private life would be painted with what happened tonight.

"I've never been with a man before. I am not sure

what I am to do." Her anguished whisper tore at Brodie's heart.

"I do." His excitement grew, knowing his assumption of her virginity was correct, for it was well known not all nuns were pure.

Shinae watched large-eyed as Brodie quickly removed all his clothes except for the tartan around his waist. He certainly was well proportioned. She had told herself that she had embellished her memories of what she saw the night before. If anything, however, she had not realized just how attractive her husband was. Brodie flashed her a mischievous smile, and Shinae realized she had been openly staring at the broad expanse of his chest, thinking about what it would be like to twine her fingers in the crisp, curling hair there.

Brodie moved toward her; the heat of his hazel gaze burned her from the inside out. Softly, he slid his fingers down her cheek before brushing his thumb along her lips. Her eyes locked on his, and he felt her shiver and her body stiffen, but she did not pull away. Before her nerves took over, Brodie claimed her mouth once again with his own, deliberately using his own desire to ignite Shinae's. With a gentleness he had not known he was capable of, he continued kissing her until Shinae relaxed into him, her mouth softening.

The feel of her lips returning his embrace caused Brodie's body to react, demanding more. Holding the back of her neck, Brodie groaned and gently bit Shinae's bottom lip, encouraging her lips to part. Slowly, she started to relax, opening for him, letting his tongue find hers.

A low rumble of satisfaction escaped from deep within him and a small thrill shot through Shinae, leaving her tingling from head to foot. Brodie felt solid and strong, and he smelled good. Last night, he had smelled like rainwater, but he must have bathed just before they married, for now she was enjoying the enticing combination of soap and maleness. She had never before found herself captivated by the way a man smelled, but Brodie's scent fascinated her.

She instinctively welcomed him into her mouth without question and without reservation. His hands began to move downward to her waist. They seemed to burn right through her gown, scorching the skin beneath. The hot, sweet, sensuous kiss went on and on, suffusing her body with an aching need for something more.

When Shinae again released a soft moan, Brodie almost ripped the thin material from her. She had no idea what that sound did to him. He was at the brink of insanity.

Slowly, he trailed his mouth down her cheek and to her neck. His long fingers freed the ties on the side of her bliaut. Breaking his kiss only for a second, he pulled her chemise over her head. Her slender form had belied the curvy woman beneath. He raised Shinae's head, recapturing her mouth, and used his tongue to distract her before she panicked at realizing she wore nothing beneath. He tasted her again, as his thumbs brushed gently over and over her nipples, relishing in her response.

Shinae fisted her hands in his hair, not willing to let her husband go for even a second. A part of her shouted in protest at their physical state, but Shinae ignored it, along with the fear of what was to come. She wanted this. No one had ever created such overwhelming desire in her. She had not thought it possible, and yet her heart was racing and her body was screaming to be touched.

Brodie quickly undid his leather belt, holding his tartan in place, and let them fall to the floor. Shinae gasped and Brodie let out a guttural groan as he scooped her up into his heavily muscled arms. He lay her down on the bed and then leaned over to kiss her once again.

All thoughts of caution left Shinae when his chest touched her breasts. Taken by surprise, Shinae instinctively clutched at his shoulders, acutely aware of her body's reaction to his caresses and she started stroking his chest, unable to stop herself.

Without lifting his mouth from hers, Brodie pushed the blankets out of the way and lay down on top of her, propping his upper body on his elbows, careful not to put too much weight on her at first. Shinae plunged her hands once again into his hair as he kissed her eyes, her cheeks, her lips, as if he could not get enough. It terrified and exhilarated her at the same time.

Shinae felt her body arch toward him as his mouth slid down her neck again. Brodie was making her burn. She did not think she had the strength to continue when his hand brushed the side of her breast. It terrified her but wanted him to continue stoking her breast, and then his thumb grazed her nipple.

Lifting his head, Brodie sucked in his breath at the sight of her rosy nipples. Shinae froze. "What's wrong?" Fear that he saw something lacking and no longer found her desirable swept over her.

"Not a single thing," Brodie growled and cupped her breast, relishing the softness of her skin.

Fear had suddenly awakened her to what was actually happening—and what was about to happen. Shinae could not relax. She thought she knew what took place between a man and a woman, but everything Brodie was doing and making her feel was unexpected and overwhelming. She had lost all control and ability to think when he kissed her. It was both terrifying and exciting.

"Just let me touch you, sweetheart. I need to touch you like this. Need to feel you." And then his mouth was on her breast, and she was once again lost to sensation.

Brodie took one nipple into his mouth while he grazed his thumbs across her nipple before catching it and squeezing carefully. He switched breasts unaware of his murmuring husky remarks. The taste of the pink bud sent a shudder of sexual tension through him. Once again, he had to fight for control, not wanting to move too fast and frightening her again. But his concern left him when her fingers raked up his back until they reached his neck and held his head in place. Arching into his touch, she cried out from the pleasure, which only made his lower body grow even more painful with need.

He took her own hands and placed them back on his shoulders, encouraging them to explore. With a quivering, tentative touch, she caressed the length of his back as he seared a path down her abdomen and along her thigh. She began to writhe beneath him, not knowing what she wanted, only that she wanted more.

She began to lightly bite his shoulder, using her teeth in ways that made him shudder. Brodie paused to kiss her, whispering his love for each part of her body. Shinae arched her back, offering her breasts, wanting him to return. She had no idea being with a man could make her feel this alive. But even if she had, she knew deep down that she would have repeated all her decisions, just so they would bring her to Brodie.

Slowly, his hands moved downward, skimming either side of her body and down her outer thighs. Shinae felt hot everywhere. Her nipples had grown painfully hard under his caresses, demanding his tongue, but he refused to return, slowly kissing the inside of her legs. Something within her was screaming in shock, that no one should be able to do this to a woman, but she did not stop him. She did not know what to do with the onslaught of sensations other than allow him to keep them coming.

Brodie could not believe how passionate Shinae was. Virgins shied away from touching and kissing the body, but she not only accepted his touch but eagerly welcomed everything he did. "*Áille. Is tú mo shonuachar,*" he whispered as he kissed her stomach. For that was who she was—his most beautiful soul mate.

Shinae framed his face and pulled his lips back up to hers. "Aye. *Is tú mo shonuachar Annsachd.*"

Brodie almost choked on the joy he felt. That she could feel the same after such a short period was a miracle from God. His very own *mìorbhuil.* He was so happy he did not listen to those who doubted the wisdom of their marrying so quickly, disbelieved the longevity of their relationship, and endlessly spun nonsense in his ear to walk away while he could. Never. Never would he want anything more. They had no idea just how lucky he would always feel, knowing that Shinae was his.

Brodie heard a deep groan and could not tell whether the sound came from him or her. He never wanted to stop touching her. He was completely entranced by the softness of her skin. His fingertips were busy tracing faint circles along her thigh, feeling her muscles jump with each contact. He wanted to lose himself in her, to forget everything that had happened up until the moment they met.

With each circle of his fingertip, she could not help but moan in delight. Her skin burned and the ache between her legs intensified and, with it, his touch rose higher.

He pulled away and looked deeply into Shinae's eyes. Nothing but her need for him stared back, searing into his soul. Everything was going to be all right; at that moment, he knew nothing could ever go wrong again.

Shinae's thoughts shattered the moment his hand touched her. It felt wrong, personal, and invasive, and then he began to massage her sacred place, gently draining all her doubts and fears. As he began to move his hips, his arousal rubbed against her inner thigh. It awakened a response deep within her.

She forced herself to breathe as Brodie stroked her slowly, parting her with his fingers, opening her. She closed her eyes and splayed her hands across his broad chest. She gasped in astonishment when he used her own moisture to lubricate her small, swelling button of desire. Whatever he was doing no longer felt wrong. It felt wonderful. It had to be right.

Brodie wanted to lap her up. Her opening felt warm and liquid and sweet, like thick honey, and he wanted a taste, but he refrained. This was all new to her, and he wanted to enjoy every minute until the end.

He felt her shudder as he slipped his questing finger

inside her snug passage and then went lower still to find the sensitive flesh just below her soft, wet channel. Her body clenched in reaction, and Brodie forced himself gradually, gently past the tightness.

He repeated the action slowly and deliberately, easing his finger into her and then teasing the small nubbin of female flesh. He did it again and again. Increasing the pressure, he pushed another finger deep into her and another, until he felt her barrier, and a powerful wave of possessiveness overtook him.

He managed to wrench his mouth from hers. "*Muinín dom*," he whispered in her ear. "Don't ever be afraid of me. After this, I won't ever hurt you again." He kissed her long and insatiably. "I could never hurt you." Brodie prayed she understood what was about to happen. He wanted her to experience nothing but pleasure when they came together, and for that to happen, he needed to break her barrier now.

His breath came in small pants that matched hers when he felt the barrier once again. His head bowed until it was only a few inches from hers. Locking his eyes to her vivid pale green ones, he quickly pushed his finger forward through the barrier. Pain flashed through Shinae's eyes, and her fingers curled into a fist. A sharp cry filled the air as her body stretched, all her barriers broken.

Shinae had known what he was about to do, but her aunt's explanation of the pleasantries of lovemaking was wrong. It was not at all pleasant.

Upon hearing Shinae cry out, Brodie went completely still. She looked wildly desirable, framed by her luxurious curtain of dark hair. She was natural, surprisingly unselfconscious, and incredibly seductive; a fantasy with creamy thighs and pearly skin. He fought the desire to immediately bury himself inside her and reminded himself forcefully that tonight was just as much about her as it was for him. Maybe more so.

Her shuddering breath almost melted his resolve. He turned her head, kissing away the tears that fell from the corners of her eyes. He started to move his fingers again, moving them up and down. The more he roused her passion, his own grew stronger. He almost roared out in relief when he felt her small hands gripping him instead of pushing him away.

Another few strokes and she began rocking with him, drawn to a height of passion that a few painful moments ago she did not think possible. "Brodie," Shinae breathed out as his fingers worked her rapidly. "*Is féidir?*"

As the remnants of her release strummed deliciously through her body, he pulled his hand out. She glanced up and inquired huskily, "Is it always this good?"

He held a soft tendril of her dark hair for a moment before brushing it away from her temple. "Aye. There's more . . . and it gets better." Brodie grinned unexpectedly, a perfect slow, sexy smirk.

Answering him with a kiss that was both sweet and aggressive, Brodie fought for his remaining anchors of control. His shaft was straining for her body. He needed to be inside her, badly.

He encouraged her legs to open and, in one, smooth motion, he moved to align his body with hers. He could feel her body's resistance to his invasion. It gave him the strength to keep his promise and hold still long enough for her to adjust to him, allowing only pleasure, no pain. But the hot, silky feel of her channel closing around his shaft was almost driving him into a frenzy.

Rocking his hips forward, he pressed into her. Sweat beaded on his brow when her slick warmth surrounded him. He eased in and out of her, trying to keep himself from pumping too hard. In and out, he basked in the exquisite feel of her soft flesh around his shaft. Her arms grasped his back; her nails dug into his flesh as if she could bring them even closer.

"No one's ever held me this way," he stammered.

"How is that?" Shinae asked, barely able to speak.

"As if you'll never let me go." Brodie took her mouth again, and at that same moment, he drove into her swiftly, filling her completely with one long, powerful stroke.

The pain was soon forgotten. They were a perfect fit. Shinae began to move eagerly with him, arching her hips to take him deeper inside. She welcomed him into her body, and a hot tide of passion raged through both of them. Their bodies moved as one with the other. The act of being together was a raw act of pure possession. No one would know this experience. He did not have to share her with anyone. Shinae was his.

She lifted to him in blatant surrender, and he slid into her in one last thrust that wrenched a loud cry of surprise from her throat. He swallowed it with a kiss that went on and on while he held himself completely still, filling her, holding her, claiming her, while his body seemed to dissolve into one molten mass of need. Then Shinae fisted her hands in the blankets and bowed up from the bed, her entire body tightening as tiny explosions ignited within her body. Seconds later, Brodie's own dam burst, and he roared his climax, his head thrown back, his eyes tightly shut.

When he opened them, he could only stare down at her. She was so beautiful, lying there beneath him, her eyes half closed, panting in ecstasy. This moment was better than anything he had imagined.

As the remnants of Shinae's release continued to thrum through her body, she glanced up and inquired huskily, again, "Is it always this good?"

Brodie wrapped his arms around her and flipped them both over, so he was on his back and her on top of him. Then, he buried his face in the curve of her neck. Shinae held him tightly as his body shook violently. She raked her fingers down his back and gently cooed as low, choked tears escaped him.

No longer would he live in the past. Only his future lay before him.

Brodie watched her, constantly feeling the need to reach out and stroke her cheek, her arm, anywhere that would not disturb her. Gently, he rolled her to her side and tucked her curves into his own contours. He was filled with an amazing sense of completeness as a deep feeling of peace overtook his being.

He would have fallen in love with her even if their mating had been lukewarm, but it had been a raging inferno, of lust, passion, and need.

Just thinking about all the women and men who had

encouraged Shinae to rethink her options made his anger grow anew. Giving her a slight squeeze of possession, he calmed down his jealous thoughts. He never had been a possessive man before, and he would have supposed that being married would dispel any reason for him to be jealous, and yet, now that she was his, he felt a ferocious need to be overprotective. He was not a violent person, but just imagining someone with the gall to try to take her away . . . he was apt to kill such a man.

Shinae was his. He had been waiting for her all his life just as she had for him.

CHAPTER FIVE

Shinae woke with a smile on her face and stretched her limbs to bring them back to life before collapsing back onto her pillow. Never had she slept so well. After coming together twice more in the night she was a little sore, but it was a good soreness.

She heard someone outside of their door talking and quickly got up to dress. She was in the middle of putting on her shift when Brodie came in carrying a tray. He kicked the door closed and walked over to a small table and put down the tray of bread, nuts, and jams. Then he grabbed her at the waist, pulled her to him, and leaned down to brush his mouth gently over hers.

"Are you as famished as I am?" he mumbled.

His mouth had moved down and was now nibbling on her neck. From the tray he'd brought in, Shinae had initially thought he meant actual food, but now she was not so sure. With a low growl, Brodie pulled back. "It's good you're wearing this thing," he said, fingering her chemise's shoulder strap. Then, abruptly, he slapped his hands together and picked up a piece of bread, covered

He also knew that those eyes would have been on Shinae if they had not wed. More than once he had given a young man a look that made them reconsider even offering her their congratulations.

"And what about Dunlop?" Shinae asked. "He watched Isilmë wherever she went and whoever she danced with."

"If you say so. What I saw was pitiful." He stopped talking, hoping Shinae was not offended, but Isilmë was the worst at dancing. Even awkward children were better.

Shinae was offended and took up for her friend. "She lived in the abbey all her life and never had a chance to dance or hear lively music. I at least was able to enjoy the activity until I lived at Dryburgh Abbey." Shinae slipped on a pair of leather shoes and started lacing them, ignoring his quirked eyebrow, as shoes were typically the last thing people put on when dressing. "Do you think Dunlop was jealous of all the men surrounding her?"

"Nay," he said, helping her tighten the laces of her bliaut on her sides. "Dunlop is never jealous. He knows every pretty lass here, and not one has he felt even slightly possessive about."

"Do you feel that way about me? Possessive, I mean."

Brodie did not answer. There was something about Shinae; she calmed him even as she excited him more than any woman ever had. Putting his large hands on either side of her face, he kissed her lips softly, but with so much possessiveness she could not doubt that she was his and his only.

He let her lips go and pulled her close to him, his

heart beating rapidly. He had been without love in his life for so long, his capacity to recognize the feeling had nearly died. For the past eight years, he had pushed aside any hint at the notion of surrendering to love. Yesterday, when she had met him in the chapel, he had envisaged a future alongside her . . . but last night had significantly escalated his feelings. He was not capable of thinking of anyone but her.

"Let's finish getting ready before I toss you back on that bed." His tone was both playful and serious.

"I just need to fix my hair."

"Leave it down."

She glanced at Brodie to see if he was serious. Seeing that he was, Shinae shrugged her shoulders and sat down to brush her hair. "I'm not too sure what everyone will think, but if you insist," she said mischievously.

Brodie stopped putting on his second shoe and frowned. "I've changed my mind. Put it up into a tight bun. In fact, where's your wimple?"

"It burned in the abbey fire," she replied in a nonchalant tone. Quickly, Shinae plaited the sides to help keep the tresses from constantly getting in her face, but left most of her hair down and flowing. Rising back to her feet, she went to where she had put her knives when she had undressed for her bath the previous day. Finding the two leather covers, she laced one sheath around her upper thigh and another around her waist underneath the purple bliaut. She then reached up for the knives and remembered she had not been able to find them yesterday when she had dressed for their wedding. She had no idea where they were. "Where are my *sgian-dubhs*?"

Brodie's brow furrowed. "You have no need for them anymore. You are safe on McTiernay land and I will be with you today."

"Where are my *sgian-dubhs*?" Shinae did not shout the words; however, the low, dark rumble of her voice was far more ominous. "I have worn them every day since I learned how to use them as a young girl and that includes while I was a nun. Now, where are they?"

"You plan on stabbing someone?"

Shinae refused to shout like a McTiernay, especially on the first day of her marriage, but she could now see why wives yelled at their husbands. It was because men thought their women should just go along with whatever they thought best—even when they clearly were wrong.

Shinae pointedly stared at Brodie with her arms crossed until he grumbled a few condescending words, spun on his heel, and went to grab the items next to his sword. He threw them toward her in rapid succession, anticipating they would land on the bed where he had aimed. To his shock, she had plucked both out of the air. After ripping the thread holding the right pocket together, she sheaved the small one on her waist and the larger one on her thigh.

"I'm not against a woman keeping a weapon on her. I mean, Lady Laurel wears one. I just never expected my *wife* to feel the same need."

"I didn't expect to need them the day the abbey was attacked and burned down. But without them, I would no longer be part of this world."

Brodie was not sure if he believed the dramatic inference

she made but quickly decided that while unexpected, he really did not care if she wore dirks. He was not going to start fighting like a McTiernay on their first day of marriage.

Grabbing the rope handle, Brodie pulled open the door and followed Shinae out and down the chapel's spiral staircase and out into the sunshine, barely avoiding Isilmë, who was hugging Shinae very tightly.

Shinae finally said her goodbyes to Isilmë, who had stopped her just as she stepped out of the chapel. The woman was excited about being able to join the McTiernay seamstresses and weavers. Her skills made her a perfect fit for the position, and no doubt once the quality of her work was seen, Isilmë would be deluged with requests.

"Where are we going?" Shinae asked Brodie, who was nearly dragging her to the castle gate in his rush.

"I thought today we would go out and watch the harvest being brought in," Brodie said flatly. Shinae initially thought he was still ruffled from her insistence at wearing her dirks. However, when she had seen his look of growing impatience while Isilmë kept rattling about her news, she knew otherwise.

She too had lost her chipper mood due to her short interlude with Isilmë, but for a different reason. Unlike Isilmë, she had nothing in particular to keep her busy.

She allowed Brodie to help her onto the large horse, and then he swung up behind her. He urged the horse forward, but did not encourage the animal to go faster than a walk.

Brodie was initially glad neither or them spoke. He was afraid if either of them did, in their current moods, it would turn into an argument. Maybe the McTiernays enjoyed a good, lively debate at the top of their lungs, but he did not. Besides, he would lose. After a quarter hour of riding in silence, he realized that all the noise in the village was not compensating for hearing her voice. "What were you and Isilmë talking about for so long?" Brodie asked in a pleasant tone.

"Oh, about how she is going to work with the other seamstresses."

Her lackluster response worried him, and he wondered if his prior attitude was behind it. "I'm sure Lady Makenna would let you join them as well if you wished."

She snorted softly. "I do *not* wish, and if I were to join them, I'd only embarrass you and my sister. I can sew when necessary, but only when I must." Shinae was glad he could not see the expression of disgust she felt at the idea.

To her surprise, Brodie burst out laughing. "Then I shall do my best to never let a needle or thread touch this skin." He lifted her hand and gave it a quick kiss.

"But she got me thinking. I've always been busy all my life. Now what will I do? After five years living as a nun, I'm afraid my skills are limited to prayer."

"I understand."

Shinae rolled her eyes. She hated platitudes, even those that people meant. "I doubt it. You have people who depend on you, men you train. I'm sure the laird depends on you for leadership and many other things."

"*Mì-cheart.* If that were true, I wouldn't be here with you."

She twisted around as far as she could to get a good look at his expression to determine if he were telling the truth. "You don't work with the soldiers?"

"I help when and where needed, but I have been given no task to oversee them regularly. That responsibility belongs to Colin's commanders."

"You truly don't do anything?"

Clearly the concept was inconceivable to her, which explained why she was so antsy about her own lack of direction. Thinking about what he had said from her point of view, Shinae was probably thinking that she had married a vagrant. The thought did not sit well. He was her husband and she deserved to understand.

"Eight years ago, one of our allies lost their commanders and most of their seasoned soldiers during a fierce battle. I agreed to help Laird Mahon Donavan rebuild and train his army. It was supposed to be temporary, but we both quickly realized that training completely unskilled men would take much longer. Three months ago, I returned."

"It took eight years?" Shinae asked incredulously.

"Aye," he answered, knowing it was only a half-truth. He had done more than just train; he had helped with clan disputes, led the people when the laird was away, and even functioned as steward when necessary.

"So now you are looking for something else to do as well," she said as relief swept through her body.

She was glad Brodie was no longer a soldier. When she had lived with the Culdees, too often was she called to nurse those who were injured, either by fighting the English or one another. It was common for soldiers to be severely wounded, and the thought of Brodie dying, or even almost dying, was not something she could contemplate. She had just found him. Having him ripped from her life was unthinkable.

Brodie felt a light shudder go through her and wondered at the cause. He had been looking for something else to do for weeks, but truth was, there was nothing available that used his skills. His experience and knowledge of leading men and guiding a clan was useless. He had no interest in becoming a farmer, a furrier, a stonemason, a carpenter, or any of the myriad of jobs that were available. He was meant to lead and make decisions, and yet nothing close to such a role was vacant. Until one of Colin's commanders decided to step down, Brodie was at a loss, but he did not want to tell Shinae and have her worry.

"Be at ease. I don't sit around and twiddle my fingers in boredom."

"Who is this Laird Donovan?" she demanded. "And why didn't he ask you to stay? Why did you agree to leave?"

Brodie's heart jumped at the questions and her defensive tone. She had just given voice to the very thing that had been haunting him since his return. He knew several clansmen and women had doubts about their speed to the altar, but Shinae's questions assured him that he had not. He'd marry her again if he could.

Taking in a deep breath, he held it and let it go with a lot of the apprehension that had been tormenting him.

He gave her a quick hug and whispered in her ear, "I had my reasons."

Shinae gazed at the land in awe. It was like summer sunlight. There were several fields, and each was brimming with a type of grain—wheat, rye, or bere. Scythes and sickles shone in the sun. Men were calling for water jugs as they gathered handfuls of grain into sheaves. Once they had enough sheaves, they were grouped into shooks to dry. The clanswomen and children followed the threshers gathering the stalks that had fallen aside.

Unlike most clans, Laird Colin McTiernay ensured most of his clansmen enjoyed a rich and varied diet, believing it made them healthier. Healthy men were able to produce more, which led to greater funds to support his army, his castle maintenance, his servants, and the feasts that could be expanded outside the great hall to include almost everyone. When the weather was good and the crops bountiful, as they had been this year, the Lammas Day banquet—held the last day of the harvest—was open to all. Because Colin had invited his brothers and their families, the festivities and bonfires would continue both in and out of the castle until Lammas Day. One was held the night before in celebration of her and Brodie's marriage. It had included wild boar, venison, and rabbit, as well as an array of fruits and fritters.

Fresh meat was a luxury, but bread and ale made from barley was a staple of life wherever one lived. Shinae knew this, but she had never seen what work went into getting such a necessity. She was witnessing the beginning of the harvest process before the cereal grains were ground into flour, then kneaded into dough for baking.

Someone called out for Brodie and, getting his attention, waved for him to come over. After giving her a quick kiss, he got down, went over to the farmer, spoke for a bit, and then came back. Helping her off the horse, he said, "There is a big push to get these fields in today so they can move to the ones to the east and outer borders. We need to get them stacked and drying before another storm comes."

She could tell Brodie wanted to go. It looked like arduous work, but he was not the type of man who watched others labor as he looked on.

"Go," Shinae encouraged him. "I think I will join the women." She was just as eager to do something. Many clans had their farmers as well as their families work only their own fields, but Colin McTiernay had started a tradition that all who could participate were expected to help with the harvest. This brought the crops in faster and lessened the chance for loss from surprise bouts of cold or rainy weather. She glanced down to the pretty, dark green bliaut she was given by Meriel the day before. It was simple, but lovely.

As if he could read her mind, he kissed her forehead. "It's dirty work, but it'll clean." Then, before she could respond, he bounded off in the direction of the threshers.

With a sigh, she headed off to the fields with a smile,

glad she had worn her leather ankle boots rather than the laced slippers Meriel had provided.

Shinae put the soap and cloth down before sinking below the water to clean her hair from the day's dirt. She then closed her eyes and relaxed her neck on the rim of the brass tub, letting the healing heat of the bath's water ease her body's aches. Some of the clanswomen had quit when she did, but they were going home to start their evening meal. When Dunlop stopped and told her to get on his horse, it had not taken much to convince her to do as directed. When she got back to find the overly large tub full, hot, and waiting, she silently thanked the Lord for Lady Makenna and quickly got in.

Shinae slightly jumped at the feel of fingertips delving into her hair, encouraging her to stay as she was. With eyes still closed, she let herself be pampered, probably for the first time since she was a young child. To be touched in such a way was both alarming and stimulating. She released a large groan when Brodie removed his hands, chuckling at her displeasure. The sound caused her to open her eyes and smile as she watched him disrobe.

Usually, Brodie would have stayed with the threshers until the last man was ready to leave, but that was before he had someone to come home to. Again, marriage was proving to be quite agreeable.

He nudged her forward in the oval tub and sank into the warm waters behind her. Water rose to the top and spilled over, but neither of them cared. Shinae picked up the small piece of cloth and rubbed the lavender soap on it until the lather bubbled. She then turned and began to wash his chest, neck, and arms before releasing the cloth to him to wash his face. She moved to the other side of the tub and tried to calm her breath. She had always considered herself to be demure, if not a prude, but with Brodie, her desires to physically touch him, look at him, and kiss him took over, pushing all her nunlike thoughts and ways to the back of her mind.

Brodie dunked his head into the water and scrubbed his hair, uncaring that he would smell of lavender. Once done, instead of putting the cloth over the rim, he leaned over to Shinae's side and started sliding the cloth slowly up her leg. "I think you missed a spot."

Shinae giggled. "I disagree. I washed myself thoroughly before you arrived." She moved in pretense to rise when his strong arm tugged her to him, ending any ideas about her leaving his side.

The cloth he had been holding now floated somewhere in the water, leaving his hand free to continue wandering. Gripping her thigh, he opened her legs to him, uncaring of the additional water sloshing over and onto the rushes as his hand found her warm and slick. He studied her face as he began to tease her. Shinae's eyes were closed, and she bit her bottom lip. Brodie moved his finger inside her, ever so slightly, and began to stroke her outer flesh with a careful thumb. There was nothing he wanted more than this. Watching his wife melt with just his touch.

Shinae began to undulate her hips to his rocking finger. He loved her reactions. They were real, not false, like the widows he had been with. They had had needs just as he had. Touching and teasing, ensuring their pleasure had not been part of the act.

He took her mouth in a scorching kiss. As his tongue danced with hers, his fingers made slow, maddening movements along her sex. He could see the pressure begin to build and quickened the speed. One finger, then another, her breaths became short and fast. He could actually feel her heart pound against the wall of her chest. Sheer happiness filled him when her body clenched, and she shuddered with pleasure.

Without a second's hesitation, he scooped her from the tub and carried her dripping in his arms to the bed. Gently lying her down, he covered her with his massive body, pushing himself between her legs. "I need you with every beat of my heart, every breath in my body. I am not strong enough and way too impatient to wait."

With the last bit of control he possessed, Brodie eased himself into her. "I will never stop wanting you," he whispered, his hazel eyes locked onto her green ones. Slow and gentle, he began to move. She was no longer a virgin, but her body was still new to lovemaking, and healing.

A flush rose in her cheeks and he stilled himself. With her voice just above a whisper, she grabbed his neck and said, "I've never felt so . . . desired." Then her hands were everywhere, raking his back, her lips seeking his mouth, desperate for more.

Brodie was surprised by her aggression and began to move slowly, determined to be gentle.

Shinae threw her head back, thrust her breasts upward, and let out a soft, needy moan. "Faster."

Hearing her plea, Brodie went wild. Pulling back, he thrust hard, and then again, feeling her body respond to his, oblivious of anything other than his primal, animalistic mission to claim her again and again.

Meeting him thrust for thrust, he could not stop his fast-approaching climax anymore. His body shook with a fierce tension until he exploded, his relief pulsing through him with every heartbeat.

Letting out a sigh, he lowered his forehead to rest against hers. "I swear, you will not know a moment's regret in marrying me."

Shinae smiled. "I will never be sorry I married you."

Shinae popped the last bit of her hard-boiled egg in her mouth before rising. "It's late and I need to get to the village quickly," she said, licking her fingers.

"You don't have to go every day," Meriel asserted with agreeing nods from the rest of the McTiernay women, who were finishing with their morning meal. "We have healers."

Shinae just smiled. "You, sweet Meriel, love to stitch and embroider, as does Isilmë. Such a tedious chore to me is bizarrely amusing to you. Ellenor loves entertaining the children, and you three," she said, pointing at Lady Makenna, Laurel, and Raelynd, "actually *enjoy* the constant onslaught of questions and decisions needed to manage this place, especially with all the bonfires and feasts each night. For the past five years, I have been unable to help families in need, and I am sincerely thankful you are letting me do it."

"Letting you?" Makenna snorted. "The healers are really midwives, and they help when they can but are not nearly as experienced. Your support enables them to go to the fields and gather what they can to help feed their families. You are the one who is a godsend."

"Then I will see you all later today."

She beamed them a huge smile and quickly left before being pulled into another conversation. They were a chatty bunch and she enjoyed their company, though it was rare they asked her for her opinion.

She had been married for a little more than two weeks and every day she had awakened to the feel of Brodie's arms holding her close. Sometimes they made love, but usually, when dawn broke, he kissed her lips, quickly dressed, and went to help with the harvest. Thankfully, the threshing was almost done, but next all the dry shooks needed to be collected and hauled to the various barns and places of storage to protect the yield for winter. Then the farmers would prepare the land for winter crops and, in the early spring, the cycle would begin again.

Shinae knew that Brodie worried about how he would spend his time in the winter months and could only pray that God sent him an answer . . . and soon. She also prayed for an answer to the reason she was there. During the day, the men were too busy to talk, but when evening came, they gathered in the great hall and inner courtyard to enjoy a simple bonfire with singing and dancing. That was when Shinae mingled with the men—married or single—in an effort to ascertain just who might be a traitor. So far everyone seemed genuinely proud to be a McTiernay. Not once did her inner voice speak up alerting her to possible danger. Not even a hiccup. Her one so-called ability had been useless. All seemed truly loyal to Colin McTiernay and his wife, Lady Makenna.

Cyric had pressed upon her that she was to keep silent and warn only Conan and her sister as to the danger they were in. If they had not yet arrived, he had made her vow that she would not say anything to anyone until they had. If she did, it might ruin the chances to find the assassin. If the McTiernays were aware of him and his plans, the brothers would act differently and the man would flee and attack another time, and their chance to capture the English spy would be lost. So would the chance to get more information on other clans that were at risk.

Never did Shinae suspect that she would meet some-one, marry them, and then fall in love with them. Her feelings for Brodie were growing stronger and stronger each day. Neither of them had expressed their emotions, but she could honestly say that, to her surprise, she loved him. She just wished she could be honest with him and reveal the real reason she had been driven to come to Lochlen.

Shinae walked the long trek to the outskirts of the village. When she finally arrived, she knocked on the door, nervous to see how things were faring. Opening the door, the woman inside hugged her tightly. There was an air of happiness in the good-sized cottage, and Shine could see the woman's ailing grandfather sitting

up and sipping some soup. His days were not over, as
they feared, and his daughter looked relieved.

"Does he not look better?" Sorcha asked. "Just a
small cough remains." She grabbed her basket. "I've sent
the older children with their father to the fields. Ualan
told me that they should finish the final field today," she
said with a grin. Her cheer at her father's improvement
rang out clearly. "Again, thank you so much for coming.
Soup is near the hearth keeping warm, and I will send
at least one of the children back in the afternoon."

Shinae gave her one last hug before the woman rushed
out the door to join the gleaners. She then glanced at
the older man and said, "Look at you! And you tried to
convince me that your time had come to an end. I think
Lochlen's steward has several more harvests to see."

Ros started coughing, but Shinae could see no blood.
He handed her his empty bowl, his hand shaking slightly.
"Not many," he corrected her, "but I will see the end of
this one, little lass."

Shinae felt his head, and it was still cool to the touch.
For four days, he had fought death and seemed to have
won the previous day, when his fever broke. Exhausted,
he slept nearly all day, barely taking any water. Today,
however, he looked much better and was sitting up for
the first time in a week. The man was not going to die
today or even that month, but his breathing was still
labored, and it worried her.

As the steward, Ros usually stayed in his chambers
on the top floor of the daunting *Tòrr-dubh*, but with so
many visitors and Lady Makenna needing rooms, he had
voluntarily agreed to stay with his daughter and her

family, allowing one of the McTiernays to use his room. It was through his youngest grandchild he had caught a cold, which had affected him far worse than it did the boy. Ros had an incredibly sharp wit and liked to flirt with her, as if both she and he were single and twenty again.

The cottage had two large rooms and a smaller addition that provided an area for the children to sleep. Ros's makeshift bed had been loaned to the family and was set up in the main living space.

Shinae tried to get Ros to lay back down, but he shooed her away. "Don't you pamper me, lass. I need to regain my strength and get back to my duties, not slumber. I have spent too much time letting others assume my work."

"The McTiernay wives have been happy to help. I think they would have gone a little prickly waiting for Conan to arrive without something to keep them busy."

Ros snorted. "They will muddle things up," he mumbled.

"I'm sure your apprentice will keep things how you wish them to be," Shinae said while trying once again to get the old man to lay down.

"I don't have one," Ros snapped. "For years I tried to train someone, but none had the skills to lead the staff and enforce the laird's decisions that were not exactly acceptable to the clan."

An idea hit Shinae like a thunderbolt. "What about Brodie?" she blurted out. "He practically was Laird Donovan's second for eight years! He told me that he often functioned as his steward until the laird was able to find someone to do it permanently. Oh please, what do you think? He is wasted helping out as needed, and so few are natural leaders like he is."

Ros just stared at her for several minutes. His mind was churning. "I had forgotten about him, and aye, he would make a good steward if he agrees. But there is a strong chance, lass, that he will not. Don't be surprised if he rejects the idea. Pride runs through all the McTiernays, especially that one."

Shinae almost argued that Brodie was only half McTiernay and bit the inside of her cheek to keep silent just in time. Ros was wrong. Just because she discovered the opportunity first would not be a problem. Only a fool would rebuff such an opportunity.

It was hard for her to sit still in her excitement and was eager for Sorcha to return so she could talk with her husband and let him know of her discovery. God must have heard her pleas, for Sorcha's eldest popped in just after Shinae had given Ros his early afternoon meal. After making sure all was fine, Shinae dashed out the door hoping she could convince Brodie to celebrate their good luck right after the midday meal.

She had not gone far when she heard a raucous banging followed by laughter in a cottage-size building with several additions. Brodie said that the family had abandoned it when the children married and moved out. Rumors were that the older couple had moved closer to the castle and Colin now used it for storage. Sorcha told her it was a way to disguise certain stored goods from travelers, thieves, and wild animals.

Curious, Shinae peeked inside and saw a room full of small barrels a little longer than her forearm. Most were wax-sealed, but several dozen had been opened and were now laying haphazardly on the floor. In the middle of the mess were two older boys—Braden and Gideon—pushing each other in fun as the two older girls, Brenna and Aislinn, ignored them as they stirred the contents of a large pot over a fire in the hearth. All four seemed oblivious to her presence.

"Just what is happening in here?" Shinae asked sharply, stepping inside and letting the door close behind her.

CHAPTER SIX

The smell of burned sugar filled the room. Shinae knew the smell well. Honey. She had not been involved in Dryburgh's beekeeping activities, but in certain areas, the air was infused with the smell. Only a few were trusted to take care of the bees as honey and beeswax were key sources of the cloister's income. Their candles were highly prized by the nobility, and the fermented honey used to make mead was imbibed by all those who lived at the abbey.

She glanced around at the additions she had seen from the outside. One looked to be full of honey, while the other was storing empty barrels. The right side of the main room, which was once a large cottage, had barrels stacked floor-to-ceiling and was three barrels deep. The impressions on the floor, however, implied there were at least two rows missing.

She looked at each child. All their clothes looked like they had been rolling in the dirt. The boys were on one side of the room wrestling and looked like they had already knocked down a few barrels while doing so.

The girls were on the other side of the room standing by a lit hearth, where there was a large pot of what Shinae assumed was honey.

Aislinn looked up with an imploring look. "Just a few more minutes. Brenna thinks this batch will finally work."

"She thought the same thing with the last five tries," Braeden chided his twin sister and threw one of the small barrels at Gideon, who caught it. But Shinae could see the evidence of several times when he had not.

Brenna ignored him and kept stirring the contents from at least two of the small barrels. "Do we have any more butter?"

"You used it all, so this batch had better work or we're telling," Gideon said with a grin.

As if it just occurred to Aislinn that Shinae was an adult and had made no promises to keep their secret, the girl looked back at Shinae with bright blue eyes that begged for her silence. "It's for a good cause," she quickly said with an upbeat tone. "We did this a few days ago, and it *worked*!"

"That's because no cooking was involved," Gideon sneered.

"And you used all the eggs," Braeden chirped in.

Brenna narrowed her eyes and gave her brother and his best friend the best scowling look she could produce. "*Honey meringue requires eggs*," she hissed.

Shinae remembered hearing about a scuffle in the kitchen about the sudden egg shortage and how this was still affecting what and how much cooks and bakers could produce. There was no gossip about the loss of honey, though.

"You need the white parts to make the meringue," Aislinn said, defending her friend. "And you and Gideon ate almost half of them, which means they were *good*."

Shinae let out a sharp whistle using her fingers. It startled everyone, including her. It had been several years since she had made that piercing sound. Thankfully it worked, and the room became silent. "What do you mean, good cause, and am I right that your parents do not know you are here or what you are doing?"

The boys started grinning and crossed their arms. Their haughtiness at thinking they were innocent irritated Shinae. She pointed to the honey dripping from the barrels they had been tossing. "You think your fathers would be pleased knowing you created this mess?" Both looked around. They thought they would be long gone and back in the Highlands before anyone knew; the guilt on their faces said it all.

Braeden swallowed. "We got bored waiting for the candy *they kept burning*," he said, directing his last words toward his sister.

"It's ready!" Brenna jumped up with a smile. "Hurry and pour it onto the boards," she said gleefully to the boys, pointing at two large, extremely smooth boards with a fuller carving all around the edges. A common piece of cookware used to pound out bread and shape pastries.

The boys dashed over and did as they were bid, and the gooey golden syrup slowly dripped onto one board. When it was full, they switched to the other. Focused on the task before them, Shinae was once again ignored as the girls used knives to push the syrup back from oozing off the boards before it overflowed despite the fuller. Within minutes, the syrup started to harden, and only then did they remember they had company.

Shinae shook her head and tried to look angry but was not sure she succeeded when Aislinn clapped her hands together. "I cannot wait to see Commander Dunlop and Sister Isilmë's faces."

"She's not Sister Isilmë, just Isilmë," Shinae corrected.

"One bite of this and they will fall in love," Brenna said licking her fingers.

Shinae sighed, finally understanding what this was all about. She remembered Isilmë practically dancing a couple of mornings ago. Brodie had mentioned that Dunlop had seemed unusually good-humored as well. "So, you are the ones behind Dunlop and Isilmë thinking the other is giving them sweet gifts."

Brenna and Aislinn grinned while Braeden put up his hands and made it clear that neither he nor Gideon were involved. "We are just here for the candy."

Gideon pointed at the board in front of him. "This one is all ours," he said proudly. "All we have to do is keep the girls' secret."

"And stay out of everyone's way," Braeden mumbled.

"I think it is now your secret too," Shinae commented.

They looked at each other, puzzled. They had not participated in the candy making. "And yours," Braeden pointed out, "unless you are going to betray us and tell."

Shinae waved her hand at the disorder. "I doubt I will have to say a word."

Brenna puffed out her chest and furrowed her brow. "It's not *that* bad."

"And besides, don't you want to see Dunlop and Isilmë fall in love?" Aislinn asked. "We were just helping."

Brenna nodded. "Trust us, without some help, it would take a *long* time."

"I'm not sure a bit of candy is going to get them to fall in love," Shinae pointed out.

Brenna looked affronted. "Out of everyone, Mama probably helped you the most! Because no one thinks you would be married otherwise, especially to Commander Brodie."

Shinae pursed her lips, thinking Brenna had a point and yet . . . "I'm going to have to let your parents know. This place—"

"Will be clean and no one will ever know we were here," Brenna assured her.

Aislinn nodded. "We made an even *bigger* mess at the other place we store honey, and we cleaned it all up."

"Did you replace the honey, too?" Shinae challenged.

"My father has a *lot* of honey," Aislinn said. "And the clan will be collecting it again in a little over a month." She must have seen the doubt on Shinae's face. "We have hundreds of hives. Truly!"

"And you only need a few drops to sweeten anything. It would probably have gone to waste!" Brenna asserted.

Shinae took one more look around. It was not as if they had compromised something costly, like beeswax. That would have been another issue. "I won't say anything as long as you clean this *all* up. But if anyone asks me about this, I will tell them."

Both boys patted her on the back wearing big, toothy grins. "You are the best nun ever!"

Shinae rolled her eyes. It was going to be a long time for people to forget who she was before she came to Lochlen. "But *no more*. Understand? The eggs were an issue last time."

Brenna smiled proudly. "That's why we made honey crackle today."

Shinae left the cottage almost in a better mood than when she arrived. Though they were only children, she had felt included. The McTiernays—both the women and their husbands—were very nice, but they did not exactly embrace her as one of them. Meriel was friendly, but she usually spent time with Isilmë as both had a passion for sewing and talking. When it came to Raelynd, Shinae often felt judged, and Ellenor seemed pleasant enough, but someone she was most likely not going to meet again. Brodie's decision to remind all of his Dunstan heritage by wearing the blue and white tartan kept him, and therefore her, apart from the clansmen and women as well. He did not realize how much it distanced him from others, but both problems time would solve. *One of them*, she thought with a large smile, thinking of earlier that day, *might just be solved quite soon.*

Shinae neared Lochlen's gatehouse and noticed numerous armed soldiers were standing around, their numbers only growing larger. When she finally made it to the entrance and then to the castle's inner ward, she stopped short. Her smile faded.

She was back earlier than usual, eager to take a bath and put some effort into doing her hair. Tonight, there was to be a big bonfire, and she intended to reveal her good news that night before they retired. She had been envisioning all the ways Brodie would convey his appreciation on her way back and none of them started with a heated look on his face. Whatever was going on was bad, for Brodie was not alone in his ire. All the McTiernay brothers appeared like they wanted to hurt someone . . . and badly.

She quietly stayed close to the castle wall as she made her way to the chapel, hoping to stay out of view. It was working until she passed the windows of the great hall. Meriel saw her and waved at her to come in.

Shinae entered the huge room and made her way to the main hearth, where, to no surprise all, the McTiernay women were gathered. She sat down and waited for someone to explain.

"Did you learn anything when you were in the village?" Makenna asked, her tone laced with worry.

Baffled by the question, Shinae shook her head. "The only indication there was something wrong was all the anger I saw rolling off the laird and his brothers."

Raelynd nodded. "I walked by them and you could almost touch their rage. The only time I felt such strong negative emotions coming from Crevan was after Conor's stabbing."

Laurel shuddered. "Let's not talk about that. It is something I would like to forget." She then pivoted to

Shinae. "We may need your herbal skills in case the men come back injured. We should make a list and prepare ourselves."

Shinae recoiled at the notion. Her husband was one of the men out in the yard, and Laurel made it sound like the clan was about to go to war. She had just learned of a way to keep Brodie safe from injury and it was too late.

"Shinae?"

"I . . . um have wormwood, mint, and balm."

"We have myrrh for wounds as well as yarrow and Achillea. I'll let Gert know to go and fetch them, as well as to reach out to the midwives to be prepared," added Makenna.

"Are you sure there is going to be fighting?" Shinae reached down and confirmed both daggers were in place.

"No, we are not saying that at all," Meriel cooed, as if she were calming a crying child. That was when Shinae realized that tears were slowly rolling down her cheeks. "But *if* we are told there is to be a battle, we need to prepare ourselves and be strong, so our men don't worry about us when they are gone."

Shinae nodded and wiped her cheeks dry, an icy fierceness overtaking her. If anything happened to Brodie, the world would learn just how deadly she could be with a knife. She stood up. "I need to know exactly what is happening."

Laurel motioned impatiently for her to sit down again. Shinae crossed her arms and arched her left brow in defiance. Laurel may be married to the McTiernays' chief and she may have the other women obedient to her commands, but Shinae did not want her to think she was subservient. That was something her abbess found out quite early into her stay at Dryburgh Abbey. She obeyed God's commands and usually complied to people's requests when that was what they were, *requests*. To Shinae's surprise, Laurel smiled appreciatively.

"I see you have much more fortitude than you led us to believe."

"Because I agreed to marry Brodie so quickly?" They all nodded. "I married him for my own reasons, not yours, and he did the same. No one forced marriage upon either of us and I think that would have been obvious by our age. If we were so weak, we would have succumbed to the pressures when we were young."

Shinae spun around, intending to march out when she heard Laurel say, "*Sàsta*. I knew when I first saw you that you were one of us. You just needed to discover it yourself." Laurel rose to her feet.

"I am not one of you," Shinae corrected, turning to look at Laurel directly in her storm-colored eyes. She was not a McTiernay and neither did she think of herself as a Dunstan.

"Aye, you are. You are a strong woman who stands by her man," Makenna added, rising to her feet. The others followed. "Not behind or ahead, but by his side."

"And just as he is your strength, you are his," Ellenor asserted.

"Tell me that we are wrong," Laurel challenged again, with a commanding tone and mannerisms, and yet Shinae did not feel as if she was being condescended to as before.

"I am not unskilled with a blade and I will prove that if necessary."

Thinking such a revelation would be shocking, Shinae was again surprised. "As will I with my sword, and Laurel with her bow," Makenna said. "And until they are ready to inform us of what is happening, we will wait here."

Shinae tightened her jaw. "And you actually believe they will tell us what is happening?"

Laurel flashed her a wicked smile. "Oh, Conor will absolutely tell me. All of our husbands will out of respect to us."

"And maybe a little fear as to what would happen otherwise," Raelynd said with a smirk and resumed her seat. She was the least friendly of the five women, but also the most forthright—a quality Shinae admired.

Shinae returned to her seat. She was not accustomed to trusting people and never with something as critical as her heart. But with lack of options and knowledge of what had riled their men, she had no choice but to follow the McTiernay wives' lead and pray that Brodie would let her know before he rode off.

"I'm sorry, I must go," Brodie said as he anchored his halberd to his waist, along with the addition of a couple of long knives and a dagger. Next, he quickly thrust one arm through the right armhole of a leather harness, followed by his left arm. After sheathing two swords in the leather slots on his back so they formed an X, he secured the harness and returned his attention to her.

Shinae sat quietly and simply watched him prepare for war when she said in a voice that was eerily calm, "I understand you must go, but can you at least tell me why?"

Brodie searched for the right words to refuse when Shinae rose to her feet, went to the chamber door, stood in front of it, and pulled out her own two weapons. "Because trust me when I say this," her voice still disturbingly calm, "I will not simply sit and wait for your return when you disappear dressed as you are."

Brodie exhaled and clutched the lid of his trunk for several seconds before replying. "I promise to explain all when I return, but saying anything now would only leave you with even more questions that I cannot answer at this time."

"Laurel and Makenna assured me their husbands would let them know and that you would respect me in the same way. Is this not true? Because if so, I might be inclined to follow you and join the fight."

Brodie jerked at the thought. Shinae was not threatening him, she was warning him, and he had a gut feeling that she really just might try to follow him. Suddenly, a *sgian dubh* appeared next to his hand, shaking back and forth.

"The next one will be in your thigh, forcing you to rethink your plans."

Brodie slammed down the chest lid at the threat. He was about to dare her to make such a move when he looked at her in the eye for the first time that evening and saw that Shinae was serious. He had been avoiding her misty green eyes since he charged into their chamber and saw her staring out the window, waiting for him. Now when he looked at her, he saw she was not a woman trying to humble her man, but a wife very afraid that she might lose him and not even know why. But he could not explain what he did not know.

There could be a simple explanation for the missing honey, but even so, that did not change the complexity of the situation. And if the border reivers *were* involved, there would be a battle and people would be hurt and possibly die. Shinae did not need to hear that. But her worried expression made it clear that she would not allow him to leave her ignorant.

He marched over and grabbed her face between his hands and kissed her long and deep. If the positions were reversed and he had a knife in hand, he suspected he would have started with her thigh.

Gasping for breath, she pulled her mouth free. A sudden impulse to say how much he loved her rippled through him, but he stayed quiet.

His thumb swept the curve of her cheek in a gentle caress. Taking her hand, he went and sat them both down on the bed. "Truth is that none of us know what is going on and what will happen. A major theft happened once again, and this time the impact to the clan and our allies is serious. Colin needs to remind his neighbors that he is not alone and has asked his brothers, Dunlop, myself, and fifty of his men to pay a little visit to the reivers. Only they would dare to come onto our land and steal so much from us. It has been too long since they have seen our might, and it seems they need a reminder."

Shinae wanted to ask why it was he and Dunlop who

had to go, not Drake or Callum. But she knew the answer. She and Brodie had no family, whereas Drake and his wife Ceridwin had two children. Callum was Schellden Highland commander sent to help protect Meriel and Raelynd nor did he know the area. Such knowledge was not needed to defend Lochlen, but it might be critical if he needed to be riding or fighting on the rocky terrain.

Shinae just nodded her head and let her tears come. He stood up to leave, and she remembered that she had yet to tell him her good news. Knowing that he had an important position that was challenging and all the things he desired was waiting for him when he returned might give him just a bit more motivation to come back whole and well.

Dunlop watched his friend jerk the reins to his horse much more fiercely than was necessary. Whatever was bothering him was not lessening the farther they were from Lochlen. Brodie had specifically volunteered to follow the army to ensure there were no problems, which was unlike the soldier Dunlop remembered. Brodie led his men, not the other way around. But because two skilled horse riders were needed to ensure there were no stragglers or issues, Dunlop agreed to ride with him. But the waves of anger Brodie was sending meant his mind was not thinking about what was going on around them and would be poor support if a fight did break out. The man needed to release whatever had him riled, so he could pay attention when necessary.

"Are you going to tell me or not?" Dunlop asked, his

own emotional state far from his usual jovial one. "We are alone. No one will hear what Shinae did or did not do to make you so angry."

"Shinae betrayed me."

Dunlop suddenly pulled back the leather reins that he had been holding loosely, bringing the animal to a stop. It forced Brodie to do the same, and Dunlop doubted that as long as they were riding, his friend would explain the accusation. Dunlop needed to hear what happened to this couple that was so different and yet so good together. He needed to understand in order to avoid the mistake of entangling his life and heart with a woman.

"She has no faith in me. No trust. No *respect* for me as a man. Shinae aids other families and thought she could take care of me as well. But I promise you that I made it abundantly clear that she in no way will ever have control of my life."

Dunlop sat stunned. Whatever Shinae did, it basically resulted in Brodie feeling extremely humiliated. If what his friend was saying was true, he would be similarly outraged.

"And she told the women! Who no doubt ran to their husbands, and now I am a mockery to all," Brodie huffed. "I can just hear them squawking about how I needed my wife to find me something to do."

Murt, if that was true, any man would be frothing at the mouth. But Dunlop had a hard time believing that Shinae would do something like that. "Just what is it that she suggested to everyone for you to do?"

"Take over for Ros when he passes away."

The old steward had been having problems with his

lungs and it was unlikely he would make it through the upcoming winter.

"You would become Colin's steward?" Dunlop asked in a shocked tone. It never occurred to him that Brodie would want to work directly for the laird. He did not even wear the McTiernay plaid. Then again, the thought of Brodie as steward made sense. He knew the people, the castle, and, more importantly, had actually done the work when he was supporting Laird Donovan.

"I can see why you might have wanted to have come to this idea on your own, but—"

"Ros is alive and getting better. The mere thought that I should lay in wait, eagerly anticipating his death, is disgusting to me."

"Put that way, it would be to anyone," Dunlop said in confusion. "But who said you would have to wait? The man could use the help now, and not someone young and inexperienced. With an apprentice, he would have to show and explain all that was involved. However, with someone like you, who already knows what needs to be done, Ros can guide you in the ways Colin likes things done. It might just be the relief Ros needs. The man is getting old and cannot do all that he once could, and yet he still needs to feel essential. You could take over the stressful or physical responsibilities." Dunlop paused. "You have to admit that no one is better suited to take over for Ros than you. No one else knows the job."

Brodie started breathing heavily, and Dunlop suspected the words he had just spoken were the very ones Shinae had said. And they were not the ones Brodie wanted to hear.

Brodie twisted in his saddle and glared at Dunlop. "Do you know *when* Shinae chose to inform me, *me*, the man she married to ensure she had a home after running away from the abbey? *After* she announced it to everyone! I bet even little Brion was told that she found me something to do."

Dunlop reached out and punched Brodie in the jaw, almost knocking him from his horse and to the ground. He was lucky that the distance impeded the full force of his fist. "You can say thanks later, and I pray to God that if I ever say something so vile about my wife you will do the same for me." He wringed his hand and wiggled his fingers to ensure nothing was broken. "Now say you understand me before my other fist finds your face again."

Brodie moved his jaw back and forth. He had forgotten his friend's strength and long arm span and did not want a second reminder. "I heard you."

"Good. Let's catch up to the others, during which time you will tell me *exactly* what happened."

At first, Brodie dismissed any insight provided and tried to lure Dunlop to his point of view. After hearing all that Brodie had said, Dunlop wondered if Brodie had seriously misinterpreted things.

"She has no faith in me," Brodie mumbled.

Dunlop snorted in disgust. "I would say she proved the opposite. A steward is a position that comes with the weight of a lot of responsibilities, including making decisions that not all will like. After what you did and said to her, I'm glad you have no interest in the position.

Good stewards do not leap to conclusions—especially negative ones."

Dunlop mostly listened when his old friend was in a mood, but not today. With each claim Brodie made, he countered it.

She had no faith in me. . . no trust that I could find work and take care of our future. "Sounds like she was just happy at the idea, believing you would be just as eager as she was. You don't realize how burdensome your mood has been to others since your return. I'm not sure many of us could have withstood it much longer if Shinae had not come into your life."

You don't understand. She was jubilant at the idea and told everyone what she had done. She held no respect for me as a man. "Maybe so, but then again, maybe she suffered from the same thing you do. Pride. Hers was about you, and instead of appreciating that fact, you scorned her for it."

Dunlop had to get Brodie to recognize that Shinae was not gossiping; she had been sharing her news because she had been happy. Not for herself, but for Brodie. "I understand why you are upset, but you two are new at being married. She used to be a nun, and from what Isilmë told me, they lived in an isolated environment. They had to keep all their emotions, thoughts, and feelings to themselves or be verbally flogged for not adhering to expectations. Shinae just escaped from such a place. It's a good thing you no longer like her, for I doubt she likes you either."

Dunlop could see that those words had been a punch to his friend's gut. He prayed it made a difference.

* * *

After that they rode on in silence, but instead of feeling anger, Brodie's mind was spinning with what-ifs. *What if she left? What if she never spoke with him again? What if he had truly lost her? What if Callum or another was giving her comfort? What if they were whispering that she could do better, and Shinae believed them?*

Rage once again swelled in his chest, this time choking him. He would shed someone's blood in the most painful ways possible and with no remorse if someone thought they could be her shelter. He was still angry about what she did, but his reaction, his words just might have broken their new relationship. Of all the blunders he had committed in his lifetime, this one was the worst of all. Whatever he needed to do to repair their relationship, he would do it.

Life without his wife was unthinkable.

Shinae remained curled in her chair with her head on her knees, staring at the fire. Even wrapped in a heavy blanket, the bedchamber had never felt so cold and lonely. No one wanted her around. Certainly not Brodie.

The women had gasped when she told them about Ros. And it was not a good sound. She tried harder to explain that it was the opportunity Brodie had been looking for. Just as she had done to Ros, she initially dismissed all the women's hints that she might have hurt his pride and trust by speaking to them about her conversation with Ros, forgetting that her husband had told her about his frustrations in confidence. If only she had listened to them.

Later, long after the men had departed, Meriel had stopped by to ensure her that this would pass. It was the first bump in a long marital road, and just as soon as they thought they were doing well, a little bairn would enter their life and prove them all wrong.

For a few minutes, Shinae felt comforted by the words and believed it really would all be fine, that Brodie would forgive her, and she would forgive him for all that he accused her of. Then she asked a simple question.

"Just what was stolen?" The answer was simple, and yet it was also devastating. Honey.

Shinae knew she had promised the four youngsters that she would stay silent, but men were riding into reiver territory armed and unknowing that the real thieves were their own children. Immediately, she revealed what she knew, but the second she explained as much, everyone exploded. If possible, their words had been far harsher than Brodie's. They did not even try to understand or remember that she had not grown up in a clan and had truly been ignorant of the importance honey played for a clan to thrive.

Each clansman's family was given twelve casks of honey throughout the year for a myriad of things beyond being a food sweetener and a means to make mead. Anytime one was injured, honey was part of the salve to help prevent sickness. They used it to preserve apples and other fruits. Mixed with milk, it was a beverage for small children and she, herself, had been using it, combining it with vinegar to reduce Ros's fever. It had been so little, she had not thought the loss of a few barrels when there were so many still left as significant.

If losing almost half their supply had happened in the new year, it would have been much easier to recover their losses. In the spring and summer, almost all the honey was harvested with only a fraction left for the bees to help them rebuild their hives. However, in October—the last honey harvest of the year—was different. The beekeepers only took about half, so the colony survived throughout the winter and lack of pollen. The amount of winter honey the bees produced was nowhere near enough to replace what was lost.

What was even worse was that there were agreements in place between Colin and several clans to receive a certain amount of honey throughout the year. Too many of Colin's neighbors lacked beekeepers and did not know how to properly grow and nurture the sensitive insects, and many lost full hives. They had agreed to combine their hives with the McTiernay clans, and for the last few years all had what they needed. After what the foursome did, there was not enough for both the McTiernay clan and those who were promised multiple large barrels of the sticky substance. Like her, none of the four children knew about the impact their candy making had created.

Shinae should have immediately told someone about the situation, and she would have if she had known its importance. Makenna had made it very clear that was no excuse. Because she had kept such a foolish secret, the men were most likely going to attack the border reivers for unfounded retribution. Lady Makenna had even said that she hoped Colin rejected Brodie as a steward for having such a witless wife.

Shinae heard the door creak open and close. Footsteps approached, and she knew it was Isilmë. "The women have sent a commander—the one called Drake—to reach the men in time with a message for them to return."

Shinae sat as she was. The news should have eased her pain, and she was glad her admission was stopping the possibility of combat with the reivers. However, Isilmë relaying the news meant that everyone knew what the McTiernay children did, and that Shinae had kept their immature secret instead of telling the clan leaders. But the image of Brodie's angry expression, learning that she was partially responsible for putting Colin's men in danger, only increased her pain. "Please leave."

Isilmë crouched down. "Let's just go. You and me," she whispered, sitting on the floor next to Shinae's chair. "Gert came into the room where I sometimes sew with the weavers and told us all what had happened between you and the McTiernay wives. For those women to say those things to you when it was *their* daughters who helped create the situation . . ." she whispered angrily, refusing to call them by their names or titles.

"It is I who should go." Shinae sniffed. "They like you. Even before this, Brodie could not stand to be around me."

"We go together," Isilmë said steadfastly.

"What about you and Dunlop?"

Isilmë swallowed. That was the one thing holding her here. Never had she dreamed someone like him might be interested in her. But he had told her, just before they left, how lucky he was to have met her and hoped that she felt the same way. "What about him? Aye, we have flirted, but we have shared no promises, and it is unlikely he ever would want to. We are too different, and eventually I would be where you are now. Miserable. Let's leave and not tell anyone. No one would miss us, and those that did notice would probably be thankful we are gone."

"Where would we go?" Shinae had a hard time thinking about going anywhere that was away from her husband.

"Let's go back to Melrose. The people were friendly there and we know the way."

Running away did not sit well with Shinae. She was married and her vows had been said in earnest. She had not done anything wrong. Ignorance, not maliciousness, guided her path, but the response to her missteps had been merciless. But most of all, she had not yet been relieved of her vow to tell her sister about the danger she and Conan were in. Still, she needed to leave Lochlen as Isilmë suggested and went to the only respite she knew of where she could pray to God for help with getting her emotions under control and a path forward.

"I know just where to go."

The day had not been cold or hot, but the cloud-covered skies had made the afternoon breeze cool, giving her a chill during her walk to Frank's cottage. After she had gotten a fire going, Shinae had sat quietly and thought about the last time she had been there. In Brodie's care, she had gone from miserable to content and relaxed. In his arms, she had felt safe, but when he had left, her feelings had been ripped apart. To discover he would say those vile things to her, she was not sure she could open herself to him again. Maybe leaving would be the best thing to do. She just first needed to meet with Mhàiri and disclose all that she knew.

Shinae wondered if it had been Brodie who had come back to refill the stack of wood by the hearth. Whoever had done so, she was glad they had. The room was finally getting warm enough so that she stopped shivering. Unwrapping herself, she sat down and moved the blanket to her lap.

When Isilmë had abdicated her vows, never had Shinae thought she would become such a good friend. Isilmë had been furious about how Shinae had been treated by both Brodie and the McTiernay women and wanted to come with her. Shinae had barely been able to convince her friend to stay at the castle and made Isilmë promise to let her know all that was happening upon her return. Her red hair swirled around her head in the wind as she threatened to come get her if she did not return. Shinae doubted her friend even remembered how to get to the cottage. She spent most of her time in and around the castle, whereas Shinae preferred to be away from it.

She was becoming well known in the village, as her name was being shared as a healer who would help when someone in a family was sick or injured. Sometimes the day had flown by as she helped several families and sometimes her self-assigned duties were few. On those days, she usually took long walks, appreciating the freedom and enjoying being alone. It was during one of those walks she had found Frank's cottage—the place Brodie had taken her the first night they had met.

She had met the jovial owner her first week at Lochlen. He was short, round, and stout, with short wisps of gray hair on his head that he compensated for with a long, gray-brown beard that tapered just past his shoulders. Brodie had explained what had happened and Frank reached up and joyfully slapped her husband on the shoulder, telling him that he was welcome to use his cottage as long as he was staying with his daughter. Shinae decided that as Brodie's wife the open invitation also included her.

Shinae paced inside the small room and let go a big sigh. Being alone without any fear of a McTiernay wife coming by and sniping at her was exactly what she had needed. She felt bad that Brodie was upset about her suggesting he become the next steward, but the only thing she would change was sharing the idea with the women before him. She had made the mistake that the wives and her were becoming friends. But about the suggestion she had made about Brodie becoming the next steward, she had no regrets.

What did Brodie think she should have done? Ignoring the idea because *he* had not been the one to think of it was nonsensical. Pride was a good thing, but having too much of it made people fools. Learning and avoiding each other's irritants was part of marriage. For their relationship to continue, they were just going to have to find a way to deal with them without turning on each other.

Makenna, on the other hand, Shinae was finding harder to understand or forgive. She understood how the McTiernays argued with one another and had witnessed their verbal spats at least half a dozen times in the two weeks she had been at Lochlen. They could continue to argue with one another however they wanted, but when speaking to her, they would be civil. Next time Makenna or any woman again said such things, Shinae would follow through on her instinct. How she wished she could revisit those moments and slap the woman as hard as she could.

The sound of a couple of horses neighing and stamping outside the cottage caught her attention. Shinae pursed her lips. A minute later, there was a knock on the door, having Shinae reaching for her knives. "Shinae, I'm coming in, but I promise it is not to criticize or berate. There are things you should know, and then I will leave." It was Laurel.

The thin woman slipped through the door and closed it quickly to keep the heat in. There was only one chair and Shinae was not in a generous spirit. Laurel looked flawless as usual, completely unfazed at having to come this far. She handed Shinae a small bundle wrapped in cloth and sat down on the rushes. Then, after taking off thin leather gloves, she put her hands up to warm them by the fire. "I would apologize for Makenna, but that is something she should do herself."

"I don't think a simple apology will rectify things

between us." Makenna had made threats not just to Shinae, they had included her husband.

"I should say not. I'm not sure what I would do if anyone said the like to me."

"I plan on slapping them. Hard. Even if they are right, I will not tolerate anyone to say such things or in such a hateful way."

Laurel gave a small nod at the thought. If she had the power to end all the fighting that happened around McTiernay Castle, she would make it so. But even then, it would be a waste of time. Highland men actually *liked* to bang up their bodies and brawl. The verbal attack made by Makenna, however, had been in every way wrong.

Once the men returned, Colin should have discussed the issue with Brodie, who would then explain to Shinae the consequences of keeping secrets that could impact the clan. "Makenna was actually humiliated and furious with Aislinn and took her anger out on you. My three will have to face their father when he returns, which they do *not* want to do."

Shinae sat quietly for a minute. Conor was a large, very tall, intimidating man. "What will he do?"

"I'm not sure. It will take him a while to calm down. Gideon is the son of his elite commander, who remained to oversee and manage McTiernay Castle while we were away. I suspect Conor will order both boys to stay in their rooms and wait until our return to McTiernay Castle to speak with Finn and decide. In the meantime, waiting for their punishment will scare them plenty."

Laurel turned to look at Shinae and with a puzzled look

said, "My son Braeden has never acted so unbelievably stupid. I truly think someone turned off his fifteen-year-old brain. He actually thought we would leave and no one would be the wiser." Laurel took in a deep breath and slowly let it out. She was so calm and serene-looking that one could easily miss the tension in her voice.

Shinae unwrapped the bundle Laurel had brought and saw that it contained some cheese, bread, nuts, and berries. Immediately she ate one of the berries. Lack of food had not helped and with that little bit of nourishment, she already felt a little less hostile. These were fresh, large, and juicy, and Shinae ate one after the other. Berries grew in Scotland wherever there was a spot, even in this rocky area of the Lowlands. The summer weather and the longer daylight hours made it ideal for berry growing.

"I thought you might be hungry."

"I wasn't," Shinae countered, "until I started eating. Now I am ravenous." She pulled off some bread and offered it to the striking woman. Laurel put up her hand and shook her head. If she expected Shinae to ask her about what she had come to say, Lady McTiernay would be waiting for a long while.

"I saw Brodie when the men left. A thundercloud of anger seemed to hover over his head, and it had little to do with the theft. I'm not sure what happened between you two, but if I were to guess, it was about your excitement about him becoming Lochlen's next steward."

"You tried to warn me."

Laurel nodded. "With more experience, you will learn which of us can detect what information can be shared and what should be kept secret, and those servants who do not know when it is not their news to divulge to others—even inadvertently."

I'll not share anything with anyone again—including my husband, Shinae thought to herself. *Especially the secret concerning my sister.*

"I can see that you would like to stay here a little longer, but you should know that a herald had been sent to intercept Colin and the troops to say the culprits have been found and that they are not border reivers. The men are on their way back and are expected at Lochlen within the hour." Shinae arched a brow at the message's brevity. Laurel shrugged slightly. "I think the details of who and why the honey was missing might be better handled when they get back. Their tempers would only grow if they knew it was their own children."

Shinae imagined Laurel to be right and planned to still be at the cottage when Conor and Colin learned who was really behind the honey pilfering and why.

Laurel stood up, dusted off her hands, and put back on her riding gloves. "There is one other thing you should know. Laird Mahon Donovan has been spotted with about a half dozen soldiers. They crossed our northwest borders last night and are expected before nightfall."

Laurel said no more, but she did not need to. Brodie was already in a sour mood and this would not improve his demeanor. Shinae's inner voice told her to be by his side when Laird Donavan arrived, but just the thought of speaking to him right now made her uneasy. She had yet to let go of all that he said, and she doubted she would for a while longer.

Laurel opened the door and Shinae quickly said, "Thank you for the food."

Laurel pivoted and said, "When you return, I suggest taking the blanket when you leave. With all the clouds blocking the sun, it has gotten nippy outside."

When Shinae walked through the outer wall gate to Lochlen Castle, she could tell by the sounds the men had already returned. Most of the soldiers were mulling around the inner and outer wards, unknowing if they were still needed or if they could leave. She quietly used them as cover and walked to the Pinnacle Tower, where Isilmë had said she was staying. She climbed one flight of stairs and knocked on the first door she saw. When it opened, she breathed a sigh of relief. "I was afraid that you might be with the weavers," she whispered. It was clear she was not planning on escaping Lochlen like Isilmë earlier suggested.

"Nay, I returned early to get ready for tonight," Isilmë said, ringing out her wet hair as she stepped aside to allow Shinae in.

"*A shaoghail!*" Shinae pleasantly exclaimed, stepping in. The moderate-sized room had large windows that faced the inner ward letting in a lot of light, and yet it felt small due to all the material lying about. Several pieces of uncut cloth were intermixed with numerous clothes belonging to both men and women that were in various states of disrepair. "And I was afraid you have been bored when I was helping in the village."

Isilmë squeaked with happiness. With her elbows

locked, she clasped her hands and swung her hips back and forth. The large smile she wore made it clear that the chaos of the room was something in which she took a lot of pride. "I cannot believe all the gifts God has given me since leaving the abbey—you, being here, and getting to do what I have always wanted. The steward who is responsible for all castle maintenance asks the seamstresses for help with anything sewn—you know, sheets, curtains, seat cushions, and such stuff. When not busy with that, the seamstresses are working on these enormous, detailed tapestries, which is what they enjoy doing. As a result, they have little time or desire to handle any garment requests, so most people have to handle their own needs. But the unmarried soldiers," Isilmë said dramatically, "are the worst. Most don't even try to fix any holes or rips, and those that do—" She let her voice trail off and shook her head.

"Let me guess. They now come to you."

Isilmë's brown and green eyes brightened. "They do! Women are now even asking that if they could get me a bit of cloth, whether I would try making them a bliaut! Even Laird McTiernay wants me to coordinate with the steward to get soldiers who are most in need, new léines and kilts. Lady Meriel, who is a skilled seamstress, is teaching me all the new styles and various ways to embellish gowns."

Her happiness was infectious and for a few minutes, Shinae forgot about her own despondency as Isilmë grabbed her hands and started them dancing in a circle. Breathing hard, Isilmë stopped, shoved all the marred clothes to the foot of the bed, and plopped down on the vacated spot. Pointing to a mostly covered stool, she said, "Just push that stuff off and sit down."

Shinae did not want to do that as there were no rushes on the floor, and she was afraid of making any of the pretty material dirty. She opted to sit down on what she hoped was an unused blanket on the ground.

Isilmë sat up, reached under a couple of dresses for a brush, and started combing her dark red hair in long strokes. It did not remove the wet curls, but it did calm them so instead of seeming disheveled, the red locks rippled down her back. Seeing Shinae's raised eyebrow, Isilmë lifted her chin defiantly and said, "I want to look especially pretty tonight. Dunlop asked if I would go for a walk with him after tonight's meal."

"Dunlop?" Shinae repeated incredulously. Had Brenna and Aislinn been right? "I did not even think you liked each other. Every time I see you two together, you are quibbling over something."

Isilmë shrugged defensively. "The McTiernays quibble all the time. Couples do that."

Her friend spoke as if Dunlop and she were courting and had a future together. Shinae had no idea that the two of them had gotten so close. The night of her and Brodie's wedding, she herself had seen them arguing quite fiercely, and then later the two had pretended to not even know each other during the celebratory banquet. Dunlop and Isilmë came from two different worlds and the two together seemed wrong for many reasons. He was a rake . . . or had been. Isilmë knew even less than her about attracting men and then keeping them. But something must have opened the doors to communication again, and Shinae wondered if it had been Brenna's honey meringues.

"You and Dunlop are a couple now?"

Isilmë pursed her lips and looked down and to the right. "Nay, well, maybe, he's never said anything, but it's not like I have a father around for him to ask about courting, so I'm not sure if we are. Then again, he did kiss me."

"He kissed you!" Shinae cried out in shock.

Isilmë started bobbing her head. "And before you ask, I really liked it. He made me tingle all over, and my stomach started doing flips. When he stopped, I just wanted him to do it again."

"And did he?" Shinae pushed.

"Not immediately, but earlier today he pulled me aside for a quick kiss before he left." Isilmë leaned over and in a hushed tone asked, "Does Brodie ever want to kiss you with your mouth open?" Shinae nodded. "And is it . . . enjoyable?"

This time Shinae took in a deep breath and tried to be careful with her words. "It is wonderful with the right man, but please know that a kiss—of any kind—is *not* a promise. I think most of the time it is just a reaction to a primal need that men have," she said definitively, in hopes to rein in her friend's expectations. "And if it is not with the right person, it is not at all pleasurable. When I lived with the Culdees before my time at Dryburgh, several men came to visit me who were interested in marriage. Most of them tried to entice my interest with a kiss." Shinae pulled in her chin and shuddered slightly.

"Did anyone know?"

"I doubt it. You're the only person I've told, with the exception of my sister. And let me tell you, *none* of their kisses—even the gentle ones—were in the least bit pleasant. And those that had their mouths open?" Shinae winced again just thinking about the slobbery onslaughts she'd had to halt with a tip of her *sgian dubh*. "They will make you want to wash your mouth with soap."

Isilmë started to giggle at Shinae's facial expression. "I'm so glad you came back and we did not leave. So much has happened this afternoon, and *you* were the main topic."

"How? What? Did you tell them where I was?" Shinae asked, thinking of Laurel's unexpected visit.

Isilmë quickly shook her head. "I said nothing to anyone. But all know you disappeared."

Shinae let go of the breath she had been holding. "*Buìochas le dia*. I don't want anyone to know that I have returned just yet."

"Even your husband?"

"*Especially* Brodie," Shinae confirmed strongly.

"Earlier, he was running around, barking at everyone, looking for you. Don't worry; he already came here. I chose to hide under my bed. After seeing the state of my room, I doubt he will come back."

"I hope you are right," Shinae remarked.

"Dunlop came by too. I felt a little guilty, but I hid from him as well. He would have told Brodie I was here, who would have stormed in here demanding to know where you were. I wasn't sure I could keep quiet under his stare. Your husband can be scary when he's angry. No wonder you left."

Shinae's stomach started to knot again. The twisting sensation was almost overwhelming. "He's still mad at me, then. Well, fine, I am more than a little angry with him." The admission sent a stabbing pain right through her heart. Hours away had changed nothing. Without thought, she brought her knees in tight and hugged them.

"I don't know," Isilmë countered. "His shouts and growls sounded more desperate than angry. And why should he be mad at you? *He* was the one in the wrong. He was horrible to you and should be down on bended knee begging for forgiveness and promising that he will never make you suffer like that again." She crossed her arms and stuck out her chin. "If Dunlop ever tries taking his anger out on me, he will learn that I may be short, but my memory is long and my hair is red."

Shinae's gaze flew to Isilmë. Her friend was now standing, looking quite serious.

A knock on the door made both of them freeze. Isilmë went to the door and cracked it open just enough to see who it was. Only then did she relax. Shinae, however, tensed when she heard the female's voice on the other side.

Lady Makenna had come to visit.

Without asking, the lady of the castle pushed the door open, stepped inside, and closed it. Isilmë then shoved everything from the stool and offered it to the woman. "Thank you for letting me in."

Isilmë glanced at Shinae and rolled her eyes as if to say she had no choice. "What can I do for you, my lady?" Isilmë asked.

"Nothing, really. I just need a small respite and everywhere I go there is one or more of my sisters-in-law, ready to make a comment or suggestion on how I manage my home, raise my children, or speak to my husband. Today has been especially awful," Makenna paused and looked briefly at Shinae, "which I probably deserve after saying what I did to you."

Shinae thought it was the beginning of an apology, but Makenna only continued to rattle on about her children and all that was stressing her. "And just *where* does Colin think Laird Donovan and his men are going to stay? Lochlen is not a small castle, nor is it littered with extra bedchambers. It was hard enough to arrange everyone's accommodations in the first place. Then, with you coming—I truly am glad you are both here—but it was stressful, and if you had not married Brodie, Shinae, I would not be surprised if both you and Isilmë had to find a way to stay in this room."

Makenna then looked around the chamber and took in its chaotic state. "And Colin thinks our girls are messy . . . you almost rival Meriel. I guess such mayhem is needed to be creative."

Obviously uncomfortable, Isilmë tried to change topics. "And what can I do for you, my lady?" she asked again.

"Nothing. I just wanted to go somewhere no one would think to find me. And when I saw Shinae sneak into the tower, I decided to do the same. I assume that is why you are here," she directed at Shinae. "It's the same reason you left—to avoid talking to anyone."

"Or have them talk to me."

"*Exactly*," Makenna said, oblivious to Shinae's reference to her behavior earlier that day. "Don't tell anyone, but I am tired of the other wives offering their opinions on simply everything. If I didn't get away and come here, I was going to explode and say things I shouldn't." Again, Shinae waited for her to make the connection to earlier that day, and when it did not come, she realized it most likely never would.

"What are you going to do about the new arrivals?" Shinae asked.

"The only commander that sleeps within the castle is Dunlop, and I guess I will have to make him sleep elsewhere. Laird Donovan and his men will just have to accept sleeping in one of the gatehouse towers or sleep outside with the others."

"Have you ever met this visitor?" Isilmë inquired.

"Aye, a few times. Laird Donovan is a brute of a man and sometimes is called the Lion because he once had wild yellow hair, a bushy dark beard, and roared when he spoke."

Like everyone in Scotland or even England, Shinae had never seen a lion, but it was said that long ago Romans had repeated stories that were passed down about the great creatures. It had become a heraldic symbol for many Scottish clans.

Curious to learn more about this man who had dismissed her husband, Shinae was about to ask questions when the sound of a ram's horn was heard. Lady

Makenna took in a deep breath. After holding it for a couple of seconds, she let it out and stood up. "*Go raibh maith agat*," she said to Isilmë, thanking her, and then turned to Shinae. "I'm sorry we cannot talk longer, but as Ros has become sickly once again, I will need to make sure the rooms are prepared for our latest guests."

Shinae vacillated about whether or not she should go as well, for she still had not resolved her feelings. But the newcomer was Laird Mahon Donovan, and if positions were reversed, she would want Brodie there at her side, even if he was justifiably angry with her.

Brodie stood in the outer ward with feet apart and arms crossed. Three men slowly made their way through the outer gate, wearing the Donovan purple-and-green plaids. He visibly scowled at the older man. Laird Donovan's crazed hair might have noticeably grayed in the last few months, but he still looked like the Lion he had known for years. Mahon rode with a two-man escort; one rode with an air of unearned arrogance, the other with an air of unease.

Brodie had no idea why Mahon Donovan had come to Lochlen Castle and did not care. For eight years he had served as the laird's elite commander and second in charge and then, without warning, Mahon had summarily dismissed him. And though the laird had not outright said so, Brodie knew Taveon, a scoundrel who could be manipulative and dishonorable, would do anything to be named the next Donovan heir. The second soldier was a younger version of Mahon. A hulk of a man, he had thick eyebrows, dark eyes that looked almost black, and wore his shoulder-length dark-blond hair tied at the back of his nape. His nose and chin were patrician, but the rest of his face was severely angular, which only accentuated the semi-scowl he was wearing.

Once close, Taveon jumped down and tossed his reins to the stable boy, missing him. "Get those and be sure to do your work well or I'll box your ears." Then, with an extended arm and a large haughty smile, he said, "Brodie."

Brodie took it briefly before returning his fists to his side.

Taveon noticed Brodie's silence. "It's good to see you again. Your help has been missed."

The cheerfulness of Taveon's voice did not reach his eyes, which reflected a high degree of resentment. Something had him vexed.

Brodie's hand ached from it being clutched so tight. He moved his fists to his hips, but it did not help relieve the tension growing inside him. He heard the McTiernay brothers walk out into the ward, Colin shouting out Mahon's name with uncalled-for enthusiasm. Brodie suspected Colin was not as happy as he sounded, just thankful to have something else to divert his attention from his remorseful child.

"You are looking fine and fit," Colin shouted happily as Conor joined his approached. It rankled.

Brodie fought from interrupting and reminding them all of just what this man did three months ago. *And why shouldn't they show their liking of Mahon?* he asked himself. He was their ally. What happened to him had nothing to do with them. They had no issue with the thorny old man, and neither had they ever met Taveon or his massive companion.

Brodie felt like he was going to explode and was about to turn and leave when he felt a soft hand join with his. The dainty fingertips squeezed his palm and he squeezed them back. The pressure that had been building inside him suddenly began to ease. Shinae might not like him at the moment, but from her just being there, standing at his side, he knew she was still his.

CHAPTER SEVEN

Shinae stood back when the Scot offered her husband his arm. Brodie's reaction was that of disdain, but he took it, if only briefly. The other two Scots dismounted just as the McTiernays cheerfully arrived. The older one had to be Laird Mahon Donovan and was just as Lady Makenna had described.

The laird gave a male version of an embrace to Colin and, with a nod, acknowledged Conor. Meanwhile, every muscle in Brodie was pronounced. He needed to calm himself before he did or said something he would regret. She slipped her hand in his and instantly felt him begin to relax; not a lot, but enough to keep him from exploding.

"Good to see you, Mahon," Colin said, clapping the laird on the shoulder. "Either your herald announcing your arrival was lost or your intent was to surprise us."

"We were able to finish our harvest last week and it is rare you McTiernays gather together within traveling distance. So, I decided to come here and introduce you to my heir, Edwin," he said proudly.

Shinae saw Brodie's head swivel to Taveon, but it was the giant man who stood next to him who nodded and stiffly greeted Conor and then Colin. Her husband looked genuinely shocked. "*Gabhaim pardùn agaibh,*" the man stiffly apologized to all and mumbled something about coming there unannounced not being his idea.

Though unusually tall and massive around the chest, Edwin Donovan was almost more uncomfortable than Brodie. Whatever he was feeling, it was hidden behind a rigid, unexpressive mask. Shinae glanced around and saw that most of the castle staff had paused and were staring at him, half in awe and the other half in fear.

Edwin stepped closer to Shinae's side to allow Brodie space to shake Mahon's arm. The body stance of both men was that of caution. Shinae expected her husband to step back and reclaim her hand when Taveon stepped between them and overtly looked her over. "Your eyes could entrap a man's soul," he said in an affectionate way that made her feel in need of a bath.

Brodie did not speak, but rather lunged at the man, though before he could make contact, Crevan and Cole caught his arms and pulled him back with the other McTiernays. Colin stepped forward and congenially introduced her. "You may remember Brodie as a single man when he lived with you, but he was married recently, and this is his wife. And like me and my brothers, he is very possessive of his woman."

Shinae was not exactly sure how she felt about being called Brodie's woman but was excessively glad when Taveon acknowledged Colin's unspoken warning and took a step back. The instant he did, Shinae felt she could breathe again. Her gut was screaming that the man was unpredictable and interested in only things that aided his personal plans.

Edwin, on the other hand, was a mystery. Her instinct was neither to like or dislike the man. He looked both impervious to danger and yet vulnerable at the same time. His eyes kept darting around, assessing the McTiernay soldiers, which made her uneasy.

The small crowd started moving to the inner gate and then the great hall, leaving her and Edwin standing there. Then, barely looking at her, he said, "Good day, my lady. I must join them." And before she could correct him and say such formality was misplaced, he was jogging to catch up with them.

Brodie was among the throng. They were halfway to the hall and not once had he looked back. Shinae's heart wilted. Her hope that her husband needed her, that she had helped him in a small way, had been misguided. She headed toward the outer gate, wanting to be alone.

She had taken for granted all the silence and time for reflection she had had at the abbey. Going to Isilmë's room was not an option, as Lady Makenna had claimed it as her sanctuary, so Shinae started the long walk to check on Ros. It was a legitimate destination, one she could easily explain if necessary. And hopefully on her way there, she could figure out a way for her and Brodie to connect again.

Shinae eyed the old man sitting in a chair just outside the cottage door, saying goodbye to the only villager she had seen. He was gnawing on a wheat straw and quickly stood up when he saw her. She shook her head in mock disappointment. "You seem awfully spry for someone who is supposedly once again struck with illness."

Ros pretended a cough, pasted on a mischievous smile, and replied, "My sudden improvement *was* something of a miracle." He grabbed the back of the wooden chair and pulled it back inside to the table and sat back down. Shinae pulled out one of the other table chairs and joined him. "Where are Sorcha and all your grandchildren?"

"Out working in the fields, but the sun is starting to set, so I expect them back soon. The laird arranged the final feast to be in three days, and while the harvest is near done, there is still much to do. Almost everyone who can work will be out in the fields until there is no light to work by." He tapped her hand. "I thought you would be getting ready for tonight's welcoming of Laird Donovan."

"Brodie and I are no one of consequence and will not be missed."

Ros studied her. "You may want to be no one of consequence, and if it were anyone else visiting Lochlen, it might be true that your absence would not cause alarm. However, you are married to Brodie, Laird Donovan's second for several years. He *will* have to attend. You are also Mhàiri's sister, which makes you related to the laird. Distantly, but you too should attend.

Shinae rolled her eyes without realizing she had done so. The evening meal was not something she wanted to be present for, but Ros was correct—she would be expected to be at her husband's side. To refuse would be publicly airing their newlywed woes, something most probably all knew by now.

"I have another good reason you should attend," Ros said when he saw that she was still wavering about going, "You need to eat. Your stomach is growling." He returned her slight smile. "But regardless of what you decide, I am glad you came by."

"And why is that?"

"I've almost fully recovered from whatever struck me, and I believe that is due to you. Since you were here last, I've done some thinking."

He sounded serious, and it made Shinae nervous.

"I'm old. I'm not saying I plan on dying soon, but I will be dead if I continue doing all I have been. Lady Makenna has had to step up to help perform some of my duties, but many things are still going unaddressed. In the past, that knowledge would have bothered me immensely; it hasn't this time, and I realized it is because I am no longer the only one who knows and can do all the duties being a steward entail. There is now someone for me to relinquish the role to, who can effectively take over after a few weeks, letting me enjoy the last years of my life."

"If you are thinking of Brodie replacing you, I can tell you the answer is no."

Ros waved his wrinkled hand dismissively. "That's because the original suggestion came from you. But I wonder if he would be open to coming to see me so that I can explain that I am not making him an offer out of pity, but just the opposite. There really is no one who can do the job without years of training, which is the single-most reason I have not turned it over to someone before. Brodie is also the one person the laird would readily accept, knowing his background experience."

Shinae rubbed her lips together and thought about all that Ros had said. "I agree that my husband is the ideal person to become Lochlen's next steward, but he is completely closed to the idea because he thinks it makes him look weak because it originally came from me."

"Nonetheless, you tell him to come see me. Tell him he either comes and gives me a solid explanation for him rejecting my offer, or I go to the laird and we will make the decision for him."

Shinae's jaw went slack. "My marriage would never survive if I say that," she stammered.

"*Amaideach!*" Ros stated glibly. Shinae stared at him. He may think the matter ridiculous, but he was wrong. Her horrified expression must have conveyed as much. "Trust me. *You* telling him will help your future as a couple more than you realize."

Shinae shook her head in disagreement.

Ros clucked his tongue. "You think your husband is not interested in your opinion when it comes to anything involving him."

"That is *exactly* what I *know*."

"Incorrect," he countered. "While relaying my message may upset him a second time, his anger will not last long. Brodie is an intelligent man. He will come to realize that you will not cower and remain silent when you have a viewpoint that he may not like. It is best your proud man learns this now, before habits are forged that will be difficult to break."

Shinae blinked. She was not weak. Her nature may be generally compliant, but that did not mean she would let anyone—including Brodie—suppress her opinion. She placed her hands flat on the small table and stood up. "I will think on what you said. I'm not sure you are entirely correct, but your words have given me much to consider."

Ros tapped her hand and gave her a wink. "Trust me. I was married for many years and my wife trained me well. Not a day goes by that I am not a better man for it."

His choice of words puzzled her, but instead of exploring what he meant, she gave his thin hand a squeeze, said goodbye, and left to go back to the castle before the sun disappeared.

Brodie glared at Shinae, and she glared back. He was trying to intimidate her into submitting to his will. Shinae almost smiled at the thought before she caught herself, but she now understood Ros's meaning about training one's spouse. Brodie needed to learn his scowl— no matter how fierce—was never going to work in obtaining her acquiescence. Rational discussion with logical reasons would go much further to persuade her to comply with his declarations. Bullying tactics would never work.

"What was I supposed to do?" she said as she turned around in her chair and resumed brushing her hair.

"You should have told him that I made it clear that our future was none of his business and that *I* will decide where we will live and how I will provide for my family," Brodie growled, pulling off his shoes and preparing for bed.

He wanted her to respond in kind by raising her voice and being argumentative. Shinae refused to take the bait, robbing him of his attempts to make himself feel better about his aggressive tone and choice of words earlier that day.

"Why should I have told Ros any of that?" she asked in a calm manner. "He just made an offer, one which seems to be perfect for you both."

"Why are you doing this, pretending not to hear my opinions and sharing what should be private conversations between a man and his wife?" he asked as he slipped between the covers.

"Conversations, hmmm," she said in a contemplative manner. "That is quite a stark contrast to what you just said about single-handedly deciding all major decisions for your 'family.' Hopefully, just hearing me say that aloud has you recognizing that such a tyrannical stance would never work between you and me."

Brodie bent his arm and rested his head on it to stare at the ceiling. He felt the urge to start yelling again but fought it back because he refused to once again break the promise they had made to each other at their wedding. Shouting at each other was not how they would interact when they disagreed. Talking, however, was not working either. "We will converse again when you are reasonable."

"Until then, I guess we will disagree. You will be a

stubborn, deaf mule, and I will continue to be a woman with opinions and enough self-confidence to voice them. Oh, that includes to my friends when I feel that getting outside input is necessary."

Despite her fancy use of words, he knew what she meant. He tilted his head to look at her directly in the eye. "You wish to embarrass and belittle me to my clansmen, then."

Shinae returned his stare. "Do you know what I figured out today? One is only 'belittled,' as you put it, if they believe that what others think of them is true. People see you as inadequate only when that is how you see yourself." She put down her brush and climbed into bed, lying on her side with her back facing him.

"I realized much today as well, part of which is how much I miss sleeping outdoors with my fellow soldiers!" he clipped.

Shinae yawned. "It's an excellent night for it. Sleep well."

It was not until a full minute later that she heard the door slam and him stomping down the stairs. And to her surprise, she found her mind did not plague her as it usually did when there was conflict between her and another. She rose, locked the door, and quickly fell asleep.

There was loud banging in her dream, and it was not for several minutes before she awoke enough to realize that the noise was coming from someone insistent upon awakening her.

She looked at the window and saw that it was still

dark outside. "Who is it?" she grumbled as she grabbed her plain robe and put it on, hoping it was not Brodie.

"It's Makenna. Open the door." The door rattled, as if she was trying to enter. Shinae sighed. Lady Makenna was not an evil woman, but she would take some getting used to.

Shinae shuffled over to the door and freed the latch. Immediately, it was pushed open, and seeing a frazzled-looking Lady Makenna sent a jolt through Shinae as she leaped to the conclusion that something had happened to Brodie. "Where is he? What happened?" Shinae demanded, panicked at what it could be.

Makenna waved her hand dismissively. "It's not Brodie, but Edwin, Mahon's heir. Someone stabbed him tonight and Laurel needs your help."

"Of course." Shinae quickly slipped on some shoes. Grabbing her herbal bags, which she had replenished during the walks she had taken the past couple of weeks, she followed Makenna out of the tower to one of the two gatehouses. "I assume Laurel is already there?"

Makenna bobbed her head. Shinae was relieved. She was good at attending the infirmed, but suturing stab wounds was not something she had done in several years, and while her stitching was adequate, it was not preferable. If Laurel had not been available, she would have asked Isilmë for help.

Both women darted across the dark inner ward and headed to one of the main gate towers. "Laurel's tending to Edwin but asked for a midwife to stay with him. You helped Ros and Mhàiri told us that you liked caring for those injured or sick."

Following Makenna up the stairs, she stopped at the door on the second floor, where there were several women standing about. None but one—Laurel—was doing anything.

Shinae edged her way to the bed. Edwin was lying on his stomach, allowing only half of his face to be seen. It was taut with pain. The unusually shaped wound was on the left side of his lower back and deep. It was definitely a stab wound, but it was much larger than that of a knife would cause, and yet not wide enough to be a sword. She had not seen a wound exactly like it before. "Do you know what kind of weapon injured this man?"

"I do not," Laurel answered tensely, never pausing what she was doing. "For something to have penetrated straight through him without hitting a main organ, either makes him incredibly lucky or the blade's handler never actually wanted to kill him—just injure. I suspect the latter. It's hard to imagine that they had not known what they were doing. Look how clean the stab wound is; daggers can be that sharp, but this wound is the same size on both front and back."

Out of habit, Shinae touched Edwin's forehead. He was warm, and the inflamed injury showed all the signs that a fever was coming. She started digging in her bag and pulled out small leather sacks of coriander and chamomile. "He's already running a fever." She looked around and saw nothing she could use to grind the ingredients together. She looked up, and Makenna was the first person she saw. "Please get some cloth, and if possible clean sheets, for it might be best to wrap both front and back wounds at the same time. Ellenor, would you ask someone in the kitchen for a mortar and pestle, as well as some water? Raelynd, please bring a mug and a pot of hot water that we can hang it in the hearth to make tea." Shinae issued several more requests, which helped clear the room. When Makenna returned, Shinae sent her back out to get Isilmë.

"*Go raibh maith agat*," Laurel mumbled her appreciation as she focused on her stitching. She snipped off the string just as Shinae had the poultice ready and dabbed it on the wound. He had a high pain tolerance and only winced when Laurel encouraged him to lay on his back and started working on the second stab wound. Taking the chamomile tea from Raelynd, Shinae lifted Edwin's head so that he could take a few swallows before he went limp from the pain.

Once Laurel finished bandaging both wounds, she and Shinae joined the other women who had been softly discussing about what happened. There were several conjectures, but no one knew any more than she did; Edwin had been stabbed from behind by a coward. Shinae's thoughts had leapt to that of the unknown attacker and wondered if Edwin had been just a practice attempt, and that his real attack would come when Conan and her sister arrived.

Edwin's eyes opened and he glanced around. Indistinguishable noises were coming from the outside. He vaguely remembered waking in the night and being given some soup and chamomile tea, but soon afterward he fell back asleep to escape the pain.

The night sky was starless and did not provide enough light for him to discern who was the slumped female asleep in the chair. Eyeing the window, he could see the sky was still dark, but based on the noise from the castle staff starting their morning duties, sunrise was imminent. Such clatter would be part of his life now, and he wished he could be back on his farm where the sounds were that of roosters, hungry horses, and cows needing to be milked.

Edwin barely raised his right arm when he decided to run his hand through his hair. It was worth the pain. He sniffed. Lord, that stench was him. How long had he been unconscious? He was just about to waken the sleeping woman when he saw a second figure keeping to the shadows, skulking toward his bed. Edwin narrowed his eyes to fake slumber and could only make out the man's height, which seemed to be average.

Weaponless and with limited mobility, Edwin concentrated on the figure's neck, knowing he would have only one punch to put the man down. But then the figure suddenly shifted to the woman in the chair.

As soon as Edwin spotted the long glint of silver being aimed toward the sleeping figure, he did the only thing he could and shouted, "Watch out!" which was neither descriptive nor compelling. Incredibly though, it worked. The man quickly made his way to the door, no longer caring about being quiet. The sleeping woman was suddenly awake and grabbing something from her side. She threw it at a dark figure just a second too late. Edwin was shaken, for he did not know who belonged to the nearly lethal shadowy figure. Whoever they were, they were not part of his plan.

The woman, now fully awake, quickly lit a candle, and he could see that it had been Brodie's wife who had been tending him. "Did you see who it was?" He looked at her apprehensively; his voice raspy.

"Nay," she replied, obviously trying to sound calm and not as shaken as he knew she must be.

"How long have I been asleep?"

Shinae went to pull her *sgian dubh* from the door. "Three days have passed, if you count the night of the stabbing." Edwin blinked at the comment. Her speech was soft but composed; it was as if nothing had happened. And based on what he could prove, nothing had. Mahon would believe him, but there would be little the laird could do.

"I changed the poultice on your wound to a mixture of frankincense and yarrow, which seem to be working well. There is very little redness and you only had a low fever the first night." The soft timbre of her voice had a calming effect, but it was not enough to keep him in a sick bed. Someone had come to this room with the intention of killing the woman, and Edwin had no notion as to who it was.

He swung his legs over the side of the bed, glad the léine he was wearing was long enough to cover him while sitting. He waited to be told to lay back down, but the pretty but disheveled woman did not object to him rising as he expected she would. Instead, she watched as he attempted to stand up. The pain was excruciating, and he felt weak and feeble. Unable to stand any more of the agony, Edwin fell back on the mattress with a squawk as his wound notified him of his stupidity. The throbbing finally started to recede when he stopped trying to raise his legs, which were hanging off the bed.

"Do you need to try again?" Shinae asked sweetly. Her tone was soft and noncombative. It was as if she had known that deep down he hated looking helpless and having to ask for assistance.

Edwin grunted out a negative reply and let her gently place the blankets over his middle. Next, she slowly picked up his legs and spun him so that he was once again in a vertical position on the bed.

Edwin hated being confined, especially to a sick bed. He wanted to tell her to just go and let him be, when she pulled up his shirt, letting the blanket hide his private parts so that she could examine the injury. "The stitches have held and your wounds did not reopen with that little stunt, but I think I'll put on another poultice on each wound." She got up and brought over a bowl of thick mush and gently covered one wound. Helping him turn on his side, she pushed down the wrap slightly and applied the poultice to his back, before moving the wrap back in place. "I must say I am amazed at how quickly you are recovering from wounds such as yours."

"I've always been a fast healer," Edwin touted in strained tones as he tried to lay flat on his back. Hopefully, he had achieved his goal and the pain he was experiencing was worthwhile. Squeezing his eyes shut, he took several deep breaths until the sharp pains began to dissipate. Only then did he realize that the kind woman had gathered the bowls, mugs, and whatnot and was about to leave.

"Where are you going?" Edwin asked in far more of a panic than he'd intended.

"To go eat and get clean now that you are awake. Don't worry, I will see to it that someone brings you some soup to eat." She flashed him a smile and disappeared behind the closing door.

He tried, but could not recall her name.

Unable to sleep, Edwin lay there, not moving, staring at the ceiling, trying hard to think over what had happened. Some might suspect Taveon, but there was no proof. The man was always friendly and openly acknowledging to all that Edwin was Mahon Donovan's heir, so any suspicion could be pushed aside.

There was a knock on the door and his heart started racing. Just as fast, it deflated when Edwin saw a young priest enter with a tray of food and a kettle. "I am Father Tam." He set the tray down. "You look better. All will be glad to hear how well you have responded to Shinae's ministrations." He put the tray on a table and said, "I can help feed you if you want."

Edwin's brows went up at the idea, and he forced himself to a sitting position, refusing to allow the man to know how much pain it was causing him. The priest quickly propped him up with pillows before handing him the bowl of soup. Edwin found himself starving and quickly finished the bowl and the loaf of bread, thinking the priest would gather the dishes and leave, but instead the young man sat down and stayed. Neither of them said a word, for neither of them knew what to say. Edwin could have tolerated the silence, but the clergyman had started snoring. His rhythmic breathing was giving Edwin a headache. Thankfully, the father's snoring became louder and louder until he woke himself up. Father Tam asked about his pain, and Edwin assured him that he was fine. He would have said as much even if it were a complete lie.

After what felt like hours, the door creaked and immediately the priest jumped up from his chair. He greeted Shinae and quickly left, nearly tripping over his robes. Just seeing her enter the room, Edwin felt better. He did not think he would after what had happened, but she appeared serene. She must not have told anyone of her near-death experience. It was either that or he had been hallucinating.

"Who are you?" he inquired.

She chuckled softly. "My name is Shinae."

Shinae! That was her name.

One of her brows was cocked. "Men are such prideful creatures," she said with a sigh. Without asking, she removed his pillows, laid him down and assessed the bandages. "There is still no bleeding, but I know you are in pain. Why would you needlessly suffer? Father Tam would have helped you lay back down."

Edwin shrugged. "It's as you said, my pride," he said gruffly as she fluffed the pillow and helped him relax against them.

"Tea?"

"Aye." He actually wanted some ale, but the tea was helping with the pain and was probably accelerating the healing. Still, he needed to leave this room before he went mad. "Aren't you afraid of rumors being spread about us being alone together?"

Shinae actually burst out laughing. "Nay. I've been nursing Scots since I was young, and though I am now married, I think most still see me as what I was—a nun. Besides, people come in and out of here frequently. You just don't know it because you are asleep."

Edwin arched a brow. Perhaps they did when she was here, but not when the priest was. "Your husband does not mind?"

"Brodie has been staying outside the castle, ensuring that Lochlen and Laird Donovan's soldiers behave," she replied with a wink.

Edwin's eyes opened wide. Brodie. Her husband was the famed Brodie Dunstan. Every day Mahon told stories about the man's skills as both a commander and a leader. "I was told he had not wanted marriage."

She smiled at Edwin, handed him his tea, and said, "Lucky for me that they were wrong." He took it and slowly drank down its honeylike sweetness. "How old are you, may I ask?"

"I am two years shy from being thirty."

"Me as well."

Edwin fell silent, unknowing what to say next and yet not wanting the deafening silence resume, he said. "I'm a farmer."

Shinae took his empty mug and refilled it before giving it back. "I think you mean *were* a farmer."

"Nay, I still am. I know nothing about being a soldier, let alone a clan leader. Never aspired to be anything other than what I am, and I certainly don't want to change now."

"It will be different," Shinae commented, "but I'm sure Laird Donovan will teach you all you will need to know."

She sat down again, and Edwin pasted his stony expression on his face. Riding past all of Colin's soldiers practicing with various weapons, moving as if it were second nature to them. Mahon had been clear about expecting him. He was to assume the title of the "Donovan Lion," who would continue growing the Donovan army until it was once again a formidable force. The man refused to see the truth. How would he be able to do that when he was barely adequate at wielding a blade?

"I am not the lion," Edwin had stated firmly.

Shinae shook her head. "Not yet, but in a few years, you will be."

He gave her a disgusted look. "You don't listen any better than he does. I never wanted this. I don't want to be a laird. I don't want to lead people, live in a castle, and be adored by all Donovan clansmen and women. *I already have a life.*"

Shinae just sat still, and he could tell she was choosing her words carefully. Finally, she nodded her head. "Then tell the laird and let someone else assume the role."

"Tried," he said with anguish, staring up at the ceiling's wood planks. "He has Taveon who can take my place and who is a natural leader, while I am not." Edwin looked at her. "Mahon just assumes because of my size that I am."

"You are being so resistant to the idea that it makes me think there is another reason you wish to reject an offer few would."

His black eyes grew large, as if she had stumbled onto a secret he had been holding.

Shinae studied him and then, after a few minutes, pressed her lips together and nodded her head. "Does your reluctance center around a woman?" she asked, probing into his thoughts. She saw him swallow and knew she was close. "Have you met someone?"

Edwin's thoughts flew to Aline, and how she would be furious with him right now if she knew the circumstances behind his attack. He felt Shinae's green gaze on him, waiting for him to reply. "I have, but I have the impression that Mahon is not keen on me having a wife."

"Brodie felt the same way about marriage and so did I, if I'm honest. Then we met, spent some time together, and changed our minds," she said with a sad smile, and Edwin was curious as to why. Her pretty countenance was made to be happy.

"Does Brodie know how lucky he is?"

Her gaze snapped to his. "I hope he thinks so."

"For you are a very bonny lass as well as very kind."

Shinae stood up and retrieved his empty mug. She put it on the tray. "*Go raibh maith agat*," she said, thanking him. "And you are a powerful man that any woman would—"

Before she could finish, the door swung open, hitting the stones of the wall. Brodie marched over, picked her up, and threw her over his shoulder. He scowled at Edwin. "She's mine," he growled and left.

Edwin smiled. *Aye*, he said to himself, *Brodie knew exactly how lucky he was*.

"Put me down!" Shinae hissed as fiercely as she could while pounding her fists on his back.

"Not a chance."

"You are hurting me, you *buthaigir duine*."

"Wrong there, *eudail*, my parents were married when I was born."

Shinae started to really struggle then, and he realized his gait was causing her chest to bounce against his shoulder. He did not stop but shifted her, so that she was cradled in his arms. The man may have promised not to yell and fight in front of everyone, but he was perfectly willing to make a spectacle of himself and her.

"We were just talking," Shinae hissed.

"Don't care. I know what I saw."

"Oh, really? In the few seconds you were in the room?"

"It was enough for me to tell that man was interested in you," he commented as he started up the chapel's winding staircase.

"He's not interested in me, you *cábóg dúramán*. He likes a woman back home and is afraid Mahon will insist that he remains single and unmarried like himself. Whatever you saw, Edwin Donovan was thinking of her."

Brodie kicked the door open and dropped her not so gently on the bed.

Shinae scrambled off the mattress. "The man is huge, but he is very shy and in a situation that he is finding difficult to cope with." Shinae could see he was unaffected. "Edwin has no desire to be Donovan's heir!"

Brodie's jaw clenched hearing her mention the man's name. "It doesn't matter what Edwin does or doesn't want. He *is* going to be Mahon's heir."

Shinae threw her hands up in the air. "He *knows* that. But he feels unprepared and is afraid of what will happen if he is in charge. The man is, if nothing else, scared."

Brodie thought for a moment and decided Shinae could be right. He'd only met Edwin the night of Laird Donovan's arrival, but he remembered seeing the man's discomfort. Mahon's heir was impressively large, and while he looked the part of the lion, he did not embody the title. He might eventually gain confidence, but Brodie hoped he did not become all of what the nickname "the lion" meant. He would caution the man not to make the same mistake of avoiding marriage, especially if he found a woman he liked, maybe even loved.

Brodie had spent the last three nights on the cold, hard ground in an effort to punish Shinae by his absence only to learn that she had been contentedly nursing Edwin back to health. It infuriated him that he had not been able to sleep, and she had been just fine. Her hair was glossy and soft, as if she had just washed it. She obviously did not feel any remorse for trying to direct his life. The frustrating woman had probably not even thought about him.

He watched her tug on the ties to her bliaut and then pull it over head. "What are you doing?" His wife could arouse a monk just by looking at her, and if she was thinking about seducing him into forgiveness . . . after three maddening nights alone, he would let her.

"I've been up each night catching only minutes of sleep in a very uncomfortable chair. I am going to bed. Do what you want," she said and quickly unlaced her shoes. She then climbed into bed, keeping as close as she could to the edge of the mattress. Seduction was the last thing on her mind.

Brodie yanked off his belt, kilt, and shoes and slid into bed, doing the same as she, hovering on his side of the bed's edge. Unfortunately, the heat coming from her had him wanting to turn around and pull her close. Just as he was about to turn over, he heard her deep intake of breath. *Murt!* She had fallen asleep, not desiring him in the least. Brodie forced himself to leave her alone despite knowing it would mean another night without sleep.

CHAPTER EIGHT

Dunlop studied Edwin as most of the tables were broken down to allow for dancing. The man had been stabbed six days before and had recovered enough to attend this last celebration as long as he remained seated. The festivities should have been a couple days prior in conjunction with the completion of the harvest, but Laird Colin had waited until the young Donovan could come to the event. Dunlop knew his laird did not especially want the feast to be a celebration of Mahon's arrival as it had been unexpected and disruptive, but not to have even a small one would strain a currently strong relationship.

All those there really had come to celebrate Lammas. Starting tomorrow, the farmers would be back at their fields, preparing the land for winter crops. The next large, clan-inclusive celebration would not happen until the Feast of Jesus's Nativity.

Dunlop shook his head in disgust as he watched Brodie sitting near the front table, holding Shinae on his lap, forcing her to watch and not participate in any of the activities. Several men had started to approach them, but they all just as quickly turned and walked away to find another dance partner without saying a word. Taveon had tried several times and finally succumbed to staring at her from across the room. The man's ungentlemanly behavior was on full display and he obviously did not care.

Brodie had gone with Shinae during her visits to check on Edwin, and even sat in the room when visiting with the McTiernay wives. He was acting like a tyrant and, mysteriously, Shinae did not fight him, but all could see his foolishness in thinking Brodie believed such tactics would break her. Dunlop suspected his friend's deplorable actions only infused her with resolve, for if anyone was as stubborn as Brodie, it was his wife. How Brodie had not seen that yet was truly bewildering.

Joyful laughter filled the great hall, and Dunlop immediately turned and stared at the bewitching redhead as she enjoyed herself. Her smile, her laughter, her delight at being at Lochlen could not be mistaken as anything but genuine.

A sweet-looking female headed his way with a coy expression that in the past would have had his full attention. Now, all Dunlop knew was that she was blocking his view. With a frown and a swish of his hand, he dismissed her and, thankfully, she took the hint and moved on to someone else.

The great hall was full of boisterous men and women. All had been invited, from Colin's soldiers to swordsmiths to candlemakers and seamstresses. Most could not fit inside the great hall so people were constantly moving in and out of the room, repeatedly interfering with his ability to watch Isilmë from across the room.

When Dunlop could finally see the other side, he snarled.

Now it was Callum who was with her.

He must have just returned to her side, for he was handing Isilmë a mug of ale with a big flashy smile. The man's chiseled jaw and unusual blue-green eyes seemed to draw the attention of every unmarried woman in the room. Isilmë was obviously included among them, enjoying being in his company. In Dunlop's opinion, Callum was too good-looking, which meant he was not to be trusted. Dunlop's own physique was comparable, but beyond that he knew women would desire the Highlander over him, with his bald head, ordinary hazel eyes, and crooked nose, which had been broken twice.

Another clanswoman he probably knew but had forgotten moved into his line of sight and started talking to a man. Between them, they effectively blocked his entire view. He counted to three. "Could you pick another place to flirt with each other?" he asked more gruffly than was needed. But just in case they had not understood, he angled his thumb toward the back of the room, hinting for them to move.

After giving him a dirty look, they both left the area. He did not care, for once again he could watch Isilmë. Unfortunately, he was not liking what he was seeing. She was not only *still* talking with Crevan McTiernay's commander, he was fingering one of the red ringlets framing her delighted face. The two of them huddled together seemed to fit in perfectly with all those around them. Cheery couples. That was all he could see—genuinely happy couples. Old couples, young couples, expecting couples, ones who had been together for years and newly married twosomes who could not stop stealing kisses from each other. All of them so very blissfully happy.

In the past, Dunlop had not cared as he was usually among the just-for-tonight couples. Then he had met one feisty, petite, not-his-type, freckled redhead, who had her own way about doing and saying things. All innocent, completely honest, and so very enticing. Isilmë had him all mixed up. And it was all Brodie's fault.

A few days ago, his friend had been furious and, based on rumors, Shinae had been just as mad as well. He thought all was good when Shinae had stood by her husband to welcome Laird Donovan. When she had publicly placed her hand in Brodie's, it gave many witnesses the impression that they were a team. Never had Brodie looked prouder. Dunlop wanted *that*. All of it. To love someone who felt the same way about him? Even now Shinae sat on Brodie's lap, and he looked so pleased that he was her husband. None of the disasters, jealous outbursts, and disagreements had put a wedge between them.

Brodie was right. Dunlop so wished he had the same thing and knew it was within reach.

He was debating how to approach Isilmë when he saw it. She flashed Callum a mischievous smile, which he returned. Dunlop felt his usually well-controlled temper start to rear and took a step toward Isilmë as Callum pulled her into a dance that had just begun. The circle of people dancing was growing rapidly, leaving little room for those just watching. Callum clasped Isilmë's right hand with his left and slowly, the large circle of dancers started to move to the left, stepping with their left foot, and then the right foot joined the left, making a clapping sound. Again and again, faster and faster, the group moved in time to the beat of the tympanum and the stringed cithara.

Isilmë's gold-and-black dress swirled around her tiny ankles. Dunlop grimaced. She was laughing the same way she always did with him, and he felt another surge of jealousy—something he had been feeling a lot since her arrival at Lochlen. The foreign emotion had arisen without warning many times in the past couple of weeks, and it did not make any sense. *Isilmë was just not his type.*

She was short, had freckles all over, and her figure was far bustier than the women who typically tempted him. Isilmë was also annoyingly argumentative and incredibly oblivious to people's reactions to her blunt, honest opinions. No coy bone in her body, she was socially naïve and was unaware how attractive she was. It did not make sense that it was *Isilmë* whom he found interesting. She was the one he sought out in the morning before he left for the day. She was the one who always gave him an honest answer to any question. She was the one he wanted to laugh with and comfort. It was Isilmë he thought of when lying in bed trying to sleep.

The dance finally ended, but seconds later he could hear the strings of the cithara being plucked. They were going to start again. Dunlop started marching over to her, with one goal—to stop all flirtations—even if he had to throw her over his shoulder like Brodie had. But just as he moved toward her, Isilmë surprisingly started making her way to him.

"Can you believe how fantastic tonight is?" she asked. Pure joy was beaming out of every pore of her face. "At the abbey, I never could eat, dance, talk, laugh—"

"—flirt—" he growled, and Isilmë just grinned.

"—or simply *smile*. Something you haven't done all night," she remarked, lightly tapping his chest. "I thought you would be enjoying yourself as this will be the last celebration for a while. Everyone is so merry. Why aren't you?"

Dunlop glanced over at Brodie. Shinae was still on his lap, smiling to people, but Dunlop was not fooled. Not once had she spoken to her husband or anyone else, and it was beginning to be noticed.

Isilmë followed his gaze to see what he was looking at. Realizing it was Shinae, she turned back around and beamed him a smile. "Don't worry. She will forgive Brodie eventually, but not until he sincerely apologizes."

He was not as sure. He suspected Brodie wanted to express his regrets, but Dunlop had a feeling that his friend was waiting for her to apologize first. Dunlop may not have any experience being a husband, but he did know that trying to control a woman who had any spirit always put you on the losing side. Even when you won, you lost." Dunlop grimaced and shook his head. His friend had a long way to go to make up all the pain he had and still was causing her. More than once Shinae had tried to rise, especially when Taveon was nearby. Each time, Brodie held her down tightly. Now, it looked like he was sitting her across his legs in such a way that she could not get up unless he released her.

"She hasn't forgiven him yet," Dunlop said flatly, "Maybe once they are in their chambers and he kisses her, he might have a chance."

Isilmë looked up. "You men really know nothing about women."

"I know more than you do about men, and identifying the bad ones."

She pointed to a small crowd of women surrounding the Schellden commander. "Do you mean Callum?" She then pointed to another jovial group. "Or Taveon?"

"You and Shinae both need to stay away from him," his eyes glaring at the arrogant man.

Isilmë had no compulsion to speak to Taveon. He was friendly enough and definitely good-looking, but his constant boasts were tiresome, so it was not difficult to agree to stay away. "Taveon comes near Shinae one more time, Brodie is going to become violent, and the witless man is going to leave with a black eye and a broken nose."

Isilmë rolled her eyes. "That is ridiculous. Taveon flirts with everyone. I think he does it to Shinae because he knows it makes Brodie jealous." She paused before continuing. "I know without a doubt Shinae does not like him. In truth, he makes us both uncomfortable."

The shaky tone of her voice alarmed him. He turned his gaze back on her. "Did he do or say anything to you?" Dunlop's voice was deep and clipped. "Or . . . Shinae?" he quickly added. If Taveon had, the man would not suffer just a mere fist to the jaw.

Dunlop's hands enveloped Isilmë's. He was not going to let go until he got an answer. Isilmë's forehead wrinkled in confusion and shook her head. Dunlop closed his eyes, pulled her in close, and dropped his chin to rest it on her head. "Women do not realize the power they have over their men. We need constant reassurance."

"I don't understand," she said, the sound muffled by his léine. "Reassurance of what?"

Slowly, Dunlop relaxed his grip and released the breath he had been holding. "That you are happy and well."

Isilmë was still puzzled, but enjoyed being close to him. She was disappointed when he started to let her go. Just by breathing in his scent, her heart was pounding, and her legs had gone weak. All week, Dunlop had given her mixed indications of what he felt for her. Whenever they met, they would talk about inane things—their day, the people they had encountered, any gossip they thought the other might find interesting. Right now, the ease she usually felt with him had abandoned her. It was hard to converse when all she could think about was whether he wanted to kiss her again, but lately he always backed away. It was so confusing that she had babbled her problem in the sewing room that afternoon.

The women were all chatty and liked to ask questions about her life as a nun as she worked on repairing and creating gowns. She had returned the borrowed garment to Ceridwin with a few embellishments. The woman had not only been very appreciative, she had shared the changes Isilmë had made on her bliaut with others. Any fears as to what she was going to do at Lochlen to occupy her time had gone completely away. Several clanswomen had approached her to see if she would do the same for them. Since then, many McTiernay clanswomen had been eager to play matchmaker, saying she should be married.

You need to use your eyes, duine óg, *bat your eyelashes at a man and it will draw him to you,* one of the seamstresses had told her. Isilmë decided to try it.

Dunlop pulled back slightly. "Why do you keep

doing that? That thing with your lashes? Is something in your eye?"

Isilmë stopped their flutter; her shoulders slumped in disappointment. She did not have many features she thought men liked, but her lashes were long and dark, and she had hoped blinking her eyes rapidly would entice Dunlop to kiss her again. She must have been doing it wrong, for he had been completely unaffected. While eating the evening meal, she overheard one of the soldiers say that women were a constant stream of mixed personalities, which was true, but in her opinion, men were far worse at misleading women with their ever-changing comments and behaviors.

Isilmë had thought that Dunlop might have feelings for her. She definitely had them for him. She was not sure when she had lost her own heart, but before she realized what was happening, she had fallen in love. And from what the seamstresses had told her about the signs to look for, she had hoped Dunlop was likewise falling for her. Over the last week, he had sent her unexpected gifts such as honey meringues, which she was told indicated Dunlop really liked her. Isilmë knew now that he had not been the one to actually give them to her, but he had gladly taken the credit when she thought he had.

It had only been a handful of weeks since Dunlop and Brodie saved them from death's door in the freezing rain. Isilmë had thought Shinae mad when she married Brodie, but if Shinae felt the sensations Isilmë experienced when Dunlop even lightly brushed against her, she wanted to be mad right along with her. Many nights, Isilmë had lain in bed at night wishing for Dunlop to burst into her room and give Lady Makenna and Lady Laurel a reason to force them into marriage too.

Losing hope that Dunlop was or ever would be in love with her, Isilmë said despondently, "Nothing. Nothing is wrong with my eyes."

Isilmë backed up and was about to turn and walk away when Dunlop grabbed her arm and lightly tugged her back to his side. "You are not going anywhere."

Isilmë pursed her lips together. Her pride was hurt by his disinterest, and she felt her anger building. "Why? We've talked and now I am saying goodbye."

His grip got tighter, and she almost winced. "It took all night to get you by my side and you are going to stay right here until I let you go."

Isilmë glared at him. If he thought she was going to allow him to physically restrain her like Brodie was doing with Shinae, he did not know her at all.

"And just how long will that be?" Isilmë asked, attempting to wrench her arm free. "Because Callum is waving for me to come back, and I feel like dancing."

Dunlop glanced up and saw she was right. His focus had only been on Isilmë since she had started toward him. "Don't even think about it." There was a snarl to his voice.

"And just what does that mean?" She waved her arm at Shinae, still restrained on Brodie's lap. "Everybody can dance but ex-nuns?" Isilmë really wished she could pause time and ask her friends what Dunlop was trying to convey, but his demeanor had changed from protection to what felt like hostile possessiveness. She felt like he was talking in riddles.

Dunlop just looked at her. Isilmë had not been flirting with Callum in an effort to make him jealous. She had no clue what she was doing to him. Still, whether he liked it or not, Dunlop knew he could never let her be courted by or even flirted with by another man. "Women drive me batty," he growled. "Always have. They talk about foolish things, and I had assumed with the pleasure you get from making these silly dresses—" Dunlop flounced one of her voluminous sleeves. "—that you would turn out to be like every other female. Pretty and nothing else. You're not."

"I guess I should thank you for the odd compliment nestled within an insult," Isilmë said crisply, completely at a loss to the point Dunlop was making. Her heart was reading into his words, but his possessive tone gave her the urge to flee. "Callum is walking this way. I am fairly certain he wants to dance again."

"Nay." His dark tone held no chance for argument.

This time Isilmë successfully wrenched her arm free. "And why not? Unlike you, Callum is not only impressed with my abilities with a needle and thread, but thinks I make a good dance partner."

"He can think it, but nothing else."

Callum was almost within hearing range. "I don't believe your opinion matters to him."

"Oh, it will. He takes one more step and I'll give him a thrashing he'll never forget."

Isilmë fully faced him and poked her right index finger into his chest. "Listen to me. I like our friendship, and I'll even admit to enjoying your kisses, but that does not mean that I will allow you to dictate when and with whom I can dance."

Friendship. He did not like the word all of a sudden. What was between Isilmë and him could not be defined so simply. It was too vague, too imprecise, and it covered too much territory. Long ago, he had promised himself to never allow his emotions to become involved with a woman, but what he felt for Isilmë would last forever.

"Just wh—" Before Isilmë could finish, his mouth crushed hers. He cupped her face in his hands and was surprised when she lifted her arms to his head and held him there. Her soft lips were tightly closed, but this time he was going to give her a kiss that could not be mistaken for friendship. His body had an immediate reaction to her timidity. He gathered her closer to his chest, planning to increase the kiss's intensity, but the music started again, making him aware that they probably had an audience. He finally forced himself to move just enough away to see her face. Framing it with his hands, he pressed brief kisses on her forehead. When her heavy-lidded eyes finally looked into his, he whispered. "You are mine. Not just right now, but forever."

Isilmë wanted to stop time and rewind it over and over again. She would never tire of hearing those words. "I love you, Dunlop, and I think I always have."

Dunlop felt a rush of exhilaration run through him. In sudden fear of her waking tomorrow and changing her mind, he whispered, "Marry me." He was determined to get Isilmë to pledge herself to him right then.

Tears formed and started rolling down her cheeks. Dunlop kissed them away, and as he did, she whispered, "I love you, too." The three words were soft but clear, and he embraced her once again, mumbling against her lips that he did not know the words that would adequately express his love for her.

Shinae quickly stepped inside the room and closed the door to their bedchamber, leaning against it, fighting the tears she had been holding back. She was not exactly sure why she was having such an emotional response to Isilmë and Dunlop's wedding announcement. They had announced it to all within hearing in the great hall. No date had been declared, but she did not think it would be very long. Shinae was happy for them; she really was. But she was envious as well. They seemed so sure about their feelings, publicly proclaiming their love for each other.

A tear fell. Not once had she or Brodie exchanged such binding words.

The door nudged and Shinae stepped away. "Trying to keep me out?" Brodie probed.

She had known he was going to follow her here as soon as he realized that she had not joined the throng of well-wishers. "Of course not."

He raised an eyebrow as if he only marginally believed her. He put a hand behind her neck and tilted her head up. With his free hand, he wiped her tears. "I see you are still mad at my keeping you with me."

She shook her head and took a step back. "Not mad. More . . . disappointed." She went and sat on the bed.

Brodie tossed two logs into the hearth and blew on the red embers to get the fire going. *Disappointed*, she had said. The word was like a punch in the gut that he had not expected. He wanted to be her hero, the one she leaned on, and shared all her deep thoughts and feelings. He'd rather have her mad than disappointed. "I don't know what to say. I'm sorry I reacted the way I did when you told me about Ros, but I still do not like you meddling in my affairs. And then to come home to find you've been nursing another man, practically day and night? How do you expect me to react?"

"For nearly twenty years I've been taking care of myself. I did not marry you to hover over me, afraid of what I might be thinking whenever I speak to another man. I can remain loyal to you without you holding me in your lap, or lingering about, proving you have claim to me. And as for Edwin, he was asleep nearly the entire time I was there due to the herbal tea I was giving him. The priest and Isilmë also tended to him. The night we met and we talked I realized *you* were the first man I actually felt comfortable talking with. And since we married, we haven't done much of that, and I realized watching Dunlop and Isilmë tonight that we hardly know each other."

Brodie flinched. He was not so sure she was right. The night he found her, he had talked more than he had ever conversed with anyone, revealing things he had never shared with anyone, not even Dunlop.

She was scaring him, and he could not stop the growing ache of foreboding that she was leading up to something that would destroy him. "What are you saying?"

Shinae blinked her crystalline green eyes at the fear she heard in his voice and answered his question with the truth. "That we should talk more and get to know each other better."

Brodie's growing anxiety lessened a little. He took off all but his léine and sank into the room's single chair next to the hearth. With his elbows on his knees, he rested his head in his hands and reminded himself that she had not said they weren't meant to be together. That she was not leaving him. He took several deep breaths and sat back. Shinae was across the room with her back against the headboard.

He wanted her closer and decided what they needed was another chair in the room. When the McTiernays finally left and he and Shinae were able to move into their permanent bedchamber, he would ensure there were at least two padded chairs for them to sit in.

After returning with another chair, he asked, "What is it you want to know?"

Shinae bit her bottom lip and looked at the ceiling, ignoring the chair he had brought in. "Anything . . . everything. How about I ask a question and then you?" He smiled at the change in her demeanor. She was actually eager to learn more things about him. Surprisingly, he felt the same way.

"What is your favorite color?" she asked.

"Green. Yours?"

"Purple. Your turn."

Brodie leaned back in the creaky chair and stretched out his legs. "What's your favorite time of year?"

"I'm not sure I have one. There are good things about them all. Yours, however, is fall."

"How did you know?" he asked with furrowed brows.

"It was the way you talked about the harvest and that it was the first sign of the next season coming when the weather was at its best."

Brodie pointed at her, indicating it was her turn, and she grinned at him. He would sit and do this all night if it meant she would continue to smile at him.

Back and forth, they talked about activities they enjoyed and those they despised. Foods both loved and disliked. People most influential in their youth. Favorite foods and beloved childhood memories.

Brodie was surprised at how much he was enjoying this odd conversation. Yet these were all things one typically knew about the person they were going to marry, and some of the information could change how they saw each other. "Things you find especially annoying," Brodie put forth, suppressing a shudder of fear.

Shinae started to look around as she thought of her answer. Her first inclination was to say something about people getting mad, expressing their opinion, and then walking away without giving her a chance to either explain or at least tell her side of the situation. After several long seconds, she decided against it. "Parents who mistreat children, dogs that won't stop barking, nosy people or anyone who likes to talk only about themselves and . . . gossips."

Brodie cocked a brow and stated, "People who feel that yelling is necessary to make a point, hypocrites, those who assume they know everything, and little lies people tell to make one feel better."

"Really?" Shinae asked rhetorically. "Well, I don't mind that last one. If I look awful or get fat on all this rich food, I want you to lie and tell me I look beautiful. I don't care how much untruth there is to your words. Until I met you, I had not had a single compliment in over a decade. I've discovered I like them."

Brodie slapped his knee and started to laugh. The deep, rich, infectious sound made her join him. On impulse, he stood up and went to sit beside her on the bed. "I love your laugh," he said and pushed her hair back over her shoulder.

Shinae bristled when he said the word. *Love.* So he *could* say it. But it was not her he loved, it was her laugh. Deep down, she knew she was being ridiculous, and yet it still hurt. This entire time they had spent talking and not once had either of them touched on the subject of love. It was like they both wanted to avoid the answer to the question they were too afraid to ask.

Brodie picked up her hand and began to lightly stroke it. "Why did you rush out of the hall tonight?" he asked in a soft but earnest whisper.

The question made her uncomfortable, but she answered it honestly. "It was the way Dunlop and Isilmë looked at each other, speaking so openly about what they felt for the other."

Brodie's eyes popped wide open, and after several seconds, he stood up and went back to the hearth before turning to look at her. His lips were pinched together in a way that made it seem like he disapproved of such openness. "That's Dunlop, but it is not me."

Scooting over to the side of the bed, Shinae silently unbraided her hair and then removed all her clothing except for her shift. She then slipped under the covers and turned on her side away from him.

Brodie just stared incredulously at her, glad she could not see him totally mystified. "Is it because Dunlop said he loved Isilmë and I haven't said the same to you? Because you haven't said those words to me either."

She flipped over and narrowed her eyes. "That's what you have been waiting for? You won't say them until I do?" She was practically calling him a coward. "I haven't said I love you because I honestly don't know what love is. I've never been in love before!"

"Well, neither have I!" he retorted sharply. Technically, he had not yelled his response, but his eyes had darkened indicating his unhappiness.

"I guess we are now very clear about our feelings," Shinae said glibly and turned back on her side.

Brodie raked his hand through his hair and began to pace. "Honesty and loyalty is what I can promise you, and I expect it in return. I know I love my mother even though I haven't seen her in years. But what I feel for you is far different from that."

Brodie stopped pacing and looked at her. Her back was facing him, but he knew she was listening. He sat down on the edge of the bed and gently twirled one of her strands of hair around his finger. *Shinae*, he thought to himself. It had become more than just a name to him. It had become synonymous with comfort, safety, and passion. With her, he had everything he needed. "I never thought you were out there. Before I met you, I was happy but lonely. Even when around lots of people or those I call friends, I felt alone. I had become accustomed to it. Then I met and miraculously married you, and suddenly life changed. I had a companion for life, and it scared me. What frightened me the most was the idea of losing you and that kind of fear I have never known before. You fill up places in my heart I never knew were empty. You are everything I ever wanted in a partner and more than I dared hope for."

When he said *partner*, Shinae twisted her head so that she could see him. Their eyes locked, and she felt that overwhelming warmth in her heart that she had felt that first night when they were alone and in that small cottage.

Brodie saw the steady glow of tenderness and desire in her eyes. He knew that she saw the same expression mirrored in his own gaze.

As the meaning of his words registered in her mind, Shinae felt as if she were being pulled along a strong current and carried over the edge of an emotional waterfall, knowing he would catch her.

"All I know is that each time I see you, or am with you, or touch you, my soul reaches out for more."

Brodie watched as her eyes looked into his. She said nothing, but her gaze was filled with a hunger that matched his own. That knowledge shook him and he could no longer resist. He seized her lips and kissed her hard, claiming her lips, his tongue plundering her accepting mouth. She gasped as he lowered his body over hers and when on top, he gripped both of her hands in his. A soft feminine sound escaped her, and she began to meet him with every sweep of his tongue.

There was no teasing, no seduction; he needed her more now than ever before. Too much had happened that day that could have ripped them apart, but she was still his and he was still hers. Slowly, his mouth started moving down until he encountered her shift. "You're overdressed," he said huskily.

She giggled. "So are you."

He pulled briefly away and quickly freed himself from his léine. Shinae slowly started pulling the white linen chemise up as she admired his perfect form, her gaze lingering shamelessly at his obvious arousal.

Impatient for her to finish, he pulled the shift over her head before resuming his kisses. He roamed the valley between Shinae's breasts before giving one quick suckle to each red bud. The rosy peaks grew to pebble hardness.

His tongue then made a path down her ribs to her stomach. She writhed beneath him, eager to touch his skin. He let go of her hands and they immediately went to his back kneading and clawing his skin and shoulders.

His own hands began a lust-arousing exploration of her soft flesh as they made their way across her silken belly to the swell of her hips and then farther downward, skimming the sides to her thighs. Shinae's whole being flooded with desire as waves of longing washed over her like a relentless rippling current. Instinctively, she arched her chest toward him, her body aching for a more intimate touch. She could feel the evidence of his desire hard against her thigh. For a moment she closed her eyes and rocked her hips against him once and then again, reveling in the power that movement had.

Brodie loved how Shinae responded to his touch. Nothing was artificial. Every moan, every reaction was honest, real, and because of him. Fueled by her pleas for more, he caved to his overwhelming desire for them to be connected once again. He pushed his palm against her sensitive core, and slowly rubbed her most sensitive flesh. His fingers circled her entrance and she arched further, pressing her backside higher, allowing him to ease into her entrance. "Please, Brodie, please," she begged, her body quivering in his arms.

"Please what?" he asked.

"Touch me."

He smiled and delayed no longer.

Shinae groaned as he finally slid one finger into her wet sheath, all the time watching her face and how pleasure washed over her face as her tight sheath clenched around him.

He slid it out and in one more time, and Shinae started begging him to go faster. Desire for him was taking over her mind, and she wanted nothing more than to feel him, not his finger, inside her. The revelation that her thoughts were so wanton excited her all the more.

"First things first," he said as he pulled his finger out.

Shinae was about to very loudly protest when he forced her legs farther apart. He paused briefly to press hot, nipping kisses along the inside of her thighs. She tightly gripped the bedsheet and let out a soft cry as Brodie slid his tongue past her curls and ran up her moist slit. She started to shake with pleasure as his tongue moved back and forth. Her heart beat faster and soon she was panting.

Her back bowed when his tongue delved deep into her. He lapped up her liquid core and her hips began to rock into his caress as pleasure raked through her. Shinae began to thrash her head on the pillow. Higher and higher he took her.

He groaned heavily against her, and the vibrating sounds sent her once again to another time and another place. Crying out, she again arched her back as she was hurtled beyond the point of no return. Every pore of her body was tingling as pleasure rippled through her.

Shinae barely realized that he had straddled her and

shifted his hips onto hers. She gasped at the touch of his heated member and her soft whimper almost drove him to the brink of insanity. Brodie leaned his head to hers and nuzzled her ear with his nose. "I need you, Shinae," he breathed. His shaft was straining for her body, demanding to be inside her.

With a relieved groan, Brodie thrust himself inside her. His mind flooded with bliss and did it again. In a slow rhythm, he eased in and out of her, trying to keep himself from pushing too hard. In and out, he basked in the exquisite feel of her soft flesh around his shaft. She had wrapped her legs around him, and he could feel the tightening of her heels along his back, urging him to move faster.

Immersing himself in the feel of her soft, warm body, he leaned down and claimed her mouth, more forcefully than he intended. Her need for pleasure matched his own, and soon both their hips were undulating in unison, short, smooth, rolling thrusts, moving into deep, long ones, repeating the sequence again and again.

Their breath mingled as his mouth brushed over hers before taking it over. His tongue plunged in and out, following the cadence of his body. Thrust by thrust, the tempo intensified. He could feel her peak along with him and kept going, determined to wait until she climaxed even more wildly again.

"Shinae," he groaned into her neck, very nearly a prayer. He was sweating with the exertion . . . with the effort of trying to hold off the end until she was there to meet him.

With a choking cry, Shinae let herself be taken over the edge, her body clenching and spiraling out of her control. She could not stop the scream of pleasure that had come from somewhere deep inside her as wave after wave of a sheer pleasure took over. His mouth on hers heightened the effect, bringing her pleasure that seemed to go on forever.

Brodie heard her sweet screams. They were wild and joyous. His release came in a hot, deep, hammering surge of waves, leaving him breathless, sweat-sheened and utterly shaken. Unable to keep his shaking arms from holding himself above her body, he collapsed by her side. They lay exhausted, side by side, and smiled at each other with the look of two well-satiated lovers.

CHAPTER NINE

Shinae squeezed Brodie's arm, draped across her stomach. She was on her side as he was nestled as close as he could get to her. Their bodies were still moist from their lovemaking. Usually neither of them noticed as they drifted off to sleep, but Shinae was not tired. Dunlop and Isilmë had made their announcement only a few hours into the evening, and Shinae had left directly after. And now she was wide awake.

"Brodie," she whispered. "Are you sleepy?"

He pushed up onto his elbow. "Nay." He looked down into her eyes, seeing that she too was wide awake.

"Why did Colin send out two heralds?"

Brodie shrugged his chin. He had not been aware two had been sent. "More than likely to cover more ground and quickly let Conan know he was to get to Lochlen as soon as he could."

Shinae closed her eyes, wondering if that was wise. Right now, Conan and Mhàiri were far safer than they would be at Lochlen, where someone evil was lying in wait. "Will you tell me what the brothers decide to do?"

He smiled, kissed her forehead, and mumbled against her soft skin, "Aye. But I doubt anything will be determined until Conan arrives."

The clan's merriment and revelry had tapered off a little, but it could still be heard out in the courtyard. Brodie sat up. "Are you hungry? I did not eat much tonight."

At the mention of food, Shinae realized she had not eaten all day and her stomach was about to start talking quite loudly, letting all know it was not happy. She sat up alongside him and pulled the sheet over her chest. They may not have been married long, but it was long enough to know that such exposure tended to distract her new husband. "I'm famished."

Like quicksilver, Brodie jumped up, threw on his léine, and haphazardly put on kilt, belt, and shoes and vanished out the door. A second later, he reopened it, poked his head in, and gave her a big grin. "Anything you want?"

She beamed a smile at him before answering. "Bread and butter. Oh, and some venison, if there is still some left, but if not, any type of fowl will do. And some carrots and potatoes." She bit her bottom lip in thought.

"Anything else?" he teased.

"Something to drink," she answered, completely unapologetic.

Shinae blew him a kiss before he shut the door, then rolled out of bed. She donned her chemise and then, rubbing her arms, went over to the small stone hearth. The fire was once again nearly out. She added two large logs before stoking the ashes to get it roaring. The warmth created by the sun and captured by the castle's stones had just started dropping when she had left the great hall earlier. Now the outside temperature felt like it had continued to drop.

She was just putting the poker away when Brodie returned, which was must faster than she had expected. He came in carrying nothing but a chair. He placed it near the fire and tapped the back of the chair for her to sit down. Shinae instead put her knee on the padded bottom and leaned over the chair's back to kiss him, hoping it conveyed her appreciation. His comedic grin let her know that it did. With her own lips curved into a large smile, she turned back around and properly sat down and realized he had brought back only the chair. "I thought you went after food."

"I did, *ban-chéile*, but with all you asked for—"

"—you wanted honesty, and I am honestly famished." She glanced at him, her eyes asking why he had returned without any nourishment.

"As am I." He leaned over and pulled the tie on both shoes so he could remove them with his toes. "I went to the kitchens. They are building a plate for us." Brodie sat back with a huff and just as he did, there was a knock on the door. Jumping back to his now bare feet, he went to get their food. Seeing him juggling a large tray, two mugs, and a tankard of ale, Shinae rushed to help. The only table in the room was the small one by the window next to the bed, Brodie placed the tray on his seat, then took off his kilt, laying it down in front of the fire so he could set the food and tankard on top of it.

Shinae moved down to sit by Brodie on his blue-and-white tartan. She pointed at the new chair. "I feel bad.

All your hard work is going unappreciated, sitting there unused."

Brodie wiggled his dark blond eyebrows and said, "It'll get used very shortly." He had purposefully found one with no arms.

Once again, he could not believe God's blessing. Shinae sat there eating, her hair mussed from making love, her light green eyes sparkling as if she was the luckiest woman in the world when he knew it was he whom fortune had blessed.

"The celebration sounds like it is still going," Shinae mumbled as she licked the juices from the meat on her fingers.

"It is, but it will soon wind down. It is the last large feast the clan will have for while. No doubt there will be a bonfire for St. Crispin's Day. But you won't see something like all the celebrations we've been having until Christmas."

Brodie popped the last piece of bread into his mouth, swallowed the rest of his ale, and rose up to stand behind her empty chair. He playfully wiggled his brows at her, and Shinae hesitantly moved to sit down. He began to stroke her hair. "I need to ask you to do something, and I don't want you to call me names in your head."

Shinae brushed the crumbs from her chemise as he moved to sit on the chair opposite him. "I promise. No mental insults. Only aloud." He gave her a slight grimace, and she realized he was being very serious. It made her nervous.

"I don't want you talking to Taveon anymore. I don't want you anywhere near the man."

Just the mention of the man's name and every fiber in Shinae's body went on alert. She waved her hand back and forth. "No need for the warning. The man makes me feel uncomfortable."

Brodie saw her visibly shudder and went to kneel in front of her. With his hands lightly on either side of her face, he asked in a soft tone that was laced with fear, "Did Taveon ever hurt you? Say something about me? Scare you?"

She shook her head and removed his hands. "I just don't like him. The way he smiles with that smug look all the time. He's hiding something, and not having a clue to what it is bothers me." Brodie stared at her for a moment and saw nothing but the truth staring back.

Shinae just watched him, knowing that he was battling himself. Something had occurred between him and the man Brodie had trained and elevated. She silently wished that Mhàiri and Conan had already arrived, and that Cyric's message was no longer a burden she had to carry. It was a weight she had been carrying too long. Taveon was the first man her instincts had warned her against since arriving at Lochlen Castle. Not every man she had encountered was warm and friendly, but nor had they triggered her inner voice to say, "*Stay away from him.*"

Brodie went back to his seat. He learned forward with clasped hands and balanced himself on his knees. "I mean it, Shinae. Keep far away from him when you go to help those in the village. Let the other McTiernay women entertain and see to his and Mahon's needs. Just avoid the Donovans altogether."

Shinae got down on her knees and inched up so that

she was between his legs. Placing her hands gently on either side of his face, he closed his eyes and savored the feel of her light touch. She waited until he opened them again. "I will."

He stared at her and knocked over his chair as he sank down on the blanket, his face still in her grasp. His palms then took her own cheeks and pulled her close. His lips met hers gently, searching, seeking, and she welcomed him without question, without reservation.

He moaned as she sated a small portion of his desire for cohesion. He picked Shinae up, never breaking their kiss, sat down in her armless chair, and carefully straddled her on his lap. Shinae's hips automatically began lifting, wanting other body parts to merge. Needing some relief from his aroused state, he moved her on top of him.

Being in a dominant position was a whole new experience for Shinae, and he found himself so extremely fond of her constant shuddering that he lost control until they both exploded in ecstasy once again.

She lay against his chest, whispering that she had never been so happy.

He kissed her head. "Thank you," he began softly. "Thank you for being born, for being you, for being my wife, and thank you for promising to stay away from Taveon and Mahon." Immediately he regretted his last words.

She slightly stiffened and sat up so that she looked him directly in the eye.

"I will, but I don't understand your insistence. I know that Laird Donovan dismissed you without warning, and I would be angry too, but after eight years I thought you at least parted as friends. Now you want me to stay away from him as well?"

"Where Mahon is, Taveon will be."

She raised her dark brows, removed herself from his lap, and redonned her chemise. making it clear that his pithy answer would not suffice. She wanted to know more about him and Mahon.

Brodie waited until she sat down across from him. "Laird Donovan and I . . . well, we have a complicated relationship. To understand it, you would have to know Mahon's history, and why Colin and he are allies." She just looked at him, clearly wanting him to continue. "Do you want the whole story or just a quick summation?"

"I think I want the whole one." She gave him a small grin, encouraging him to continue.

Brodie sighed and sat back. He had not told anyone about why he had stayed with Mahon for so long, or why he had thought he had a chance at being the next Donovan laird. But the aspect of telling Shinae gave him a severe case of anxiety as it had when Dunlop hinted for explanations. It was time someone knew.

"You know a bit about me and how I am both Highlander and Lowlander. Mahon too had a mother who sent him north to Clan Mhuirich, located just south of where I was, with the Sinclairs."

"Did you know each other?"

Brodie looked at her incredulously. "Nay, we did not know each other. He is nearly twenty years older than me and no longer lived in the Highlands by the time I arrived. However, he and I came from the Lowlands to the Highlands in the Caithness region when we were young, although for different reasons.

"Mahon's grandfather was, as you would expect, at one time Laird Donovan. He had three sons and one daughter. Mahon's father—Ruaraidh—was the third son born to his father's second wife. Ruaraidh married and had one child, a son."

"Let me guess. Mahon."

Brodie gave her a single nod. "For six years after Mahon was born, he, his mother, and his father, lived happily together until tragedy struck when Ruaraidh supposedly died fighting in the Battle of Largs."

"You said *supposedly*."

It was not directly part of Mahon's story, but it was an interesting tidbit, so Brodie told her anyway. "The way Mahon explained it makes the accounting of what happened to his father somewhat suspicious. It was reported by several Donovan soldiers who had been at Largs that Ruaraidh was very much alive and uninjured when the battle was over. And yet he never made it back home.

"No one questioned Ruaraidh's disappearance—lots of things might have happened that would explain his death. However, a week later, Mahon's grandfather died in his sleep. Again, understandable; the man was old. But rumors started when, within days, Ruaraidh's eldest brother and the clan's new laird, also died from a supposed accident. Somehow the laird's horse was spooked and lost its footing. When it reared, the laird fell off and the horse fell as well . . . on the laird. A week later, Mahon's uncle succumbed to his injuries."

"*A dheagh-thighearna,*" Shinae said softly, in slight shock. Supposed was right.

"This made Mahon's brother, Tearlach, the new laird

of the Donovan clan. With no emotional ties to the Donovan clan and the possibility that her son might also be considered a possible threat from his uncle, Mahon's mother moved north to live with Clan Mhurich, where she was raised."

"How did Mahon come to be laird?" she asked impatiently. The story so far had nothing to do with why Mahon Donovan arrived at Castle Lochlen or brought Taveon with him, but she was fascinated by it and wanted Brodie to continue.

Brodie hid a smile at her eagerness to hear more. It was a somber story, but admittedly, it was interesting.

"Now Tearlach was thirty years old when he became laird and allegedly was highly ambitious. Mahon believes the suspicious nature of his father and grandfather's deaths was the real reason behind his mother taking him and journeying north to live, train, and grow strong." Brodie shrugged his shoulders.

"It makes sense. I'd probably do the same and protect my children from any more *unfortunate accidents*." The last words definitely were said sarcastically.

"Child*ren?*" Shinae repeated, emphasizing the concept of there being more than one.

Brodie shrugged. He was not keen on the noises, messes, and chaos little people caused, but a wee little girl running around and an older brother to protect her appealed to him.

Shinae pretended to swat his leg, which was now outstretched before him. "Continue," she urged.

"Tearlach ruled for nine and twenty years, and history does not record him favorably."

"How so?"

"Oh, nothing mysterious or remarkable, just that under Tearlach's rule, the Donovan clan was guided into ruin in every way you could imagine. Tearlach spent too much time eating and toying with women to guide his people. His army was small, untrained, and completely unprepared for Edward I when he invaded the Lowlands."

"That's so awful."

"Aye, it was, but you might find this interesting. Tearlach died the exact same way his father did. A horse fell on him."

Shinae's eyes grew large. "*A shaoghail*," she whispered under her breath. She thought her family a little odd because her father was a traveling merchant and took his family with him, but it included nothing sinister. "What happened then?"

"What you would expect. Mahon became laird."

"Tearlach had no sons or daughters?"

"He never married, but rumor was that while Tearlach had several bastards, none of them survived to adulthood. When he passed, the clan eagerly sought out new leadership and summoned Mahon to return and be their new chief. He came to a clan in the Lowlands, with people and traditions he did not know, and a place he barely remembered. At five and thirty, he had to give up his family, his friends, his ranking position in the Clan Mhurich army because of duty. Laird Mahon Donovan was not and is still not interested in power.

"What he returned to was a pitiful clan that had once been moderate in size that was made weak and mocked by its neighbors. Mahon worked tirelessly over the next decade, growing the clan and protecting its clansmen from the English. He built relationships with neighboring clans, such as the Dunstans."

"Wait, that's *your* name. I assumed something had happened and no other Dunstans existed."

"They do in a way. When Colin became laird, most of the younger Dunstan clansmen and women started calling themselves McTiernays and soon wore the dark blue and green. Many of the older ones combined names, calling themselves Dunstan-McTiernays."

"You don't, though," Shinae said, pausing between each word.

"Aye." Brodie admitted. "At first, it was because I felt a loyalty to my father and when I went to help Laird Donovan, it wasn't an issue that I still wore the Dunstan plaid. When I returned to Lochlen, the home of Colin McTiernay, everyone had gotten used to being known as McTiernays, whereas I had not."

"So why is Laird Donovan *here*?"

"Mahon says that after he ensured his own clan's harvest was brought in, he wanted to stop by to see the McTiernays as it has been five years since any of them had come down to visit. He wanted to introduce his heir, his aunt's only child."

"You don't believe him."

Brodie shrugged his shoulders. "Mahon is an honest man, so it is true he wanted to personally visit with the McTiernays, introduce Edwin, and get assurances that their alliance is still strong despite sending me back. But I overheard one of Mahon's soldiers say that it was Taveon who encouraged the visit. And until I know why, I want you nowhere near him. And until we know who stabbed Edwin, I don't want you going anywhere alone."

Shinae knew those orders had been given to all the McTiernay wives, but she was not sure she would have argued regardless. Maybe the man who stabbed Edwin was the same person she was to warn Conan about, but it was just as possible there were two murderers walking among them. The pressure of holding this knowledge to herself was no longer a burden she could carry alone.

"Do you consider having secrets being dishonest?" Shinae asked, nervous as to how Brodie might answer.

"Secrets?" he repeated, and his eyebrows arched in surprise. When Shinae said nothing, he answered, "Nay, almost everyone has them." Shinae was about to release a sign of relief when he continued. "Then again, it depends on the nature of the secret and who it's being kept from. Of course, between you and me, there should not be any secrets. Don't you agree?"

"What about when you made a promise? I mean, even if there were no impediments when you made the pledge, but later one arose, are you not still bound by your vow?"

Brodie was getting a sinking feeling in his gut. "It is not dishonest to keep a secret already made, but if you were not to share it with me, it would feel kind of like a betrayal. I don't want to know secrets made between women about new gowns or what is being served for the evening meal, but most other things, aye, I expect to be told. Preferably before any promises are exchanged. Wives should especially share any promises to be silent with her husband and vice versa. I want to know about your squabbles, things you are excited about or dread.

I would like to share mine as well, knowing that it would stay just between us. That kind of openness, however, is new to me, and probably to you as well. We will just have to be patient with each other."

Patient, Shinae repeated to herself. She sat still, staring at the fire, thinking. It was like a quiet foreboding had come over Lochlen with Taveon's arrival, and she was the only one who possibly knew why.

She had made a vow to Cyric about keeping what he told her to herself until her sister arrived. Only then was she to let Conan and Mhàiri know the danger they were in and who the traitor was if became known to her. The tardy couple was supposed to have arrived already, but she had learned the couple was known for being significantly tardy to most events, more interested in mapping Scotland and its clan borders. No word had been received giving any insight to their intentions. Though unlikely, they could decide not to even come.

Shinae stood up and started pacing. The promise she had made did not seem that difficult at the time, but she had not been married then, nor did she expect to be carrying the burden for so long.

Brodie watched Shinae in silence, waiting until she was ready to speak. Something was obviously bothering her, and he had a dreadful feeling that he was not going to like what it was. First, though, she needed to tell him.

"I have a secret." She waved her hand, clearly nervous. "Undoubtedly, you have surmised as much."

That foreboding feeling he had was getting worse.

"Do you know Cyric Schellden? I believe he is related to the McTiernays."

Brodie shook his head no. "I've heard of him, and I

think we briefly met at Conan's wedding. He's a Schellden, so he's most likely related to Craig and Crevan's wives, Meriel and Raelynd."

"He also works as an attaché for King Robert."

Brodie sat upright and took a deep breath. He had assumed Shinae's secret was about her, but her mentioning the king meant it was something far different.

Shinae wrung her hands. "Oh, I don't know where to begin."

"At the very beginning. Even if you think I know things, tell me anyway, just to ensure there is no confusion."

"There is more than one beginning. To understand one, you must know the other."

"Then tell me the one in which you are involved."

Shinae nodded and sat back down. "When the English army was being driven out of Scotland this past summer, they were burning abbeys as they went. I was at Dryburgh Abbey when they attacked. Most of us were in the dining hall eating the midday meal when the English struck. They came in through the main door to the hall and the abbess ordered everyone to escape using the door that led to the kitchens and then out the back. To help gain enough time for them to leave, I stayed to help delay the English soldiers who barged in."

"You *what?*" Brodie had not intended to shout or interrupt, but he had not been able to stop his reaction. "You *delayed* them . . . by yourself?" He knew she meant fought. "What were you thinking?"

"I was thinking that I needed to save my fellow sisters," Shinae replied sharply. "I did not really intend on killing anyone, I was acting on instinct. That was when—"

"You *killed* someone?" His voice again rose in volume as he envisioned her having to defend herself against trained English soldiers. They would have no care that she was a nun, not if she thrust herself into their path.

Feeling defensive, Shinae snapped, "I killed four. The fifth man I only injured and Cyric took the man with him."

Brodie stood up and raked his fingers through his hair. He was angry. He knew Shinae had lived through it, but just the *idea* that she had been put in such mortal danger was still terrifying. He moved to stand behind the chair he had been sitting in and gripped its back, his knuckles turning white. "Go on."

Shinae looked at him and wondered if she should continue, but she had no choice now. Deep down, she had known that Brodie would be upset but he was livid. And if he was that upset now, he was never going to want to see her again when he knew it all. "I was fighting the last one when a Scottish man—Cyric—came in and stopped me. He did not seem upset by what I did or what I could do, just the opposite. He was delighted. I did not find out why until he came to Melrose a month later. He told me I needed to go to Lochlen Castle and—"

Brodie continued to remain where he was. He had better never meet Cyric Schellden again because he was not sure what he would do if that were to happen.

Shinae licked her lips. "And he asked me to spy for the king."

"Silence!" Conor roared. The room that had started so quiet that it echoed anything Shinae said had grown to a cacophony of angry voices. Conor then signaled something to Colin, who abruptly left the room.

Shinae had hardly said more than a few words when the McTiernays' puzzled expressions had transformed into stiff angry ones before they erupted all at once. Conor sat eerily silent letting everyone release their initial shock and anger upon hearing her story. Despite his silence, it was clear as clan chief, he was in charge. Though only visiting the Lowland McTiernays, which were under the leadership of his brother Colin, this matter would be decided by him.

"Repeat what you just said one more time, but this time start with Cyric's return," Conor McTiernay said in a low, solemn voice.

For what felt like hours, they had pummeled questions at her, repeating their shock at the secret she had been carrying. Talking over one another, cursing loudly, only bits and pieces of her answers were being heard. It had been frustrating, but surprisingly preferable to the weighty silence now filling the room.

Shinae swallowed and began to explain once more that Cyric had sent her to warn Conan about the danger he was in, and that she was to tell no one else, especially not Conor or any of the McTiernay brothers. Each time she said as much, it only seemed to make things worse. When she had first told Brodie, he had immediately risen to his feet, dressed, left the room, and returned just a couple of minutes later. He had then pointed to her gown, rumpled on the floor, and ordered her to put it on quickly and meet him in the great hall. He rushed back out of the room, and Shinae knew he was waking the McTiernays. Cyric had been right. The moment someone else knew the promise he had made her make, the entire family would be alerted, which most likely was going to signal the traitor that something was happening.

She should have never said anything.

Looking each McTiernay in their striking blue eyes that were riveted on her, Shinae's already rapid pulse increased. She had been placed in the center of the half circle made by seven padded chairs facing the hearth. A few logs had been added to the hot embers and were now ablaze, but to her the room was cold and unwelcoming. Not all the chairs were occupied. Brodie stood by the hearth, arms crossed, his body rigid. She knew he was mad that she had kept such a serious secret from him but was not positive that all his anger was aimed at her, or if it might be at the horrible situation.

Conor reached over and lightly took her hand and his storm-colored gray eyes softened. The gentle gesture gave her the encouragement to continue. "Who did Cyric talk to that told him we have a traitor in our midst?"

With a slight shrug of her shoulders, Shinae answered. "I honestly don't know why he thought the McTiernays were in danger."

Colin reentered the room and to Conor said, "It is done."

Conor asked, "How many?"

"Two on horses, one to Conan and another to Cyric."

"W-w-what exactly did he say again?" Crevan asked, his voice, despite his stutter, clipped and full of tension.

Shinae winced at the snapped question. "He told me that over the last decade Edward II had converted a handful of Scots to betray their country by infiltrating large influential clans . . . and when word came that it was time, they were to kill someone important to the clan's chief." Anger-filled mumbles started again. Conor rubbed his thumb soothingly over the back of her hand and sat still until his brothers had stopped their grumbling.

Shinae felt tears slip down her cheek. Brodie did not seem to care about the rough tones being used, or that it was Conor, not he, who was comforting her. Then again, he was the one who called them all together, knowing it would result in a nasty inquisition.

Taking back her hand, Shinae continued. "Cyric told me that based on the other clans who had not been fore-warned, it was always the most vulnerable targeted. The McTiernays were next and the assassination would happen when the clan brothers all gathered together this summer. Cyric told me Conan and my sister are the most vulnerable out of the six of you. All know they travel around without any protection other than what they can provide for themselves." She glanced at all five brothers. "You all have armies, soldiers, personal guards. Conan and my sister do not."

"*Cyric* really told you all this?" Craig posed incredulously, practically accusing her with his tone that she was speaking falsehoods. "He told a helpless *nun* that Scottish clans were being attacked by someone close to the clan chiefs. Why?"

Shinae said nothing and looked over wide-eyed at Brodie for support. He still refused to look in her direction. His icy expression worried her more than anything else. It was the same unemotional look he had given her when he had left to gather the McTiernays.

Feeling abandoned and in need of protection, she

narrowed her eyes and covertly touched her daggers through the hidden alterations of her gown. Having the bottoms ripped out of each pocket gave her easy access to the weapons strapped and sheathed on each leg; suddenly, she felt the need to assure herself that she had not forgotten to put them on before she left.

"To weaken them, and in return weaken Scotland and the king's ability to prevent England from invading once more," Conor answered, looking at Craig with a steely gaze for several seconds.

Conor sat back, looking far more relaxed than she suspected he really was. "Clans Hamilton, Steward, and Kennedy all have lost someone in the last year. Hamilton's mother, who was a strong matriarch, one day never woke up. Some suspected her drink had been laced with hemlock. The wife of Laird Steward, who was known for her exceptional riding skills, mysteriously died after being bucked off her personal horse. Kennedy's daughter went into premature labor. Both she and the clan's next heir did not make it. I knew of the deaths but never thought they were anything but accidental until now."

Cole snorted. "So, the king doesn't warn any of the lairds, but informs a nun with instructions to tell Conan he was in danger?" he said in disbelief. Like the others, his deep voice and demeanor carried another, unspoken message. *There was more that she was not telling them.*

Shinae said nothing and looked again at Brodie for support. He still refused to look at her. Realizing he was not going to help her, she straightened up, pushed her chin forward, and felt her timidity disappear. She was on her own. "I do not know why Cyric asked me instead of sending word to you. Perhaps it's because my sister is Conan's wife. Then again, it could be that as a former nun I wouldn't be suspected of anything nefarious, allowing me to mingle with a variety of clansmen in an effort to learn who was less loyal to the McTiernays—after all it wasn't by choice they lost their Dunstan name. As a nun, Cyric could have thought I would be true to my word and keep silent because he feared if you knew, you would announce such knowledge with a noticeable meeting, such as this, alerting the castle that something was amiss. It also might be that *Cyric watched me single-handedly kill four English soldiers* and knew even if I was caught, I could defend myself."

Craig grunted and a couple of seconds later two knives whizzed by him. All eyes but Conor and Colin's gaped at the two wobbling knives embedded in a disassembled trestle table leaning against the wall. "I threw two so all would know that you were not my target," she told Craig. Her own hostility at their treatment was evident.

Suddenly, Brodie moved. He was behind her, with his hands on her shoulders, encouraging her to sit back down. She did so, and he gave her a squeeze. It was the first indication in hours that he *was* there and that she was not alone.

Conor eyed her. "You have made your point." He then held each of his brothers' eyes for long enough to make it clear that all snipes were to end. "I think our anger comes not only at learning our younger brother is in danger, but that you have been as well."

Another squeeze. This one much stronger.

Calmer, Shinae told them what she'd found. "Since I arrived at Lochlen, I have been praying for Mhàiri to be delayed until I could figure out potential suspects. Anyone behaving oddly, and while a few people are disgruntled—something expected in a clan this size— not a single person has seemed suspect until a week ago."

Crevan hissed, "Taveon."

"I cannot prove it, but when I was tending Edwin someone snuck into his room and tried to kill both of us. Thankfully, I awoke in time to throw my knife at him. I missed, but it frightened him and he immediately fled the tower."

"You never told me that," Brodie whispered in her ear, more than a little upset at discovering the attempt along with everyone else.

"I don't think the attacker wanted me in particular," Shinae tried to assure them. "He probably didn't realize I was there at first."

Craig looked at her appreciatively, "That knife skill of yours could work to our favor." He glanced around to his brothers. "Think about it. Taveon hates the idea that he was not named Mahon's heir, which explains why he went after Edwin. And all saw Taveon's cold stare at her all night. He probably wants her dead as well. She would make the perfect bait during. . . Dunlop's wedding? When he goes to strike them again, we'll be ready and catch him in the act."

Conor looked dubious. "We don't know if the traitor is Taveon. Cyric said the most vulnerable *McTiernay*, was the killer's target, not Donovan."

Brodie was incredulous. None of them seemed to understand what she had just revealed, and if they thought for one minute he would let them use her as *bait* . . . "Her name is Shinae and she is my *wife*," Brodie emphasized.

Shinae took a deep breath. It was the first time Brodie had spoken, and it was now clear that at least some of his anger was directed toward the men who had been questioning her.

"She did not volunteer to know this information, nor should she have *ever* been asked to spy or almost be victim to a dangerous killer. Three things none of you have bothered to acknowledge," he snarled.

Brodie then helped her up and led Shinae out of the room.

Brodie swept Shinae into his arms the moment the great hall doors closed behind him. The day had been an incredibly long one, and he was amazed Shinae could even talk, let alone endure, the last couple of hours. He had known that questions would be asked and that their anger would accompany her story. He watched them with a cold stare that had silenced a few of them. But in the end, they had started to take out their fear with doubt and nastiness.

Brodie tucked the soft blanket from years of use around his wife. He could not remember a time when someone had done it for him, but he instinctively did it in hopes that it made her feel safe. He just wished it could have been his arms wrapped around her.

"I'm glad you are not mad at me anymore for keeping my secret."

With her back to him, Brodie could not tell if her eyes were closed. He kissed her neck. "I was never angry with you, but I'll admit to wanting to murder Cyric. If he and I were to meet again, he would learn very quickly how much I treasure my wife. The rage going through me is from knowing he so casually put you in danger."

Several seconds passed by and he thought Shinae was asleep when a soft, "He didn't" came.

Brodie did not argue. She was wrong, but would never believe it because of her skill with small blades. Tonight, however, explained many things that had bothered him, but he had kept his doubts to himself mostly just to keep peace between them. Since the day after their marriage, Shinae had been uncomfortably friendly with every man at Lochlen. She did not flirt exactly. There was nothing exactly wrong with how she acted and as far as he knew, it had not caused any gossip, but he had witnessed her friendliness with the male gender time and time again. Especially during the feasts. It was the perfect setting to mingle and chat with anyone and everyone—something Shinae seemed more than interested in doing. He had even hovered over her a few times. Nothing really had changed and the conversations had always been innocuous—their marriage, did they plan to have children, did they consider themselves Dunstans, and if Brodie planned to rejoin Colin's army. In reality, she had been searching for the man planning to kill Conan.

Shinae might be clever enough with her blades if attacked straight on, but not if it were done covertly. To purposefully send her down in search of someone intent on murdering someone else was inexcusable.

He kissed her shoulder. "I must return."

"Wait," Shinae whispered, rolling over. "Why?"

Brodie held still for a moment, stood up, and went to put another log on the fire. When he came back, she was looking at him expectantly. He did not want to answer, for it would only lead to more questions, and the problem with smart wives was that they asked smart questions. Shinae desperately needed to sleep, and his answer would only rile her again. He did not want to tell her even a small lie after all they had been through, so Brodie did the only thing he could think of to get out of answering her simple question and started to undo his belt to get undressed.

"Good question. They are all probably back with their wives, because nothing can be decided until Conan arrives." It was possible, but he doubted it. The McTiernays were more likely discussing next steps as no one was around. Meeting in the middle of the day might arouse the suspicion Cyric had foreseen.

Shinae yawned. "I wonder what is taking Conan and Mhàiri so long. I thought they would have been here by now."

"Expect him to arrive in the next day or two, depending on how long it takes Conan's heralds to find him," Brodie said, slipping between the sheets and pulling her back against his chest. "Mmmm, much better than some drafty room with tired, angry men."

"Is that where Colin went? To send someone to get Conan?" Shinae asked and heard him whisper, "Aye," in her ear.

She snuggled closer and let things happen as they always did when their skins touched. Their mating was indulgent, rapacious, and gratifying. Brodie held her suspended between two worlds, until they both were too exhausted to do anything but hold each other, entwined in each other's arms.

He lay there, listening to Shinae's slow and consistent breaths, wondering if what he was feeling was love. His own parents had spoken the words freely and often. He vaguely remembered them kissing and hugging each other frequently, and he could only recall a couple of times they ever raised their voices to each other. As a young child, he never had thought about their loving relationship and how rare it was. Later in life, he assumed those couples who fought had underlying issues in their marriage. Perhaps they were not as compatible as they thought when they first wed. He had even thought that about Laird Colin and Lady Makenna. All could see how much they loved each other, and yet all were aware that they infuriated each other too.

Until today, he had not truly understood how one spouse could absolutely, to their very core, infuriate the other and yet at the same time love them just as fiercely. He now understood why the McTiernays, who all had an inclination of erupting the moment they felt anger, stayed not just together . . . but *happily* together. If a couple did not argue periodically, it most likely meant one of them, or maybe both, were suppressing thoughts and feelings that would eventually erupt, possibly creating a rift in the marriage. Misunderstandings were more easily handled when addressed at the moment of occurrence.

He sent a silent vow to his father that he would fight

with anyone who threatened his wife. Shinae was never going to be in danger again.

Brodie slowly pulled his arm back and carefully got to his feet, glad he had not awakened her. He had lain there thinking for probably half an hour, waiting for her to fall into a deep state of sleep. He quickly dressed and closed the door as quietly as he could before heading to the great hall.

He approached the doors and stepped inside to snores. He was not surprised that the McTiernays had passed out rather than returning to their chambers. They must have talked until they fell unconscious. Brodie doubted he missed much. Very little could be decided until Conan arrived. The only reason he had left Shinae's side was the off chance that the brothers were still considering using her to lure the killer into a trap.

He had noticed that no one else had been invited to their earlier interrogation. Dunlop and Drake had been absent, but not by accident. The only reason he had been allowed to attend was because it was he who had brought Shinae's revelation to their attention. He had no idea if they intended to include him in future discussions, but he was going insert himself regardless. Shinae was no longer going to be entangled in how this unknown killer would be found and dealt with. He understood that Conan was the intended target, but the man's wife was Shinae's sister, and everything Conan said to Mhàiri would be relayed to Shinae. Just the knowledge Mhàiri relayed to her would compel Shinae to get involved. To think otherwise would be foolish. To believe he could prevent it was even more foolish. The most he could do was ensure he had a say in any decisions the McTiernays made.

Brodie was about to turn back when he saw the movement of a leg and a foot, highlighted by the main hearth's dying fire. The large chair the person was sitting in was the one Shinae had been using when she told all about the vow she had made. Brodie began to walk toward the outstretched man wondering which McTiernay had yet to retire.

He had thought it would be Colin, as he was laird of Lochlen, but it was Conor McTiernay—a man he both knew yet didn't. The mighty chief was known to be fair, demanding, and a great strategist, but that was concerning battles and how to fight and win wars. Just how the great clan chief handled complex, elusive situations, however, Brodie did not know.

Conor did not look at him when he approached but waved his hand at the cushioned armchair next to him. After Brodie sat down, Conor spoke in a deep, casual tone about nothing in particular. "I like these chairs," he said in a deep voice, just shy of a whisper. "They are large, comfortable, and the backs are high enough one can recline and still have their head supported."

This Brodie already knew. He also knew their rarity as most lairds only used hard, wooden chairs made of oak. "These are the ones Laird Dunstan had ordered when he was still laird, but it was your brother Colin who commissioned them to have cushions added."

"It's the McTiernay way. My father started it. He was not a vain man, but he did believe that presentation was a large part of influencing other lairds' opinions. They are also far more comfortable."

Brodie sat and gazed at the fire, wondering how he could state that he wanted to be there when the McTiernays spoke to Conan. After several minutes of quiet, Conor spoke. "Your wife is a brave woman."

"Aye, brave and smart and reckless."

"Makes you feel lucky, doesn't it?"

Brodie gave it a thought and found that he agreed. Foolish and boring had no appeal. "A complicated woman does keep it interesting."

"A spirited one does as well. Women without the conviction of their opinions are limp, unable to make a stand. It appeals to some, but not me."

Brodie listened but wanted to get back to Shinae. "What did I miss?"

"Not much," Conor answered. "We don't know enough yet."

"Do you think Shinae is right? That it's Taveon?" Brodie asked, unable to disguise the apprehension he felt.

"Could be, but I wouldn't wager anything on it."

Shinae just lay there, on their bed, exactly as Brodie had left her. She had not moved a muscle; even her eyelids remained closed, but she was far from asleep. Mentally debating what she should do—if anything. It was obvious that Brodie did not want her involved and was livid that she ever had been involved. And she understood why. There was one, possibly *two* killers within Lochlen's walls with the freedom to wander about and strike at a whim. She had no proof that one of them was

Taveon except her heavy dislike of the man and the attack against Edwin was too suspicious knowing how much he had been wanting to be named the Donovan heir. The malevolent glint in his eye every time he looked at Brodie gave her the chills. A few times he caught her watching him, and he just curled his lips into a disturbing smile as if to say, "I won."

Just the memory of it made Shinae want to acquiesce to Brodie's request and avoid him at all times. But that promise was made before her revelation. She should forget the whole thing, and just focus on her sister's imminent arrival. And yet, a nagging inner voice said that she needed to do something. Just what she needed to do, however, remained a mystery. On that subject, the fickle voice remained silent.

Shinae rubbed her eyes and slowly sat up, still feeling drowsy. Brodie usually rose when it was *fàire*, but not her. She and the early morning sun did not like each other. Lying back down, Shinae snuggled against her pillow, intending on getting a couple more hours of sleep. A rapid tapping came from the other side of the room, and by the third time, it was obvious they were not going away. Shinae grabbed a robe and threw it on.

The door creaked as she opened it a crack, wondering who it could be. "Mornin', me lady." A heavyset but cheerful gray-haired woman with small blue eyes, noticeable jowls, and plump cheeks was carrying a tray of items, including what smelled like warm mulled mead. Shinae's mouth began to water and she opened the door wide for the woman to enter.

"I was told to send this to ye early this morning and ensure that ye got the freshest of breads and that the mulled mead was hot. Seems like yer sweetheart wants to make sure ye get plenty of food, and by the look of ye, I can see why." Her mouth twisted humorously, and she playfully wiggled her thin eyebrows. "Newlyweds need to keep up their strength, for their nighttime play—or daytime when both are available."

Shinae gasped, her eyes widening in surprise at the woman's forwardness. It was obvious the servant was just teasing, and while Shinae had heard such remarks made between others, never had anything so forthright been said to her. Such opinions were just not said where she came from.

Seeing the shocked look in Shinae's green eyes, the woman clicked her tongue. "Oh, Lordy, ye really were a nun," she said under her breath.

She placed the tray on the small table, shoving the candle and a small washing bowl to the far back against the wall. Then, picking up the pewter mug, she shoved it into Shinae's hands. Shinae almost dropped it, the metal was so hot. She started switching her grasp between hands every few seconds until her skin became accustomed to the heat.

"Ah, now don't get all twisted up about a few jests, *stìorlag*." Her hands on her hips and her powder-blue eyes darted between Shinae and to the floor in front of the hearth, where there were scattered dishes on the blanket Brodie had laid out. "But I am glad to see that mess by the fire and this," she said with a bit of mirth, pointing to the messed-up sheets on the bed. It was obvious that more than just sleeping had occurred in it. The servant immediately started to pull on the sheets. "Might as well take these now and get them washed so ye two can use them again tonight."

"I . . . I . . ." Shinae stammered. There were so many thoughts and questions swirling in her head, she was unable to form a sentence or even a question before the woman started talking again.

"Father Tam, now that's another one needs to learn how to relax. Maybe it's because the maids are putting too much starch in his laundry. Foolish man likes it. I'll talk to them about that."

Some nuns had liked to add starch to the water, but Shinae never did. The resulting stiffness made her garments uncomfortable and itchy for days; it was weeks before it was comfortable to wear. She preferred to use soap made from ash lye and animal fat. Once clean, they would lay everything out on the grassy ground, hoping the garments would dry before the sun dropped.

"I *never* want that stuff near anything I or Brodie wear," Shinae blurted out.

"Ye are a little wiser than Father Tam . . . he's still young and has much to learn." She continued to gather the sheets on the bed and started to chuckle. "The young man got all squeamish about asking if he thought ye and yer man did anything but sleep at night in his bed. And he's the one who married ye!" She gathered the sheets in her arms and threw them in the hall. "*Laundry!*" she shouted loudly and then came back in. "Where does the man think bairns come from?"

"Probably a good thing he is a priest and doesn't need to know," Shinae responded without thought.

"Ha!" the woman barked out.

"I'm sorry, but who are you?"

The older woman did a sloppy curtsy. "I'm Gert. I don't have an official title, but you can think of me as the castle keeper." Gert leaned over the bed and whispered, "I'm sorry we have not met before, but his lairdship's brothers being here has kept me on the run. If they weren't so nice, I probably would have been down on me sickbed with Ros, he's the castle's steward," she explained.

"Oh, I've met him," Shinae said, thinking of the ornery old man. She sipped some of the mead; it was delicious. She extended out her arm and offered Gert her mug. "This is wonderful. Please try some."

Gert furrowed her brows in astonishment. "Ye're a *bòidheach* on the inside as well as the out, aren't ye?" And took a sip of the mead. "Aye, this is a fine batch. Glen, me husband, is wicked good with the liquids. He's in charge of the buttery, and a wise choice said by all who drink his ale and mead. His cider is not me favorite, but the children seem to enjoy it well enough."

Shinae took the mug back and sat down, still puzzled as to what a castle keeper was. Dryburgh Abbey never had castle keepers and she had never known anyone who had. The steward ran the abbey, and she assumed he also handled the domestic affairs of the household. "Just what does a castle keeper do?"

"Aye, 'tis strange, but I overheard of Lady Laurel and Lady Raelynd discussing their housekeepers and all that they did, and I realized that is exactly what I was, except Lochlen is certainly no house. Every clanswoman takes care of her home, her family, and their needs. They are housekeepers. Me? I'm a castle keeper," Gert stated proudly.

Shinae waved for Gert to sit down and join her. "How does Lady Makenna feel about you calling yourself her castle keeper?"

Gert scratched her head. "I don't think she knows, but I doubt she'd mind, as I've been doing this since about the time when Lady Makenna had her second child. Ros started slowing down, letting me handle more and more of what needs to be done so he could focus on the responsibilities he actually enjoys—overseeing wages, the stables, any discipline that needs to be done, interacting with the laird's commanders, procuring wares, filtering disputes, and so much more. The castle help was only getting a bit of the direction needed. That man was more than happy to let me see to the kitchens, weavers, candlemakers, chambermaids, and any staff supporting the castle."

Gert took a last gulp, slapped her knees and stood up. "*Mo chreach*, I need to move on, but am glad to know you and your husband will still be here when everybody leaves. Now I need to go and see about our latest guests and ensure their needs are being attended."

Shinae stood up as well to close the door after Gert swished out the door and down the hall. Just as she was about to lower the latch, she reopened the door and peeked out. The sheets had disappeared. Gert was a lively woman with a gift for gab. The kind that had at one time irritated her. Now it felt welcoming in a way. And it gave her a very clear idea of what to do next.

CHAPTER TEN

Shinae looked in the great hall and saw all the McTiernay brothers inside and asleep in chairs or lying on the main table. Brodie was not among them. She closed the door as softly as she could and was about to go look elsewhere for their wives when she spied several women carrying mounds of household léines, under-clothing, and linens. She knew immediately what was happening, remembering all too well the wash days at the abbey. Newer nuns did not only wash their own things, but those belonging to anyone who was considered senior or important.

They would store their dirty stuff for weeks until a beautiful day came, perfect for washing, smoothing, and drying. First, the newer nuns had to carry everything out to the river—washing tubs, soap, and washing bats. She personally had only used bats to swirl the clothes in the tub, but these McTiernay washerwomen had access to dolly legs. They looked like small milking stools on a long stick, which made it easier and faster to agitate the cloth.

Suddenly, she saw Gert exit *Tòrr-dubh* scurrying to

Forfar Tower, barking orders to the washerwomen as they headed toward the gate. Shinae waved to her, catching her attention. "Oh, I am so glad to see you," she said, hurrying to Gert's side.

Gert furrowed her brow in puzzlement and shifted her load to rest on her hip. "And why is that? We just spoke not even a half hour ago."

Shinae beamed her brightest smile. "Because I suspect you know everything that goes on in this place."

Gert proudly puffed out her chest. "Aye, I do. So what do you need, *sìochaire*? It's a fine day and I've ordered the laundresses to buck everything for at least two hours. I need to be there, otherwise there'll be a lot more chattering than bucking." Bucking involved lengthy soaking of laundry in lye, which was a way of whitening white and off-white cloth.

"*Gabh mo leithscéal,*" Shinae apologized, "but do you know where Lady Laurel is right now?"

"Aye, third floor of the Canmore Tower." Gert nodded in the direction and with a "*Slàn agat!*" she left with a cheerful parting.

Laurel opened the door a crack and gave Shinae a displeased look. "I assume this is important as you are usually the last to rise," she said, opening the door and waving for Shinae to enter.

Growing up, making shelters, sleeping on the ground of the small rooms at the priory and abbey, Shinae had thought her and Brodie's chambers were nice and somewhat roomy. She now understood what people meant when they said something was luxurious. Laurel waved to one of the high-backed, dark red-and-blue padded chairs.

"It is important," Shinae assured Laurel, hiding her envy. Even just rising from bed with her hair slightly mussed and a crease across her cheek, Laurel looked attractive. "Have you spoken with your husband since the party?"

Laurel went to go and pour two mugs of water for them. Handing Shinae one, she sat down and said, "I have not, but as Conor never returned last night and your impromptu arrival, I am beginning to think that more happened last night than his getting drunk on ale and passing out with his brothers."

Shinae took a swallow of the tepid water and reconvinced herself that keeping what she knew to herself was not the right thing to do. As she explained all that had happened in the early morning hours, the more awake Laurel became. When Shinae reached the part when Craig suggested she become bait, Laurel rose to her feet. "Oh that most certainly is not going to happen. I absolutely cannot believe the man suggested it nor can I believe the others did not immediately squash the idea."

"They might have, but Brodie shuffled me out of the room right after that."

"We need more information, and then we need to gather the wives."

"How?" Shinae asked. "How do you intend to find out what our husbands are planning?"

Laurel winked at her. "By asking for help from two of the best eavesdroppers I know." She went to the door and whispered to the chambermaid sleeping just outside her door to awaken and go to fetch her two oldest daughters.

Shinae was baffled. "Isn't it too late to discover what they decided?"

Laurel went to her chest and pulled out a sky-blue ensemble. "Nothing has been decided," she said confidently, "and it won't be until Conan arrives, which will probably be sometime today. I would wager all my clothes that once Conan and Mhàiri heard Colin's herald that he stopped dragging his feet and is rushing to come here with Mhàiri at his side."

A surge of joy went through Shinae, followed by another surge—this one of fear. "I must tell Mhàiri all that is happening, and that she and Conan are in danger the moment she arrives."

"Of course," Laurel replied, stepping behind a screen to dress, "hopefully by that time we will have learned what the men are planning or hopefully they just come out and tell us. Unfortunately, it seems they are intending to keep us in the dark until they deem it time to let us know."

"If Brodie had his preference, I would remain clueless until the killer was found and successfully executed."

Several minutes later, the sharp taps of two hands could be heard on the door. Before Laurel could welcome them in, the door opened, and Brenna and Bonny came in and walked directly to their parents' bed, collapsing on it. Both looked like they had fallen asleep in their clothes, probably because they had. They had made merry as a result of being released from their confines to attend the last night's feast.

"I'm glad you both came so quickly."

"Rosina made us," Brenna mumbled into the blanket. "She doesn't like us."

"That's because she only likes Brion," added Bonny, her eyes practically closed. "She's constantly playing or cuddling with him."

Brenna grumbled, "Better him than me."

"True," Bonny said while yawning.

Shinae had been told that the woman assigned to help with the younger children had been with Lady Makenna for years. With five children, Makenna did need help, especially with the surge of visitors and their children. But with her fondness of the little boy, one would have thought Rosina was Laurel's nanny, not Makenna's.

"Well, I still thank you, for I have something I would like you to do." Just as the moans started, Laurel added, "You will need to promise to keep it a secret. I will decide what and when to tell your father." Brenna's eyes popped open, but when her mother added, "And unfortunately, it involves eavesdropping." Brenna sat up suddenly quite awake, poking Bonny to pay attention and make the necessary promises.

A few hours later, just as Laurel predicted, Conan and Mhàiri rode in on the herald's horse through the front gate, eager to know what was so urgent. The unfortunate herald had been told to return to Lochlen, driving their covered wagon that carried all their things.

Once inside, Conan had briefly kissed his wife and then gone directly to see his brothers, leaving Mhàiri to hand the horse over to a stable boy to cool and feed. The moment she passed through the main gate all the McTiernay wives gathered around Mhàiri, hugging her, expressing how glad they were to see her again. Even though it had been five years since she and Mhàiri had seen each other, Shinae could see how tired her sister was from riding much of the night and suggested that she go and relax. They could talk later. Mhàiri did so without complaint and followed Makenna to their temporary bedchamber in *Tòrr-dubh*. Shinae was thankful Mhàiri had not resisted, for what she had to tell her little sister needed to be heard with an alert mind.

While Mhàiri slumbered, it gave Shinae the opportunity to see the one person she needed to speak with before all the wives gathered together again. Someone who would be just as affected by the men's current plans to find and capture the unknown killer.

"*My* wedding?" Isilmë repeated.

"That is the men's latest idea."

"Well, they are going to have to think of another way, because when Dunlop tells the world that he loves me, *it is going to a perfect day*. It will be a celebration where all the focus will be on Dunlop and me. It *will be* something I will remember the rest of my life," she said definitively and in raised tones.

"I want it to be that," Shinae assured her friend. "I don't want them trying to lure a killer into a trap using your wedding as a distraction."

"But this man . . . this killer, you said he tried to attack you with a . . . weapon?" Isilmë asked incredulously while pointing at the *sgian dubh* that Shinae now wore at her waist where all could see.

"Aye, but the blade wound was not one I've ever seen

before. It was narrower than those made by a dirk, and longer."

"And you believe it was Taveon?" Isilmë had a combined look of disbelief and shock. "He's always so jovial and nice to everyone."

Shinae rolled her eyes. To her it was obvious that Taveon was what he appeared to be. "He seems nice." *And vulgar*, Shinae mentally added. "Brodie does not trust him at all. And I have witnessed that Taveon only considers himself when making decisions."

"I thought everyone liked him. The women certainly do. I was not interested because I'm attracted to Dunlop."

"Perhaps, but sometimes I think Taveon likes to irritate Brodie by flirting with me."

"You're married! Why would he do that?"

Shinae decided she needed to sit down, and the only place was Isilmë's bed. Rather than moving everything to the floor, she sat down on the pile of léines and bliauts as she had seen her friend do when they last met. "I don't know. Maybe to keep Brodie from wanting to return to help Laird Donovan, or maybe I'm wrong by suspecting him."

Isilmë waved her hand and changed the subject. "Go back to this notion of using *my* wedding as a means to catch this traitor. Who knows about him?"

Shinae bit her bottom lip. "I'm not sure yet. I've only told Brodie, who of course told the McTiernay chief and his brothers." She swallowed and continued. "And Laurel . . . who told Bonny and Brenna, asking them to come help."

Isilmë stopped pacing. "Help with what?"

"Laurel directed them to eavesdrop on the men and learn what they are planning. I only know about their wedding idea because I was in the room when they first started discussing how it could work. Now that Conan has joined them, Laurel and I hope her girls discover that they have changed their minds."

Isilmë shook her head in disagreement. "That does not make sense. Why would Taveon attack Edwin? And why would he go after your sister's husband? If he's like his brothers, he would need to sneak up on the man. Are you *sure* Taveon's the traitor?"

"My instincts are telling me that Taveon is hiding something quite sinful and that he knows more than he is saying about the attack on Edwin. Yet you bring up a good point in that we are doing *exactly* what the men are, latching onto one possibility and discounting the rest."

Isilmë nodded and went to look out the window of the small room.

Seeing her friend was deep in thought, Shinae rose up from the bed and said, "If you don't mind, I need to go see my sister."

"That's right!" Isilmë squeaked as she spun around. "It's been a while since you have spoken to her."

More than a while, Shinae thought to herself, but remembered Isilmë did not have any family. "Five years. And I want you to realize that just because we are not with the Church anymore, I still consider you a sister."

Isilmë hopped over several layers of uncut cloth and hugged her. To Shinae's surprise, she found herself returning the embrace. "Aye," Isilmë said, letting Shinae go. "Sisters that share thoughts and opinions with each other! Can you imagine what the abbess would think if she saw us now? You, married, and me, who also will very soon be a wife."

An image of Isilmë's notion appeared in Shinae's mind, and the abbess had a look of disgust on her face that she often wore. "I am not sure she would want to trade places with us, despite how content we are. She enjoys her power."

Isilmë rolled her hazel eyes. "She does, doesn't she? But I also think that deep down she would be envious, especially if she truly knew how happy I am."

Shinae gave her one last squeeze. "I really do need to talk to my sister before Brenna and Bonny return."

Shinae left and was halfway down the stairs when she turned and came back. "Isilmë, we are gathering in the chapel to discuss other ideas and ways to catch this allusive traitor. Join us if you want; just don't tell anyone I invited you."

"I will tell you *exactly* why it took us so long to get here," Mhàiri said with frustration. "Conan. I love him dearly, but he is the most headstrong man in Scotland, and as soon as we received the invitation, he got it in his mind that Lochlen Castle would be swarming with children. And not just children, but loud, argumentative, unable-to-hold-a-conversation-of-any-interest *McTiernay* children." She shook her head just remembering their numerous conversations. "Even seeing Bonny again could not persuade him to get here earlier."

"Well, that fits the descriptions Father told me of your husband. But you are . . . happy?"

Mhàiri produced a large grin. "Beyond what words can convey. I'm living my dream. Aye, Conan might have some characteristics that are less than ideal, but when it is really important to me, he yields to my wants. So when Conan said that he wanted to visit the Earl of Moray and see the great Pele Tower the earl built near Duns a couple of years ago before we came here, I agreed. But that was because I knew you would still be here even if everyone else got tired of waiting and left Lochlen Castle to head back to their homes."

"And how was the grand Pele Tower? Worth the delay?"

Mhàiri wrinkled her nose, reminding Shinae of when they were young. She was taller than her little sister and her eyes a much lighter shade of green; otherwise there was little else to tell them apart. Both looked remarkably similar, with their olive complexion, lower lips that were slightly fuller than the upper, and dark, brown hair that almost looked black. "It was a tower house." Mhàiri shrugged. "I did one drawing of it. None of its features held any interest. Of course, I pretended otherwise. The earl kept promising that it would one day become the grandest estate for miles, that he was going to add on, and his descendants would do the same. The tower, he claimed, was not an end, but a beginning." Shinae laughed as her sister impersonated the earl. She wiggled a finger like their mother used to when she disapproved.

Mhàiri rolled her eyes. "I will admit that his wife, Isobel, decorated it very nicely. I might have been more impressed if I had never visited any of the Lowland castles. Some of them are rather stunning. More often than not, the laird or his wife would ask us to stay while Conan mapped out their lands."

Mhàiri took a deep breath and continued, as if she had all these stories about her adventures and no one to share them with. "Anyway, Isobel—she's married to the Earl of Moray—"

"I gathered that already."

"Well, she is King Robert's sister, and you would not believe all the stories she told me from their youth. Did you know our king speaks three languages and that he and his brothers would use it to play pranks on their educators? But for the most part, she claims King Robert was boring and read all the time, preferring learning over leisure." Mhàiri slapped her knees. "I have stories that will keep you tickled for days, but I want to know about you. What happened after I left?" She gestured at Shinae's bliaut. "I thought you had decided to join the Church."

Shinae took in a deep breath and trilled her lips together so they buzzed.

"I remember you doing that whenever Father asked you a question you did not want to answer." Mhàiri giggled. "Oh, how it infuriated Mother."

Shinae joined her and laughed at the memory. "She used to tell me that I was not going to grow up and be thought of as a lady until I learned to act like one."

"If only she could see you now. Married, as beautiful as ever—she would be proud."

"And Father?"

"Um, I don't think he would welcome the return of the buzzing sound you like to make, but he will be thrilled to see you again, especially knowing you are completely free of the long arm of the Augustinian Church."

"How is Father?"

Mhàiri shrugged her chin. "The same as you remember, maybe a bit grayer. I think he wants to be a grandfather and has given up on Conan and I ever expanding."

"Do you not want children?" Shinae asked, surprised.

"I might someday, but not yet. I'm just enjoying being married and traveling, visually documenting Scotland's landscape."

"You've been doing that for five years!"

"I know! It's the life I had always dreamed of having but whenever Father and I meet, he alludes to us having a child in almost every sentence he utters! The man is annoyingly persistent, but I love him. He would have been by to see you, but he is spending the summer with friends in Spain. I'm sure you will be the first stop he makes. And don't say you have not been warned."

"I won't," Shinae said with a large smile. Mhàiri had not changed much, but she was softer around the edges.

"Before you tell me why Conan and I have been summoned, first tell me how is it you are no longer a nun, married and had the wedding ceremony without waiting for me? Laurel made Conan and me wait for *weeks upon weeks*. I do not exaggerate."

"If it's a wedding you want, my friend will soon be making her vows."

Mhàiri shook her head. "Not the same." She studied Shinae and noticed she was squeezing her fingers. "Why did the herald chase us down? Why the urgency for us to come?"

Shinae took a deep breath, held it and then let it go.

Once she explained the urgency behind the request for them to come to Lochlen Castle immediately, Shinae knew they would talk of little else. So she decided to work up to it. She told Mhàiri about how Brodie had saved her and that when they met, both knew they were in the presence of the one person God had created specifically for them.

Mhàiri crinkled her eyebrows. "And what is your Brodie's opinion about the knives you never go anywhere without? I mean, if you were wearing them when you were a nun, I can't imagine you not doing so now."

Shinae pulled out one and then the other, both much faster than Mhàiri would have thought. "Aye, I carry them, and you are correct that Brodie does not prefer me to do so." Shinae shrugged her shoulders, hinting that while she cared about his thoughts and opinions, her wearing the daggers was not something on which she would compromise.

"You have had disagreements about them," Mhàiri guessed. Shinae rolled her eyes, but that just encouraged Mhàiri to ask more. "And do you lovebirds yell and get into juicy fights as Mother and Father did?"

Shinae gave her sister a point-blank stare. "One of the many reasons I love my husband is that, like me, he doesn't feel one must holler everything they feel or think. When we disag—" Shinae suddenly forgot what she was saying as it dawned on her what she *had* said. She loved Brodie. And she did. Very much. How he had come to mean so much to her in such a short time was unbelievable and yet it was true.

"I heard that he found you in the bedchamber of

another man and carried you on his shoulder back to your chamber *in the chapel*."

Shinae pulled back. Mhàiri had only arrived a few hours ago. "Who told you about that?"

"Bonny. When I saw her running across the courtyard to greet Conan as he exited the great hall. He looked stunned. She's a *very* smart little thing, although she's not so little anymore. She's on the verge of becoming a woman. Conan only gave her a brief hug before going back inside the hall. Anyway, Bonny then showed me where Conan and I were to stay and gave me some of the highlights I missed because Conan had delayed our arrival. After her summary on the honey incident, I'm thinking that Conan is right. That is just the sort of family drama we want to avoid." Mhàiri paused and asked, "So are you going to tell me about you and this Brodie or you are going to explain what this urgent message is all about?"

Suddenly, the prospect of telling her sister about Cyric suddenly sounded more appealing than talking about her love life. And so for the next five minutes, she spoke about the English attack on the abbey, how she defended herself and ensured the safety of her fellow sisters. She then told Mhàiri about Cyric, and that he had found her a month later.

"That's all he told you?" Mhàiri squealed, incredulous. "Someone is going to kill the most vulnerable of the McTiernays—*my husband*—during this family gathering and his eldest brother encouraged him to *come here* rather than to stay away?" Mhàiri was mad and started to pace.

"Compared to his brothers, Conan is the most exposed

of the six McTiernays. But without his prey, this killer might go for someone else. *Chruitheachd!* They might already be planning to do so."

Mhàiri's pace picked up speed. "We need to find out who it is—that will give us an idea of what to expect."

Shinae held up her hand to stop her sister and said, "And that is why all of us women are gathering together in the main chapel this afternoon."

"They want to do *what*?" Mhàiri shouted. "Six McTiernay brothers, who are known to be some of the best minds in Scotland, came up with that ridiculous idea and then decided to act on it?" She raised her hands and looked up to the heavens. "I cannot believe that my very intelligent husband agreed to this nonsense."

"Mhàiri, shh, Brenna and Bonny are still here," Rae-lynd chided.

"Maybe they should stay and help. They certainly could not do worse than their father," Meriel chimed in.

Both Brenna and Bonny looked pleadingly at their mother. Laurel waved at them to join the group. Ordinarily, she would not have considered the idea, but they were bright and interpreted things differently. And that is what they needed right now. Different ideas.

Raelynd raised her eyebrows questioningly. Laurel dismissed her silent admonishment and said, "They would only go find a way to eavesdrop on us," she said in surrender. "Who knows, they may come up with ideas we would not think of."

Shinae was not sure about young girls being involved with such a dangerous and very real situation. Brodie was going to have a conniption when he found out about *her* being involved in the discussion, but she was not a mother and Laurel was theirs. "So, what Brenna and Bonny learned was what we knew this morning: our husbands want to use Isilmë and Dunlop's wedding to set both a diversion and a trap. Only instead of Shinae being the bait, Conan would be."

"Dunlop won't agree to any of this," Isilmë declared. "He will not allow our ceremony to be interrupted with all the chaos chasing this . . . this killer would cause, even if the plan worked!"

Bonny sat with her legs crisscrossed in her chair. "He already agreed," she said matter-of-factly.

Brenna bobbed her head in agreement. "He did not even hesitate," she stated flatly and then saw Isilmë's face had turned bright red. "Um, he also said that his only condition was that you were not to be put in any danger."

Raelynd leaned over and whispered to Meriel, "Maybe letting them stay was a good thing."

Isilmë dropped her jaw and one could practically see the clouds of anger that had formed around her. "I don't believe it! Did he really think I would agree to this?" she shrilled.

Shinae could not help it and felt a tiny amount of joy, discovering that Isilmë and Dunlop's perfect relationship was in fact just like everyone else's. Seems her husband-to-be also did things before he discussed it with the "most important person in his life."

"He wasn't going to tell you," Brenna answered hesitantly, obviously unsure if she should repeat *all* that was said. "Everyone agreed that the less their wives knew

the better. They wouldn't lie, but neither would they—"
She looked at Bonny for help, knowing her mother was
not going to be happy.

"They wouldn't volunteer information because all
that would happen is 'the women would get riled up,
causing their plan to fail.'"

Laurel pursed her lips so hard, they were turning
white. Bonny was only eleven, but she clearly considered
herself part of their group. She was the smartest one in
the room, yet she was still naïve about a lot of things that
Laurel still wanted to protect her from. And what she
wanted to shield her and Brenna from the most right now
was the glib attitudes about women her father and uncles
had conveyed, especially when they actually felt quite
differently. It was just when they all got together, a need
to prove how patriarchal they were came over them. The
longer they were together, the stronger their prejudicial
attitude became.

"What do you two think about their plan?" Mhàiri
asked calmly. When she had lived at McTiernay Castle
prior to marrying Conan, she had come to like the little
girl as much as her husband did. That was when she realized Conan could be a jerk, but gender had nothing to
do with his opinion. Ignorance was what he could not
abide, even when there was no reason for someone to
have knowledge of a particular piece of information.
Mhàiri did not think she would ever change that aspect
about him, but since they became husband and wife, she
was helping him to keep his more offensive opinions to
himself.

"It's not going to work," Brenna replied, shaking her
head. "I watch people, and those around the castle are

already noticing that something is going on. The killer probably suspects we are overly sensitive to all that is happening."

Bonny nodded in agreement. "He won't attack during or even after the wedding. He'll suspect it's a trap."

Brenna looked at Mhàiri and added, "You need to catch him *before* the wedding, when he still thinks his identity is unknown."

"His identity *is* unknown," Bonny corrected.

Mhàiri stood up and hugged both girls. "I've missed you, *boireannach toinisgeil*."

Makenna clapped her hands and said to the group, "So, *we* all agree, nothing is to happen during Isilmë and Dunlop's wedding."

"And just how are we going to prevent that?" Isilmë huffed, keenly interested in the answer.

"Just as Bonny said, we figure out who he is *before* the ceremony," Laurel answered. "And let the men take care of it from there."

"I definitely like that idea," Isilmë piped in. "But how when we don't even know who it is?"

"Well, whoever they are must be nearby. They also have access to us. We have one suspect. Let's start there," Laurel simply stated.

"You could look for something in his room that proved he was the one who hurt Laird Donovan's commander," Bonny suggested.

"He's Laird Donovan's *heir*, not commander," Brenna hissed at her sister, who shrugged her off.

Laurel tapped her chin. "If we could find the weapon, we would most likely be able to use it to identify Edwin's attacker."

"How are we going to find the exact blade? Practically every male carries one," Makenna put forth.

Shinae nodded and said, "I always keep at least two on me."

"Me too," chimed in Mhàiri, pulling out hers.

"As do I. And I know Laurel carries at least one," stated Ellenor, showing her recently polished *sgian dubh*, before sliding it back into its hidden sheath. "But that still does not answer Makenna's question."

Laurel replied, "Edwin's wound was unique and so the blade that made it, is probably recognizable."

"It would be impossible to identify the exact dagger," Ellenor said wide-eyed at the prospect of searching hundreds of daggers.

"Edwin was not attacked by a dagger of any kind," Laurel countered. "His wound was unique and therefore, so must be the blade that made it. Something much longer as well as thinner than a knife. Such a unique blade is most likely recognizable."

"A sword possibly?" Ellenor put forward.

"Nay," Laurel answered. "A sword's blade is too wide and would have lacerated his innards. Edwin is fortunate the weapon had not punctured anything vital. He just lost a lot of blood. The skin was also not shredded but smooth, which means that whatever was used is very, very sharp." She threw her hands up in the air. "Honestly, I don't know what it could have been. I'm just hoping when we find it, there will be no doubt."

Shinae had taken care of Edwin, and Laurel was accurate in her description of his wound. She could also confirm that the blade that had been held to her neck was too long to be a knife.

Isilmë turned to Shinae and whispered, "Am I the only who has never even held a weapon, let alone doesn't know how to wield one?"

"You will learn," Shinae said. "After you marry Dunlop, he will teach you what you need to know."

"Hamish, one of Conor McTiernay's chieftains, had almost lost his wife from a crazed rival. Since then, all the brothers have insisted their wives become at least competent in self-defense," Ellenor explained.

For years, Shinae had thought her and Mhàiri's skills with their knives were highly unusual among females, and yet all the McTiernay wives claimed to have a proficiency with not just knives but other weapons as well. It seemed McTiernay husbands held similar opinions to that of her father—their women needed to always be able to protect themselves if needed.

Unfortunately, all their knowledge of weaponry did not advance an idea of what weapon was used to attack Edwin.

"I wonder," Lady Makenna said, tapping her index finger against her lips. "If it could be my Secret. It went missing several months ago. It's a sword, but an unusual one, made just for me when I was much younger. It was just like Laurel was describing—shorter than a real sword, but longer than a knife. It is also much thinner and lighter."

"Someone took it?"

Makenna shook her head as she fought back her tears at losing one of her most prized possessions. She always prayed she would be reunited with it, but it looked like someone else found it first—and used it. "Nay. Last year, my younger children and I were playing by hiding something of one another's in Canmore Tower. Almost everyone hid whatever it was they had, somewhere obvious. Then our little Connor, who was only five at the time, thought of himself as a big boy by taking my sword. I should have noticed, for it was next to me. But he must have picked it up when I went to go get one of the 'hidden' items. Then we were interrupted, and it wasn't until a couple of days later I realized it was missing. I asked the children if they had seen it and Connor owned up to taking it—he just could not remember where he hid it. I wonder if Connor hid my sword in the gatehouse weapon room? For that is where all the Donovans are staying."

Everyone looked at one another, agreeing that it was looking like a good possibility, when Meriel, who had been sitting quietly listening to everything but saying little, spoke up. "Last meal will soon be served and we all need to get ready, and I want to check on my son, Shaun. So, I suggest we come back tomorrow morning with ideas on how to keep the men occupied while we search the gatehouse rooms."

"I'm telling you, it will work," Brenna argued as she and Bonny trudged up the winding staircase.

"It's dangerous. I don't want to think about what will happen if we get caught."

"Can you imagine how happy Mama will be if we find it? Think about it—she was the one who asked us to eavesdrop *and* to stay and help make plans. Mama *wants* us to help."

Bonny had to admit that Brenna might be correct. "Aye," she answered grudgingly.

"*And* it will be like a puzzle. I know no one who is better at puzzles than you."

When she saw Bonny's interested expression, Brenna pulled her into a quick hug before opening the door into the room they were sharing with Makenna's eldest daughter, Aislinn. All the visiting offspring were staying in a bedchamber belonging to one of Makenna's offspring. Machara, who was not yet nine, had her own room and was sharing with Ellenor's daughter, Elle, who was the same age as Bonny, along with Raelynd's twin three-year-old girls, Aeryn and Laire. The boys had even less room; Braeden and Gideon along with Ellenor's son Chrighton, were staying with little Connor, while Brion slept with Makenna's youngest sons, Lachlann and Alec. The noise level in the tower indicated that all of them were inside the tower getting ready for the evening meal. Only the eldest four children ate with the adults; the younger ones went to the great hall early so they could be put to bed.

When Brenna and Bonny walked in, Aislinn stopped brushing her curly, red hair and glared at Bonny and Brenna. "I may be younger than you, but I am a year older than Bonny and this is *my* castle. Where have you been?" she asked, clearly upset at being left behind. "And why didn't you tell me so I could come with you?"

Brenna sat down on her own makeshift bed and Bonny sat on hers.

"Are you going to tell me? Or should I tell Braeden and Gideon and have them force you to let them join as well?"

Brenna did not want that at all, but the only way to keep Aislinn quiet was to let her to come along.

Their cousin listened to an abbreviated version of what had happened. Aislinn chewed on her bottom lip and then asked, "Why didn't you ask me to come with you? I would have liked to listen, too." Her face was pouty, but when Brenna asked her to help them with the next part, Aislinn perked up again.

"Your mama thinks her weapon is hidden in a roomyin the gatehouse," Bonny stated.

"Do you know who is staying in which room?" Aislinn asked eagerly. "I am *very* good at finding things." Brenna raised her brows in obvious doubt. Aislinn scrunched up the bright blue eyes she got from her father and added, "And I am the only one who knows what Mama's Secret looks like!"

Brenna beamed her cousin a large smile, but Bonny still looked doubtful. "If we are going to do this, we need to go now, when everyone has gathered for the last meal."

Aislinn nodded in agreement and tucked a loose strand of her red hair behind her ear. "I'll tell Machara that we decided to have a picnic. She'll be upset that she wasn't invited and be all the more eager to tattle to anyone who comes by and asks where we are."

Brenna nodded in agreement. "Sometimes little sisters can be quite helpful without even knowing it."

Knowing Brenna could only be referring to her, Bonny was tempted to ask her to provide one example she had successfully tricked or manipulated her, but refrained as her stomach was starting to rumble. "We'd better get something from the kitchens so they can vouch for us."

Aislinn's blue eyes widened. "Good idea! Mama seems to always know when I am up to something she would not approve of." He eyes twinkled in anticipation. "After the honey disaster, I did not think I was ever going to get to do anything fun again."

"Is this it?" Brenna asked, holding up a long dirk that was resting on the window frame. They had gone directly to the room Taveon had been sleeping in.

Bonny just rolled her eyes. They were looking for a miniature sword. Something that looked like a man's weapon, just smaller. Still, every knife or dagger they found in Taveon's room Brenna held up for Aislinn to examine. Once again, her cousin shook her head. "Her sword is much longer than that. Also, Mama polishes the steel often, so it shimmers in the light."

"We'd better hurry up. Once the sun goes down, the only way we will be able to see is with a candle, which will alert anyone looking at the gatehouse that someone is in here," Bonny hissed at her sister. "Oh, and there's nothing here!"

Aislinn looked at Brenna and shrugged her shoulders. "I'm going to look in Edwin's room," she said with glee.

"This is not supposed to be fun, Aislinn," Bonny chided her.

"It is to me. My mama plays a hiding game with my younger siblings. She says I'm too old and clever to play anymore," Aislinn explained, and raced down the stairs to the chambers below.

Bonny hated being young, but young *and* smart? It sometimes was a burden and almost always a constant frustration. She had nothing in common with her peers, and even adults who somewhat knew what she was capable of rarely believed her because of her age. They would whisper, wondering how she could know how to solve disputes, fix problems, or notice things no one else had. Her mother tried to be open-minded, but she mostly "corrected" her youngest daughter to prove that her little girl still needed her "mama." The only one who could ever match her wit was her Uncle Conan, and he should have arrived at Lochlen Castle weeks ago. In her opinion, he had delayed his arrival on purpose. Why, however, was a mystery.

Bonny went downstairs and waited at the door for them to realize there was no weapon in Edwin's room either.

Aislinn sighed. The room had very little in it, making it difficult to hide anything. "Maybe it's hidden," Aislinn said, dumping out the contents stuffed into a large saddlebag. "Why would someone keep this filthy thing in their trunk?" she asked, holding up a léine for all to see.

Bonny was about to ridicule her cousin when she noticed it was stained and took several steps closer. With a timid hand, she reached out and touched one of the dark spots. It felt hard and smelled like iron. Then she lifted it to see if there was a hole that went through the garment. Nothing. A bloody shirt could be easily explained away for he was attacked. Neither was it a weapon; therefore, it was not the evidence their mothers were looking for. She tossed it back into the trunk.

Brenna picked up the léine. "That is blood, so I'm bringing this."

"If we find Mama's Secret, then what?" Aislinn asked, looking to see if it was stashed under the pillows or under the bed.

"Let's find it first," Brenna answered. Realizing Bonny was just watching them. Brenna was not happy. She was about to scold Bonny for not participating in the search when Aislinn gasped. Both Bonny and Brenna looked over at their cousin, who was holding a short sword with dried blood from its tip to halfway up the blade.

"This is it!" Aislinn shouted, and then realized she might have accidentally alerted a passerby of their presence. Dropping her voice down to a whisper, she said, "It was right behind this curtain, which even my little brother Connor knows is a bad hiding place."

Brenna went and plucked it out of her cousin's hands. "It's the same as the shirt. Bloody. But why would Taveon hide the sword in Edwin's room?"

"Because he did not think anyone would look here," Bonny mumbled, thinking the answer quite obvious.

"Ohhh, Mama is *not* going to be happy that he didn't clean it," Aislinn remarked, forgetting just why it had blood on it. She looked at Brenna and asked, "We found it, so what now?"

Before Brenna could issue a foolish decision such as bringing it to their room, Bonny barked out an order of her own. "You, Aislinn, go get our parents while I put it back behind the curtain. And Aislinn, don't tell them why, just that we need to show them something and it would only take a few minutes." Bonny hoped that by seeing they had found the weapon, it would calm some of their expected ire.

Aislinn nodded and vanished to do as bid.

Brenna crossed her arms and sat down on the bed. "That was a bit high and mighty," she mumbled irritably.

"You should know," Bonny replied unapologetically. "You've been ordering Aislinn about since we arrived at Lochlen, using her to help make the rest of us follow your decisions. Bad ones. If you had agreed to search my way, we could have found this much earlier," Bonny said grumpily and tucked the sword back behind the curtain.

"What's the fun in that? I like searching other peoples' rooms. It's as if we are looking for treasure, and it's clear Aislinn feels the same way."

Several minutes passed by in silence. Brenna was intentionally ignoring her, but Bonny did not care. She had let herself get caught in Brenna's excitement. *Never again*, she promised herself. Never again was she going to just recklessly follow Brenna because an element of whatever she was doing or planning piqued her curiosity. She just prayed that her parents only saw the positive from their outing. "I do not think I am going to eavesdrop with you anymore. There are other ways of learning what is happening."

"Trust me, I was not planning on including you from now on either," Brenna snapped back.

Brenna never even tried to see what she was doing from other people's point of view; therefore, she never had any regrets, even when she got herself and all those around her in trouble. After learning about the problems they had put the clan in with their honey disaster, Bonny had felt deep remorse. Her sister and twin brother, however, were only sorry they had been caught. They did not aim to break rules, but they did not mind when they did—especially if it was entertaining. Bonny did not get the spike of pleasure they did from taking risks. She would rather read a book, even if it was one she had read before.

"Are you ever going to *grow up* and stop listening in on people and getting in trouble?" Bonny finally asked.

Brenna's gray eyes went dark. "And just who would have Mama reached out to for help when she needed someone to eavesdrop on our papa and uncles to discover their plan? Not you if your nose was buried in some boring book. I am willing to break the rules when—"

"When what, Brenna?" came a loud, deep, and very angry voice in the doorway. "How you explicitly disobeyed my rule about the *one thing* you could never eavesdrop on?"

A contrite Aislinn suddenly appeared in the doorway and then stumbled as she was pushed into the room by her father. "Go stand with your cousins," Colin said in a voice that was vacant of emotion. It terrified not only Aislinn, but Bonny. Brenna, however, failed to apprehend just how furious their parents were.

"Father, we were just—"

"Not another word will come out of your mouth, Brenna, or so help me I will get a switch and use it until you cannot sit down for a week," Laurel warned as she stepped up next to Conor, making room for Makenna to come in.

Bonny shivered upon seeing her. Their mother had overheard Brenna as well.

Brenna's eyes about popped out of her head upon seeing her mother. In the past, they would be forbidden to leave their rooms as punishment, and usually that was just a few hours, but never did they *physically* discipline her. That was reserved for Braeden like when he and Gideon got into a fist fight in the middle of the courtyard and knocked two carts over in the process, breaking them both. Their father had been fuming and though her brother never admitted it, she saw how he had hesitated that night before slowly sitting down.

On the other hand, her sister Brenna was not inclined to believe she would ever be seriously punished—and certainly not for finding the weapon. Once her parents and her aunt and uncle knew what they had found, everything would change and all the adults would be grateful.

Bonny knew otherwise. Her mother's anger was in part for their dangerous, independent decision to raid the visiting guests' chambers rooms, but her mother was likely to be significantly more upset at Brenna for announcing to all that *their mama* had asked them to listen in on their father. *That was* really *not good*, Bonny thought to herself. Usually she would immediately start to explain the logic behind her misbegotten decision to follow her older sister's lead, but she sensed that right now an explanation would only make things much worse and therefore, kept her lips tightly together.

"I assume you found the weapon."

Bonny looked at Aislinn, who pointed to the curtain, and then back at her father. His voice was calm but fearsome. She preferred him yelling. The anger rolling off him right now was terrifying her.

Colin stepped up to Brenna and snatched the léine from her hands and then went to the curtain and pulled back the heavy curtains to reveal a small, bloody sword. He picked it up and with a stone face showed it to his wife. Makenna nodded her head once, her green eyes sparked with fury seeing the state of her prized possession. "Was this what injured Edwin?" he asked Laurel.

She took the small sword and examined the size. Even if Taveon had wiped it off, she would know if it was the weapon used to stab Edwin in the back. It was the right width and was long enough to penetrate both sides of the body. "Aye," she replied and handed it back to Colin.

He immediately marched out of the room still holding Makenna's sword, exited the gatehouse, and proceeded across the inner ward toward the great hall, where a small group of soldiers was still enjoying their meal. Makenna, then Laurel, quickly followed in silence, leaving all three girls with Brenna and Bonny's father.

Conor looked at each girl for a long minute. Then rubbed his forehead and sighed with enormous disappointment. "Go directly to bed. We will discuss this later." Immediately, he added, "I am sure your father will want to talk with you too, Aislinn."

Bonny swallowed, knowing there was going to be a very loud, intense fight taking place between her parents later that night. And when her uncles learned how all their wives had gathered together and made their own plans, she suspected her parents would not be the only ones expressing their feelings about today's activities. Only Aunt Mhàiri and Uncle Conan would not be fighting, but their reaction would be the worst punishment of all. Uncle Conan was someone whose opinion of her meant more than she could describe. The pain of seeing the look of disappointment in her uncle's eyes was going to be the worst of all.

Now, instead of being his favorite niece, he would think she had become her sister Brenna—a mischief-maker.

CHAPTER ELEVEN

Colin banged open the great hall doors and went to where everyone had stopped eating in midmotion upon seeing their furious laird. He signaled all those still eating at the banquet tables to leave. One look at his and Conor's expressions they all immediately rose, grabbed what they could and vacated the room. Even the servers had quickly abandoned their duties. Only those sitting at the main table near the large hearth remained.

Colin then looked directly at Taveon, while holding out the sword Makenna referred to as her Secret. "Mahon, I respectfully ask that you stay silent as I get some answers, but you will get an explanation, that I promise." With his arms crossed, Mahon did not look pleased by the politely phrased request, but after a moment, he dropped his head down and back up.

Conor handed the sword to Colin, who then approached Taveon. "Did you use this to attack Edwin?" he asked Mahon's defiant commander.

For once, Taveon was not smiling and making light of the situation. He stood up, ignored Colin, looked

Conor directly in the eye, and said, "Nay" in an insolent tone.

Unfazed by the commander's impudence, Colin asked, "Did you hide Makenna's sword in Edwin's room?"

"Nay," Taveon replied again without elaboration.

Colin pivoted to Edwin, whose dark eyes grew large when the thin sword slammed into the wooden table in front of where he sat. "This was found in *your* room, not Taveon's, bloodied and hidden behind a curtain." Despite his size, Edwin looked shaken.

"And this blood-soaked léine was found in *your* room." Colin threw the dirty léine hard at Taveon. "I believe its owner was wearing it when he attacked Mahon's heir."

"Combing through my chest? Such inhospitality." Taveon started clucking his tongue. Then he threw the shirt back at Colin. "I did not attack anyone," he asserted.

Conor paused for a moment and narrowed his eyes. Despite how he appeared, Taveon was nervous. "But it was you who *stabbed* him."

Taveon did not answer. He just crossed his arms and stood in silence.

Conor then shifted his gaze to Edwin. "So, if Taveon stabbed—not attacked—you with a blade that was hidden in your room, I can only conclude that you two conspired together to allow it."

Edwin squirmed in his seat. "Aye, but it was my idea." He then glanced at Taveon, who was now glaring at him venomously.

Mahon could no longer keep silent. "Is this true? *A dheagh-thighearna*, why?"

Taveon stayed silent. As if he was being interrogated by the enemy, he put his hands behind his back, spread his legs shoulder-width apart, and moved his eyes to stare straight ahead at no one and nothing in particular.

Edwin took Taveon's hint and kept his lips sealed.

Colin turned toward Conor, who shrugged his shoulders. They both knew they could do much to encourage Edwin to speak, but torture tactics performed in front of their wives were not an option. In addition, if Taveon was the one the English had sent to kill Conan, he would not talk even if he were on the brink of death. The only explanation Colin could think of for Edwin's mysterious behavior was that he had been threatened, and that whatever Taveon had over him still existed.

Colin nodded his head to his commander. "Drake, take both of them to the dungeon. My brothers and I have a lot to discuss with our wives. Mahon and I, along with my brothers, will gather together in the morning to discuss how we will proceed."

Drake opened the door and signaled for Colin's soldiers hovering near it to do as Colin ordered. Within a minute, four of Drake's men tugged both Taveon and Edwin out of the room.

To Drake, Conor signaled him to wait for further instructions. "Ensure they are put in the last two cells and that they are next to each other, not across. Then instruct your men guarding them to retire for the night." Drake's face was not the only one that looked puzzled, but a moment later, he curled his lips into a wicked smile and left.

* * *

All three girls immediately dashed across the courtyard and only spoke when they reached their shared bedchamber. Bonny immediately undressed, braided her long hair, and climbed into bed, and rolled on her side so that her back was facing them.

Aislinn sat on her mattress, shaking. "M-my father is s-so-so mad."

Brenna tried to calm her, reminding her that tomorrow he would be calm and all would be all right, just like the last time. "Remember how mad Uncle Colin was about the honey? But he forgave us, and that had affected the entire clan!" Aislinn just held her head and cried. "Help me, Bonny, help me make her understand," Brenna said to Bonny's back.

Across the room, Bonny heard her sister name all the reasons she no doubt planned to use with their own father of why they eavesdropped, and all the positive outcomes that had come out of the forbidden activity. Last on her list was how it was somewhat their fathers' fault for creating a need for her eavesdropping.

Aislinn sat up and glared two bright blue beams of anger at Brenna. "*I* did not eavesdrop. *You* did. And don't you dare tell me or my papa or mama that they are to blame for me going where I knew I shouldn't. I think Bonny was right in the tower—I'm never going to join you in any of your schemes again."

After almost a minute, Bonny rolled over to see why it had gone quiet. Brenna's dove-gray eyes actually looked surprised by her cousin's hostile reaction. Only when Aislinn pointed to the bed where her cousins had been sleeping did Brenna stand up and prepare for bed. After she slipped under the covers, she whispered, "You'll see. It will be better tomorrow and when by the time we're home, all will be forgotten."

Turning back around, Bonny whispered, "If I were you, Brenna, I would pray that Father *does* bring you home. I doubt Mama will support you if he decides not to . . . not after you betrayed her."

Brenna sat up and pointed in the direction of the great hall. "Because of what they *overheard* me saying?" she hissed, pointing out the hypocrisy. How could they be angry over something she had done when they had virtually done the same thing?

Whether her sister was intentionally being naïve or really was a fool, Bonny no longer cared. Brenna really did not understand what had happened or the high price they both would pay. "You broke promises tonight. The very ones that gave them a reason to trust you."

"Well, if I did, so did you. I had company while overhearing Papa and his brothers talk—all with Mama's approval."

"And you made her a promise to never say a word and let *her* tell Papa. You may not be sorry for what we did— you never are—but I am going to think of every way possible to gain their trust back."

Brenna gaped at Bonny's back for several seconds before finally lying down with a huff. She did not think her parents would send her away as Bonny hinted, but even if they did, she made two promises to herself:

Never to stop listening in on others and never discover all that she could about what was going on around her.

And *never* again let another soul know.

* * *

Conor lay with his arm behind his head. Laurel lay next to him, also looking up at the ceiling, listening to various arguments coming through their open window.

After all these years, you don't trust me.

I think you proved why I don't *trust you to keep me informed or tell what is going on!*

"I wonder if we sound like that," Laurel murmured.

"Probably worse," Conor answered.

Aye, I will! came a fierce shout from another tower. It sounded like Raelynd. A second later Crevan bellowed something unclear that ended with *just see if I don't.*

Laurel sat up slightly with a growing smile, before leaning over and giving Conor a soft, lingering kiss. "I think we should fight like this more often." Conor looked at her puzzled. "With someone else making our arguments for us," she explained.

"But this way we don't end all hot and passionate." Conor pulled her closer to deepen his embrace when several strands of her hair tumbled into their mouths, quickly ending the kiss.

"Before I forget, just what did you ask Brodie to do?" Laurel asked as she sat up to quickly braid her hair.

"What do you mean?" he asked. His innocent-sounding question would mislead many, but not Laurel.

"I meant, what did you whisper to Brodie so that none of us could hear?"

"Oh, that. I just suggested he and Mahon do a little eavesdropping of their own. Colin once mentioned that the *Tòrr-dubh* dungeons echoed. I sensed that Edwin had a lot more to say and it would be a shame for one of us not to hear it."

"Very clever. But don't you feel even slightly hypo-critical asking Brodie and Mahon to spy on them?"

"Not even a tiny bit." Conor started stroking her cheek. "Might even resolve some things."

Once again, a soft breeze carried the sounds of heated voices through the windows. The weather that night was just the perfect temperature. "What do you think about changing our solar windows to casement ones like these?" Very few of McTiernay Castle tower windows had hinges that could be pivoted outward using a crank attached to its frame.

Conor chuckled at Laurel's attempt at changing the subject. "It's too cold where we live at night, especially the way we like to be dressed when we sleep. They'd never be open."

Laurel rolled over to her side facing him and let her fingers run lightly over his chest. "But we have other ways to stay warm."

Because we thought your plan foolish and ill-conceived!

Laurel waved her right index finger toward the bicker-ing couple. "Now, Makenna makes a good point there. I'm actually surprised you were considering it," she whis-pered, regarding the men's plan as explained by Brenna and Bonny.

"I doubt we would have executed it in the end," Conor agreed. "I was waiting until later to talk with the man everyone felt eager to blame before I formed any firm ideas about what to do next."

"I was thinking the same thing when we McTiernay

women were discussing things. That's when I mentioned that we needed evidence."

"Were the girls there?" he asked, annoyed because he already knew the answer.

Laurel winced and lay back down on her back. "In my defense, I thought if I let Brenna and Bonny stay and feel involved, they would not be tempted to find a way to spy on us and make their own plans. I honestly thought it had worked."

Fighting voices could still be heard, but not as distinctly as they were initially. Conor moved his arm around Laurel's shoulders and pulled her close again. "We have to do something about Brenna," he softly stated and kissed the top of her head.

Laurel knew he was right. She hated sending their firstborn away, but nothing they tried was working. To Conor, Brenna would always be his precious bit of sunshine and, as her mother, Laurel always found it difficult to punish her daughter the way she needed to when often the information was helpful to whatever was happening. "I agree."

"Think Crevan and Raelynd would take her?" Conor proposed. "Brenna would be a day's ride away, and Raelynd is naturally firm."

Laurel shook her head. "Ellenor. She has Brighid, and between the two of them, they will keep a fixed eye on her as well as expand her knowledge of other languages."

"I'll talk to Cole tomorrow while you speak with Ellenor."

"Afterwards, I think we should prepare to leave," Laurel added.

"Cyric should arrive tomorrow and I suspect he will

leave with Taveon directly afterward, once he sees what was found in Edwin's room. Let's wait until that mess is over before we make our announcements. Mahon could come back with information that might surprise us all."

"What if Conan wants to stay a few more days?"

"He very well may, as his wife's sister is staying here, but the day after tomorrow, we will depart."

Laurel climbed up on top of him. "I suggest we should take advantage of our privacy now. It will be several days before we will be at McTiernay Castle and are alone once again."

Conor's mouth broke out into a large grin only a few others had ever seen. "Don't you worry . . . I will figure out a way."

He closed his hand around the back of her head and brought her mouth down to be ravaged by his.

Isilmë stood right in front of her doorway, uncaring who heard her. She did not remember ever being so upset about anything, but Dunlop's demands brought out something inside her that was almost scary. Dunlop, however, was far from being scared by her defiance and kept shouting about how she would learn her place as his wife. He would not interfere with her sewing, but she was never again to get involved with a man's activities or decisions. Something Isilmë refused to accept.

"Before I could walk or talk, I've been told what to do and when to do it. And I will never let anyone have power over me in such a way again! You knew this before you asked if I would marry you, so do not think because I agreed to your proposal that anything has changed."

Dunlop raked his hands along his bald head as if he still had hair. "I don't want to control you. I want to *trust* you, but how can I, knowing you don't discuss things with me first, but instead go to Shinae or Makenna, or . . . Gert?" He visibly winced at the thought, before continuing. "I don't know what to say other than just as much as you don't want to be controlled, I don't want to be married to a harridan determined to make me look like a fool!"

Isilmë's hazel eyes sparkled with fury matching Dunlop's own glare. "I was already in the middle of things before telling you was even an option. Nothing spoken was one of my ideas, but I will admit that I supported anything the women put forward *that did not involve my wedding!*"

Dunlop's glare shifted to one of consideration. For the past half hour, they had been repeating the same accusations, more focused on making their points than actually listening to the other's point of view. "I did not think nuns knew how to raise their voice."

The sudden change in direction caught her mouth wide open in shock. Without thought, Dunlop leaned over and caught Isilmë's face between his hands and enveloped her trembling lips with his before she could respond.

Isilmë resisted at first, but Dunlop kept holding on to her head between his hands, urging her to her tiptoes, kissing her long and deep, capturing her tongue, and drawing it into his own mouth. Unlike before, when he had tried to kiss her similarly, Isilmë would always pull back. But tonight, her arms softly twined around his neck, but with enough pressure that urged him to continue.

As he kissed her mouth hungrily, thrusting his tongue deep, his need for her began to grow. Dunlop thought how alive he had felt the first time he had kissed Isilmë and the sense of certainty that she was the one for him. His need to have her pulsed through him and his hands moved to her sides to free the ties to her bliaut. Suddenly, he let go and took several steps toward the staircase.

Isilmë touched her buzzing lips and said the first thing that came to her mind. "Do not ever shave off your beard."

Dunlop brightened and paused his descent. "Don't worry about that. I have plans to use it the night we marry." Then, with a wink, he shouted, "*I love you, Isilmë!*" and then vanished down the stairs.

Isilmë leaned back against her door and whispered, "And I love you, Dunlop McTiernay." No one in all of Scotland was as lucky as she. The love in his eyes had been bright and clear, and she knew it would last her for the rest of her life.

Conan and Mhàiri sat in front of the fire, listening to all the muffled shouts coming from elsewhere in the castle. "If we had children, that would be us."

Mhàiri bobbed her head in agreement. She was glad they had waited to start a family. Their constant travel did not dissuade her of the idea of having children. Outside of the priory, she had never been anchored to one spot and preferred the nomadic life. Maybe someday they would add another to their lives, but any idea about having a baby soon had completely disappeared with this trip.

"And Bonny! My perfect, brilliant little niece—even she participated in the mayhem of this place!"

Mhàiri looked at him in disbelief. That was how he saw the girl, and while her behavior was surprising, she was glad Conan had witnessed it. For five years, he would periodically mention how he missed her and the discussions they had. Mhàiri had never been jealous of the child, but she had not remembered Bonny being perfect or angelic in all that she did, as Conan had.

Mhàiri shifted in her chair and watched him stare into the unlit hearth. "The weather is ideal. Why don't we consider leaving day after tomorrow?"

Conan swiftly turned so that he could study his wife's expression and determine whether she meant what she had said. "Are you serious? What about time with your sister, Shinae?"

Mhàiri shrugged her shoulders and stood up to brush off the twigs of grass that made up the fresh rushes. "We will be in the Lowlands for a good while longer and can come back to visit. Besides, she just got married, and you remember what we were like."

In one smooth motion, Conan rose, took a step toward her, and swept her into his arms. "I remember how it's still like that," he said as he wiggled his brows. But the bright blue orbs quickly grew serious as he slowly slid her body down his chest. "I'll never stop loving you."

Mhàiri's green eyes twinkled as she met him halfway when he bent down and began his unhurried caresses that proved he had meant every single word.

* * *

"What was Mahon thinking, announcing *you* as his heir?" The sneer was evident from just the voice. Placed in separate cells that were next to each other enabled them to speak to but not see the other. One did not have to see Taveon to envision his face. The venom in his voice conveyed every disparaging thing he thought of Edwin.

"*But it was my idea,*" Taveon whined, repeating what the large fool had said earlier. He rested his head against the stones separating him and Edwin. The floor he was sitting on was cool, giving him chills despite it being dry.

"What do you mean?" Edwin loudly whispered, sincerely confused about Taveon's frustration. "I told you that I would refuse becoming Mahon's heir and I did— multiple times. Mahon just kept insisting that I looked like him in his youth, and he could instruct me on how to be laird with time. It was those meddlesome girls that messed everything up. I was just hours away from telling Mahon that *it was I who asked you* to stab me."

"I know, I know. Mahon was to think you a coward and then ask me to become his next heir." Taveon closed his eyes. "Where did you get that joke of a sword anyway? Lady Laurel and that Shinae woman immediately recognized that your wound had not been made with either a dagger or a broadsword."

"I found it among the various weapons stored in a room on the bottom floor of the gatehouse. Seemed like the perfect length for me to clasp the handle and stab myself."

Taveon wished he had just kept walking. But just as

Edwin managed to get the nerve to stab himself, he was passing his door and heard the muffled scream. He had glanced inside and witnessed Edwin attempting to stab himself in the stomach, he had almost let him. Only Mahon's unpredictable reactions of Edwin's death enticed him to intervene. Now he was stuck in a dungeon, probably banished from the clan. He somehow needed to convince Mahon not to do either.

"You are lucky I came by when I did, and even luckier that I do happen to know where to stab someone without it being deadly." Taveon picked up a small rock lying on the dungeon floor and tossed it against the far wall. "We need to figure out why I stabbed but did not attack you."

"Why not just tell them that you stabbed me because I asked you to?"

"You did not ask me. You were already doing it as I was walking by your chambers *with your door open*, about to make a mess of things."

Edwin shifted and became defensive. "I'd like to see you get the nerve to stab yourself. I doubt you could have either. And I did not hear you protesting the idea at the time. And *you* also left the door open as well after you disappeared, leaving me lying there in my own blood. If I did not know better, I think you enjoyed wounding me."

"Maybe I did." Taveon shrugged his shoulders on instinct. We made a bargain. You were to refuse Mahon's offer and I was to get what I always should have had."

"Well, it was your man who forced us into this situation, for I certainly did not hear you offering an alternative that would stall our departure to the McTiernays for several days." Edwin sensed his fellow conspirator's dark scowl. Neither man liked the other and only dire circumstances had caused them to collaborate.

"I wonder if Beitiris made it to Jedburgh Abbey," Edwin pondered aloud, but to himself.

"I'm sure Duff got her to the abbey safely. The old steward gambles with Mahon's coffers, and he knows what will happen if he fails."

"You'd better hope so," Edwin growled.

For the first time, Taveon was vaguely wary of Edwin. The man was huge, but, in many ways, his actions were timid. "Who is this Beitiris and why was she hiding in your cottage?"

The sound of Edwin rising to his feet echoed in the air. "Why do you suddenly want to know now? You made it clear that you cared not who she was or why she wanted to go to the abbey in secrecy. Your only thoughts had been about me publicly renouncing my becoming the next Donovan heir."

"I don't know," Taveon replied and decided it was because he was bored, and talking would help him occupy time. "I'll admit to being slightly curious as to why anyone would be willing to sacrifice himself over a woman."

Edwin was silent for a time, and the quiet was making him nervous. He did not know what was going to happen tomorrow, though technically it should be nothing. He was the one who had been stabbed and he was not asking for justice.

"Fine," Edwin said, pacing in the small cell. "Beitiris is my younger sister by a few years. When she was a girl, an older woman skilled in the art of medicinal herbs recognized that she had an unusual instinct with herbs. She tutored her, teaching my sister how to recognize them, as well as when and how much to use for various ailments." He paused waiting for Taveon to make a comment or fake a yawn but heard only silence. "Now, while many midwives are aware of herbs for pain, fever, and common ailments, Beitiris knew how to use even the most poisonous herbs, such as nightshade. Only someone with highly unusual skills could treat someone with the deadly berries to induce healing, not death. Beitiris is one of the few who has that ability. All know it, and that was why she had gone north, helping nobles with their ailments, when Mahon made his announcement."

"What happened? She make a mistake and kill someone?" Taveon asked, giving Edwin the first clue that he was paying attention.

"Nay, but it was her proximity to the death of a young child from eating the deadly black berries that led many in the royal court to suspect her. Unfortunately, the child was the beloved nephew to one of the king's close allies. The child's death was one of high prominence and someone needed to be blamed."

Taveon let out a chuckle. "*Murt*, that is some bad luck. Unless she is lying to you."

Edwin's hands curled into tight fists, wishing they were in the same cell. Never again would Taveon speak ill about his sister. "To my knowledge, Beitiris has never lied to me."

Again, Taveon snorted in amusement at not only Edwin's naivety, but that the question angered him to such a large degree. "If you say so, but when a person's life is at risk, I've learned they are capable of doing and saying anything. Even to their brothers." Edwin heard him shift to lay down. "Let me guess. By some miracle, your sister made it to your home and you've been hiding her."

"Aye."

"And *that* is why you came to me for help. Because you knew I would do about anything to become the next Laird Donovan."

"Let's just say I suspected you knew someone who owed you a favor and that I had the ability to give you what you so desperately wanted." Edwin sat back down with his back against cool stones. "I actually wondered just before you stabbed me if you were going to kill me."

"It had crossed my mind," Taveon confirmed, "but I was trying to make everyone think that it was this 'feared and mysterious killer' who attacked you. And just in case anyone thought it might have been me, I assumed you would absolve me from being your assailant by saying you saw me elsewhere just before, *not* announce to all that I agreed to help you with a ludicrous idea that no one would have otherwise believed."

"But it's the truth."

"For a moment, I thought it was a ruse to get me to make a mistake and reveal our little ploy."

"Little ploy, my arse," Edwin countered angrily. "You would describe it far differently if you were the one with a blade shoved through you."

"You're lucky that I knew just where to stab you and how to use that blade. Any other man would have caused extensive bleeding and far larger wounds that you'd have possibly died from."

That reminded Edwin of a question he had had. "I have been meaning to ask you why you threatened to kill Shinae when I was recovering?" Edwin asked.

"I have no idea what you are talking about," Taveon said while yawning.

"You were dressed in black and were pretending you were about to kill her."

"Are you serious?" Taveon asked, unable to tell if Edwin was trying to blame him for something or actually was being sincere.

"Aye, I'm being in earnest," Edwin said, annoyed that Taveon thought he would just make it up.

Taveon rolled his eyes. "Why would I do something that would attract attention? You must have imagined it. The whole thing about this would-be aggressor in your room and after some ex-nun is complete nonsense."

Edwin said nothing and let his eyes close. He would have agreed except he *had* seen it. If it hadn't been Taveon, then Lochlen Castle still had a dangerous killer lurking about.

"Edwin?" Taveon questioned.

"Aye," he replied in a low tone.

"Tomorrow, don't say anything when the McTiernays question us. They already know all they need to and nothing you said was dishonest."

"You still think Mahon will offer you the lairdship after knowing you willingly stabbed me?"

"I have no doubt. By refusing to let you attempt to wound and most likely kill yourself, I was able to save your life by doing the deed myself. He wants a legitimate Donovan heir so badly that he'll even believe my rendition of events."

"I needed to delay our return to give your man Duff more time to get my sister to the abbey and safe," Edwin argued. "But I did *not* want to kill myself."

"Fine, but it looks like you did. You thought it would ensure Mahon finally listened to you and accepted that you'd rather die than be his heir." Taveon adjusted his arm as a pillow. "And tomorrow you will say just that. But know that if Mahon doesn't then turn to me to be his heir, your little sister will pay the price."

CHAPTER TWELVE

As the echoes of Shinae's release ebbed away, Brodie stilled and cradled his wife's face between his hands. The trust that grew between them in the moments he took to relate what he had overheard in the dungeons had pacified their souls. The small action of telling her before anyone else was a symbol of how they would go forward.

He drank in her misty green eyes and then kissed her mouth—long, hard, and deep. "You complete me."

He murmured love words into her open lips until she could no longer breathe, and then, only then, did he let go. Shinae's legs were still wrapped around him, her hands rubbing his arms, his chest, his back, as if she could not get enough of touching him. He rolled to lie beside her, pulled her back up against his chest, and nuzzled his face into the crook of her neck. He could not get enough of her either.

"I love you, Brodie," she murmured with a sigh against his arm. "You make me feel things I've never felt before. These emotions are so intense I'm . . . afraid of someday losing you." Her heart melted as she waited motionless for his response.

Those three softly spoken words shook him to his core. Only his chest moved from breathing. *Afraid*, she had said. Of all things, he never wanted her to be afraid.

He rolled her to her back, holding himself up by his elbows so as not to crush her, and saw the honesty of her fear. Gathering tears of true vulnerability shimmered in her mint-green eyes as she stared up at him.

Shinae felt her chin begin to quiver as he stayed silent. "I . . . understand that you cannot make me any prom-promises, especially after all that has happened." Instinctively, she tried to turn back and curl protectively into a ball.

Brodie could feel her closing herself off. He had been silent too long. Not in just that couple of minutes, but since he promised to love, cherish, and worship her for the rest of his life. He had thought many things but had never said them.

"Never think anything you say could ever drive me away. Nothing could do that. I cannot ever lose what I have with you. My *need* for you is not just in my bed but in my *life*. Do you understand?"

After several seconds of silence, Shinae pulled back, her disbelief evident. She did not believe him, and Brodie felt the stirrings of true panic. "No," he said, keeping her facing him, "before you say anything, I want to tell you that I love you. Please hear me," he pleaded. "I've loved you since the night we met, but I wouldn't let myself truly believe it. For years, I only thought about clan needs, not my own. My life was nothing but making decisions, seeing everything as only right or wrong, good or bad, with nothing in between. But that night and every second since I have been different. My outlook has completely changed. I think about the future with elation, not dread, and when you came to my side when Mahon arrived . . . I loved you before, but right then was when I consciously grasped that I am deeply in love with you."

Shinae shook her head as her memory of those events were quite different. "You did not seem pleased."

Brodie's expression became one of anguish, realizing that he had hurt her. "And I never will be happy when another man flirts with you. *You are mine.*"

Shinae could almost believe that if he had stayed with her. "You just walked away without a word."

"I swear I did not want to go with them, and when I finally broke away and turned around, you were no longer there. My *bòidheach,* before you, my life was cold and hollow; there was no one I could trust and depend on. Every day we are together—even the ones we weren't in um, agreement, I continue love you more and more. I just did not realize it at first. But I do now. I finally am living my life fully. If not for you, *sonuchar,* I would never have known love at all. You are the only woman for me. You are my heart, my love, my soul mate."

Shinae's tears were steadily running down her cheeks, but when he saw the smile on her face, Brodie felt a brief moment of elation before he lowered his head to kiss every tear away, and then he captured her lips in a deep, sensual embrace. He slanted their mouths together again and again, and Shinae melted into him, filled with so much happiness she feared she might burst with it.

When he finally let her go, he rested his forehead

against hers, with his eyes closed and breathing rapidly. "I so love you."

Shinae raised her head and softly whispered in his ear, "Prove it."

Brodie wiggled his brows. "It will take time," he warned.

Her eyes twinkled at him. "It better."

With those words, he could wait no longer and lowered his head till their lips barely met. Shinae's lips parted in anticipation; her entire being seemed to vibrate with desire. Brodie slowly increased the intensity determined to take his time, making sure it was a long, gradual kiss full of controlled passion—far different from the raging course of fierce need that rapaciously grew below his waist.

His tongue swept into her, spurring her desire and need for him. There were no misunderstandings or worries—all were forgotten.

Shinae kissed him back. Thoroughly. Completely. A kiss so full of feeling that it brought unexpected tears once again to her eyes.

A soft moan of dissent escaped her when he reluctantly pulled back and saw that her vivid green eyes had closed during their kiss. Her eyelids fluttered for a moment before she stared up at him with a slightly dazed expression.

Seeing the love in his gold brown eyes, Shinae's mouth curled upward as she wrapped her arms around his neck and pulled him toward her, determined to turn up the heat. Sweeping her tongue across his lower lip, he moaned and slanted his head, deepening the embrace. Her hands and fingernails caressed his back and arms, loving the feel of this muscles. They made her feel frail but also incredibly feminine.

Brodie palmed her backside and she moaned into his mouth as she tunneled her fingers into thick hair and held on to him. He kissed a soft line along her womanly jaw before moving to her earlobe, flicking it carefully with his hot, wet tongue, pulling it fully into his mouth.

Shinae shuddered, arching her back as Brodie released her lobe and began to drop a line of searing kisses down her neck as he slowly made his way to her chest. His mouth continued its descent, and Shinae tightened her fingers into his slightly wavy hair. His lips never stopped their unhurried pursuit. Her tongue started to trace circles on his shoulder; she could feel the muscles twitching beneath his skin.

Brodie's body was on the verge of losing control and he needed to change his focus from the sensations she was creating in him, back to her. Grabbing her hands, he stretched her arms above her head as his tongue flicked lightly over a nipple. Shinae cried out and began to squirm beneath him. The wonderous feelings caused by something so simple once again coursed through her.

Brodie smiled as he took her other breast into his mouth. With only his left hand, he held both her delicate wrists so that his right could begin its own caress of her other breast. She writhed against him. Her breathing was erratic. Brodie smiled. His wife thought she needed him badly, but her need was still not enough. He looked down on her, silently vowing to wring every ounce of passion and desire from her. Only then would he free himself to find his own elation.

Shinae stared up into his amber-colored eyes, eyes

that held her captive, commanded her as they roved possessively over her body. He cupped one breast, filling his palm with her softness, his thumb feathering across the rosy tip, bringing it to a hard peak. His lips took her hardened nipple, sucking on it till it throbbed. He turned to the other one for the same attention.

"So beautiful," Brodie moaned against her skin. "You are so very beautiful." When he once again covered her breast with one hand, her eyes rolled and her head fell back as her body arched to his touch.

"*A ghràidh!*" Shinae breathed out as his lips latched around the straining peak. "More!"

Shinae's nails scraped along his scalp, gasping as he sucked her sweet berry between his teeth. She pressed up against his mouth, wanting—needing more. Her breath stuttered as Brodie backed away.

Lying down beside her, he swept a hand across her silky skin. He adored all of her, loved every single last part of her, body and soul. Her lips caught his in a deep, meaningful kiss. Her hand wound around his sex, lightly touching his tip with her thumb. Quickly, he pulled her hand away.

"Next time, *a bòidheach,* you can do that. But tonight I want you to experience my feelings, to know my feelings without any doubts. You do that," he said, gently taking her hand in his grip, "I cannot control my desire to possess you. Previously, we came together in fierce need, letting passion take over as we joined." He paused and gently kissed her cheek. "Tonight, you are mine. I am going take my time to enjoy you, and take you to limits you can only imagine."

He moved farther down her body. His lips were hot

and moist as they ran a path from her navel to her hip and then down to her thigh, murmuring over and over, "You are so beautiful...so very, very beautiful . . ."

His fingers began to knead her thighs, his mouth barely skimming over her warmth as he caressed one inner thigh with his tongue, the softness of her skin brushing against his lips and cheek. Shinae thought she'd die if he did not stop this slow act of seduction.

She arched into his touch, desperate to feel his fingers touch her between her legs. She tried to wind her arms around his neck, as the need he was stirring within her grew into a ravishing hunger. Finally, his fingers met her core. She gasped once more, mindless with an overload of sensation and yet craving more.

When she started to tremble violently, with exaggerated slowness he withdrew his fingers. Shinae cried out in protest, but when she felt his hands on her inner thighs, pushing them outward, it suddenly occurred to her what was about to happen .

"Brodie, don't. Not like that. I don't want you to do that. . . I've never . . . " She started to struggle, but he paid no attention to her stammering pleas. His fingers clamped gently into her soft skin, holding her knees in a bent position. Then his tongue gave her the most intimate of all kisses.

Shinae gasped at the unfamiliar caress. At the first touch of his lips on the soft mound of curls between her thighs, her legs nearly gave out. She tried desperately to retreat from his mouth's silky touch, but Brodie held her by her hips, and when his tongue began to explore, her knees did buckle. Her panic changed into unnerving desire. As he drew her into the moist heat of his mouth, her body went liquid with need. Shinae thought she was going to die from the pleasure.

She moaned a soft whimper. The primitive erotic sound nearly drove Brodie mad. He needed to touch her channel, watch her squirm, feel her explode.

He ran his fingers down along the dark, moist slit. He was rewarded with a loud cry that echoed through the room. He felt the tightening of her heels along his back, pulling him forward. Her back bowed when he slid his finger past the curls and deep into her. He began to stroke her expertly, adding a second finger, bringing her tighter and tighter, keeping at it until she was mindless and could stand no more. Her body clenched and released in a flood of pleasure.

His shaft was straining for her body. He needed to be inside her, badly. "Tell me you want me inside you. That you need me. Say it, Shinae."

She felt his hard arousal against the junction of her thighs and was not sure her body could handle any more sensations. Her mind was flooded with bliss, and she could not imagine him bringing her that high again.

"Shinae!" he begged, and hearing his desperate plea, she nodded. With a relieved groan, Brodie shoved himself inside her snug passage. Not hard, but not as gentle as usual. He groaned as Shinae closed around him, hot and wet and clinging.

Brodie started to move within her, and impossibly, her body was once again alive. He plunged between her thighs, burying himself in the warm softness of her. He felt her body clench around his with each stroke. Brodie's back was slick with sweat and his muscles trembled beneath his skin. He was losing control and his body demanded he increase the passionate rhythm.

He thrust harder and faster, making her gasp for air, yet she could not seem to get enough of the hot, thick feel of him inside her. She lifted her hips from the bed. She felt as if he was taking her to heaven.

His desire had become painful, a pain Brodie could no longer deny release. He pressed his face into the curve of her neck. Shinae clutched him to her, riding each thrust, hardly aware of the passionate moans she was making. And then it was there again. The hot pressure was building and building until her entire body was in danger of exploding.

Brodie's gaze never left her eyes as he pumped into her harder and faster. "Aye," he hissed. He felt her body tightening around him just seconds before she cried out, "Brodie!" Gasping, his own body exploded as wave after wave of intense pleasure assaulted her.

The world washed away, and only she and Brodie remained.

He slumped on top of her, holding himself up by his elbows so as not to crush her. They struggled to catch their breath. He rolled to lie beside her and pulled her against him. She nuzzled her face into the crook of his neck. Brodie closed his eyelids. He could not get enough of her.

Shinae's lovely body was draped over his in the most gratifying way. Her leg trapped one of his, her arm folded over his chest, and her mess of dark hair fanned out behind her. He'd never felt more relaxed in his life, never so content.

They lay there like that, basking in each other for a long while. Not speaking, just touching, kissing, loving each other. Shinae had never felt so completely loved or cherished in her life, and she clung to him tightly, not wanting the moment to end.

They had mended each other—heart, mind, and soul.

CHAPTER THIRTEEN

Brodie glanced at the window and saw the first rays of dawn shine through. He could hear the neighing of a horse and the muffled greetings coming from the courtyard. It had to be Cyric, which meant things would start happening.

He tried to remove his arm without waking Shinae but failed. "Stay," her soft voice begged. "Don't go; it's too early."

Brodie was very tempted to do just as she asked. If her body was as drained as his was from last night's activities, she might not rise until midday. "Are you fine?" he asked, hoping he had not bruised her in one of the times they had come together.

"The only thing that would injure me is if you left." Shinae yawned and intensified her grip on his arm.

"Cyric is here, love. I have to go and join the men."

"Nay. Donovan's men are not our problem. Mahon was with you and overheard all that you did in the dungeons, and it was his men who caused all madness the last few days. Let the old laird handle it. He sent you away with no explanation, so you have no obligation to him."

"Such an ungenerous position for a nun," Brodie said teasingly.

"Ex-nun," Shinae corrected him.

He pulled his head slightly back and saw her eyes were closed. He gave her a soft kiss on her forehead and continued to stare at her, feeling completely shocked once more that she was actually his, not just in marriage, but that he had her heart.

He snuggled down in the bed and tightened his arms around her. He could feel her lips curl into a smile just before she flipped over to her other side and wiggled her backside up next to him. Taking the hint, he pulled her in close and shut his own eyes. She was right. Conor and Colin were more than familiar with all the events, and they were not going to ask Brodie to be involved in deciding Taveon and Edwin's outcome.

"Sleep, my love," he whispered in her ear. "I will not leave until we both are ready."

He could feel her soft intake of air and knew she was asleep once again. The jabbering noise outside lessened, and he suspected the McTiernay wives and most of the brothers were still in bed as well, after some vigorous making up.

I am yours, forever and always, he said to himself, and then joined her in slumber.

* * *

A soft yet persistent pounding sound echoed in the room. Shinae slowly lifted her eyelids and she saw the room was bright with light, indicating it was mid-morning. The pounding continued and Shinae turned over to ask Brodie to send them away. Seeing he had left, she was tempted to shout for whoever it was at the door to come in when she remembered she was not wearing anything. Getting to her feet, she snatched her silk robe and tied it around her waist.

Shinae opened the door a crack, thinking it Gert or one of the chambermaids, when Isilmë pushed it wide open and charged into the room, noticeably upset. "You won't believe what I was just told, and believe me, you will want to know this as well, for it affects you too." Shinae slipped behind a curtain and dressed in a light blue bliaut—another gift from Meriel. "Don't you want to know?" Isilmë's voice asked with a slight shrill quality.

"I did not realize that I needed to ask," Shinae said, trying hard to cut off a yawn as she put on her slippers.

"One of the chambermaids told me that because neither Dunlop nor myself are related to the McTiernays and that there are to be no more feasts, we—" she pointed between the two of them, "are no longer allowed to eat in the great hall but have to get our meals in the kitchen until we move out of the castle."

Surprised, Shinae just stood there, staring at her friend. She had not thought about where to eat her meals since she first arrived. Isilmë had a point, though. The chamber she and Brodie were using had been provided only temporarily and only because her sister was married to one of the McTiernay brothers. She was not. Her husband did not even look like he belonged to the clan.

"But Brodie and Dunlop have eaten in the hall for almost every meal, even before our arrival." Shinae's mind raced. She was not a servant, and even if she was, she had seen the small room they had placed Isilmë in and there was no way she and Brodie could fit in one, even if it was offered.

"Dunlop is a commander and once we are married, I can then dine with the other leaders and their wives if we are not eating in our cottage, which is the most common choice." Isilmë looked at Shinae in horror at the aspect.

Shinae tried to calm her friend as well as herself at the idea. "That doesn't appeal to you? Having a much larger place to work? All that privacy for you and Dunlop?"

Isilmë's hazel-brown eyes grew large. "I know *nothing* about cooking. You did all the skinning and seasoning of the food when we journeyed here; I just held it over the fire. Not to mention the meals we ate at the abbey were routine and limited." She sat down in one of the chairs and whispered as if it were a shameful secret, "Since we arrived, most of the time I haven't recognized most of what has been served or what we were eating."

Shinae opened and closed her mouth several times, before realizing what she was doing and kept it shut. Most likely she would also be living in a small village cottage. Worse, she did not remember ever seeing a vacant cottage whenever she ventured out of the castle walls. First Brodie would have to build them one, plus the furniture. In the meantime, once the McTiernays left, the chaplain, Ros, and everyone else displaced due to the large number of visitors would want their own chambers back. Thank goodness she was familiar with living outside, for it looked like that was where she was going to be staying for a while. Where she ate her meals seemed a minor issue.

"Where does Dunlop live now?"

The question only raised Isilmë's anxiety. "With his men! Either outside or in the gatehouse, where the many soldiers supporting the protection of the castle live. They all bunk in the same room." Tears rolled down her freckled cherub cheeks. "I am going to live in a cottage like Ceridwin and their children do! I'll be so busy trying to do the laundry of two and prepare food that I'll never have any time to sew again!" she wailed and threw her face into her palms.

Shinae just partially listened as Isilmë agonized over her future. What would happen when all left was something she had not considered. Wherever they lived, she wanted to be in a position to support and help the community as she had always dreamed of being able to do. If Isilmë was correct, she too would be too busy with personal matters to help anyone.

"It will be an adjustment, but our husbands will have to be patient with us as we learn skills our past never taught us."

"*Mo thruaigh mise!*" Isilmë shrieked. "Once Dunlop learns any of this, he is not going to marry me!"

The door opened again, and Gert stepped through.

"What's all the wailing about?" she asked Shinae while pointing her finger at Isilmë.

"She doesn't think Dunlop will want to marry someone ignorant of taking care of a home."

Gert nodded. "She may be right. But all that can be taught, lass," she said confidently. "And I saw yer love for each other that night he asked ye to be his. That man's in love. He'd eat his kilt if it meant ye were in his bed at night." Then, she squinted her eyes and added, "Well, maybe for a week. Men like their food almost as much as they like their night activities."

The frank statement startled Isilmë and ended her crying. Gert clapped her hands. "Dry that face of yers. Somebody important came earlier this morning and I was told to fetch ye both to the great hall immediately."

As soon as Shinae opened the door to the great hall, she scanned the room. Cyric jumped up and headed toward her. Brodie's eyes were locked on him the entire time. Dunlop had saved Isilmë a seat next to him at the head of the center trestle table where the commanders and their wives were sitting. Her worried expression changed to one of sheer joy by the gesture. Shinae saw that Brodie had done the same for her, but Cyric had halted her ability to get to him. "I am relieved to find you looking far prettier and happier than when you left Melrose."

Shinae arched her left brow and crossed her arms but said nothing. Cyric coughed to clear his throat, but continued to grin appreciatively at her. She had not said anything, but based on her stance and Brodie's deadly stare, he knew what they were thinking. "Umm, uh . . . my associates have scolded me on my decision to send you in my stead as the mission could have been dangerous."

At that Brodie rose to his feet and went to stand beside Shinae with his hand on her waist. "It *was* dangerous, or did you miss the part where a knife was about to plunge into her throat," he said through gritted teeth.

Cyric outstretched his arm, palm upward and gestured to all the people by the hearth. "But look how it all ended. You both found love and are happily married. Two of Laird Donovan's men were revealed to be fools, and Conan McTiernay is safe and unharmed. All is well."

Shinae was not so sure about the accuracy of Cyric's assessment. In her mind, the reason he had sent her to Lochlen Castle had not been resolved. Taveon and Edwin's shocking plan did not address the fact that supposedly someone was planning to kill Conan. "Are not my sister and her husband still in danger?"

Shinae felt Brodie give her a little tug, forcing her to leave Cyric's side. Only after she was sitting down between him and Mhàiri did she feel him relax.

Cyric directed his answer to her despite all in the room being interested in the answer. "Aye, it does, but I doubt there is immediate danger any longer. Whoever they are, the killer knows by now that we are all aware of his plan to murder Conan, and what was once an easy target is no longer. It is probable he is in England, getting new instructions."

Shinae's gut started churning in disagreement, and

she looked at her husband dubiously. Cyric was wrong, and she suspected that he did not believe what he said any more than she did. Brodie just shrugged his shoulders. In a low, private voice, he said, "The threat may be still out there, but Conan has been forewarned. He is a superior swordsman and, like you, Mhàiri always has access to knives. They will be fine."

Shinae could not decide if Brodie meant what he had said. Something was causing her inner voice to say they all had it wrong, but until she could identify just what it was, she said nothing more.

Colin eyed Cyric as he made his way back to the main table. "When do you plan on leaving?"

Cyric shrugged nonchalantly. "Soon. I am not returning with anyone, so I can leave tomorrow for Stirling Castle, when Conan and Mhàiri depart."

Hearing the unexpected news, Shinae turned to her sister. They exchanged anguished looks at the little time they had been able to spend with each other.

Colin was perturbed by Cyric's answer and challenged his decision to return alone. "What do you mean, you are returning to Stirling by yourself? I may be holding Donovan's men, but I expect them to leave with you."

Cyric shook his head back and forth. "Why should I take them? They are your problem, not mine. I had intended to bring back the man threatening the backbone of Scotland—our chief. The two men you are holding are a mere menace and should be left in Laird Donovan's care. King Robert has no desire to meddle in clan issues, and therefore I do not either."

Mahon Donovan had spoken very little after overhearing Edwin and Taveon's confessions. For someone once referred to as "the lion," the old laird looked defeated. Since discovering the truth about the two men he had blindly trusted, he had not known what to do. It was as if what happened eight years before was happening again. "They are my responsibility, and I will bring them home and decide what to do with them." He then coughed and looked at Brodie. "It seems I am in need of your services again."

Brodie almost choked on the ale he was drinking. The man had to be desperate to ask if he would return in front of everyone. But even if the request had been made in private, with the promise of the lairdship, the answer would have been the same. "I cannot accept. I have already accepted Ros's offer to become the next McTiernay steward."

Mahon pinched his lips and finally gave a single nod of acceptance. "An honorable position that holds a great responsibilities, and one that ensures stability to a newly married couple," Mahon answered. His face said it all. He had known that it had been highly unlikely Brodie would accept his offer, but he had had to try.

Brodie took pity on the old man. For many years, he had considered him a friend. "Talk to Garron about becoming lead commander. He does not want to be laird, but he is bright, has a lot of common sense, gets along with the men, and is good with a variety of weapons. But you will have to adjust some of your thoughts on marriage. He is happily married with three children. He will not give up his time spent with them."

Mahon nodded. "Perhaps such a change is what the

clan needs. Colin, have your men bring Taveon and Edwin to the courtyard. I hope to leave within the hour." Then, with a small smile at Makenna, he added, "Thank you for your warm welcome, Lady McTiernay. Hopefully this frees a room for Cyric to use."

Makenna's cheeks turned pink, for that was exactly what she was trying to figure out when Cyric had announced he was staying.

Colin and Conor saw Laird Donovan leave with his guards and Edwin and Taveon tied to the horses on which they had arrived. Once they were out of sight, Colin waved Brodie and Shinae to follow him back into the hall. He normally would have had this conversation in his dayroom, but currently that was less private than the hall.

He went up to the hearth and swung around the chair in which he had been sitting at the main table. He indicated for them both to do the same. Brodie moved both chairs and waited for Shinae to sit before he did the same. The feeling in the air was not one of cheer, and Brodie reached over to hold his wife's hand. Partly to give her comfort and partly to receive it.

Colin clasped his hands together, and rested his elbows on his knees. "I have enormous respect for you, Brodie. I did before you left, and I still do now. After that many years supporting Mahon as his primary adviser and second in charge, I am aware that you are the only one who is knowledgeable enough in the duties of a steward to assume them immediately. Ros has been exemplary in his execution of all that was expected and has been critical to my being able to focus on the various aspects of being a McTiernay chieftain. His duties cannot be performed by anyone else, outside of Conor. But I cannot agree to you becoming the next McTiernay steward."

Shinae's back stiffened defensively. "And just why not?"

Colin shifted his gaze from Brodie to Shinae's flashing green eyes. Laurel had been right about the two of them getting married. He had known Brodie years ago, and when he came back single and with no interest in changing that status, he had thought his sister-in-law's matchmaker inclinations were incredibly shortsighted and highly arrogant. But Conor insisted Laurel had a knack for seeing connections between people and let it be.

"For several reasons," he said to Shinae, and then shifted his gaze back to Brodie. "My rejection mostly centers on two facts. One is your refusal to wear the McTiernay plaid, and secondly, you are not a McTiernay, or even a Dunstan-McTiernay. You are simply a Dunstan, something you proudly announce daily by what you wear. So how can I expect McTiernay clansmen and women to respect you and all the decisions you would have to make as steward? You are not one of them. I will not give an outsider any role within my clan, especially a prestigious and trustworthy position. You can stay here, help as you have been, or even start your own farm if you are willing to live a bit farther out. But I can offer nothing else." He shifted his eyes to Shinae and then back to Brodie. "Your blood is not Donovan blood. That is why Mahon never considered you to be his heir. One day it occurred to him that he may have given you the impression that he would name you as the next laird— an idea he had never once entertained."

"And when did you come to learn this?"

"Two nights ago, he, Conor, and I stayed up talking and the subject of you came up."

Brodie squeezed Shinae's hand reassuringly so she would know that what happened between him and Mahon was in the past. "Mahon was right," Brodie stated, surprising Shinae. But she stayed quiet. "I was just too hurt and angry to realize it. But God's path for me is here with my fellow McTiernay clansmen and, most importantly, Shinae."

Before Colin could end the uncomfortable conversation and leave, Brodie continued. "For a long time, I felt that I owed it to my father to represent him and his pride in being a loyal Dunstan. When you arrived and assumed the title of laird after Alexander's death, I was actually relieved, as well as were most of my fellow soldiers. At that moment I saw myself as a McTiernay, and you had allowed me to continue wearing the Dunstan plaid. I suspect you did it less out of respect for me, but more for Alexander Dunstan. It was because you took over his role and changed the Dunstan clan to McTiernay that I just assumed it was possible for Donovan to do the same, except I would become a Donovan. I respect Mahon, but there are several opinions and philosophies I did not hold. But as time passed, my thoughts on marriage and family and a few other things shifted to better align with him. It was not until the night I met Shinae that I realized how fortunate I was that Mahon sent me back to the place I had truly felt was home and where I belonged."

"So, what are you saying?" Colin asked with a twinge of impatience.

"That I have been a McTiernay wearing a Dunstan tartan, and when I stop wearing the Dunstan kilt to that of the McTiernay colors, it will not be because I've just now decided to become a McTiernay for your approval to a prominent position. It will be to show what probably most of this clan already knows—that I already am one of them."

Colin sprouted a huge grin and his bright blue eyes lit up as he extended his arm out. Brodie, who also rose to his feet, grabbed the outstretched forearm. "Good luck. Ros will be hard to follow, but if he did not believe you could perform to his standards, he never would have offered the stewardship to you."

"*Mòran taing,*" came Brodie's crisp clear voice that was full of appreciation.

Brodie and Shinae left and went back to the chapel and their room. Neither of them had discussed where they would stay when the McTiernays left for their own homes. Only after they were back in their temporary room did Brodie give her a light kiss. "Ros said he had a few things to get and to give him today to get them out. It will be ours starting tomorrow." He appeared and sounded calm, but Shinae could tell that he was eager to start as soon as he could. Months without responsibilities had been very difficult and now to have a position of prominence—one that not only was needed by the laird and all the clansmen—but was also challenging made him eager to begin. It was hard for him to pretend not to be as jubilant as he felt.

"I did not know you went and saw Ros."

"That day when I left to sleep with the men and calm down gave me some interesting insight. Like usual the men were chatting for a while, and I tried to sleep. Their main topic was the same as most nights—their longing for what I found with you. Someone to come home to at night, a comfortable bed, and a woman who believed in him and made his home one he was keen to get home to. The ones that were married spoke about their futures and the next steps they were taking to improve their lives of their families. And it occurred to me that I never provided such to you."

Shinae shook her head. "Not true, I always knew you would figure out a way to provide for us. What I worried about was you finding something not just to do to pass the day, but something that gripped your interest, made you happy."

"I realized my foolishness that first night and went to see Ros the next day. Speaking with him, we both recognized that I was ideal for taking over. Before I had the notion that request was in part out of compassion for us." Shinae gave him a solid thump on his chest. "I know, and it was not long into our conversation when I came to the conclusion that there was no pity at all. He had been wanting to quit for a couple of years but felt he could not if it meant leaving the responsibilities to someone unfit for being steward. He really did need someone. Being steward for Colin is a little different, as there is a greater expectation for the steward to oversee all at the castle, not just assist. The clan requires a lot of oversight—more than I realized—and he needs a steward who would enable him the time to spend with his wife and family."

Shinae had witnessed Colin often talking, playing, or reprimanding the younger three boys and encouraging his elder daughters. "Did you know Colin and Makenna want more little McTiernays?"

Brodie shrugged his chin. "Does not surprise me. He likes to tell his soldiers that he is a two-family man. One is the clan and the other is his wife and children. It is probably the most striking difference between him and Laird Donovan. Mahon does not believe a good laird can effectively split his time between the clan and a family."

"Is that why you never married?" Shinae asked him, a little surprised the laird had such an influence over him.

"In part," Brodie answered. "But mostly I think it is because I had not met you. I truly believe that if we met, even when I was still with Mahon, I would have chosen you over his mistaken ideas about giving everything one had to the clan, and only the clan. Laird Donovan's a good man, but I'm glad he forced me to leave. Otherwise I would never have learned that with him I was content, but not happy. That did not happen until you first spoke to me. I'll treasure that moment forever."

"That is hard to believe. I now know what I looked like—and smelled like—and I don't even think a starving dog would have come near me if I was waving a large piece of meat."

Brodie broke out in a large grin. "Your clothes were pretty ripe, but you smelled divine."

She arched one eyebrow, knowing he was lying but then changed her mind. She remembered a lot from that night as well, and none of it was negative. Only the good.

"I'm going to go see Isilmë. She was all in a panic about having to eat in the kitchen and not the great hall."

"Dunlop wouldn't let that happen. Lady Makenna insists her friends dine with her most nights. She likes the company and to hear all the latest gossip. I know Colin likes the women to be there for distraction, so he and his men can discuss things."

Shinae gave him a playful swat, but mentally acknowledged that he was probably right.

Brodie leaned down to give her a quick kiss. "I think Mahon is going to leave in a few hours. I know that both the Laird and Lady Makenna would want you there to show that despite all that has happened, we still consider him an ally."

Shinae nodded and headed toward the Pinnacle Tower. About halfway across the courtyard, something made her pause and look back. Brodie was there, watching her with undeniable love and pride in his eyes. She waved at him and whispered another prayer of thanks to God for all that he had given her.

Shinae finished brushing her hair and crawled into bed. She had waited up for Brodie but finally gave up and was just getting comfortable to go to sleep when the door opened and he came in. For the first time, she saw her husband truly exhausted, not from physical exertion but mental.

"Sorry I'm so late. When Ros came over for his belongings, he saw me and asked if we could go over some things. I accepted, not realizing how late I would be."

A soft giggle came from Shinae. "I know. I was there, remember? When I eventually left, you looked like a little boy given an entire custard pie."

He gave her a slight smile and disrobed before sliding between the sheets, gathering her close to him. He mumbled in her ear that it was probably going to happen again in the next few days. She was about to tell him that she understood when she heard the deep intake of his breath, indicating he was already asleep. Once again, that feeling of peace and happiness flooded her senses, and she started to doze off as well.

Then, all of a sudden, she rose to a sitting position. She was sweating and in a state of terror. She felt like she had just closed her eyes, but the dying fire proved she had been asleep for at least two hours. Shinae had never been prone to nightmares, but the way her inner voice was screaming at her, she needed to remember just what she had dreamed.

Taking several deep breaths, she got her heart to slow down and was about to lay back down when her memory abruptly returned. Everything clicked. Why she had been attacked, Cyric's warning, and, most of all, Conor's announcement that everyone intended to leave and return home the next day.

Throwing off the blankets, she jumped out of bed and

started hunting for her robe. "Brodie, wake up and get dressed." He moaned and buried his face in his pillow. She thumped him on the head with her pillow and saw just one eye open a smidgeon, giving her a disgruntled look.

"Get up!" she ordered forcefully. "I know who the killer is."

"Who?" Brodie mumbled. "Mahon left with Taveon and Edwin hours ago."

"Not them," she said with an exasperated tone while trying to stick her arm down the wrong sleeve. "Ever since everyone started assuming it was Taveon, I fell into the same trap, ignoring the parts of Cyric's message that did not fit. That the traitor had been entrenched for some time at Lochlen and had been biding their time until they could attack."

That did get Brodie's attention. He raised himself onto his elbows and started to process what she was saying. A handful of seconds passed by as his foggy brain cleared before he got up and began to throw his clothes back on.

"The McTiernays always get together at Christmas but have not been able to the last few years because of all the snow and blizzards. This is the first time the traitor has had access to Conor and Laurel's children. *Brion* is the most vulnerable McTiernay."

Brodie had almost finished dressing when what Shinae was saying suddenly made sense. "Rosina."

Shinae briefly nodded and started looking for her slippers. "Makenna's nanny has been helping with the younger children, but she has a strange attachment to Brion."

When she finished putting on her shoes, she saw Brodie standing at the door waiting for her. "You go get Conor and Laurel and tell them what you just told me. I'll go and check on Brion."

Shinae saw the glint of silver sheathed on his back as he sped down the stairs.

Shinae dashed across the courtyard, praying she was not too late. There had always been something not right about the woman and the odd attachment she had with Brion. Once inside the tower, she ran up a flight of stairs and banged on Conor and Laurel's door. She shouted for Laurel, hoping it would awaken everyone. Finally, Laurel came out into the narrow hallway completely alert, as if she could hear the anxiety in Shinae's voice. Shinae did not even wait for her to ask what was wrong. "Rosina is the killer."

Laurel's blue eyes grew dark and were now the color of a North Sea storm. "Brion," she whispered as everything clicked into place for her.

Conor must have been listening because he pushed Shinae to the side and in only his léine began running. Shinae and Laurel followed him and were halfway across the yard when they saw Brodie emerge with most of the children following him. He had searched every room, including the small area where Rosina had slept. All her things were gone.

Laurel crumpled when she saw Brodie look at Conor and shake his head.

Without warning, Laurel rose back to her feet and

started heading to the gatehouse, shouting out loud to fate. "You tried to take my life, then the lives of my first-born, my husband, and my baby boy. You *lost*. You will not take my son away from me. Do you hear me? Brion's alive and he's mine!" Her voice was ferocious. But all her bravado disappeared the moment Conor caught up to her and she collapsed in his arms.

He knelt down on the ground, rocking her in his arms, whispering her promises that he would find him and bring him back to her. That no one could take away what God had given them.

Colin appeared with Conor's kilt, belt, and weapons. Shinae took over comforting Laurel and saw that all the wives were coming over. Like her and Laurel, all of them were in robes, and some were without footwear.

By the time Conor had cinched his belt and secured his weapons, horses had been brought out and saddles were on them. The stable master, who slept in a small building next to the stables, had roused all the stable hands, and they worked feverishly to get the horses ready. All they had left to do was getting the bridles on.

"They'll find him," Ellenor whispered to Laurel. "He most likely is hiding somewhere and Rosina is just trying to find him."

Shinae knew Ellenor was just trying to help, but it gave her an idea. Maybe Rosina had not yet left and was hiding.

Shinae found the older girls huddled together, crying. "Aislinn, Brenna, Bonny. You three have been in and out of every hidden room and hiding space in this place. If

Rosina is hiding somewhere in Pinnacle Tower, where is she?"

Both the girls and boys stared at her wide-eyed, still in shock over what was happening.

"Brenna," Shinae said sharply, attaining the eldest girl's attention. "Do you remember the day I caught you in the honey shed? How did you all get there without anybody seeing you leave—or, more importantly, return?"

Without warning Conor was there waiting for the answer. Brenna blinked, but her younger sister, Bonny, understood Shinae's line of questioning. "There's a small dirt tunnel under the tower that splits. One way leads to the great hall; the other is much longer and goes out to the village."

Laurel heard a sharp voice. "Show me," he demanded. Laurel and the three girls immediately left. Shinae instructed the wives to stay there and let their husbands know what they were doing before they left.

Weaving around goods that had a few weeks earlier filled the room for all the feasts, Shinae found Laurel and Brenna on the floor, trying to find the rope that would open the entrance to the tunnel.

"I did not know that was there," Makenna whispered. "I've lived at Lochlen my entire life and Colin has been here for nearly ten and five years."

Shinae saw that the men had not ridden off, but had joined them—all but Brodie.

"I swear, I didn't know either until Brenna showed me," Aislinn vowed, hoping her mother believed her.

"I don't doubt you," Makenna said and gave her daughter's hand a squeeze.

Conor's large hand appeared and helped open the heavy door. No one but his daughter would have found the thing. She had a knack for discovering hidden tunnels, doors that looked like walls, and ways to get anywhere she wanted with no one knowing. He was not surprised, and suddenly grateful of his daughter's unusual skill.

Laurel waved for Brenna to step back and started to go down when she solved the mystery behind why nobody knew about the tunnel. It was barely large enough for her to go through. Stepping back up with some assistance from Makenna, Conor asked Aislinn, "Where does this go? I'm going to need you to take me there."

Brenna looked at her father, and then her mother, who had an intense look that was more prominent in her storm-colored eyes. She then looked at Shinae, who could tell from Brenna's frightened face that she had no idea how to get there from above the ground, only underneath. "Does it open near where you found the honey?"

Brenna's eyes lit up and she bobbed her head. "Close to there, but it took a while to get there using the tunnel."

Laurel hugged her. "That's fine. You and Bonny take this candle and go through the tunnel like you did before. But this time, when you reach the end, get out but don't leave that spot. All right?"

Colin spoke up. "I know the area." Shinae had not seen him enter the tower, but a second later, both he and Conor had vanished.

Shinae followed the crowd and exited the tower. Her eyes started to dart around, looking for Brodie. She was about to go search for him when it struck her where he was. He had already left on a horse and was out searching for Brion before Rosina took his life.

Laurel could feel the eyes of all the McTiernay women on her, including Shinae, Isilmë, and, somehow, Gert. They were watching her in silence as they could not think of anything comforting to say. She paced from one end of the hall's giant hearth to the other, knowing if she stopped she would break down and scream in fear, scaring her children.

Shinae had no intention of telling Laurel to sit down or give her empty assurances about everything being fine. Like the rest of the McTiernay wives, she was afraid Laurel would verbally rip their heads off, and they were right. She would have.

The men had left on horses nearly two hours before. Dunlop had come back and informed them that the exit's door had been left open and easy to find. Based on the intermittent footprints they had been able to make out; they knew the direction Rosina was heading. They could only guess when she and Brion had left, but based on the lack of blood, they did not think she had hurt him. By now several others had joined the search, exploring other trails—eventually they would find them.

Dunlop returned to update their progress. He went over to Isilmë, who was standing near Shinae and her sister. He squeezed her hand and gave her a small smile. "I'm glad they included you, my love. Times like these, the McTiernays—especially the women—close themselves off to outsiders. Your personality will help keep things calm until we get back." Then, with a peck on Islime's cheek, he exited the hall to rejoin the search.

Isilmë whispered so softly, Shinae could barely hear her. "How am I supposed to do that? Make jokes? Tell stories about the abbey? Talk about my wedding?"

Shinae did not know how to answer and continued to twirl her *sgian dubh* in her hand to reduce the anxiety she felt. Isilmë saw that her sister Mhàiri was also doing the same thing. "Do *all* of you carry weapons?" she said aloud.

The women looked confused, but each had their knives out and available for use. They had not even been aware they had them in their hands. Isilmë looked at Meriel— the only one sitting down—and then looked back at the tense group. "Can you all actually wield the daggers you are holding? Or do you just carry one for comfort?"

Mhàiri stopped and stared at Isilmë, as did everyone else.

The unexpected question did exactly what Isilmë hoped it would. "Until I met Shinae, I had never heard of a woman who was proficient with any type of weapon."

"Most don't know." Mhàiri was no longer spinning her blade. "It would defeat the purpose."

"I didn't," Ellenor admitted. "It had never occurred to me to carry one because I didn't know how to use it. After being kidnapped and almost killed, Cole made me train each day for more than a year and always keep one with me."

"I as well," Raelynd added. "After Conor and Laurel's attack five years ago, Crevan insisted that I become comfortable with a dirk and still insists I carry a *sgian dubh* with me at all times."

"Laurel is best at archery," Meriel interjected. "And Makenna is fierce with her sword."

Laurel huffed. A growing anger was replacing her fear. "I'm also quite proficient with knives, as Rosina will soon find out."

"Craig and his brother made Raelynd and me learn and carry a weapon at all times," Meriel imparted, pulling out her blade, hoping to keep the discussion away from Rosina and Brion.

Makenna and Ellenor glanced at Shinae and Isilmë and started smiling at Isilmë's confused expression. "You do know that they are Laird Schellden's twin daughters and are married to the McTiernay twins, Craig and Crevan," Makenna clarified.

"I did not," Isilmë replied, wide-eyed.

"Nor did I," Shinae added.

Laurel stepped forward. "I think many more women are knowledgeable with at least one weapon. Definitely far more than men realize. They may not carry their knives on them, but I suspect most cottages have a weapon to which they have quick access." She turned her fists clutched in an effort to keep thoughts that he was forever gone from taking over. "I should never have let him sleep so far from me. Not at his age."

"I wonder . . ." Isilmë intentionally did not finish her thought, hoping it would get their thoughts off Brion and capture their curiosity.

Isilmë elbowed Shinae in the ribs and angled her head for her friend to follow her. All eyes were on them now. Shinae did as her friend wanted and followed her to the other side of the great hall. "Just what are you up to?" Shinae whispered, needing some clarification.

"I'm shifting Laurel's thoughts to something else until the men get back with Brion," she answered optimistically. God would save the little lad. "Lady McTiernay's mind is full of bad memories and she needs to quit thinking of them before she goes mad."

"By talking about weapons?"

"It was not my intention, but it worked for a while, and this will too."

Shinae still did not understand what Isilmë intended, but she understood the purpose and just did as instructed. They went to the right side of the hearth and lifted the heavy, round, targe resting on two bottom spokes.

Makenna saw what they were doing and raced over to stop them, but it was too late. They had removed the shield and were laying it on the table. "This targe belongs to my husband and he used it during the last clan conflict we had," she said lightly fingering the defensive weapon.

The walls of the great hall had stained wainscoting fourteen feet high, enabling items such as tapestries and weapons to be hung on its walls. "*Buannaich*! That will work," Isilmë said excitedly.

Makenna fingered the large shield. "Colin said it had saved his life, so I restored it and added the crests."

The targe itself was made of a single piece of birch wood, stained walnut-colored leather, and goat hide on the back with two straps attached for a man to wield. Brass rivets lined the outside circle, as well as the large brass knob in the center. Tacks divided the targe into four pieces, and in each piece the leather was etched with the McTiernay crest—an eagle clutching a tree branch of Highland mountain ash. Makenna lightly fingered it.

"No wonder the laird loves you so much," Isilmë said as she took some ash and drew two circles on the wooden backdrop.

She then handed the bowl of ash to Shinae and asked her to walk thirty paces from the shield backdrop and use the ashes to mark a line. The hall was only wide enough for three trestle tables, but its length allowed four tables end to end—twelve tables altogether. Currently, the great hall was configured as it normally was. Only the main table shaped like a wide U and the first three tables were left standing. The rest had been dismantled until they were needed again.

Makenna's brows bunched and she was about to order Isilmë to stop whatever she was planning and for the shield to be rehung when she saw a *sgian dubh* whip through the air and land very close to the dead center on the backdrop.

Shinae marched right over, pulled the knife, gave it to her sister, and said, "It's been a long time, little sister." Mhàiri scoffed, stood at the line, and let her blade fly, and it too landed near the middle of the circle.

Makenna could see Raelynd watch, itching to try, but this was *her* home, and that meant the Lady of Lochlen was going next. Laurel, however, beat her to it. She went to the line and then took several steps back and her own knife went sailing, landing just outside the inner circle. Makenna went next and then Raelynd. All the women took turns, even Isilmë. They were in their sixth round when they heard the men enter the castle.

Laurel immediately bolted out of the room and the group waited for Makenna to recover her dagger and join them before rushing outside to verify the screams they heard were those of joy and not sorrow.

Laurel was kneeling on the ground hugging an un-injured Brion, thanking the Lord for his return. She squeezed him for nearly a full minute when her baby boy began to wriggle to get free. "Mama, why did you scream? It was just me!"

His little smile was infectious and the tension they had been feeling for the past few hours was finally easing away.

Laurel kissed the soft dark hair on his head and wiped her tears only for them to return again. "It was a good kind of scream." Brion looked at her with skeptical eyes, the exact unusual shade of blue his mother had. "I am just so happy to see you."

"You are crying happy tears?"

"Aye, very, very happy tears." She rubbed their noses together. "I'm so glad you're back home. Why did you leave without telling me?"

"I don't know. Rosie told me to go with her, but I didn't like where she took me. It was a dark, dirty tunnel, and I told her I wanted to go back, but she said I would have a lot of fun if I kept going. Mama?" he asked with his forehead scrunched up as if he was afraid of what she might say.

"What, my *balach beag milis?*"

"I didn't have fun." He wrapped his little arms around her. "Please don't let her take me there again."

Laurel shifted him in her arms, sad to think it would not be long before she would be unable to hold him like this. "Never again, I promise, and your papa sent Nanny Rosie away so you don't have to worry that she will make you go with her again."

Brion squeezed her neck tightly. "*Tha gaol agam ort*, Mama."

"*Tha gaol agam ort*, my sweet little boy."

Conor, seeing the tight hold she had on Brion, reached out and took his son back into his arms. He suspected it would be some time before her youngest child was able to leave his wife's sight.

Laurel licked her lips and almost demanded for Conor to give Brion back, but turned around and hugged Isilmë instead. "*Mòran taing*, for what you did in there," she said, pointing to the great hall with her chin. "I don't think I could have continued waiting and worrying. As each minute passed, I was losing hope and you distracted me."

"You knew?"

"Aye, but it was clever. An activity that both distracted and gave me a way to release some of my aggression. Now, if you could do me one last favor before you go over to Dunlop, can you run and find Lady Makenna for me? I would like to talk to her about an idea you inspired."

The small group of McTiernays was growing larger by the minute as all the children came out, and soldiers, castle staff, and even kitchen workers came outside to see with their own eyes that the sweet little boy was back safe and sound. It seemed that in the past few weeks,

Brion and all the children had been everywhere, meeting all those that worked in the castle. He had wedged a piece of him into their hearts.

Brodie was profoundly happy for the chief and his wife, but he was eager to find Shinae. He had been keeping an eye on the chapel and knew she had not gone there. He peeked inside the great hall and saw his wife had indeed sneaked away. "What are you doing?"

Shinae smiled up at him. The strain of knowing about this unknown assailant had never stopped weighing on her. When everyone seemed so dismissive, trying to convince her and themselves all was well, it had only made things worse. She had been sleeping poorly for the past few nights, and last night she had slept hardly at all. "Straightening up, before the servants come in and are distraught at the damage we caused. Would you help me with this?" Shinae pointed to the heavy targe.

Brodie lifted the beautiful shield and was about to put it back on its perch when he saw more than a dozen notches gouged into the wood. "What were you doing?"

"Throwing knives." She pulled out a dagger. "I think this is Meriel's, but I don't know for sure. I'm sure its owner will come looking for it. Oh, I know. I'll give it to Gert to figure out."

"Ahem." Brodie stood near her with his arms crossed, trying to look serious. From her lack of concern, he knew he was failing.

She gave him a wink. "Laurel needed a target and Isilmë and I made one. We were all distressed, waiting on news, having no idea how much longer it would be or if the news would be positive. Too much longer, one or more of us was going to burst. So Isilmë suggested that we throw our knives. She even joined us."

Brodie imagined the short, freckled woman attempting to throw even the smallest of knives and physically winced. "Did she break anything?"

Shinae lightly thumped him on the chest, and he started grinning. "I'm liking this thing you've started doing when you want to scold me about something I said or did. It's kind of endearing."

Shinae lifted her hand and almost walloped him again. After a couple of seconds, she decided to do it anyway, and gave him a solid thump, but this time with a bright smile that warmed him all over.

"To answer your question, *nay*, Isilmë did not break anything, but Dunlop will definitely need to spend some time training her."

Brodie chuckled. "I'm sure they will both enjoy that activity."

He wiggled his eyebrows and Shinae just rolled her eyes and went back to straighten the targe, ensuring the crossed lines made of brass tacks were perfectly straight up and down as well as horizontal. She stood back and noticed that three gashes were not hidden by the targe. "I wonder if I can convince Lady Makenna to *not* replace the wood or, even better, give it to me."

"Why would you want to keep it?"

Shinae looked at the beautiful shield and touched it softly. "To hang in our bedchamber, of course. I have yet to see the room, but we could use it for your targe. You don't use it often; at least I haven't seen you wear one since Isilmë and I arrived."

"That's because I do not have one. I just grab one out of the weapon room."

Shinae clucked her tongue. "Well, I will see that is corrected. If you are particular about how it should look, let me know, but I would like to attempt to design one."

"Fine, if it makes you happy."

She spun around for a couple of seconds. "I'm sure Makenna will let me make it."

"Again," Brodie asked, "why?"

"For decoration!"

Brodie took a deep breath, but when she spun around and beamed at him, he realized she had been teasing him. Another first. "You know what you have just done, don't you?" he asked.

Shinae tilted her head to the side. "Gotten approval for our first of many things that will bring joy into our everyday lives?"

Brodie started tickling her, and immediately she yielded. "Stop, please stop," Shinae implored, and he finally let go so she could catch her breath. "Just what have I done?"

He pulled her close. "Not done, but unleashed." She looked at him quizzically. "You've officially, though indirectly, made it clear that you not only like to tease but enjoy *being* teased. I approve. In fact, I cannot wait to tease not only you, but our children." Shinae's jaw dropped. "It will be all in good fun, of course, otherwise it is not teasing but tormenting, and that I will not a—"

"Our *family*?" Shinae croaked.

"Mmm-hmm. I'm thinking a dozen."

She stared at him for no more than two seconds before she started to laugh, but then she could not stop. Her laughter was infectious, forcing Brodie to join her, which caused her hilarity to grow until her stomach began to hurt and she was gasping for breath. Unable to stand anymore, she collapsed on the bench next to her husband, who was only just getting control of himself. Leaning back against his chest, she slowly got her mirth back under control, but it did not lessen the happiness she felt. "I want the wood for a memory of today," she finally explained. "Today was the first time in my life I've experienced pure joy. Every dream I've ever had, every wish I secretly wanted, God has fulfilled. And with you as my best friend and husband, I know that all my secret dreams will come true as well."

If he could, Brodie would have taken her right there. Even a single kiss would have caused him to lose control. So he caressed her hand and kissed the top of her head. "As steward, I don't get bedchambers," he said softly.

Shinae's head tilted upward as all the things Isilmë was worried about came flooding back. Brodie saw the panic in her eyes and took pity on her. He had meant it earlier, that he loved to tease and be teased, but not create suffering. "The steward actually has several rooms in *Tòrr-dubh*."

Her liquid green eyes grew even more beautiful as she slowly sat up and turned around. "*Several?*" Outside of the king, the laird, the abbot or abbess, she did not know of anyone who had more than one room unless they had their own cottage.

"Aye, several. We will have the entire top floor, which has three rooms, all with at least one window—our bed-chamber and one room for you and one for me."

"But I don't need a room."

"I thought you liked to polish your knives at night, and a private space where you can practice your maneuvers. And did you not just mention your desire to design and make me a personal targe?"

Shinae's mind started racing. She would have a place people could visit, where she could collect and prepare her various herbs. Brodie had kept talking, but she had not been listening until he said, "And, eventually, a nursery."

He had her full attention then. She wanted children, but not twelve. Unfortunately, whatever his thoughts had been about the subject had already been spoken as he moved on to tell her that he would also have room on the second floor, which would be used to support his duties, such as dispensing funding and castle mainte-nance duties to all the staff, giving him time to manage and address noncritical clan issues.

"Would you like to go see them? We can take a look, then come back to the great hall. We are starving, and Colin asked the kitchens to serve us early."

It took no more encouragement for Shinae to leave and head toward *Tòrr-dubh,* their new home.

Everyone ate until they could eat no more. The meal was simpler than usual, but the kitchens had put together what they could. Shinae only knew it was close to the best meal she had ever eaten, she had been so hungry.

Finally, the meal was over and all had been cleaned. Each time she or Brodie stood up to leave, Colin indicated for them to sit back down. The soldiers, however, left when they had consumed what they could. There had been no battle, but they had been famished nonetheless.

Once the soldiers had left the room, Makenna instructed the trestles to be unassembled, and Colin waved for the doors to be opened, where clansmen and women began to pour in. Colin knew that everyone—not just their wives—would want to know what had happened and decided to withhold detailed explanations until after they ate, and could provide enough space for all interested who wanted to hear the story of Brion's kidnapping. Colin's hope was to reduce the rumor enhancements gossip generally included.

Colin waited until the hall was completely full. The doors were left open and someone with a loud hailer was outside, repeating the laird's words. Colin began speaking and was at the part of finding the tunnel's exit when he stopped talking and swallowed half of his ale. Shinae was impressed and whispered to Brodie, "He is a really good bard. Lacks poetry, but I'm enjoying it, and I can envision all that happened when all of you left the castle." Brodie flashed her a quick smile and turned back to listen to Colin as he continued.

"Once we located Brenna, she showed us where the tunnel came to an end, which several of you have traveled across maybe even daily it was so well hidden. Only then did some of the worry we held about little Brion still being alive disappeared. There were two sets of footprints, but no blood. Brion was alive. Knowing that, your chief became like a feral beast and started to track them. Conor saw even the smallest things from crushed grass to rocks recently overturned—everything indicating where Rosina was taking Brion. I, my commanders, or any of my brothers would have noticed them as well, but our chief? He was especially quick. If he had not been, I'm not sure this tale would be a happy one."

As Colin waited for his mug to be refilled, Shinae leaned over and whispered to Makenna, "Does he do this often?"

"Nay," Makenna replied. "I'm just as shocked as you are."

Colin looked over the chattering crowd and waited for them to go silent once more. "The most frightening thing was the need for us to go as fast as we did, for we were nearing Hadrian's Wall." He stopped and gave his clan a chance to digest the seriousness of what that meant. English soldiers always patrolled the Wall, and if Rosina had gotten to it, she and Brion would have been escorted into the heart of England, most likely never to be heard of again.

Brodie whispered in Shinae's ear, "We were not exactly near the Wall. It would have taken us at least two more hours, maybe longer to get that far. Time I suspect Rosina thought she had and would have had if you had not woken everyone up to go after them. Brion had stopped being able to walk and she had been forced to carry the lad or leave without him."

Shinae shifted her attention back to Colin, who had already begun speaking again.

The crowd grew even more quiet. "The only way we

believe Rosina could have gotten so far so fast is if she left far earlier than we originally thought. Many of you were most likely still awake when she tricked Brion into following her."

The crowd gasped, but Colin kept speaking. "Then we found them. Rosina, however, did not see us. How was that? We heard Brion asking her to go back home. His frightened cries could barely be heard, but because of them, we knew to leave our horses and travel by foot. When we got near, I went around behind Rosina, while Conor walked straight toward her and Brion. Seeing her raise a sharp dagger, I quickly grabbed her wrist and twisted it, forcing her to drop the weapon as well as Brion.

"Upon seeing his father, Brion ran into his arms, asking if he could go home. When his father, your chief, promised to take him back, the little lad fell right to sleep with his face nestled securely on his father's upper chest. He did not even wake when his father got back on his horse, still holding the lad."

Colin paused to let his clan absorb and relay what he had described. It did not take long when shouts were heard asking where Rosina was. "Still tied to the back of your chieftain's saddle," Cyric called out.

"Why didn't ye just kill the woman?" a voice shouted out.

"Believe me, I wanted to," Conor bellowed, and both inside and out of the great hall you could hear calls for it to be done.

Cyric held out his hand to quiet them. "She *will* die," he assured them. He was surprised that he had been able to keep her alive at all. "She is a spy for the English, and

King Robert wants to have her interrogated before her head is severed off her body."

Cheers erupted and several heads bobbed up and down in approval. Colin continued with his recount of what happened. "By forcing her to walk, she begged to stop and get a drink of water. So we stopped and gave her one," he told the now-quiet crowd. Cyric smiled slyly. "But only after she started talking." Again, the crowd roared with approval. He waved for them to calm and let him finish. "Rosina, as many of you know, came to Makenna and me three years ago, supposedly after losing all her belongings and her husband to a clan raid. This was true, but an English spy convinced her that it was the *Scottish* lairds who were to blame, unable to save their own people. That they deserved to lose someone they loved. So Rosina had come to our clan, fooling everyone, helping to take care of our littlest son, Alec, who had just been born. We McTiernays typically get together once a year in winter to celebrate our Lord and new year, but that year we did not because of the terrible snowstorms Scotland has been having this far south.

"For three years she waited while Makenna and I were unknowing that we housed someone also eager for the McTiernays to gather together. Her orders were to poison the chief's youngest son. But the weather still made it too dangerous to travel that year nor the next two. Rather than risk another delay, my brothers and I decided to celebrate Lammas Day. By now Rosina was supposed to have killed Brion and disappeared, but something unexpected happened."

"Tell us!" his clan began to chant.

"Brion was no longer two years of age, but five—

Brion is the age her only child was when his life had been taken. When she first saw your chief's son, she saw him as her own child, and so she changed her plan. She would still get the reward from the English by making the McTiernays pay, but she would do so by taking him and raising him as her own. *Buìochas le dia*, that did not happen. All rumors about a mysterious killer roaming throughout the castle can now desist. The danger to Lochlen and its clansmen and women is gone."

Shinae was engrossed in the story when all of a sudden the room erupted with cheers, whistles, and shouts to their chief and chieftain. After several minutes, the volume lessened and the crowd started to head out when Laurel's voice hollered so loudly, the room suddenly stilled and became quiet as they grasped the idea that such a feminine, regal woman could yell that loud.

"Tomorrow your chief Laird McTiernay and I will be holding some Highland games, but with one small but significant change. This time the game participants *will be female*. Any woman who wants to participate in one or more event is welcome to come and be a challenger."

Even before she had finished, several men began to shout out several curses at her, as well as the women who looked excited by the idea. The rants were continuing to get louder and more disparaging, when a booming, furious voice roared "*Bí tostach!*" that rattled and scared everyone who heard it. They all knew the chief of the McTiernays to be a relaxed and generally happy man. At that moment, they learned why their chief was so feared across Scotland.

"My *wife, and your ladyship* is speaking to you, which means you will listen or prepare to spend the next month in the dungeons. And if I hear even one whispered insult aimed at her or any other female, they can spend two months in the dungeon." Conor's gaze went slowly over the crowd, looking at every man, conveying that he meant what he said.

Shinae leaned over to Brodie. "I think he means it."

He whispered back, "That's because he does."

"There are so many more here than I would have thought after last night's reaction," Shinae said with a smile as she plopped down on the grass beside her husband.

He pointed to several huddled groups of women who were participating. "There are an amazing number of women who are skilled in weaponry. I wager there are more women participating than Colin and his brothers ever considered possible. Many men are looking at their wives and older daughters a little differently."

"I meant the number of *men* present," Shinae said and nudged him with her elbow. Brodie handed her a water bag, which she took and started to drink until it was empty. She ran her forearm across her forehead. "Hardly any of them showed up this morning. Now I wouldn't be surprised if almost all were here."

Brodie chuckled and nodded in agreement. "Those that remained at home or out in the fields are going to regret not coming." He had been there since the beginning, watching and being both surprised and impressed at what he saw.

A few adjustments were made, but in general it was much like what the men did. Competitive, inspiring, and exciting. The sheer aggression displayed, as well as the arrogance women displayed walking around when they won an event was exactly how men behaved—including himself. Knowing there would be demand for more of these female games after today's success, there was one aspect that was very different, so much so it made Brodie feel uncomfortable. He was going to talk to Colin about creating a rule that stated there was to be no hugging before or after a match.

He, to his surprise, was far less bored than he expected to be. The mud wrestling alone got the interest of several men, and he and Dunlop began to wager on several of the matches before he noticed they had not been alone. Demands for the games to return would be heard by their neighbors. He would not be surprised if they were held again.

The games included traditional and semitraditional categories. The events that were traditional were ones that were closely like those performed by men in their games. The semitraditional events were those that had been modified so women could attempt to do them.

In archery, a skill many men, let alone women, lacked, Ellenor and Laurel tied, but when it was made more challenging by having to shoot while riding on a horse, Laurel was the obvious master at both speed and accuracy. There were a few women—Shinae's sister included—who also performed unexpectedly very well because they had never held a bow in their hands. Mhàiri was a lot stronger than she looked.

The best at swordplay was easily won by Makenna. When some growls came that it was because she was using her Secret sword, she had tossed it to her opponent, proving to all when she still readily beat all challengers that there was much more to wielding a blade than the tool itself. Once announced the winner, however, she collapsed and said she would never use a regular sword again, even if it was the lightest one they could find. She only watched the next few events.

Battling with dirks came down to Mhàiri and Shinae, but Shinae eked out the win. Mhàiri vowed the next time they battled, it would be she that would win.

Caber tossing was done in teams of eight. Shinae joined the McTiernay wives and quickly lost the first match and moved to the sidelines. The final two groups—one comprised of castle staff and the other of farmer wives. Both teams as well as the crowd looked shocked when the castle staff won.

The hill race was a ruthless event. There were a lot of very quick women who themselves had no idea how fast they could run. In the end, endurance was the key to success, and a chambermaid who ran up and down stairs carrying water and laundry all day took the title. Raelynd and Meriel surprised even their husbands by being part of the first group to finish. Running was something the twin sisters used to do almost every day when they were young.

One large but evidently very strong farmer's wife won the stone put. It was nearly as heavy as the rock men used, but the distance it went was still impressive.

Haggis hurling, though, was Brodie's favorite so far though the throwing of food was never intended to be an event. One woman supposedly knocked down another walking by her. Neither had come close to winning. The woman slowly got up and went over to one of the food tables, grabbed some haggis, and chucked it. Unfortunately, it did not hit its intended target and mayhem soon commenced. Laurel, who had been unfortunately hit in the head, declared that event was never to be repeated, but Brodie suspected that someday the "sport" would pop up again.

Shinae chuckled again when she saw her sister lining up for tug-of-war. She and Isilmë had successfully avoided the haggis fight, but Mhàiri had been a full participant when she was hit in the face with a fish head.

"You aren't participating?" Brodie asked, hoping Shinae would be on the losing side and end up in the muddy pit.

"Nay, those who did the caber toss can't help out. Our arms are fatigued." She gave Brodie a brief kiss and stood up. "I've got to go! The log roll will start soon down by the river. Did I ever tell you that I have an uncanny sense of balance?"

Brodie thought for a moment and realized that unless Shinae won, she would fall into the river. That was a sight he had to see. He jumped up and chased after her. Catching her, he swung her around and gave her a short but passionate kiss. "I love you, *shonuachar*."

"And I love you." Then she started running again not wanting to be late and unable to pick the best log.

"I'll have a blanket ready for you!" Brodie bellowed as she ran off. Shinae was so different from the first day they had met and stolen his heart. And yet she was the same. For years, her spirit had been caged by situation and isolation. Likewise, he had suppressed his own nature for so long he had forgotten who he really was.

Suddenly, Brodie broke out into a run and stopped the next woman who was going to try to knock his wife off the unstable log. He ignored all the outraged comments about him being a man and not allowed to participate. He just pulled off his shoes and jumped on Shinae's log with ease. "Did I ever happen to tell you that I never lost at this when I was a lad?"

The group's gripes turned into chants, shouting Shinae's name. For several minutes, each would attempt to knock the other off. They would try to stop the spin, slow it down, reverse the direction of the log, but both remained firm. Then the log started to roll faster and faster. It was clear that neither of them was going to be able to stay on. The only question was who was going to fall first.

Brodie wobbled, which broke Shinae's concentration, and both fell into the summer-heated water at the same time. Rather than get out, they just held on to each other.

This is where I belong, Shinae thought to herself, *in the arms of my Highlander*.

Connect with  U s